TIG

SUNNI MERCER

Green
Heron
Books

Published by Green Heron Books, an imprint of Storied Publishing

ISBN: 978-1-951991-16-6

Cover design by Sean Benesh

Art photography by Ann Sherman

Edited by Doug Serven and Peggy Poteet

Mercer has set the story well within the framework of Oklahoma history—reflective and relevant. The quality of the writing brings the history to life, and Mercer's descriptive ability transports us to the land. The robust characters in *TIG* are startling mirrors of the land they inhabit. They are weathered, tenacious, and resourceful. In this compelling story, *TIG* reminds us of the power of community and its potential to become a healing force regardless of the circumstances. *TIG* challenges us to consider our faith, heritage, and relationships.

Dr. Bob Blackburn
Executive Director of the Oklahoma Historical Society, 1999–2021

A vast and visual tribute to the beautiful, brittle, high prairies and those who commit to finding the meaning of home there, this geographically researched novel deeply engages with its' intertwining characters. Author Sunni Mercer shows deep reverence for the texture of place and for the flow and ruptures of time and memory on those whose faith is challenged. *TIG* allows the reader to serve as a witness to the most intimate of human tragedies and to full participation in life.

Melinda Levin
Professor and Documentary Film Director, University of North Texas

Is redemption possible? And if so, how does it happen? In this compelling story of Tig's joys and tragedies, we are invited to imagine the ways of persistent, unassuming love brings wholeness and healing. It's a story that rings with the beauty of truth and invites us to ponder the way redemption comes to all of us.

Rev. Michaele LaVigne
Pastor
Author, *Living the Way of Jesus*

Tig is a superb read. Mercer takes us on a captivating journey through the life of a disabled man—a derelict. Mercer's descriptive style will transport you to the land of red earth. You'll taste the dirt.

Joe Thomas
Executive Officer, Department of Culture and Humanities Literary Arts Division, the Chickasaw Nation

Sunni Mercer paints Tig's journey in a way that portrays the journey of many of us. Seemingly marginalized and alone, Tig recovers hope from community. Whatever our disability or ability, we all need the support and strength provided by others, and Sunni helps us find it through her artistic prose that warmly breathes hope into us.

Jim Priest
CEO, Goodwill Industries of Central Oklahoma

Sunni Mercer takes the reader deep into the life-fabric of the community of the fictional town of Arvita, Oklahoma. The author's skill for description through the use of color, texture, landscape, and human experience is remarkable, and it adds to the reader's experience of the time, place, and people. Mercer conveys the feelings, situations, and relationships that carry the story of Tig to its conclusion.

Rev. Dr. Tommy Goode
Founding Director, Moral Injury Institute, Springfield, Missouri

*For Wendell, who fostered in me a love
for the rugged plains of Northwest Oklahoma.*

For Ron and Ima Jean, whose stories gave Tig substance.

*And for Gary, whose unwavering support
has encouraged me to dance with the impossible.*

CONTENTS

FOREWORD

The low humidity and chill of the room did nothing to alleviate the beads of sweat on the nape of my neck. I stood very still, although my insides would have no part of my calm exterior. I remained invisible in the background while four individuals moved slowly back and forth in front of a lengthy stretch of gallery wall. They drew in and pulled back; they squatted down and stretched up to see. At times they nodded while making marks in small black notebooks. Other times they just stood shaking their heads, not in a negative fashion but rather in disbelief. They rotated positions, crossing each other to get to the opposite side of the room, but they never spoke nor acknowledged one other.

In front of them on a long expanse of wall, forty feet long to be exact, were forty rows of small metal objects, hung in a matrix. Each row contained six objects mounted from a few inches above the floor to nearly six feet high on a white washed backdrop. Spread across the wall were 240 small art objects, each small construct a unique assemblage made from cast-offs, rusty metal, small animal bones, old photographs, and run over bottle caps and wire. At a mere nine inches each, they commanded the room, and I knew each one intimately. They were my progeny, and this exhibit was my act of releasing them.

Time crawled. Finally, they all drew back and gathered in a small huddle to deliberate—four giants conferring. They gestured to each other, pointing this way and that, hands on hips, tipping heads, referring to notebooks, nodding again and then turning in my direction. This was the signal I desired—dreaded. I was within minutes of defending my thesis, the culmination of my graduate work. I ran over all that I had rehearsed.

Two years prior, I had decided to try my hand at assemblage art, I went out to a friend's ranch and spent some time contemplating. While I was there, I hiked to an area where an old farmhouse stood. Many years ago, it had burned to the ground. As I walked around the foundation of that old house, I noticed bits and pieces of charred debris. There were old spoons, door hinges, and rusty tools. I decided to gather them and take them back to my studio. So, I dug around for days and came back with quite a haul of usable junk. As I lay the pieces out on my table in the studio, they began to take shape. It was like putting together a jigsaw puzzle.

When the first assemblage was finished, I noticed how the rusty pieces of metal had come together to form what looked to me like a medal, like the ones they give to heroes. I thought about this notion and the basis for my thesis was formed.

Each object was made for a specific "individual." Unlike a shiny new accolade for some outward act of valor, these medals were made to honor individuals who have beat the odds just by living their lives. They represent the struggles individuals have endured and their sheer will to survive. They personify the unseen in each of us.

These borrowed bits of history wired together with bones and debris are offered as visual internal scars. Our scars are evidence to the stories of our lives—the events that have made us stronger, resilient and uniquely beautiful.

Eventually, after all the traditional obligations were met, my thesis defense was complete. One at a time, each committee member came over and shook my hand. The art historian on my committee had not come over to personally congratulate me. I was disappointed at first until I turned and saw that she was crouched down in front of the wall carefully inspecting an object. She was not finished looking. I waited several minutes out of respect. Finally, she stood straight and took her glasses off. With her patent satchel under her arm, she quietly approached. We were the only two left in the gallery.

She reached for my hand. She looked straight into my eyes and spoke while nodding her head to reinforce her statement. She said four words and made her exit.

"These are powerful storytellers."

With that I found myself alone—with 240 other souls.

—————

The medal on the front cover is the one for *Tig*.

ONE

Tig stood on a tuft of dirt and weeds at the top of the hill. His eyes looked over the rolling dunes of variegated green. The wild and untamed prairie sprawled out in all directions. He could see rugged outcroppings of dolomite and limestone, dressed with spotty mounds of indigo and yarrow coming out of the red clay bluffs. Plateaus and ravines were interspersed between the intermittent crests with clusters of golden-tipped evergreens and wayward mesquites bending to the will of the wind. Several miles beyond the swollen ripples, the land lay down like waves finding the shore. There, the short grass prairie stretched out in grids of rich auburn loam. The lowlands were fertile and coveted. They flanked the river, gracing the banks of caramel sand. At the farthest point, the azure sky kissed the ground. It spread upwards, shaping a vast dome arching overhead, and dropping to meet the earth on the opposite side. A handful of cotton billows hovered in the big sky, gently shifting on a mantle of opulent blue. Tig drew his eyes up from the valley and scanned the hills once more. *How ruggedly beautiful they are*, he thought.

All these years and the prairie looked familiar. It had been transformed in ways, yet primitive and raw. But nonetheless scarred. Much like his own, the skin of the land had been altered over time.

Tig lifted his head, letting the warm wind brush his face. Had the soul of the land also been etched by events played out over time?

Was it possible to scar the human soul in such a way, to efface its essence so that it might never be restored?

Tig's mind surged back to a time before he was marked by life. Back to a time when his senses were alive like the bluestem and Indian grass moving in gentle waves over the hills, when the scent of sage and wild onions taunted his sinuses, and sand plums puckered his mouth with their sweet pungent flesh. When he felt the comfort and sting of living, a time before becoming anesthetized by withdrawal.

"Tig! For Christ's sake, get back in the car! I could've watered the entire countryside with the time you've taken!"

Johnnie half stood up in the driver's side of the old Cadillac convertible. With one hand on the steering wheel, he stretched up high enough to see Tig standing on a knoll several yards from the road.

"I mean it, Tig! I'm not gonna wait around here all day! Get in the damn car!" He sat back down hard and reached under his seat, retrieving a small bottle. He took a deep swig.

Tig snapped back from his daydream. He reluctantly turned and grabbed a small rugged tree trunk to steady himself. As he clenched the branch, his fingers burned with a familiar pain.

Tig turned to take a final look before descending the hill. *Things are different now*, he thought. He glanced down at his gloved hand. *Very different*.

"I swear, Tig. I knew I'd regret dragging ya out here. We only have a few more miles to go, so do me a favor and stop looking for ways to annoy me." Johnnie turned the key and revved the engine. Gravel churned up and cracked against the chrome bumper as he spun out and back onto the narrow clay road.

The only way Tig tolerated his older brother Johnnie was to ignore him. On rare occasions when Tig fired back an answer, Johnnie became violent, so Tig chose to keep his mouth shut.

Unfortunately, his silence was the lesser of two evils because when he did turn away, Johnnie considered it an insult. When it came down to it, Johnnie was always antagonized by Tig.

Tig leaned against his door while Johnnie harped on. Off in the distance, a red-tailed Hawk soared up and swooped down, circled overhead and dove again, taunting some small prey on the prairie floor. Tig tried to recall when the enmity between him and his brother had first started.

He stared out over the resilient prairie, searching for answers. Johnnie accelerated as they bottomed the hill where they were greeted with an unexpected jog in the road. Johnnie jerked the steering wheel, and the car skidded around the curve. The tires churned up the loose dirt, creating clouds of suffocating dust. A powdery haze filled the car. The whiff of dry earth, the taste of dirt and gritty sand between Tig's teeth roused the dust of the past. The memory took form. Tig saw it behind his closed eyelids—the ominous black demon rising up from the horizon—and he knew the answer, the birthplace of his brother's hate.

————

Johnnie and Richard lived with their parents on a modest farm at the edge of Arvita, a small town in northwest Oklahoma. The town was situated at the far edge of Dawson County, barely on the outskirts of the panhandle. Harold and Carrie Ann Mills had purchased their twenty acres shortly after their marriage in 1925.

Like so many young hopefuls, they bought into the real estate hype. Newspaper articles and realtors led them to believe the expansion of the Homestead Act offered them a chance to own some of the best land in the Great Plains. The dry rolling hills and the marginal land that awaited them was far from the fertile river valley they expected to find.

Young and idealistic, they chose to make the best of it and with the help of neighbors quickly built their small three-room house. They dug a well and purchased a few cows, some chickens, and a half dozen pigs. Carrie Ann made curtains, and Harold planted a garden. The shiny metal blades of their new windmill turned gently, humming a lullaby over the pasture. Within a year their first son, Johnnie, was born. Shortly after, Richard came along. Both sons were birthed on a straw mattress resting on the splintered wood planks of the bedroom floor.

Harold worked at the grain elevator, and those first few years in their new community were exciting and profitable. Seasonal rains yielded an abundance of wheat. Midas-touched fields of grain stretched as far as the eye could see. Nearly chest high, the graceful shafts swayed melodically in the wind, casting a golden haze over Dawson County. The economy was crashing back East, but the little town of Arvita and many others like it out west continued to operate blissfully unaffected.

By the early 1930s, the heavens closed up, and the rains stopped. Without irrigation, crops quickly withered, and plowed fields became blankets of red clay dust. Wells dried up, and cattle had to be sold. The winds began to gust, picking up the dirt and depositing it across the prairie. Tractors sat unusable, buried in soil, and farm commodities dropped. While agricultural businesses were failing all over the country, fields as far north as Nebraska continued to surrender their topsoil to the blistering winds.

Sand and dust storms started visiting Dawson and neighboring Talgart County with disastrous regularity. With all this and the added scourge of a grasshopper infestation, the townspeople and stockmen believed the end of the world was at hand. Residents packed up what few belongings they could carry and evacuated the area in large numbers.

Those early years were tremendously difficult, everyone doing all they could to survive. Neighbors helped each other plow, dig out equipment, and repair things. They frequently shared tools and provisions. Bartering became a way of life. Food was scarce. As often as possible, what could be saved from their gardens was processed and stored in cellars.

During the endless drought and amidst the financial woes of the Great Depression, Harold, Carrie Ann, and their two boys subsisted off of their small farm. A week's worth of food might consist of a measly handful of scrawny vegetables, what milk their skinny cow could produce, and an egg or two. On rare occasions, government rations provided a piece of salt pork or a bag of cornmeal, meager provisions for a family of four.

———

By the mid-30s, the drought and the Depression were more than enough to bear, but it was the Dusters that pushed the limit of suffering. With the ferocity of a hurricane, the storms rolled over the prairie.

Precious topsoil ripped from plowed fields was caught up in the roaring wind and would cover the sky in haze. The worst were the black blizzards barreling in—mushrooming clouds from hell. They would cover everything with an impenetrable darkness of suffocating dust and dirt. In a single year, more than thirty Dusters blew through the northwest counties of Oklahoma.

Nothing Carrie Ann could do would keep the dirt at bay. She put wet towels over the windows, sealed the doors, and covered everything in the house.

Regardless, the morning after a dust storm, nothing had escaped untouched. The blankets, the pillows on the beds, the children's toys, and the dishes were all encased in inches of displaced grime.

The small vegetable garden was regularly coated with layers of terracotta powder, and what the pelting sand and lack of water did not destroy the rabbits ate. Starving coyotes were shot by the ranchers to protect the livestock, so the jack-rabbits ran free and multiplied. Thousands of rabbits covered the desolate land. With the horror of an apocalyptic pestilence, they descended on the small town, searching for food, consuming everything in sight.

Townspeople would gather. Standing arm in arm they would encircle the rodents and corral them. Then in a nightmarish frenzy, they would bludgeon the rabbits to death with baseball bats and makeshift clubs. These primitive hunts were witnessed by even the youngest in town, who alongside their elders, joined in the kill.

Harold and Johnnie participated, but Richard could not get himself to do it.

"Ah come on, Richard! You scared or what? I'm gonna kill some rabbits. I'm gonna hit them in the head and knock their brains all over the ground. Like this." Johnnie swung his arms around in wild motions, acting out the kill.

"That's what I'm gonna do. But not you, cuz you're just a baby! Lil' One wants ta hide with his mama, right Lil' One? You just a scaredy cat, ain't ya?"

Richard stood back as Harold handed his son Johnnie a part of a wooden fence post.

"Don't you worry none, Lil' One. Maybe next time you'll want to come. You stay here and watch over your Momma. Johnnie and me, we'll handle this."

Harold headed out the door. As Johnnie grabbed the door handle, he leaned over and whispered in Richard's ear. "You just a baby, scaredy cat." Then he held up his stick like he intended to bludgeon his brother on the head.

As soon as Johnny stepped out through the door, Richard slammed it shut. He was grateful to be closed up in the house with his mother. As the hunt began, Carrie Ann went about preparing dinner, but Richard became agitated. With nowhere to escape and the commotion mounting outside, he crawled under his bed, holding his ears with his eyes squeezed tight. His attempts to shut out the dull thuds and screaming rabbits failed. Ultimately, the hellish sounds visited him in night terrors for weeks.

———

In the midst of the drought, Harold watched many local stockmen stand helpless as their starving cattle were shot and dumped in canyons as part of the Emergency Cattle Purchase Program. Harold knew the few Holsteins occupying his pasture were a commodity, and he saw to it they were well cared for. Harold would labor late into the evenings, doing all he could to protect his livestock.

Russian thistles the size of small bushes dried up all over the Great Plains. They would snap off when their roots withered and commence to roll—tumbleweeds in the wind. They would summersault across the fields. Inevitably, they would snag against the barbed wire fences that safeguarded grazing cattle. When the dust storms hit, mounds of sand and dirt would drift against the trapped weeds, so much so that land bridges formed over the fences and cattle began to walk up and over dirt-covered barbed wire. Escaped cattle left unprotected eventually starved to death if the dust didn't suffocate them first.

Many of Harold's neighbors lost their livestock this way. So,

Harold spent copious hours with his son Johnnie digging out sand drifts and pulling tumbleweed off the fences. It was a painful chore. After hours of digging, their hands were covered with splinters and blisters. His back aching, Harold would stand back and survey their work. Satisfied the fence was cleared and his livestock protected, he and Johnnie would head back to the house under the night sky. The next day, another storm would come, and Harold, weary, discouraged, shovel in hand, would slowly trudge through the sand back out to the fence line. Johnnie followed close behind.

———

Pneumonia from the dust was becoming an epidemic with infants and toddlers. The elderly were most at risk. In an attempt to stave it off, at even a hint of a cough, Carrie Ann would give her boys a dose of kerosene in sugar water. Wet towels and bandanas were worn around their faces. As soon as they were available, Harold picked up ventilating masks for his family at Smith's Hardware Store. Eventually no one went anywhere without either a wet cloth or a mask over his or her face.

Although preventing the bulk of dust from entering the lungs, the masks were not totally successful, and the death rate continued to climb. The population of Dawson County was already near half of what it had been before the Dusters started. Folks were still packing up and moving out in droves. Farmers were defaulting on their loans, and suicides were not uncommon.

One neighbor stood at the gate to the Mills' home bidding them farewell, telling how he was leaving just to save what was left of his wife.

"We just can't stay any longer, Harold. Marylyn has had a nervous breakdown. The dust storms, the dirt. It just never ends. God, it just never ends. She can't take it any more, Harold. I found her wild-eyed, eating dirt off the table."

———

On a crystal-clear April morning in 1935, Harold gathered his family for church. It was Palm Sunday and a beautiful spring day. The sky was cloudless and deep blue, the sun warm and inviting. A lighthearted joy radiated from the community. This was the type of day wind and dust-weary people lived for. There was no tangible explanation for their stubborn tenacity, why they chose to stay, to continue to live in such adverse conditions. Many who knew of their plight called them foolish, even irresponsible for putting their families at risk. But if asked, folks in Arvita would say they had a strong belief rain would come to restore the crops and provide better days. So, for those who remained—for Harold and Carrie Ann—every vibrant sunny day was evidence of what lay ahead. With the strength of their convictions and the power of their hope, they put their heads down and plowed through to the next day, trusting that the worst had already come.

Harold had developed the habit of keeping his livestock in the barn, but it was such a nice day he decided that after he had fed them, he would let them roam in the pasture. Albeit not much more than a patch of dirt, the cattle appeared to enjoy the fresh air.

After the service, the congregation gathered for a picnic at the creek bed just beyond the church grounds. Roughhewn tables were covered with plates of food and pitchers of iced tea. A single chocolate cake sat on a small glass pedestal at the end of the table. This was rare treat at a time when food was sparse, and it caught the attention of all who attended.

Children and adults gathered around to admire it. With oohs and ahhs, they circled the cake as if surveying an exotic treasure. After the blessing was given, everyone sat to eat. Conversations were lighthearted, and laughter accompanied the simple offerings at the table. As the sun began to lower, afternoon rays spread across the sandy banks of the dry creek bed, creating playful shadows that danced over the rocks.

The children chased each other in a game of tag. Teenagers flirted innocently while the elders told generation-honored stories. For a time, the weight of the drought and the Great Depression dissipated, as the folks from Arvita were drawn together under the safe mantle of community.

By early mid-day, the air took on an ominous chill. Parishioners began to mention they could feel their skin tingle, a telltale sign of increasing static electricity in the atmosphere. A cool, even wind began to blow from the north. The birds and animals became agitated. Flocks of squawking geese soared loudly overhead. The barometric pressure dropped rapidly, causing dogs to howl and babies to cry. The temperature took another dip, making it a good twenty degrees colder.

Without notice, the wind subsided, and everything grew disturbingly silent and still. Carrie Ann instinctively stood up from the table and visually accounted for her small family. Harold noticed her look of concern, and he reached to squeeze her hand. She looked intuitively into her husband's eyes while the breeze lifted her dark curls. Time was momentarily suspended....

The horizon went black. The heavens roared. Huge billowing black clouds rose in the distance and began to roll like tumbleweeds tossed and hurtling across the open fields. Red and white gingham table cloths began thrashing in the wind, sending dishes and food crashing to the ground. The cake platter shattered against the hard unquenched earth. Bells began to sound throughout Arvita—a loud continuous clanging cacophony as parishioners grabbed their families and ran for cover in the church. Carrie Ann clenched Richard's hand while Harold latched onto Johnnie. The young family dashed across the church yard with the rest of the panicked congregation. Harold pushed Johnnie on up ahead of him next to Carrie Ann as she ascended the stairs toward the open door. Before Carrie Ann entered the church, she turned to motion for Harold, but he was gone.

She tried to leave to go back out, but the crowds behind her drove her farther into the church. Johnnie cried out in a panic for his father, but Harold did not hear him. Running frantically to the window, Johnnie pressed his face against the glass as the heavy shutters were closed. He began to whimper, then cry, then wail.

Richard stood close to his mother, gripping her hand as the massive door was pushed shut and the bolt forced down. The scraping of metal on metal set Richard's teeth on edge like sand caught in his gums. When the heavy bar finally dropped into the latch, the clanging thud brought a sigh of relief from the congregation, but not for Carrie Ann, who deliberately closed her eyes and dropped her head into her hands.

Knowing his family was secure, Harold tore out toward their small farm just a few blocks away. He ran down the dirt road, the black clouds pushing in behind him, darkness descending. Pulling a small hankie from his pocket, he covered his mouth and nose. Turning, Harold could see the black demon pressing in on him, so he ran faster. He closed his eyes and pressed on.

Dear God, we can't survive without the livestock. Oh God, spare my family.

Racing through the gate to the small pasture, he threw a rope over the cow and tugged her into the barn. He ran back out in an attempt to corral the rest of the cattle, to frighten them back into the fenced barnyard just as the storm closed in and covered the church steeple. Waves of sand pelted his face, slashed at his skin, and stung his eyelids. The raging wind hurled tumbleweed at him. Sharp twigs snagged his cheeks.

He threw up his hand to protect himself but the wind tore away the cloth protecting his mouth. The dirt was so dense he could not see anything. Trails of blood ran down his arms. He became disoriented, his mouth full of dirt. Coughing, spitting, and stumbling, he felt for the fence while trying to keep his mouth and nose covered. He groped for the gate, but the storm was too much. The wind-blown pellets tore at his eyes. Small pockets of red emerged on his face, as he continued to be impaled with sand, inescapable shrapnel whirling in the wind. He began to choke, wheezing as he went to his knees, then onto his stomach, planting his head between his arms, gasping for air.

After four hours of dreadful blackness and violent howling wind, the storm passed. With the help of one of the deacons, the pastor pulled up the rod and forced open the door of the church. Johnnie bolted and ran all the way home. The house was surrounded by hills of dirt and the barn had nearly drifted over.

He climbed up a hill of sand and dropped down into the entrance of the barn. There, the cow was standing, traumatized but safe in her stall. A few stray pigs roamed through the barn, while a handful of chickens pecked at the dirt-covered straw. Johnnie leaned against the back door to the barn, forcing away drifts of sand. He threw his body back and forth on the door until he finally created an opening large enough to push through. As he tumbled out, clouds of rusty dust swelled up behind him.

He tried to run to the pasture, but the sand sucked at his legs and slowed him down. In his frustration, he began to cry. He pushed on, hot tears washing the dirt from his eyes, trails forming a map of anguish across his cheeks. He slogged his way instinctively to the entrance of the field. Two cows lay stiff and cold, partially buried in a drift of sand under the battered windmill. The gate was mostly submerged, and a ridge of dirt and sand encircled the yard. The storm had dropped enough soil to completely cover any evidence of the barbed wire fence. Johnnie stood there taking in the scene around him.

Disoriented, he turned in circles. Dirt-laced snot ran into his mouth. In frustration, Johnnie lifted his arm to wipe it away. Tipping his head to his sleeve he saw it—an irregularity in the ridge. He plowed through the sea of dirt to the nearest corner of the pasture, digging frantically with his bare hands, unaware of how the grit was sanding off his skin. His hands were bleeding when he felt the worn heel of a familiar boot.

Johnnie jumped in horror. Falling backwards, he sat down hard. He couldn't move. He stared at the pile of dirt in front of him. Johnnie was still motionless when his mother and three men from the church showed up. Across from where Johnnie sat, they uncovered his father.

Buried alive, face down, they found Harold tucked between clumps of tumbleweed, covered by a pile of dirt.

Johnnie was the spitting image of his father, and they had always been together. He had followed Harold around everywhere from when he began to toddle straight through to the afternoon the church folk referred to as Black Sunday, the day his father died. When Johnnie woke the morning after the storm and realized his father was never coming back, he let out a scream that shook the wood planks of the kitchen floor, sending residual dust falling through the cracks.

The day Carrie Ann buried her husband, gentle white clouds floated peacefully across a deep blue sky. The morning sun reflected off of the sand with such intensity that it glared like new snow. Carrie Ann wanted her husband buried on their land.

Early that morning, Mr. Peterson, the local funeral director, had arranged the pallbearers. They were the first to step out of the funeral home with Harold's simple pine box. Carrie Ann and her boys were the next to darken the doorway. Taking a deep sigh and squinting her weary bloodshot eyes, she stepped off the porch. The pallbearers dropped their heads in respect as Johnnie and Richard took their place next to their mother behind the casket. A small group of neighbors and friends emerged from the Arvita Funeral Home behind Carrie Ann and quietly got in line.

The road through town was no longer defined. Covered over, it visually merged with everything around it, all disfigured, a desert of dust and sand. The mourners were shrouded in black, and they formed a line in the gritty loam. They walked ever so slowly in single file to the Mill's place. The pace of the procession mimicked the cadence of a dirge, a living yet silent requiem. As they drew near the little spot of land where Harold would rest, someone began to sing quietly, "I need Thee every hour, most gracious Lord; no tender voice like Thine can peace afford. I need Thee, oh I need Thee; every hour I need Thee."

Carrie Ann closed her eyes, and tears dripped off her chin. Richard gripped his mother's hand all the more and choked back the deep sadness rising up in him. Johnnie pulled away. He kicked the dirt in anger before breaking out in sobs. Embarrassed and knowing nothing could soothe his ache, he ran to the back of the line and lagged behind. His dark hair, the legacy of his father, stood out against the glaring earth. It glistened in the sunlight, a single black dot, the punctuation mark at the end of a long line of human suffering.

"I need Thee, every hour in joy or pain; come quickly and abide, or life is vain. I need Thee, oh I need Thee; every hour I need Thee."

The procession solemnly turned to ascend the small embankment. They stopped under a single tree. Frail shredded leaves fluttered in the soft breeze, desperately clinging to the withered branches. Beaten but unyielding, the determined little oak stood as a guardian over the plot.

The interment was simple. There were neither fancy words nor any emotional outpourings. Everything had already been said. They simply laid Harold's hands across his chest and gave him back to the prairie.

Carrie Ann and her neighbors were emotionally spent. There had been so many deaths in the past few years that the edge of loss had become very familiar. Everyone had come to believe that death was just another of the many sacrifices the prairie required. She was a restless, demanding mistress. Her many personalities—her cracked and blistered earth, her shiny rain-soaked clay, her blood-streaked sunsets, her demon dusters, her soft waving grasses, her endless azure skies—were all as temporal as the measured days of a human life.

Those who dwelled on the prairie and chose to dance with her learned quickly that to survive, they must strengthen their backs and their resolve. They were a resilient people.

Regardless, an air of sadness surrounded many a farmhouse. The sanded paint on the clapboards, the cloudy etched windows, the dead cattle, and the parched land were all haunting reminders of the sacrifice the drought, the black blizzards, and the Great Depression had cost the residents of Arvita.

Carrie Ann moved through her grief as gracefully as possible, yielding to the waves of sorrow as they rolled over her. The boys were an exception, however. Johnnie never got over his dad's death; worse, he never got through it. And Richard, well Richard just pushed it under and buried it. Just as nutrient giving loam had smothered the life out of the prairie, Richard suffocated his verve under the weight of his emotional restraint.

———

"TIG! Are ya deaf now too? I was trying to ask ya a damn question, but you're so lost in that dull brain of yours. Where'd ya put that Southern Comfort I bought the other day? TIG! Do ya hear me?"

Tig had no difficulty. He heard perfectly. He reached under his seat and pulled out the half-full bottle. His concerns about Johnnie drinking were of little consequence. He handed the bottle to Johnnie, who took a swig while juggling the steering wheel with his other hand. Tig turned toward his side of the car.

"TIG!"

Johnnie had taken on his patent whiny tone, his disgust for his brother spilling out in two condescending syllables.

"TE-GA"

Tig hated his nickname. Even as a young child he was rarely called by his birth name, Richard. For years, Tig was referred to as Li'l One until he was given the name Tig. He was never sure which he thought to be more humiliating. No one, save Johnnie, really knew how he had been given the nickname. Even his own mother could not remember when he was first called Tig, but he would never forget. The memory of the day he was branded with the name still held venom, and the recollection set him burning anew.

───────

As far as Carrie Ann could recall, the storm on Black Sunday was the last of the major black blizzards to ravage Arvita. After Harold's death, Carrie Ann relied on her boys to help her survive. The young widow and her two sons were cared for by the townspeople. They provided food and companionship whenever possible. Several relatives, friends, and acquaintances visited the Mills' home over the weeks following Harold's death.

Tig was seven years old that summer, and his Aunt Verna was paying Carrie Ann a token "here to make sure you are OK" visit. The "I care" drop in was more like an appointment than a social call. It lasted all of an hour, just long enough for Verna to say she had met the obligation of getting in touch with her widowed sister-in-law.

Aunt Verna sat across from a frail Carrie Ann in the modestly furnished room of the small farmhouse. Johnnie and his little brother Richard stood quietly off to the side of the room out of respect for their elders. The brothers would have given anything to have been somewhere else, but this was how their mother wanted it. She needed them close. So, they stood near the doorway saying nothing but fidgeting the entire time, ready to tear as soon as they were released.

Richard studied his aunt. He hated the way her nostrils flared, just enough from his perspective to display the dark hair in her nose. It matched the short frizzy dark hair on her head. Random bristles shot out from under a small faded hat pinned down tight to her skull. Her cream-toned blouse was stretched tight over her chest. It gaped open in even intervals down her front. Each small button strained to contain her ample bosom which attempted to free itself. Verna's lap spread across the chair like soft putty. The scant excesses of her skirt had flattened from the static in the room and adhered to the sides of the cushions. Tig believed they were clinging for dear life. Her heavy, beige-colored stockings were rolled painfully just below her knees where her legs were turning blue in places. The skin of her feet spilled over the tops of her clunky black shoes that secured the entire ensemble to the dusty floor.

Verna held her cup of tea, barely touching the handle with her chubby little finger sticking out. Carrie Ann thought about how people said she did this to put on "airs," a haughty display of delusions of grandeur. In truth, Verna feared the dust, dirt, and grime of a prairie farmer's house. To be contaminated by such debris would undo her pretense of having risen above the small-town life she had so quickly left behind.

"Carrie Ann, I can't get over just how different your boys are from each other. Why they are barely two years apart and Johnnie towers over Richard. Funny how they are from the same tree but as different as branches are to a twig!"

Johnnie looked down at his brother with a glint in his eye. Johnnie's relentless need to tease might as well have been printed across his forehead. Leave it to Aunt Verna to hand him some very impressive shiny new ammunition. Johnnie leaned over and whispered in Richard's ear.

"Twiggy, Twiggy never gonna be a branch, stupid little twig, snap and break, snap and break baby twig!"

Richard swung to hit his brother, but his fist bounced off the door frame instead, making a loud cracking sound, leaving a dent in the wood. Verna jumped, spilling her tea all over her lap. As she flew up out of her chair, one of the buttons on her blouse surrendered the fight and soared across the room. Verna let out a humiliating scream.

"Carrie Ann, you better take hold of that boy!"

Her hat had shifted and was covering one eye. The sight caught the boys by surprise and they began to laugh uncontrollably. Verna's anger heated the room. She turned to Richard and put her chubby bent finger to his nose.

"You're a little Hellian, aren't you? I knew you'd turn out to be a good-for-nothin'. You were always a disappointment. Oh, believe you me, I knew your father well and he must have wished you were more like Johnnie. Well, with your father gone I have half a mind to...."

"That will be enough, Verna!"

Carrie Ann had risen from her chair and was on her feet. Her eyes were intense and drawn together. Her neck strained, and her forehead pulled into a scowl.

"How dare you! You have no right to speak to my son that way." Carrie Ann threw her arm up toward the door. "You need to leave, Verna. NOW!"

The anger in her voice sent Verna wailing out the front door, one hand clenching her blouse and the other swinging her handbag. After she left, Carrie Ann doled out the discipline but not before attending to some much-needed damage control.

"Richard, she didn't mean it. Aunt Verna just...."

Richard stopped listening. What followed—the apologies, all the justifications, the condolences—were of no value. Aunt Verna's words had sunken in, forging deep into his psyche. They traveled quickly to that desolate place, to the canyon forming within, the pit where an accumulating pile of self-loathing debris was covered over with an ever-thinning layer of topsoil: Richard's absolute will to suppress.

Richard was ordered to bed that night without supper--proper punishment for his disrespectful behavior. While Carrie Ann attended to cleaning up the mess, Johnnie followed Richard into the bedroom.

"Ha Ha Twiggy. Twiggy baby don't get no supper."

Throughout the years, Johnnie's whiny tone still rang in Tig's ears. Over time, the "w" was dropped and everyone just called him Tig. No one really even knew him as Richard anymore.

The brand Johnnie laid on him that day stuck. It left a burning scar, one that had the potential of setting off a deep and frightening anger.

TWO

Johnnie's 1965 Cadillac convertible rolled with the top down from hill to hill, its weathered blue finish merging with the late spring sky. Regardless of its dented body, missing hubcaps, and broken tail lights, the car took the turns. The tires grabbed the gravel and cursed the sand as they skidded and spun. Like most of the roads in Talgart County, Rte. 426 was packed red clay with a thin covering of pea gravel. On a rainy day, the top layer would begin to run. An earthen slip would form a slimy coat over the surface, quickly turning the road slick and dangerous. Rubber tires didn't stand much of a chance of staying in touch with the surface. Although particularly risky when wet, driving on the sienna bands that hemmed the rolling hills of the prairie was always dangerous, particularly for those who drove like Johnnie.

Johnnie's cavalier approach to churning up the loose gravel at high speed was indicative of his total approach to life. He was a risk-taker, a gambler, a rogue. Johnnie never considered the consequences of his choices, for to do so would compromise the thrill of acting on impulse.

Tig's stomach lurched as the car sped up and plunged down, mound after mound. When Johnnie accelerated to ascend each hill, the wheels spun and sprayed gravel to the sides of the road. The passenger seat was left dusted in gritty clay every time the Cadillac flew around a corner.

"Hey, little brother, ya ain't lookin' so good." Johnny grinned and held out an empty potato chip bag. "Here, if you're gonna barf, use this. Don't be messin' with my car."

Tig was miserably car sick and concentrating on not losing his lunch. Johnnie, on the other hand, relished the ride like a kid on a roller coaster. His adrenaline surging, he let out a loud "Wahoo" as the car dove down and soared up again, the baby blue convertible rousing thick red puffs to settle in its wake.

Tig saw the brick structure rise on a distant hill and heaved a sigh of relief. He would not have recognized it to be the Carson ranch had Johnnie not mentioned Ron's new house. Unlike his father, Abe Carson, Ron much preferred modern brick to farmhouse clapboard. So, he tore down the house he had inherited and replaced it with a contemporary brick rambler. Much to the delight of Ron's wife, this house was filled with the latest in-home appliances. The closets were larger and the bathroom floors tiled. The stained linoleum floors of the former house were gone, and, with the exception of a few antiques, so was everything else.

Tig figured he much preferred the white clapboard house with its broad front porch shaded by the craggy old black jack oak, which too had gone missing. As Johnnie pulled onto the long gravel drive, the house loomed as a perfect brick rectangle erected against the horizon, a wide door cut into a blue abyss.

Ron was on the front steps ready to greet them as the silt-covered car ground its way up the gravel drive. Johnnie, waving frantically, pulled up close to the house. As he put the car in park, he leaned out over the door yelling at Ron.

"Ron! Good God, it's been forever brother!"

Before Tig could shake the dust from his hat, Johnnie lunged out and slammed the driver's side door. A thick cloud of dust nearly choked Tig as he reached for the door handle.

Johnnie promptly tied Ron up in a bear hug. Tig closed the door hesitantly so as not to stir up the dirt collected in the seams of the leather seats and the arm rests. Unassumingly, he approached the embracing friends. Catching Tig out of the corner of his eye, Ron turned and stuck out his right hand to grasp Tig's. Tig stood unmoved in awkward silence.

"Oh, hey Tig, forgive me man. I forgot. Here…."

Ron dropped his right hand and offered his left. Tig reached out with his ungloved hand and shook Ron's. The strength of Tig's non-dominant hand caught Ron by surprise.

"It's been a long time."

"Yeah, it sure has."

Tig lowered his hand and pursed his lips. An uncomfortable silence began to swell between them. Johnnie grabbed Ron by the arm and swung him toward the house while Tig, not saying a word, was left staring at the ground.

"Ron, tell me. How is Linda these days…."

Their conversation faded as they strolled toward the house. Tig didn't move. He was lost in his thoughts. As the two friends talked, Johnnie intermittently increased his volume so Tig would hear specific parts of the conversation. As planned every so often, Tig could make out a few words of Johnnie's and Ron's exchange.

"She's gone, Ron. Long gone, and she ain't comin' back."

Tig looked up long enough to see Ron shake his head and mouth, "Sorry, so sorry."

Ron and Johnnie continued to converse, as though they were oblivious to Tig. The words were not always clear, but the tone was undeniable—demeaning pity. So accustomed to his brother, Tig could intuitively decipher Johnnie's sentences just by observing his mannerisms.

"Nope, the (accident) likely (killed) her."

Tig was doing his level best to appear as though he was taking everything in stride. Inside he was agonizing. He burned with anger over the humiliation of what was taking place, another episode of Johnnie's display of condescension and disgust disguised as concern. To Johnnie, Tig would always be "little Twig. Snap and break little Twig." Tig was never sure if it was his weakness or his brother's vindictiveness that enabled the perpetuation of this devastating ritual.

When Tig was thoroughly humiliated, the stabbing blow came: like the coyote stalking the shrew, ambushing it, pouncing on it, injuring it, waiting for it to be most vulnerable, and then delivering the lethal bite—teeth cutting bone. Tig looked up and heard the words full well, the volume accompanied by perfect enunciation no doubt meant for his benefit.

"I know, Ron. Like I've said all along, she should've been mine. None of this would've happened had she been mine."

Tig dropped his head and felt his blood pressure pounding behind hot eyes. He shuffled his feet, milling the earth beneath his timeworn boots. Dry vestiges of the prairie wind, the soil, like Tig, had been wind-driven and left displaced. No stranger to the grind of shifting sand beneath his feet, Tig was introduced to it years ago as a boy. As inexorable as his nickname, so was his connection to the dirt.

———

It took months to sweep the last of the soil away and bring some semblance of normalcy back to the Mills' home after Black Sunday. Tig spent weeks digging out the house and barn for his mother. He removed the dirt shovels-full at a time. Soil, sand, and powdery clay rested in dunes nearly ten feet high against the windows and the back door. Loads were painstakingly dug out by hand and moved by wheelbarrow to the back of the pasture.

Johnnie and Tig would start out in the morning working together, taking turns digging and lugging the soil. Before noon without fail, Johnnie would wander off to attend to some other less demanding chore. He never managed to return. Meanwhile, Tig held tight to his post. The weight of the dirt pulled on his arms and tugged at the tendons in his neck. The handle of the shovel worked deep blisters and callouses into his palms. Frequently, the dry dust would sting his nostrils and cause his chapped lips to crack and bleed. He would just wipe them off on the sleeve of his shirt and continue working. Carrie Ann would watch from the window and marvel at how her young son had the resolve of a grown man.

It was a monotonous job that dragged through each day with no reprieve. To break the boredom, Tig would run a hymn or two over in his mind. He especially liked "Come Thou Fount of Every Blessing." He knew that one word for word. They sang it frequently at the church since the land had become so thirsty.

Other times he would challenge himself to see how much dirt he could move. He would take a piece of burned wood and mark the side of the house where the pile was when he started and then again when he finished. Each day he would try to move more than he had the day before. Sometimes his eyes would catch a swooping hawk or a scurrying mouse, and he would stop and watch. This was when a curious ritual would take place; no matter where Tig would initially be looking, his head would eventually turn and face the pasture. Many times during the day he could be seen standing, stone still, shovel in hand, staring at the field.

As Carrie Ann observed secretly from behind the curtained window, she wondered what he was thinking. Could he be remembering how his father would walk alongside, gently prodding the cows as they slowly ambled across the field? Maybe his vision was all wind, choking dust and bloody hands, images of his father pulling himself along the fence, desperate to survive on the day he was buried alive. Tig never spoke of his thoughts or what he envisioned as he fixated on that field. It remained a mystery, because Tig protected those moments of reflection, shielding them for only his heart to see.

———

"We're gonna take the back way," Ron called out as he climbed up into his oversized red pickup truck. Leaning out the window, he yelled as he pulled out in front of Johnnie.

"It'll be faster."

A spray of gravel, dust, and weeds peppered Johnnie's beat up car, adding a few more pings to the lackluster finish. The two vehicles jostled back and forth down the pot-holed drive. The short cut, Rte. 412 to the Old Macklin Place, was no more than a continuation of the prior twenty miles that Tig had endured; only worse—up and down, round and round. The winding narrow ribbon of road cut through the rugged wilderness. Fortunately, the house Tig would soon call home was only five miles away.

Tig marveled at how virginal the landscape appeared. The hills covered with unkempt terrain rolled on for miles, the trees all bent, facing due east, sculpted by the wind, each a living compass, and for Tig, pointing the way home. Tig leaned his head against the back of his seat and closed his eyes. *I never should have left.* The prodigal was finally returning—broken and alone. Faithful and long-suffering, the land had been waiting to greet him. As the wheels slowed to turn, Tig could feel the breeze and hear the soft rustling of the Johnson grass, their whispers confirming he was back on the prairie where he belonged.

Ron pulled up in front of the house with Johnnie behind. The dust settled, and Tig leaned out the window to get a good look. *So,* he thought, *this is where I will be living.*

The little dwelling built years ago had been foreclosed on and then abandoned by the Macklin family during the Dust Bowl. When the Carsons bought up all the land in the area, the Macklin's small tenant farm was among the holdings.

Weathered and witness to cloudless skies and howling storms, the modest three-room structure had seen better days. The house sat on the top of a little hill, positioned as though on a small pedestal. The knoll it occupied rolled down to a small valley on each side. There, at the lowest point to the east, was a windmill and just beyond it a wooded area. Although rusted with one blade dangling, the windmill rotated slowly. Water dripped from the discharge pipe into a large warped trough. The slightest breeze would catch the blades and they would turn, loudly squeaking and grinding together.

The sound of the screeching blades shot through Tig like a gun. He froze. His gloved hand rested firmly on his jaw as he bit his lip. Tig felt like his feet were cemented to the ground. He stared, transfixed at the windmill. Beads of sweat gathered on his brow. Tig momentarily lost his bearings, hypnotized by the grinding sounds of metal against metal, until Johnnie called out to him. "TIG. Would ya stop wasting time! We need to let Ron show us around. The man needs to get back to his cattle. Some of us work for our keep, ya know? Besides, you'll have all the time in the world to work on that windmill!"

Tig forced his attention to shift. He turned and made his way to the house.

"Tig, we did what we could to get the house ready, but without a lot of notice, well ya…."

"No bother, Ron. This will be fine, and I'm most grateful."

"Um, yes, of course. Tig, why don't we take a look inside. I don't have a key. Never seemed to need one out here in the middle of nowhere and all. I suppose we could put…."

"I'll just keep my shotgun handy. It'll be fine."

Tig stood back and took a good look at the house, as though being acquainted with a long-lost friend. From a distance, the house appeared to be rectangular, but it was actually cut out in the back forming more of an L shape. A small outhouse was positioned just beyond the east side of the main structure. From the looks of it, Tig figured the house was no more than three hundred square feet.

"I'll just wait out here." Johnnie turned and walked back to the car where he retrieved the bottle from under the seat.

The cement stucco that covered the house had been painted at one time. Now more beige than white, bits of unpainted wood were exposed from underneath the chipped cement. Most of the milk paint on the front door had been naturally sanded off. The threshold sat above a cement stoop and was located between two windows. Tig followed Ron up the stoop that led into the house.

Inside, the floors were covered with stained and torn, checkered linoleum. Bits of the covering were missing, and the splintered plank floors were laid bare, the cracks open to the earth. The walls were covered with plaster. Some of the it had chipped off, revealing the lathe beneath. In other spots, bits of horsehair stuck out. On all sides, rust-toned water stains streaked from the ceiling to the floor.

Sunlight broke into the room randomly above the walls, defining parts of the wavy corrugated tin roof that rested precariously on top of the house. Thin streaks of light stole in through the openings and raked down the distressed walls. Although there was electricity, Tig saw very few outlets. A single bulb hung on a stripped cord from the ceiling, providing the only manmade light. Intermittently, a waft of air would send the bulb swaying back and forth. There were very few windows, each with at least one cracked pane. All were etched and cloudy, some completely opaque.

"I reckon ya'd call this the kitchen and living area."

A chipped refrigerator and a small dented gas stove sat along one wall. An old cast iron pot with a large bent spoon sat next to a flowered tea kettle, which rested on one of the burners.

"Ahh, that was Linda. I told her the flowers were too much," Ron rolled his eyes.

Tig hadn't noticed. He was wrestling to get the refrigerator door open. He supported his right hand with his left and jerked up on the handle. It opened, releasing a rancid odor. A jar filled with something black and dusty sat on the top shelf. Tig shut the door as Ron apologized.

"Oh man, that must've been left from the last time we were up here huntin'. I'll bring some cleanin' supplies next time I'm out, Tig."

"No bother, Ron. I can manage it," Tig turned toward the other side of the room.

A metal Formica-topped table, large enough for two, was tucked against the west window. On it sat a stack of three plates and a few utensils, four coffee mugs, and two glasses. Two mismatched wood chairs sat at either end of the table and leaned to one side on the uneven floor. At the far end of the room was a tiny pot-bellied wood stove sitting on top of a handful of fire bricks. A worn-out arm chair covered in brown Naugahyde sat on the opposite side. The fake leather was scuffed and torn. The stuffing poked out of the seat and one of the arms.

"Ya can use wood in the stove over there, but ya need to watch it. The pipe is small, and it likes to collect creosote. Now, this here is a gas. The propane tank is settin' right out there." Ron gestured to the west side of the house.

"You'll need to let us know when you're runnin' short. I can have them come out and fill yours when they fill ours. It's runnin' about thirty one cents per gallon right now. Market says it will likely go up soon. This tank is filled right now, so it should keep ya a long time. The stove is for cookin'. Ya should use only the wood stove to heat the house."

Tig nodded as he fiddled with the knobs and checked the oven. Ron said, "Over here is the bedroom."

An opening between the two sides of the house led to a small room. It had a window facing the front of the house and a door on the opposite side to the outside.

"This door is the fastest way to get to the john."

Ron opened the back door and pointed to an unpainted shanty the size of a closet approximately fifteen feet away.

"There's no water in the house. You'll have to bring water up from the windmill down there. I left a couple pails back behind the outhouse. There's an extra small trough down by the well ya can drag up here if ya want."

Ron pointed beyond the outhouse to the squeaking windmill at the base of the bluff. Tig nodded. As they stepped back to the house, Tig walked into the bedroom. A doorless, narrow closet hosted a few random hangers. The walls were much like those in the front room, stained and aged. Tig moved to the window. Positioned almost below it was an army cot made up with a sheet, a blanket, and a pillow. The cot took up most of the room. Tig laid his hand on the sill. The window was partially open, and a draft of cool air was playing with the curtains.

"I know it ain't much, but Linda wanted to fancy it up a little bit, make it more home-like, I guess. She's always doin...."

Ron was muttering something about the room but, Tig had stopped listening and was held captive by the sheer curtain dancing in the breeze from the open window.

———

Swathes of transparent fabric flirted with her shoulders as she stood looking out the thick distorted pane. The window to her home was a small opening revealing the largeness of everything that fell outside her protection. Carrie Ann was faithfully waiting for her boys to crest the hill. Tig could see her shape backlit by the kerosene lantern as he made his way across the field. The house, like Carrie Ann, glowed with her love. His mother had been preparing chicken and noodles all day, and the aroma overtook him as he drew near. As the boys bolted through the door after school and after chores, the home she made embraced them. The table was covered with simple linens and bowls of warm food, and it always welcomed them. While they ate, Tig would run his bare feet over the hand-braided rug under the table.

Mealtime was a symphony of clanging spoons against bowls, random jabber, and laughter. After dinner, the dishes were cleared, and school books were laid in their place as the boys completed their assignments under the dim light of the kerosene lamp. Math and writing homework were more palatable with a side of Carrie Ann's fresh bread slathered with sand plum jam. After getting ready for bed, the boys would stoke the stove while Carrie Ann dusted off their shoes and shook out their trousers. Every night, she tucked them under their faded quilt. She always paused before closing the door. Standing backlit in the doorway, Carrie Ann whispered a prayer for her boys.

———

Tig never doubted home would be a safe place as long as his mother was there. A fleeting pang of nostalgia ran through him, the recognition that after all these years he still missed her. Everything he had ever imagined home should be was wrapped up in the silhouette of Carrie Ann waiting at the window.

"Well, Tig, I've gotta box of supplies in the back of the truck. Just a few things to get ya going. You'll need some tools, and ya mentioned ya had a gun. That's a good thing."

"I have my tools, so I won't be needin' any of those. Thank ya anyway. I plan to earn my keep, ya know. This won't be a free hand out. I'm not like that."

"I know, Tig. I figured we'd sit down and work everythin' out in a couple days after you're all settled in."

"That'll do just fine. Thank ya."

Ron started to leave and then turned back. He looked momentarily to the floor and then at Tig. "Tig, I need to tell ya how sorry I am about the way things worked out. Life sure ain't fair."

"No," Tig paused, "but it's all we got."

Tig dropped his head. He was clearly uncomfortable. Ron tapped him on the shoulder and then turned to leave. Tig heard the door open and shut. He remained at the window; the sun was dropping quickly, shooting tracks of deep purple across the sky. The windmill squeaked and turned as the wind shifted. A chilly draft of air forced its way into the room, leaving a fresh trail of dust on the sill. Tig reached up and pulled the window closed, and the curtains laid down.

————

As the years passed, Carrie Ann grew frail. Her lungs, like everything else, were blanketed in clay talc. Growing weaker and never having remarried, she relied on her sons to support her. She began to have periodic bouts of delirium. Her random hallucinations frightened her young sons. Soliciting support from the community provided intermittent assistance. However, the entire area was still recovering so resources were spread thin. As Carrie Ann's failing health demanded more attention, Johnnie and Tig would alternate caring for their mother. Keeping vigil by her beside meant long hours spent wiping the sweat of sickness off their mother's forehead, feeding her broth and kerosene with sugar—watching her die slowly.

What money Harold had saved had dwindled, and resources were becoming more difficult to come by. Survival on the drought-sick prairie required extreme measures. In order to endure the blustery winter months, Johnnie and Tig regularly collected desiccated cow patties. Digging them from the surrounding fields, they lugged them to the house in big pails. They'd burn them for fuel, keeping the house and their mother warm.

Throughout the hot summers, water was dragged from the well and brought to the house and garden. The boys sprinkled small amounts of cool liquid on the withered leaves, hoping to keep a few plants alive.

Johnnie learned how to use the tractor. He took charge of working the land, planting, cultivating, and harvesting what few vegetables he could grow. Both he and Tig managed the livestock. They saw to it that a pig was butchered, the ham smoked and then stored. The meat it provided lasted for nearly a year.

In 1940, the cooling rains finally came and ended the miserable drought that had bound the prairie for so long. Red cedar and green ash trees began to set down their roots and spread. Wild grasses and flowers began to fill the dirt-covered wasteland, anchoring the soil. Simultaneously, people started to move back to Arvita and the surrounding towns and counties. The river bottom area, the flat lands, began to change. Fields were plowed, but only under strict guidelines. Unlike prior to the drought, crops were regulated and rotated so as not to strip the topsoil and create another manmade disaster.

Large sections of land were acquired by ranchers who used it for cattle, lots of cattle. Within a relatively short time, the hills around Dawson and Talgart were covered with roaming hoofed spots of black and brown. In the winter months, herds of bawling cattle were moved slowly across the rolling prairie to the wheat fields. There, they grazed, fat and content on the early winter wheat. By early spring, the cattle were pulled off the fields while the wheat stooled. Within a short time, the rich soil was covered with a verdant green blanket of winter wheat set to be harvested in June. Before the wheat harvest, herds of wheat-fed cattle would be rounded up and driven to the railhead where they would be loaded and moved to market.

Things were looking up for the little town of Arvita. Once abandoned farms were again bustling with life as new families moved in and worked the land. The newest residents of Talgart and Dawson counties brought their stories with them. They told of adventure in faraway places. Johnnie was always eager to hear tales about anywhere but Arvita, so he availed himself every opportunity to gather new fodder for his wander-lusting heart. The more Johnnie heard, the more restless and discontent he became. This, compounded by his unresolved anger over his father's death and bitterness at having to spend time nursing his sick mother, made him hot-tempered. He became easily distracted, and he could seldom stick to a task. He would take his father's old truck and roam around Arvita, coming home late, leaving his chores for Tig.

Johnnie spent a lot of time with Ron Carson, a well-mannered son of a local rancher. Carrie Ann was impressed with Ron from the start, but Johnnie was adding some new acquaintances to his repertoire of friends. These individuals gave her pause for concern.

More often than not, Johnnie would come home, his eyes glazed over, his breath spiked with whiskey. Carrie Ann tried talking to her son, but invariably her attempts ended with Johnnie's explosive bouts of anger. Ultimately, his episodes caused Carrie Ann to harbor a deep fear for hers and Tig's safety. Without the benefit of her husband to lean on, Carrie Ann felt it best to avoid Johnnie. She cautioned Tig to do the same. This suited Johnnie just fine. He happily embraced a spirit of reckless abandon. For his part, he counted the days when he would no longer be obligated to live in the small white clapboard house he was convinced he had long since outgrown.

Conversely the more restless Johnnie grew, the more settled Tig became. Tig wanted nothing more than to stay on the little farm his parents had dreamed and then worked into reality. Tig was always looking for things to tinker with and fix. He was particularly adept at repairing machines. Carrie Ann marveled at her youngest son's innate gift, his mechanical acumen. As needed, he repaired the wind mill, the stove, the truck, and the farm equipment.

To provide extra income for his mother, he hired himself out to fix stuff for other folks in Arvita. New technology gave Tig something unique to learn every day. While Johnnie socialized, always looking for something to assuage his burning restless spirit, Tig repaired things. He could fix just about anything... except his mother.

During the last few weeks of Carrie Ann's life, Tig spent many hours sitting by her bedside. As he would care for her, she would talk with him, bringing up things he was never aware of.

"Tig, I know you love this little farm. It is not much, but I know your father would want you boys to have it. Pastor Davis is the executor of my will. Tig, I'm giving you the farm. Johnnie will get the truck and some of the equipment, but I want you to have the house, the land."

Tig was there when his mother breathed her last. He never left her side as she painfully succumbed to the dirt burying her lungs—dust to dust. He spent those last precious moments saying his good-byes while Johnnie was off on one of his usual jaunts. The fact that this was the second time he was not present during the death of a parent was not lost on Johnnie. His unresolved grief began to rapidly shape itself into shame and hostility. When Johnnie discovered Tig had inherited the farm, his resentment empowered an agenda. He found that goading his younger brother gave him a feeling of control. Johnnie relished the sense of power that coddled the emotional upheaval he carried inside.

Carrie Ann was laid quietly to rest next to Harold in the small family cemetery plot at the back of the pasture. According to her will, the house and property would not be transferred to Tig until he turned eighteen or was married, whichever came first. This being the case, the boys continued to cohabitate, but everyone knew there was no love lost between the brothers. The house was never the same. The emotional warmth, the glow—these things were buried with Carrie Ann.

Given the circumstances and the obligations of their existence, the brothers were forced to live at peace with each other. Both Johnnie and Tig realized it was healthier if they were not in the same place for too long a period of time, so they both found random jobs around town.

Johnnie chose to work at the local movie house. The clicking of the projector brought images of city life and soldiers marching in exotic places. Johnnie found the whole of it exhilarating, and in the darkness of the theater, he let his imagination travel to places he longed to go. Meanwhile, Tig could be heard humming to himself as he lugged a dented, well-used metal tool box around town.

———

Johnnie opened the trunk and pulled out a duffle bag and a rusted tool box and set them on the ground next to where he and Ron stood.

"He's gonna need those tools out here, Johnnie, not to mention his gun."

"Yeah. He stuck that behind the back seat. Guess he thought he might need to take things into his own hands. Ha, what's left of 'em." Johnnie guffawed.

"Johnnie, ya shouldn't be so hard on him. Ya gotta give the man credit. I mean, I can't think of anyone as determined as Tig."

Johnnie's laughter turned quickly. A look of disgust washed over his face.

"What the Hell ya know about Tig's determination, Ron? Ya weren't there. Ya ain't seen all that's happened, and you've never seen all I've done for him either. He's been nothin' but a problem these last few years, and havin' to care for him has been a burden. Ya woulda' never put up with being stuck drivin' clear 'cross the country with him in the car. I know that for a fact. He is and has always been a pain in the ass. Thank God, he will finally be on his own like he shoulda' been for years."

Ron knew he had crossed an invisible line, a thin string in the sand, a fuse that led to Johnnie's explosive temper.

"Hey, I'm sorry man. I can't imagine what ya've been through. Glad you're back though. How long ya stayin'?"

Johnnie let his hot temper cool a few degrees. Ron always knew how to disarm him.

"Don't worry about it, Ron. Ya know, I think I'll stay a few days until he's all 'stablished. That'd be the right thing. Then I'll need to get back home. The wife, ya know?"

Johnnie snickered.

Ron nodded, although he had a sense Johnnie was being quite disingenuous about doing the right thing for Tig. As much as it pained him, Ron knew the only verbal support Johnnie would give Tig would be for his, Ron's, benefit.

"Yeah, well let's get that box of supplies out of the back of my truck. Linda put several cans of beans and soup in there. I think she stuffed some homemade preserves and dill pickles in there too, along with a loaf of bread, a box of cereal—stuff like that. There's enough to last for a few days until Tig gets settled."

"I appreciate ya and Linda helpin' him out. Lettin' him use the house would seem more than enough, but all this extra you're doin'...."

"It ain't hard, Johnnie. It's the right thing to do."

"He should be fine until the paperwork is processed. They told us it would be a couple weeks, and that was over a week ago. He gave them your address since he didn't know the mailin' address here."

"There's no mailin' address here. Everythin' will have to come through Linda and me, I reckon. We'll see he gets his mail. Now, will he get full benefits?"

"He'll be on disability welfare. This'll provide him with food stamps and some medical help. This time it will be federal not state. He should be able to make it on his own, but he'll need your help to get him set up."

"I'm planin' on headin' back over here in about four days, Johnnie. I figured I'd pick him up, and we'd go down to the courthouse in Arvita and get all this stuff taken care of. Maybe take him to get a few things he'll need. Show him around and all."

"I appreciate your support, brother."

Johnnie reached up and put his arm over Ron's shoulder as they walked down the eroded drive to Ron's truck. Tig watched out the window as the lifelong friends moved as a single unit. The red ball low on the horizon was eclipsed by the two men. Their shadows stretched out and cast behind them. Tig studied the dark specters floating over the top of the road. The silhouettes moved in and out of clay fissures, deep ruts that compromised the stability of the surface. Tig reflected on how the pocked earth had been eroded from continual abrasion. It cast a distorted image of his brother, rendering him unrecognizable.

THREE

Ron Carson grew up on a large cattle ranch that covered nearly half of Talgart County. Ron's father, Abe, owned wheat fields that stretched as far as the eye could see and nearly eight hundred head of cattle, Hereford and Angus.

Every year, the Carsons would drive a small herd to the railhead in Amarillo. Ron asked his father if Johnnie and Tig could join the ranch hands on the annual cattle drive. The brothers worked out well. So, after the first year Abe Carson no longer needed persuading —Johnnie and Tig became regulars. Every spring, they joined with the Carson ranch hands and moved the cattle west to the railhead. The cattle drives afforded them an opportunity to step away from their normal routine while providing necessary income. It was a win-win situation mostly for Johnnie since he got to participate in the entire process with his best friend Ron. Johnnie and Ron were always together. All of their peers knew Johnnie and Ron's friendship was exclusive, especially Tig, who Johnnie considered persona non grata.

During the school year, Johnnie and Ron hung out together in the halls and on the ball fields of Talgart High. Individually, their strapping good looks were captivating, but when Johnnie and Ron walked side by side, the girls would stop what they were doing and stare. The thought of walking between those two boys, supported by their well-defined arms, made many a heart flutter. When Johnnie and Ron sauntered by, girls would giggle and whisper among themselves, but there was one who refused to be impressed.

———

Dottie Harns was a freckled-faced, fiery red-head with riveting green eyes. Quite a looker, she held a court of her own. Dottie was Dawson County's highly sought-after sweetheart. When Dottie smiled, nothing was more dazzling as far as the boys were concerned. She generally got what she wanted, not just because she was spoiled but because she bore a dogged determination beneath her captivating charm. Her wholesome girl-next-door beauty, stubbornness, and pluck made her a triple threat.

If anyone could match Johnnie and Ron's charisma, it was Dottie. Johnnie had pursued Dottie for nearly three years. He had every intention of staking his claim on her, and she knew it. They had dated a few times—a picnic here, a dance or two there, but nothing of any consequence.

Dottie was attracted to Johnnie at first, but his arrogance far outweighed her initial infatuation. She came to find his egotism repulsive. Knowing full well he was attracted to her, Dottie played at exacerbating Johnnie's false hopes of having her. She rather enjoyed leading him on, and she did so with great finesse. She viewed her behavior as just desserts for his impudence. So it was that Johnnie Mills and Dottie Harns had traits occupying opposite sides of the same coin.

———

Tig also attended Talgart High School, but he did not rule the halls like Johnnie. Given all their differences, many people found it impossible to believe Tig was Johnnie's brother. Tig was a good five inches shorter than his towering sibling. Johnnie had dark, nearly black hair and chiseled features, making him look as though he was of Roman descent. He had become the spitting image of his father, Harold.

On the other hand, Tig's features were commonplace by

comparison. He had mousy brown hair, unremarkable brown eyes, and a small nose that was undersized for his round face. Tig could easily be lost in a crowd, for nothing about him stood out.

Tig hated being reminded that he bore the same last name as Talgart High's resident Adonis. There appeared to be a need among the students to constantly make comparisons between the physical differences that separated the brothers. Tig's reliability and resourcefulness made no difference in this arena. More often than not, these peer assessments were done in public situations, making Tig's "nothing like your brother" moments all the more humiliating.

By the time the boys were in high school, Johnnie had completely taken center stage. He knew that using Tig as the butt of his jokes would always draw snickers from the audience. After so many years of exposure to Johnnie's tormenting, Tig was most comfortable when he could manage to stay unseen.

What no one ever mentioned was what Tig lacked in stature and natural good looks, he made up for in physical strength and dexterity. Tig was nearly twice as strong as Johnnie. He was muscular, wiry, and fast. Tig could run like the wind and turn on a dime. His most noticeable feature was his hands. They were broad and large boned, exceptional for his build, and they were strong. Tig had a grip that could crush the hand of a champion arm wrestler. For all the relentless teasing he endured, he never, not once since the day he was labeled "Tig," attempted to hit his brother with those hands, although he wanted to on many occasions.

———

When Harold died, Tig learned how to push things down inside himself, forcing fire into his belly while remaining calm on the outside. All through high school, the fire burned, and Tig continued to swallow it back. Like the thirsty drought ridden land, he craved for something to quench his scorched spirit, anything that might suspend the wasting away of his self-worth. It would come soon enough and unexpectedly.

Johnnie was particularly obnoxious on the first day of the cattle drive. He was assigned to the back of the herd with Tig while Ron was moved up front. Johnnie felt demeaned. The last person he wanted to be stuck with for three days was his brother. Johnnie was not in control in this scenario, however, so he fell in line and did what he was told, but Tig would pay.

No sooner had the herd begun to kick up dust, when Johnnie began riding roughshod on his brother. Tig moved too slowly; Tig moved too fast; Tig wasn't whistling right; Tig didn't know how to handle his horse; nothing Tig could do was right. Whenever the other hands gathered their horses together, Johnnie would ostracize Tig by cutting him off or sending him on some useless task.

For the better part of the morning, Tig managed to effectively tune his brother out. By midday he had grown weary of keeping his defenses up and the constant berating got the best of him. Tig began to intentionally lag behind. He pulled back and extended the distance between himself, the twenty five head of cattle in his charge, and his brother.

He kept his eyes on the lumbering Angus as they moved slowly up the red dirt ribbon through the hills. He lifted his eyes from the cattle momentarily to watch the weeds rustling in the breeze along the side of the road. The hypnotizing movement sent his mind on a path of its own. Daydreaming, Tig's eyes skipped across the land swells where he rested his thoughts on a field of vibrant yellow broomweed. The swaying of the horse beneath him moved in harmony with the waving field—lulling him away.

———

It was a beautiful spring morning when Dottie saddled up her prize Appaloosa. Ginger was given to Dottie as a present for her sixteenth birthday. With the right training, Ginger's bloodline promised her a future as a champion cutting horse. Ginger was spirited and unpredictable, a four year old filly that wasn't fully broken yet, but that made her a thrilling challenge for Dottie. Ginger resisted restrictions placed on her, and Dottie, on the other hand, liked to push the limit. They were equally matched in spirit. Wendell Harns permitted his daughter to ride Ginger with one caveat—she was not allowed to ride beyond the north pasture.

Owning a half-section of land, the Harns were among the wealthiest families in Dawson County. Their picturesque farm rested snugly against the South Canadian River and consisted of some of the most productive soil in the region. The fields spread out in sheets of even terrain, perfect for farming and horseback riding. Just beyond their three hundred plus acres, the river bottom flat lands swelled into short plateaus with red clay bluffs and sandy loam. Rugged terrain bordered the Harns' property. This territory was owned by the Carsons and was considered too craggy for crops and in some places too harsh for grazing.

Dottie's father made it abundantly clear that riding onto the Carson's land was not up for discussion. The answer was no. Self-assured, naïve, and stubborn—a potentially toxic mix that added to her vigor—Dottie kept her parents in a constant state of concern for her well-being. Dottie saw nothing wrong with extending the boundaries of the rules, especially if no one were the wiser.

She pushed the edge many times, unbeknownst to her father. This time, she traveled much farther than she normally did, crossing the border of her family ranch and moving well onto the back acreage of the Carson's land. Her father had good reason to forbid her from crossing over into into territory where short grass prairie yielded to the rolling mounds. It was desolate and treacherous. The ground heaved and sunk in unpredictable places. Rich loam pastures gave way to stony fields. Hills of rock blistered up from the craggy terrain. Deep gulches tucked in between were lined with serrated boulders and full of gnarled debris. While the cracks along the canyon walls, provided safe haven for an assortment of dangerous inhabitants known for their proclivity to bite.

None of this seemed of any consequence to Dottie. She rode fearlessly on, seduced by her own abandon and enraptured by the endless sky with its clouds skipping across the cerulean horizon. The late morning sun was warm on her neck as the dusty breeze swept evenly across her face. The horse and rider glided along as one through patches of ragweed, sage and yarrow. Desiring more speed, Dottie rolled her spurs evenly across Ginger's side. The horse responded and broke into a gallop. Away they went, Ginger's red splotches glistening with sweat, her mane and Dottie's hair flying in unison, whipping in the wind.

———

Off in the distance, the cattle turned and moved slowly off the road, wandering onto the grassy hills. By the time Tig became aware he had lost focus, his twenty five head were separated from the herd. He raced to cut his horse toward the hills while whistling to Johnnie, who was now nearly a half mile ahead of him with the balance of the cattle. Johnnie pulled up his horse. He turned and swore as he called out to one of the other ranch hands.

"Damn him. Hey, Joe! I've gotta go back and help Tig."

Then, setting his heels down strong in the stirrups, Johnnie reached back and smacked the flank of his horse.

"Dammit, Tig! What the Hell is the matter with ya?! Get over there and start movin' up behind those two, and I'll ease these toward the road."

After several minutes, Johnnie and Tig were moving alongside and behind the cattle, steadily driving the rogue herd back up through the gap between the hills. Their whistles and yelps off in the distance caught Dottie's attention just as she and Ginger mounted the top of a hill.

Ginger turned sharp to descend. The cattle drive was hidden by a second mound, and Dottie wanted to catch a glimpse before they moved out of sight. So once again, she rolled her spur along Ginger's side.

The horse bolted, moving too fast to manage the backside of the hill. Neither horse nor rider was prepared for the eroded gorge halfway down the hidden side of the knoll. In the instant Dottie spotted the threat, she pulled up hard on the reins.

Ginger's footing was compromised, and she jerked to a stop and lowered her head. The sudden halt threw Dottie over the front of the horse and to the ground. Her head hit the packed clay hard, her leg twisting painfully underneath her. The force of her fall pushed her forward, and she began to roll.

She tumbled over the jagged edge of the ravine—a gaping

mouth open wide in the earth. The weight of her body accelerated her, throwing her deeper into the chasm. She rolled several yards into the rock and debris-strewn gulch, all the while gaining momentum. Dead branches and saw-toothed shale scraped and bruised her skin as she revolved. A jutting ridge of limestone stopped her suddenly on a narrow ledge, wedging her between a boulder and the rim of the canyon wall. Dazed and not sure where she was, Dottie tried to sit up. She reached behind her head and felt the warm liquid saturating her scalp and oozing down the back of her neck. Her head spinning and fiery pain shooting from her leg, Dottie fell back and passed out. Ginger was gone.

———

Tig was the first one to see the flash of red, Ginger's mane blowing wildly in the wind as she ran riderless through the pass between the hills.

"Johnnie, did ya see that!?"

"Oh my God, that's Ginger, Dottie's horse. She must've thrown Dottie! Tig, go round up Ginger. The cattle will be fine. I have to find Dottie!"

With that, Johnnie turned his horse away from the cattle and raced back down through the hills.

Tig headed in the opposite direction. He found Ginger standing alongside the road, partially hidden by Johnson grass plumes waving beside her in the breeze. Tig rode slowly up alongside the nervous horse and gently slipped a rope over her head. Then he slid out of his saddle and stepped quietly toward her.

"Here, here girl. It's gonna be OK. Come now. Let's go find Dottie. Easy girl"

———

Johnnie rode alongside the gorge mindful of the unstable edge, the ever-eroding clay. Dismounting, he tethered his horse to a small tree and walked cautiously, leaning over, scanning the ravine.

"Dottie! Dottie, are ya down there?"

More than halfway down, he spotted a hint of torn aqua fabric and blood-stained denim. Dottie was pressed against the wall of the gorge. From what he could make out, she was lying on a ledge. He cautiously descended, working his way down the pocked wall of the gulch. There, a good twenty feet below the ridge he found Dottie contorted on her back and coated with dirt, her head resting in a pool of blood.

Realizing Johnnie's cattle were unattended, Ron and some of the other ranch hands were gathering in the distance, trying to gain back control of the herd. Baffled that both Johnnie and Tig were nowhere to be seen, Ron began to whistle. Johnnie could hear the commotion as the other riders pursued the straying cattle. He knew one of the hands would eventually spot his horse, so he began to holler.

"Hey, I'm down here! I'm down here with Dottie!"

One of the cowboys responded to Johnnie's calls for help, racing back to tell Ron what had happened. In no time Ron and a half dozen ranch hands made their way to where Johnnie's horse was standing. Ron dismounted his horse and walked as close as he dared to the edge. He leaned over trying to spot Johnnie.

"Johnnie?"

Johnnie was on the ledge sitting with Dottie's head in his lap. His gloves were off, and his long dusty fingers were pressing a bandana against the back of her head.

"Ron, quick. Go get your dad! We need the truck. Dottie has been hurt, bad. Quick, GO!"

Ron raced past Tig, who had just arrived and was standing with Ginger in tow. Tig dismounted and tethered the horses. He leaned over the edge to search the canyon.

"Tig, get down here and help me! We have to get her outta here!"

Tig steadily lowered himself into the gorge. Using jutting rocks and small trees as handles, he worked his way down to his brother and Dottie. When he reached them, he pressed himself against the earthen wall for stability.

"Tig, ya take her feet. I'll lift from her shoulders."

But as Johnnie and Tig attempted to lift Dottie, barely

conscious, she moaned in pain. "Wait, wait, it's her leg. Stop! We have to keep her still 'til the truck…."

The rattling of the truck grew louder as it flew over the rough terrain. Abe Carson had the wheel, and Ron held tight to the door handle as the truck spun out and skidded precariously along the uneven ground.

The thin rubber tires drew stones up from the dirt, spinning them frenetically and then shooting them out from behind the truck, pelting everything in sight. Abe set his foot down hard on the brake, downshifting, stripping the gears and bringing the truck to a screeching halt. Everything that was once stable and tied down was thrown to the front of the bed of the pickup.

"Oh, thank God they're here! Tig, get over here and hold her head while I climb out. Ron and I'll get blankets from the truck. We're gonna have to make a sling or somethin' to put her in to get her up out of here."

"Dear Lord, what happened? Is she OK?" Abe Carson stood at the edge with Ron calling down to Johnnie.

"I'm not sure what happened, Mr. Carson, but we've got to get her to a doctor. She hit her head hard and is bleedin' pretty bad."

Johnnie carefully lifted Dottie's head while he slid out from under her. "Here, Tig. Sit here."

Tig steadily maneuvered himself around to take Johnnie's place with Dottie's head resting gently in his lap.

"Put your hand on the back of her head and apply pressure. Yeah, that's right. Now stay here and don't move 'til Ron and I get back!"

Johnnie climbed slowly back up the walls of the ravine. At the top, Abe and Ron pulled him out and then they were gone. Tig sat with Dottie while everyone else who had been standing around the ledge went back to the truck to work on a rescue plan.

———

Everything got strangely quiet. Tig looked around and marveled that Dottie had survived her fall. He glanced down where dead limbs and branches jutted from the floor of the gorge. The dark, gnarled mess resembled a medieval torture chamber. He looked at the deep red walls with dozens of sharp rocks breaking through the clay. The serrated stones, forged by nature, could easily have functioned as weapons capable of tearing leather, bending metal, and cracking bones. Tig looked down at the blood-soaked bandana and shuddered. *She could've been ripped to threads.*

He could not imagine how Dottie escaped being impaled when she was thrust head first into the canyon death trap. Dottie moaned, and Tig pressed one hand gently against the back of her head while holding her very still. With his other hand, he moved strands of hair from her eyes and carefully stroked her forehead.

God help her.

It was strangely serene in the gorge as Dottie lay unconscious with her head in Tig's hands. He had never been this close to Dottie Harns. Everyone knew if he ever had, his brother would have killed him. Johnnie had eyes for Dottie. She was not only off limits but was virtually non-existent where Tig was concerned.

But now she was resting in his lap, her face turned toward him. He could not be faulted for looking. She was a painful mess, but even in this state, she was beautiful. He was surprised at how she took his breath away. Her peachy, freckled complexion was bruised and scratched. Her face was glazed with dirt, her lips chafed and bleeding. Her hair had freed itself from its ponytail and draped her head wildly. She had an earthy, wholesome look, and Tig could not take his eyes off of her.

How have I managed to never notice her before?

He wasn't certain how long he had been looking at her when Dottie abruptly opened her eyes and stared up at him. Her eyes wet and glassy made her pupils shimmer like shallow green pools with trapped light reflecting from beneath.

"Tig? Tig, is that you? What are you doing here?"

Dottie's voice was soft and raspy. She looked dazed, her confusion evidence of the concussion she must have suffered when she hit the ground.

"Shh, Dottie. It's OK. Ya took a bad fall, and we're going to stay right here till Johnnie and Ron come back down to get ya out."

"Please don't leave me, Tig, please." Dottie's eyes flashed with fear.

"I won't, Dottie. You'll be OK. I'm not going anywhere."

Dottie looked directly into Tig's eyes. "Tig... Thank you... for being here, for finding me."

Tig wanted to tell her it was his brother who had found her, but he couldn't bring himself to say it. Having Dottie Harns think of you as a hero was a rare gift, and Tig decided to savor it. *Johnnie will never know.*

"You're welcome, Dottie. Now be still. Ya have to be still and rest."

––––––

Dottie closed her eyes but not before reaching up and gently placing her hand on top of Tig's. The electricity of her touch caused him to tense up. He looked down at Dottie's small hand resting on his, and he marveled. For the first time Tig could remember, he felt a part of something greater than himself. He trembled as he experienced just a hint of what it meant to be aware, awakened—to the whole of it. The drifting clouds released rays of light. They shot into the canyon, spotlighting portions of the jagged interior walls. The sunlight reached down right to where they sat. Seizing bits of light, small glowing locks of red hair rested against her skin, accentuating the soft swell of her cheeks. All the while the prairie pulsed with life, caught up in a breeze. It wafted through Tig and comforted his scorched spirit, if but for a moment.

––––––

Ron Carsen's older brother, David, took the truck and raced off to get Dottie's father. Wendell Harns and his wife, Anna, stood at the door with Dottie's little sister, Clara, listening to the news in horror. Seven-year-old Clara began to cry as her parents ran off in different directions. They wasted no time gathering bandages, blankets, and other necessary supplies. Wendell hastily hugged his wife before climbing into the truck with David.

"It'll be OK, Anna. I'll bring her home." Then calling out from the open truck window—"Anna, call Dr. Benton!"

As Wendell and David sped past bright green fields of winter wheat, Dottie's mother, Anna, was on the phone preparing the doctor for Dottie's arrival. As they approached the rolling hills, Wendell bounced his leg up and down nervously, mumbling first, "Let her be OK," and then "How much is it going to take to settle her rebel spirit?" and then back again to, "Let her be OK."

Within twenty minutes, Johnnie and Ron stood at the edge of the gorge with Wendell Harns and Abe Carson.

"Sweetheart, Dottie, are you OK.... Dottie!" Wendell Harns shouted desperately down to his daughter.

"She can't answer ya, Mr. Harns. She's pretty beat up."

"Oh, God."

"It'll be OK, Wendell. We'll get her outta there." Abe reached over and put his arm around Wendell's shoulders to console him.

"Tig!" Johnnie leaned slightly over the ravine. "Tig, how's it goin' down there?"

Tig arched his neck and called back. "She's restin'. Think I got the bleedin' to stop, but she's gettin' pale."

Abe yelled down into the canyon.

"OK, Tig. Sit tight! We're sendin' down a sling, so be ready for it. When it gets close enough for ya to reach, catch it and grab hold of it!"

The men, along with Ron and two of his brothers, were rapidly pulling supplies out of the back of the truck. Abe Carson sent the ranch hands back out to manage the cattle until Dottie was pulled from the ravine. While David had been fetching Dottie's father, Abe, Ron, and Johnnie were making a makeshift harness-sling apparatus. Using a blanket and four cinch rings, they managed to finagle a reliable hammock to put Dottie in. They asked Wendell to bring a cast iron pulley from his barn to use for running the rope through. They attached the pulley to the back of the truck and let the rope slacken.

"Tig. TIG! Pay attention, now. Listen. We're ready to throw this thing down there. It has some tack attached to it, so don't let it hit Dottie!" Johnnie leaned over Abe Carson and shouted into the canyon.

"Tig, I'm comin' down to handle it. I'll get her into the sling."

"No, Johnnie. No! There's no room on this ledge. The edges are unstable. I think I need to do this alone. I can roll her onto it after I get it in place."

Tig shifted his weight to stabilize himself and shouted, "Go ahead! Throw it down!"

Johnnie hesitated but knew Tig was right. It was not worth the risk. "OK, Ron. Give me some more slack! Tig, it's on its way!"

Abe and Johnnie took the rope in both hands and guided the sling down. When it had gotten to just within reach, Tig grabbed it with his free hand and pulled it down toward himself. Once he secured it, he spread the blanket out as best he could next to where he and Dottie sat. He was careful not to release his hold on Dottie's head. He knew he would have to act quickly to move her so he would not complicate her injuries. He took a deep breath and without further delay he placed his free hand underneath her. Then, while in a squatting position, he slid his arms under Dottie's back, picked her up, and pivoted on his knees with her in his arms, placing her securely in the sling.

"Man alive! Did ya see that, Johnnie?! That was unbelievable!" Ron had been watching with all the others from above while Tig positioned Dottie into the sling.

"Yeah, right." Johnnie said in a matter-of-fact tone.

He had seen it too, but he certainly wasn't going to draw any more attention to Tig. "Tig, are ya ready?"

Tig placed his face near Dottie's and whispered, "OK, Dottie, just relax. I'm right under ya, and I won't let you fall."

He squeezed Dottie's hand and tipped his head back until he could see the men standing along the edge. "Yeah, we're ready. Pull her up!"

With the men on top guiding the rope, Abe put the truck in gear and gently nudged it forward. At the same time the truck was easing the sling out of the gorge, Tig was gently guiding from underneath.

With one hand, he kept some pressure under Dottie's back, keeping her from tipping or swinging into the jagged limestone walls of the ravine. With his other hand, he dug into the clay, grabbed stumps and limbs, and pulled himself up methodically.

When Dottie emerged, there was a bustle of activity. Johnnie and Ron each grabbed an end of the sling and pulled her up to safety, laying her carefully on the ground. Wendell immediately went to his knees, leaning over her, kissing her cheeks and checking her wounds. While Wendell covered her in a blanket, Abe backed the truck up and jumped out. The bed of the truck was now filled with hay, creating a soft bed for Dottie to lie on.

Meanwhile, Tig's hands emerged from the gorge. He pulled himself up and peered over the edge. Everyone had moved away from the ravine, so he hoisted himself out and stood up. His arms bruised and his hands bloodied, Tig remained motionless, silently watching the whir of activity playing out in front of him.

The men gathered around Dottie and lifted her carefully into the truck. Wendell climbed in to sit next to her. She was conscious and crying, tears coursing down her face and salty, red dirt grime covering her cheeks. Her father wiped her tears and noticed her swollen lips were mouthing something he could not understand. He leaned over, close to her face as she whispered to him.

"Sure, sweetheart. Absolutely."

Johnnie had just stepped up on to the bed of the truck to get in when Abe Carson tapped him on the back.

"I'm sorry, Johnnie, but I need ya and Ron to get down the road with them boys and catch up with the herd. We're on a tight deadline, and I need all ya'll to move along. We've lost a few hours, and we're gonna be pushin' it to make Delmargo by sunset."

"Yes sir."

For fear of insubordination, Johnnie contained his frustration as he stepped off the back of the truck. At the same time, Wendell motioned to Abe that he needed to talk with him. As Johnnie turned from the back of the truck, he spotted something on the ground catching the light, partially exposed beneath the dirt. He bent to pick it up.

"Yes, Wendell, I don't have a problem with that at all. Tig... get over here, son!" Abe Carson waved his hands in the air.

"Yes sir, Mr. Carson."

"Tig, Mr. Harns would like for ya to ride along with him and Dottie to the hospital." Abe gestured for Tig to get into the back of the truck. Tig tipped his head in disbelief.

"Don't worry, son. I won't dock your pay. You're needed here, so go, and we'll settle up later."

Tig reluctantly climbed up into the bed of the truck and sat next to Dottie, across from her father. As Wendell mouthed "Thank you," Dottie reached over and took Tig's hand.

As the truck spun away, kicking up a haze of dirt and hurling rocks against the muffler, Johnnie stood brooding. Infuriated, he narrowed his eyes in anger and clenched his fists by his side. So tight was his grasp that the object he held embedded into his palm. The biting pain caught him by surprise. His fingers flew open. The rowel broken off of Dottie's spur slipped from his hand. It fell, buried in dust.

FOUR

Tig rolled over, the chattering birds contributing to his restless sleep. Outside, tips of bluestem surfaced from the morning fog, black stubble poking out from a skin of white mist. The pebbly surface of the ground around the small house shimmered under a thick blanket of dew. The clammy spring air was heavy with moisture. Tig felt it in his bones and joints.

Stiff and aching, he groaned and rolled cautiously onto his back. He was half awake and fully disoriented. The density of the murk outside could not compete with the cloud inside Tig's head. He lingered, savoring the scant remains of a fleeting dream. He may have yielded to an extended doze had the rigidity of the army cot not intruded with a bite of reality.

He opened his eyes, reluctantly surrendering to the light of day. Cognizant of the chill in the room, he pulled the scratchy wool blanket up over his shoulders. His lower back was throbbing. Straining to get comfortable, he rolled back over and faced the blank wall. Not wanting to move again, Tig surrendered to the stiff cot. He lay still, rehearsing in his mind the scene from the night before.

―――――

As the last glow of Ron's taillights had merged with the dusk, Tig had moved away from the window and joined his brother outside.

There, he and Johnnie unloaded the convertible. Within minutes, what few belongings Tig owned were piled inside the little house. Random tools and a carton of supplies from the Carsons were added to the clutter collecting inside the front door.

Tig set the box of food on the table and started sorting through it. There were several cans of beans and soup, a jar of applesauce, a container of peanut butter, a bag of sugar, a half dozen eggs, a loaf of bread, a can of coffee, some apples, Hershey bars, a jar of pickles, and jam. Tig smiled as he considered how Linda had hand-selected the items, making certain the choices were nutritious.

While Tig carried his small suitcase of clothes into the bedroom, Johnnie grabbed his duffle bag, a six pack of beer, and six bottles of liquor out of the trunk. He slammed the hood and sauntered into the house.

"Tig, go and get that damn gun from behind the seat."

Tig shuffled past Johnnie and walked back to the car. Night had fallen and navigating the driveway was tricky. The lesions in the compacted dirt challenged Tig's sense of balance. His footing was unstable. His ankles were almost giving way on the uneven surface.

He wished he had a flash light. *Someone could bust their leg out here,* he thought. The glove compartment was usually locked, but it was hanging open. *There might be a flash light in there.* Poking his fingers around, he felt what seemed to be embossed leather.

"Wait, what the devil?"

Tig pulled the object out and discovered it to be exactly what he thought it was—his wallet.

Johnnie had taken Tig's wallet and put it in the glove compartment. Unbeknownst to Tig, it had been locked up the entire trip. Tig fumed as he recalled Johnnie trying to convince him he must have lost it at a gas station. Irritated, Tig stuffed the wallet in his back pocket and retrieved his shot gun from the back seat.

Johnnie was leaning back in the big chair, slurping on a can of beer. His feet were resting on the stove. Cigarette smoke circled his head and was rising. Puffs of smog hugged the ceiling as Tig came through the front door. The fumes caught in Tig's throat and started a coughing fit. Since childhood, he was susceptible to asthma attacks induced by smoke and dust. Johnnie knew this, but it never stopped him from lighting up around Tig. Johnnie raised the can of beer and saluted Tig. It sloshed down Johnnie's arm as he belched.

"Grab yourself one."

Tig threw Johnnie a look. "Johnnie ya know I stopped drinkin' after my accident. Don't be askin' me."

"We both know ya want it. Besides, we really should celebrate your new home, don't ya think? Why look at this little castle of yours? Bet Dottie would love to get her sweet little hands on this place and pretty it up."

Johnnie looked around the room. Tipping his head from one side to the next, he screwed up his mouth as though he was contemplating. He smirked and with a melodramatic flourish threw his hands in the air. "Oh, I forgot. Dottie, yeah, she ain't interested."

"Shut the Hell up, Johnnie." Tig drew his eyes together. "Ya can sit there and drink all night for all I care. I'm goin' to bed."

"Ya do that, li'l brother. I got the best of the deal anyhow. This chair has to be more comfortable than that pitiful makeshift bed of yours." Johnnie opened another can of beer defiantly to goad his brother, the recovering alcoholic.

Tig went into his new bedroom. *Plans, schedules, and settling accounts can be tended to tomorrow. Nothing is worth this aggravation*, he thought.

He took his boots and pants off, and he set his belt on the floor in the corner, putting his wallet under the pillow. He sat down on the edge of the wood-framed cot for a few minutes, his stocking feet planted on the cold floor. Sitting in the darkness, he eyed the dim moonlight reflecting off the window. He could see her red hair blowing in the morning sun. She was looking at him, her bright eyes laughing.

Tig rejected the fleeting thought, preventing its fire from swelling into rage and despair. He closed his eyes and swung his legs up under the blanket, shielding himself from the cold.

As Tig scanned the dirty bedroom wall, he could not recall going to sleep. The morning light arrived too soon and illuminated not only the barren cold plaster but Tig's situation. Lying there, thinking about it was counterproductive and hoping for additional sleep in which to hide was an act of futility. So, Tig halfheartedly wiped his eyes and sat up. The thick dew found its way into the bedroom. It collected on everything, including Tig's blue jeans thrown in a heap in the corner. He sat on the edge of his cot and struggled to pull the damp pants up over his legs. He slipped on his stiff leather boots and grabbed his belt.

With any luck, Johnnie has slept off that booze. It'd sure be a Hell of a lot easier to get my affairs in order with him sober.

Over the course of the trip, Johnnie and Tig had made plans. They had agreed on how to get the business issues taken care of as soon as Tig was moved into the old Macklin place. Johnnie would take his brother into town to check on the paperwork regarding Tig's government disability payments. The brothers would go from there and pick up a few extra things, miscellaneous items Tig needed to set up house. They also discussed driving back over to Arvita one afternoon to visit their parents' graves.

Tig buckled his belt and turned the corner. "Johnnie?"

Tig stopped short and stared. Beer cans and cigarette butts were gathered in a pile around the legs of the lopsided arm chair in the corner. All that remained of Johnnie was an indentation in the seat where he had planted his backside for the night.

Hmm. He's probably peeing. Gonna take some time for him to get rid of all that booze.

Tig turned toward the box of food left on the table. Longing for a cup of hot coffee, he pulled open the box. He looked perplexed. With the exception of three cans of beans, everything was gone.

"What the hell?"

Tig's voice hoarse, he choked, coughed, and spit on the floor. "Johnnie!"

He opened the refrigerator. Three cans of beer sat in a row next to the jar of mousy mold. Tig began to frantically search through the few random items left by the front door—nothing. He angrily clenched the doorknob and swung the door wide. He stood in the opening, looking out at the long driveway winding down the hill.

The car was gone. Johnnie was gone. The only evidence that Johnnie's Cadillac had ever been at the Macklin place was the tire treads embossed in the clay, newly created rifts left to erode.

Tig paused, his mouth open, trying to let the thought sink in. As quickly as a tiny lizard darted over the torn linoleum, a thought crossed Tig's mind. He dashed into the bedroom and shook the pillow.

It must've fallen on the floor. He scanned every square inch, under and around the cot, but with the exception of a couple clods of dirt, the floor by the cot was empty. Johnnie had taken Tig's wallet too. Tig flipped the cot over in anger.

"Damn ya, Johnnie!"

Tig's voice ricocheted off the walls. A flock of birds pecking on the ground just outside the window were set to flight. Tig walked back into the front room and went to shut the refrigerator door. He was unaware how long he stood there staring at the top shelf.

Three shiny cans triggered a skirmish inside his head. He stood on a familiar battlefield. Victory or surrender hinged on one small, one monumental choice. Should he or should he not drink one, just one?

The struggle seemed to last an eternity. Tig closed the door. He won the battle, but not the war. Discouragement had taken him hostage. Tig sat down hard in one of the small chairs next to the table. He flicked the butt of a cigarette off the Formica and onto the floor. Crushing the last dregs under his boot, Tig looked toward the door.

"God—Dottie, now what?"

The realization of just how alone he was settled over him like the dense fog, covering any sense of purpose with heavy clouds of regret and shame. He dropped his head and closed his eyes, sitting unmoved for a very long time, using every still moment to recharge. He gathered energy for what he knew would be a very long journey.

Tig's heart sank as he recalled his childhood home, the place where memories were made, first with his parents and then with Dottie. Dottie's vivacity and creative flair extended the life of Harold and Carrie Ann's homestead for the next generation. Her spirit filled every nook and crevice of the little farmhouse planted on the outskirts of Arvita. Tig assumed he would always live in the home he had inherited. He thought of how different his life would be now—here. His circumstances pressed in on him, leaving him numb. He stared blankly at the wall across from where he sat.

Open wounds and gaping cracks spread along the surface up from the floor to the ceiling. The fractures in the cement had filled with dust and dirt over the years. He squinted to confirm what he was seeing.

There, in the thick humid air, thin terracotta trails were hemorrhaging down the walls and gathering in small clay puddles on the floor. The skeleton of the house, the pine two by fours, all that held the small building in place, was exposed. Weathered, stripped, and splintered in places, the wooden bones were severely vulnerable. As the morning breeze stole through the cracks and crevices, the precarious infrastructure moaned and threatened to give way. The deteriorating house was nothing more than a shanty, and it creaked and grieved while Tig sat in silence. Something from deep within him called out in equivalence—and the walls of his internal house bled.

———

Dottie's recovery from her accident took several weeks. She suffered from a concussion, her back was badly bruised, and her leg broken in two places. Bed rest was followed by weeks of convalescing with intermittent therapeutic exercise.

To ensure his daughter's academic success, Wendell Harns hired a tutor. Mrs. Parkhurst was a local retired teacher, and she taught Dottie at home in the afternoons for the remainder of the school year. This way, Dottie could fully recover while not risking her graduation the following year.

Dottie's absence from school excited the rumor mill. At Talgart High, the word was that it was Tig—not Johnnie—who had rescued the damsel in distress. Regardless of Johnnie's objections and efforts to recount the story, Tig was made out to be the hero. When the girls giggled and referred to Tig as "Sir Tig, knight of Talgart County," the boys laughed, but Johnnie seethed.

Tig took his new status in stride. There was always something unassuming about Tig that no number of accolades could change. He was consistent and compliant, always wanting to do the right thing.

Although painfully shy, Tig made trips to the Harns' home to pay his respects to Dottie and her family while she was recuperating. He took Dottie candy during one of his visits. He handed it nervously to Mrs. Harns. Anna accepted the dusty box from Tig's clammy hands, smiling as she noticed the small bunch of wild flowers tied loosely to the box with a piece of twine.

Whenever Tig came around, Dottie's father would ask him to sit and visit. Wendell Harns liked Tig. It wasn't long before Wendell recruited Tig to do odd jobs and repairs around the farm. Tig dug several wells and irrigation ditches for Wendell. Although it was challenging work, Tig was proficient at excavating dirt and setting water wells. At an early age, Tig's hand at the shovel always revealed his great physical strength. Everything about his physique—his broad strong shoulders, his muscular arms and powerful hands—made him a natural for this brand of physical labor.

There were days when Tig had the added benefit of catching a glimpse of Dottie as she groomed Ginger or as she and her mother would return from the garden carrying baskets of vegetables and wild roses. Dottie always came close enough so that Tig could catch the wafting scent of the lavender soap she used. Dottie's distinctive smell always caught Tig off guard.

Just when Dottie was close enough to look full into Tig's face, he would drop his head out of respect. He never made eye contact with Dottie. It did not matter, since the image of her captivating eyes was embossed in his memory. Her teal green pupils, dotted with bits of gold, radiated light, and feral energy... he could see them in his sleep.

———

The Annual Fox Creek Social was a late summer tradition in Arvita. The dinner and dance were sponsored by the Fox Creek Ladies Auxiliary. The Auxiliary was supported by the Congregational Church, and it provided compassionate care for needy individuals and families throughout the community. The highly anticipated fundraising event brought out the entire town. Everyone would dress up in their Sunday best and proceed to the church lawn where tables were set up with colorful tablecloths and mason jars full of wild sunflowers and purple thistles. All the girls clamored for weeks, planning their menu and preparing their food. As tradition stated, each woman who participated made a box dinner for one of Arvita's eligible bachelors. The participant cooks chose who would be privileged to buy her meal and share it with her.

The menus varied, but fried chicken, green beans, potato salad with homemade bread and jam was a standard. All this and a delicious dessert, often a generous slice of pecan pie or a liberal portion of apple cake, would be placed in a beautifully decorated box. Each container was as unique as the woman who prepared had it.

The boxes were placed on the long, covered tables that wrapped around the church grounds. Once everyone had arrived, there were a few random announcements and a quick blessing. Then the cast iron church bell was rung. This alerted each woman to locate the man she preferred to purchase her meal. After the sales transaction took place, the couple enjoyed dinner together. Once everyone finished eating, all the participants walked, many arm in arm and hand in hand, to Earl Hinson's barn, where the community dance commenced.

———

It was an exceptionally warm late September evening, but that did not deter Dottie. Bursting with excitement, she came bounding downstairs from her bedroom as though her leg had never been broken. She wore a soft lavender cotton dress her mother had made for her. The skirt was full and flouncy. It swished over her petticoat as she descended the staircase. Dottie had tied three long purple ribbons onto her straw bonnet reserving one to wrap around her box

FIG   57

dinner. In the dining room, she picked up her box from the table and studied it.

Over the course of several weeks, Dottie had picked and pressed wild violets between the pages of the Harns' family Bible. Once flattened and dried, she glued them to the top and sides of her box. She thoughtfully crisscrossed the light purple ribbon around the violet-covered container making a large bow that rested on top. She looked pleased as she assessed her creation. She abruptly lifted her eyebrows, widening her eyes, as she realized the most important thing had been left off.

"Dottie, where are you off to? I need to tie the bow on the back of your dress!" Dottie was flying up the stairs.

"I'll be right back. I forgot something."

Anna Harns looked over at her husband. He was shaking his head.

"I know. That accident hasn't slowed her down a bit. I guess we really wouldn't have wanted that, her slowing down I mean. Would we?"

"No, Anna." Wendell Harns paused and lowered his voice. "Any attempt to tame her would kill her spirit. God forbid that the fire in her eyes ever goes out."

Dottie pulled open her dresser drawer and pulled out a small object wrapped in a flowered cotton hankie. She laid the object on her bed and carefully unfolded the small square of fabric. There, inside, rested the rowel from one of her spurs. It matched the one she had lost in the accident. This one was taken from the spur still attached to her boot when they cut it off before treating her broken leg. She carefully picked up the spiky metal star and went running back downstairs with it tucked gingerly in her hand.

She untied her box and pulled the ribbon through the rowel before tying the strands of satin back into a bow. The rowel hung off the ribbon like a shiny medal. She smiled at her handiwork.

Dottie's little sister, Clara, stood admiring the box.

"Dottie, that's so pretty. I don't know how you could give it away."

"You're so sweet, Clara. Someday you'll get to make one for someone special."

"Who're you givin' it to, Dottie?"

"Now that is a big secret! You will know soon enough." Dottie leaned over and kissed Clara on the forehead.

"Mother," Dottie called out, "I would like to go on ahead to the church. Could you just meet me there, please?"

"I suppose. Your father can take you and come back to get Clara and me. You go on ahead. And Dottie...."

"Yes, Ma'am?"

"Have fun dear, but please be mindful of your leg."

Dottie's eyes twinkled as she ran out the front door to meet her father, who was already waiting for her by the truck. Wendell Harns took his daughter's arm and gently helped her into the truck while she held tightly to her box dinner.

He watched as she laid it carefully on her lap, adjusting the bow and positioning the rowel so that it sat evenly in the center. The recipient was a secret but not to Wendell. He knew exactly who would get Dottie's dinner. Dottie's father was still smiling as they drove over the cattle guard and onto the road to Arvita.

The 1946 Annual Fox Creek Social was both as unique and as unchanged as those that had preceded it. Every year, the boxes were lined up in rows across the long table, and every year, each box was one of a kind. Some had bows, some were wrapped in paper, and some were written on.

Displayed together, they resembled lovingly wrapped packages waiting to be placed under the Christmas tree. As the townspeople arrived, they would congregate in a predictable manner. The young girls met near the end of the long table. There they would giggle and point, playing the match game—trying to guess which box would go to which bow-tied young man. The young women fidgeted nervously, huddled in a group by the church. They peered from a distance as the reluctant fraternity of eligible young men made their way onto the grounds. Married women attended to their small children and doted over plump-cheeked babies, while the old women sat in chairs gossiping and guarding the food.

By the time the festivities were to begin, men of all ages stood awkwardly in random locations around the tables. They nervously jingled the change in their pockets while hovering over the box dinners. The box creators hoped it was for the beauty of their assemblages, but for the men the allure was the scent of hot biscuits and smoked ham.

Dottie didn't wait for her father to help her out of the truck. She pushed open the door and was half way across the church lawn before Wendell had gotten out from behind the wheel. She moved directly to the long table and set her violet-covered box down next to a box draped in bright yellow fabric. The juxtaposition of the purple against the yellow made both boxes look as though they were illuminated.

Dottie beamed from ear to ear at the attention her box drew. Although she enjoyed enthusiasm for her creation, her thoughts were elsewhere. Dottie's eyes never made contact with those of her admirers. Distracted, she would hastily thank her devotees while looking past them into the crowd.

Where is he? She scanned the new crop of boys entering from the south side of the lawn.

Her heart raced as Johnnie and Tig appeared from behind a group of older men. Johnnie was as handsome as ever, dressed in black trousers and a crisp dress shirt with his dark hair combed back in the latest style. A late summer tan gave additional distinction to the sharp masculine contours of his face. His dark eyes glistened beneath his black brow line and high forehead. He smiled cagily as he strutted past a row of fawning girls.

Tig walked a few steps behind with his hands in his pockets. He had on a tan shirt with brown pants and suspenders. His sleeves were rolled up and his muscular arms were a deep bronze. Tig's face was also tanned, and his mousy hair had seasonal blond highlights. He wore a brown flat cap atop his head, and a few wayward curls stuck out from under it. His bleached locks and the freckles across his nose lent a playful, tousled look to his boyish appearance.

Johnnie spotted Ron and pushed his way through the crowd to join his best friend on the other side of the lawn. Tig lagged behind, greeting neighbors and folks he had done work for, including Mr. Harns. After a few minutes, he found his way to where several other boys were gathered.

What seemed like a lifetime took less than a half hour. The

pastor made the announcements and prayed a traditional blessing over the meal. Then Arvita's mayor rang the bell. Over and over, it clanged while young women scooped up their boxes and scampered like mice vying for a single piece of cheese.

Johnnie stood smugly, leaning against the fence, watching the scuttle. He was amused by the ridiculousness of the event. He felt it beneath him to take part in such frivolous romantic pretense.

Johnnie believed any number of the young women in Arvita were his for the taking. He had suggested as much to Ron, how the box dinner social was intended for desperate misfits. He supported his premise by pointing out how the Fox Creek Ladies always made extra dinners so no one was left out.

Johnnie leaned over to whisper an additional smug tidbit in Ron's ear just as Linda Ordway came up and placed a blue box in Ron's hands. Before Johnnie could say anything, Ron and Linda were off walking hand in hand in the direction of a picnic table covered in yellow gingham. Johnnie just huffed and turned his attention back to the bustling women. He spotted Dottie, her lavender ribbons waving in the breeze, trailing behind her hat, her shiny red hair casting a glowing halo behind her head.

He leaned more pronouncedly against the fence, poising himself so as to appear nonchalant when she handed him the box. He eyed her. She looked lost. She was turned in his direction, but she stared right past him.

Huh? She must have just overlooked me, he thought, and he stood upright, straightening his back. Still attempting to look unaffected, he moved a little to the right directly into her sight line.

But Dottie didn't move in his direction. She continued to look past him. Carolyn, Dottie's best friend, leaned over and whispered something in Dottie's ear. Dottie quickly swung around. She headed the opposite way, back through the crowd and toward the outer edge of the church lawn. Johnnie locked his eyes on her.

Dottie picked up speed at the fence line. She made a beeline straight for Tig, who stood off by himself quietly, modestly looking on. Johnnie narrowed his eyes. He could feel his fists clench.

"Tig." Dottie stood directly in front of Tig and arrested his eyes. "Tig, this is for you."

Tig was taken aback. He wasn't sure how to respond. After a few terribly awkward seconds, he reached out his hands to take the flower-wrapped container. As Dottie laid the box into his hands, Tig was thinking to himself, *Are ya sure, Dottie? Are ya sure?*

"Thank ya, Dottie. This is beautiful. I'd be honored to buy your box dinner." Tig reached into his pocket while Dottie slipped her arm through his.

While Tig and Dottie were finding a place to sit, Carolyn Wilson walked up to Johnnie. He was so engrossed with watching Dottie cling to his brother that he was unaware of the gift bearer standing in front of him.

Carolyn was every bit as beautiful as Dottie. Many said Carolyn Wilson had a bit of royalty in her. She was tall and stunning, with the poise of someone twice her age. Soft spoken and eloquent, her movements were fluid. Carolyn had long silky blond hair and tender gray-blue eyes. Her complexion was flawless, with a porcelain quality to it.

But with all she had to offer, she could not match the spunk of Dottie. It was Dottie's feral side that was most attractive to Johnnie. He had a penchant for the chase. The more elusive the object of his affection, the more desirable. Carolyn Wilson, on the other hand, was just way too easy to get.

———

Music and laughter spilled over into the cool night air as Tig pushed open the barn door. The shuffle of couples swirling around the sawdust dance floor sent a fog of earthen talc curling up behind Tig and Dottie as they left. Tig looked over when Dottie took his arm. The light from the barn encircled her in a dust-filled mandorla. They strolled down the path toward Fox Creek, laughing as they recounted the events of the evening.

"You are quite the dancer, Mr. Mills."

Tig turned to thank Dottie when he noticed her eyes. In the evening light, they had turned a deep shade of jade. They caught him off guard, took his thoughts captive, and twisted his tongue. He redirected the conversation hoping to reclaim his composure.

"Dottie, those biscuits and plum jam were delicious. I used to pick sand plums for my mother."

"Thank you, Tig. I am pleased you enjoyed it. I always pick with Mother and Clara. We harvested quite a lot this year."

Dottie, unlike Tig, was not easily distracted. Determined to assert her affection, she tightened her arm, pulling Tig closer. She abruptly stopped walking and turned toward him. The darker new growth of Tig's sun-bleached hair was drenched. Perspiration fixed his wavy locks to his forehead and the nap of his neck, his face still flushed from the last waltz they had two-stepped across the dance floor.

"Tig, I want you to have something special."

After Tig had purchased her box dinner, Dottie removed the rowel from the top of the box and tied it onto one of the violet ribbons. She wrapped it around her wrist for safe keeping during the meal. Now, she pulled it off and let it dangle from her fingers. She reached up, spreading the ribbons for Tig to put his head through.

He looked perplexed but Dottie nodded, letting him know it was OK. He removed his cap and leaned forward, dropping his head. The rowel hung around his neck and lay against his chest like a medallion.

"I've never met anyone as kind as you, Tig. This is from the spur they removed from my boot the day you rescued me. You deserve this, Tig. I want you to keep this so you will never forget that day."

Tig was overwhelmed. He lifted the rowel and looked closely at it. The ambient light from the half moon reflected off the metal. It glowed like a fallen star against his hand.

"Thank ya, Dottie. I'll keep this—always."

Tig carefully tucked the medallion inside his shirt, letting the cool metal lay against his bare chest. Dottie stood watching, her eyes softening.

Tig lifted his head, his dark eyes penetrating hers. There was only one other time when he had been this close to Dottie Harns, and on that day, she was half conscious. His heart quickened. He took her hands in his, leaned over, and kissed her.

Dottie threw her arms around his neck holding him tight,

returning his kiss with twice the passion. Pulling back, she looked up into his face, her eyes holding him transfixed.

"I want to keep you, Tig Mills. Can I have you?"

———

Time passed—measured by the thin dusty ray of light traveling across the floor and up the leg of the table. Tig had no idea how long he had been sitting there, but the clay puddles at the base of the wall had long since dried up. The breeze dispersed the dust so all that remained was a faint outline on the floor and thin red-veined residue on the walls. The stiffness in his back and ache in his neck indicated he had remained in the same position for too long.

He leaned against the wall, surprised to feel its warmth. Radiant heat from the sun had penetrated the west side of the house. It was mid-afternoon, judging from the position of light raking the outside of the small building. There were no clocks anywhere in the house, and the only watch Tig ever owned had been destroyed in the accident. Tig pushed himself slowly up and away from the table, his growling stomach complaining of hunger. He had not eaten since the morning before.

He took one can of beans from the box, reached down, and pulled a knife from his boot. Using the cast iron pot from the stove with his knife, he hammered around the edges until he could bend the lid up.

He slurped one third of the can and wiped his face on his sleeve. Although still hungry, he bent the cover back down.

I better ration this out, Tig deliberated. *Ron is not expected back for a few days, and I'll be damned if I'm gonna go beggin' for help.*

Tig opened the refrigerator for the second time on the off chance that something—a loaf of bread, a piece of fruit, anything to eat— might have been overlooked or have magically appeared. The cold metal shelves offered only what he would not partake. He closed the door and sat back down hard in his chair. The stained cushion was still warm and molded to his shape from the hours he had spent there. He surveyed the room.

How long could I sit here before starvin' to death?

He contemplated the thought. Moaning, Tig rested his gloved hand on his thigh. A searing burn traveled through the remaining knuckles of his right hand. He grimaced in pain. He leaned forward to get up but changed his mind. *There's no reason to move, not really. What could anything outside the broken walls of this makeshift shelter have to offer?*

Tig dropped his head, his eyes fixed on the dirty floor. He slid the worn leather sole of his boot back and forth over the grit. The sound of sand grinding beneath his feet blended with that of the screeching windmill.

Together, they created a haunting duet. The noise filled the space around him, thickening the air. Tig struggled to close his ears to the tormenting chants. His efforts failed. They broke through and called forth the shadows from the hidden rooms of his psyche. The specter of anxiety emerged.

Impenetrable fear welled up and engulfed him, claiming all sense of well-being and readying his body for flight. A disorientating haze covered his eyes, tinting the light in the room.

He began to feel the ominous sensation of separating from himself. The floor shifted and swayed. Tig's pulse raced as the walls pressed in, embracing him in their decay. Sweat ran down his forehead and his back. Wave after wave of dread seized him and dragged him into a pit of hopelessness, leaving him gasping for air and doubting his sanity.

The panic attack lasted several minutes. Tig was shaken and drenched in sweat. He wrestled with his mind, straining to focus on anything to push the fear back down. He thought about the four walls and the roof that protected him now. It was completely inadequate but all he had. The house was much like his internal shelter. For the course of his life, he had retreated and hid, had endured years of neglect. The slow rot was now revealing itself as full decay.

We have both pretty much exhausted our usefulness, haven't we?

Tig reflected on the tangible aspects of his deterioration. What kind of life would he live now, alone, an indigent, disabled? His destitution and physical impairments were grave.

These concerns, however, were less threatening to Tig's wellbeing than what festered beneath the surface, the things Tig had enabled most of his life. Tig's internal enemy had been successfully camouflaged for years. Tig skillfully dressed himself each day in a façade of strength, but beneath the brick and mortar of his resolve, the blight of self-loathing continued to rot Tig's infrastructure. Now he was stripped of any semblance of dignity, and Tig sat on his splintering throne.

He felt nauseous from his own stench. He considered the gun leaning against the door. The dark vortex tempted him. Tig continued to slip steadily, easily, down into the blackness of despair. The final decline would be easy now. *Who would know? Who would care?*

Tig shifted his weight to drop his head in his hands when an odd sound drew his attention. A dull thud followed by a clanging and scuffling—then silence. The sound was similar to that of a large coin hitting the floor, rolling and spinning before coming to a stop.

Tig's eyes scanned the linoleum. In the corner lay a small rusty object. The rowel Dottie had given him rested, barely discernible on a red clay stain. Tig reached down to feel his empty belt loop. When he had leaned over the table, the worn leather loop on his belt had given way, sending the rowel spinning beneath his feet.

Since the morning after Dottie tied it around his neck, Tig had kept the rowel tightly secured to his belt. Dottie convinced him it would bring good luck. Over the years, whenever facing an obstacle in his life, Tig would compulsively run his fingers over the object, so much so that as the rowel rusted over the years, one area of its surface shone like a new dime.

Tig moved from the chair to the corner. He bent down and picked up the rusty metal star. He held it flat in his hand and stood staring, reflecting on all the memories a single object could hold.

"Tig, you can do anything you set your mind to!" Dottie's words reverberated in Tig's ears as though she were standing in front of him. "Our lives are hinged on what we choose to do in this moment, and the next and the next. You know how to make the right choice, Tig."

Tig could see Dottie's eyes. They always glistened and smiled on the sides when she was encouraging him.

Tig walked over and opened the door, greeting the late afternoon sun. In a single act of defiance, he faced the windmill and spoke out loud. "I will get my life back. I will."

Tig turned and pulled the door shut behind him. The windmill screeched. Its harsh-clawed metal thwacks mocked and countered Tig's resolve. The rusty metal blades ground against each other called out in beats, "This izzzz your life now, Tig Mills; this izzzz your life now, Tig Mills; this izzzz your life now, Tig Mills."

FIVE

Judging from the position of the sun, Tig was fairly confident there were several hours of daylight left. He knew the best remedy for his anxiety was to be proactive. With this in mind, he considered how to make the place more livable. Getting the lay of the land ranked high on his small list of priorities. With a sense of determination, Tig prepared to survey the land surrounding his new home. Without the benefit of paper and with no writing tool in sight, Tig tore a section from the cardboard box that had contained his food. Stuffing the scrap in his pocket, he found some half-burned pieces of kindling in the wood stove. He could use the burnt end of the sticks as improvised charcoal pencils to make a list of needed repairs. The windmill was the most obvious in need of an overhaul. Tig stood in the doorway weighing the importance of addressing the windmill first.

Not today, he thought. He clenched the charcoal sticks and stepped off the stoop. He walked past the squawking windmill on down the hill to a low spot in the driveway. There, a quarter mile from the house, in a narrow valley, a stand of trees embraced the road on both sides. He turned to the west.

Pushing down the scrub and thorny bushes, he moved into the woods. Within thirty yards of where he had entered, Tig pressed past a cluster of dense cedars. A covey of quail sprayed out of the undergrowth in all directions. Tig jumped and fell backwards against the thick foliage. Startled, he shook himself off and then laughed.

"Phew. That'll get the heart pumpin!"

Curious as to the density of the trees, Tig forced his way under the cedars. The sap stuck to his skin and hair, its strong oily scent burning his eyes. He stood still long enough to hear the "see, see, see" of a warbler.

Putting his head down, Tig moved farther into the thick brush. He forced down the branches with his forearms, careful not to use his gloved hand. A branch snapped back, flying up to etch his cheek. He wiped the blood on his sleeve and pushed on.

He was about to turn back when he spotted a remarkable change in the lighting. It was coming from beyond the trees, and it beckoned him on. An open space came into view as Tig contorted himself through the last of a dense section of thicket. In the center of the copious overgrowth in the middle of the forest was an unobstructed site, an outdoor room. It was a hollow formed by a ring of cedars. The space was not much more than twenty feet in diameter. The trees created a screen encompassing the entire area. The outer edges of the ring were obscure, deeply shaded by cedar sentinels standing side by side, boughs intertwined. There the prickly thatch underfoot gave way to a chipped bark and dirt-covered rug. Directly above the space was an uncluttered view of clear blue sky with a single source of light dropping in from overhead—a natural oculus.

The forest had created a beautiful, hidden sanctuary. Tig freed himself from the clinging thicket and stretched upright. He walked to the center and looked in awe around him. He let out a deep sigh, the wonder of the enigmatic creation catching his breath.

Tig stood in reverence, taking in the fullness of the room. He let his senses experience all that was around him. Moist and dark, the hollow possessed a spicy scent of damp acrid peat. A songbird's faint and distant melody could be heard, chirping whispers just beyond the wall. There were the subtle sounds of the forest, the creaking of the cedars as they rubbed together in the breeze, the buzz of insects, and the rustling of leaves.

Tig stooped to rake his hand over the soft floor, filling it with earth and bark. He let it sift through his fingers and escape back to the ground. He gazed up at the sky, never making a sound. His silence was met with a peace that moved not just over him but through him. Before he proceeded to leave, he committed to memory the location of the hollow—the place he ordained as sacred.

———

Following the exchange of vows, wedding guests filed out from the church sanctuary onto the lawn. Side by side, family and friends locked arms, forming a large circle around the young couple. The spring air was scented with plum blossoms and fresh mowed grass. A swell of excitement moved through the group as they gathered to take part in a thirty-year-old Arvita tradition.

In a show of support and celebration, members of the community would dance in a large circle around the newlyweds. On this particular afternoon in May, the bride and groom standing on the church lawn were radiant. Dressed in gray slacks, white shirt, and a bow tie with a few wild purple hyacinths extending from his breast pocket, Tig took Dottie's hand. Dottie marveled at how handsome her groom was.

His brown eyes smiled. He had a way of looking right through her. He lifted his gaze for just an instant, long enough to look straight up at the pale blue sky. A deep sense of gratitude filled his heart.

A small cluster of lacy and aromatic violets and yarrow blossoms were stuck into a few strands of red curls pulled up on the back of Dottie's head. The remainder of her long locks flowed over her shoulders and fell freely down her back.

Tig held both hands of his bride, relishing her beauty. As he bent forward to kiss Dottie, the music began. Those gathered as witnesses began to cheer and dance around them in celebration. In response, Tig spun Dottie around. Extending one arm out, Dottie let the bouquet of prairie flowers trail behind her, the stems surrendering petals and blossoms to the breeze. Released, they floated freely through the air, showering the couple, while Dottie's cotton lace wedding dress swirled behind her like gossamer wings.

Johnnie barely made it through the wedding ceremony. As Tig's best man, Johnnie stood next to his brother during the entire service. He writhed inside when Tig took Dottie as his wife, evidence for everyone to see that Johnnie could not have the woman he wanted. While Dottie's maid of honor, Carolyn, stood with her eyes lovingly on Johnnie, he in turn saw only Dottie. The week before the wedding, Johnnie moved out of the house he shared with Tig. He wanted no part in celebrating Tig and Dottie's post nuptial bliss or in witnessing the creation of their home. Johnnie was full of bitterness when he seized the opportunity to leave Arvita behind. He wasted no time enlisting in the army.

While Dottie was hanging dotted Swiss curtains in the windows of Carrie Ann's house, Tig was turning the sod. The very next spring, Tig nurtured a small garden on the same land his mother had first planted. While the young couple admired the first sprouts uncurling through the soil, Johnnie was in basic training at Fort Jackson, South Carolina. The tomatoes were ripe on the vine when Johnnie graduated from boot camp.

The first of two children joined the Mills household in 1949, one year before the start of the Korean conflict. Ominous green-black swells rose steadily from the southwest all afternoon the day Leon Jonathan Mills arrived. Tig paced from window to window in the waiting room of Dawson County Hospital anticipating the event. The only storm that arrived that day was Leon, who tore out of his mother at dusk. He was still kicking and screaming when he was placed in his father's arms. Smiling down at his flailing newborn, Tig ran his fingers through Leon's soft tufts of black hair.

"My, my. Ya favor your Uncle Johnnie. Look at those solid hands, just like mine. You're a little tornado, aren't ya?"

Tig and Dottie could not have been more thrilled with their baby boy, who grew to look more like his Uncle Johnnie every day. Unlike Johnnie, however, Leon was enamored with Tig. Even as a small toddler, whenever Tig walked through the door, his son's excitement was easy to see. Tig could not help but recall how Johnnie had followed their father, Harold, around with the same devotion.

Tig was thankful to have avoided the draft due to a heart murmur, a souvenir from the duster years. Instead of brandishing a gun, Tig lugged a tool box.

Meanwhile, Johnnie was on the other side of the world marching the 38th parallel. No one heard much of anything from Johnnie during those years. There was the occasional generic note indicating where he was located and for how long, but that was about it. Tig was not surprised that Johnnie never inquired about him. It did baffle him, however, that Johnnie showed no apparent interest in Dottie or his nephew. When Tig and Dottie wrote to tell Johnnie they had given Leon his middle name, Johnnie wrote nothing in return.

———

The Mills family fell into the routine of raising and supporting their small family. The first years Tig and Dottie spent at Carrie Ann and Harold's homestead were pleasant. They lived a life of gratitude.

Laughter was commonplace, and the young family was content. Tig fixed things around the house, tended to the garden and live-stock, and made modest toys for his son. Dottie loved to sew and cook. The simple trappings of their prairie lifestyle and their baby growing up in a loving and nurturing environment were the things that measured success.

Tig enjoyed his work. He was satisfied earning what was needed to sustain his home. He savored left over time at the end of each work day and weekends off. Tig relished the freedom to spend his spare time as he chose, and he had no desire to pursue a prestigious career at the risk of losing his autonomy.

Leon was not yet potty trained when Dottie announced she was pregnant with their second child.

Within less than two years of Leon's birth, Evelyn Dorothy Mills was laid in the cradle near the hearth. Tig's and Dottie's hearts swelled at the sight of Leon pulling himself up to the edge of the cradle, admiring his baby sister. Evelyn lay swaddled in an earth-toned patchwork quilt her mother had made. Raking autumn light graced the top of her head, christening her peach fuzz. Her ruddy complexion was as suitable for October as the black jack leaves gathering on the lawn. She was her mother's daughter.

The first time Evelyn's tiny lids lifted, Dottie called out, "Tig look, come look. Evelyn is smiling at me with her eyes!"

Tig and Dottie sat side by side admiring the little cherub face of their baby daughter. "Look, Tig, look how her little chin is pointed and her cheeks are so full, and with your dark eyes. Why, she looks like a little elf!"

"She does. She's a little elf, sweet Elfie."

"Oh, I like that, Tig, but instead of Elfie, why don't we call her Effie? What a perfect nickname, Tig. I love it! Let's call her Effie."

———

Anna handed Effie to Wendell. Both grandparents cooed over the tiny red-head in their arms. "Wendell, she looks just like Dottie did as a baby, doesn't she?"

Holding his granddaughter in his arms, Wendell recalled how expensive it was to raise two girls. From the time Tig and Dottie married, Wendell did his best to gently convince his son-in-law to look for a steady job.

As much as he liked Tig, Wendell felt there was room for improvement. Regardless of his father-in-law's cajoling, Tig always sloughed off the notion. Nonetheless, Wendell maintained that his daughter deserved the best. Now with a second child to care for, Wendell believed security for his daughter's family was in the balance. He purposed to do something about it. Having successfully run his farming business, Wendell possessed a healthy degree of confidence. He felt it totally acceptable to research career opportunities for his son-in-law. Wendell believed it admirable that he would secure Dottie's future while enabling Tig's business reputation. Tig never sought Wendell's opinion. Nonetheless, believing he knew the best plan for Tig's success, Wendell did not consider unsolicited advice out of the question.

———

Three months later, Wendell sat at the kitchen table, across from Tig. Wendell began to make his pitch as soon as a steaming mug of coffee was set in front of him.

"Tig, windmills are all over this part of the country, and do you know why?" Wendell didn't wait for Tig to answer. He really had no intention of letting him respond.

"Well, I'll tell you why, Tig. It's because they're inexpensive, and ranchers still use them. Newspapers are saying they will soon be obsolete as more folks turn to electric pumped water. But it has been a few years since FDR's Electricity Act, and we still have folks who can't get electric pumps. In the towns, yes. But the poorer ranchers, now, they're the ones who need those windmill pumps more than ever."

Wendell's intensity grew. He was noticeably excited.

"Why in just this last year, Draford Windmill has gone out of business, leaving their pumps up all over southern Kansas with nobody to repair them or provide replacement parts. And I'm fit to tell you we will have the same problem here before we know it."

Wendell tapped his pointer finger on the table for emphasis.

"Now is the time to get into this business, now when wooden parts are being replaced by metal. Now is when you can get in on the ground floor of the windmill pump repair and replacement industry."

Wendell leaned over the table emphasizing the word "now." Tig pushed his lower back a little tighter against the rungs of his chair, uncomfortable with the sudden assertiveness of his father-in-law.

"I don't know, Wendell. I mean I think I'd enjoy it, but I'm not much of a businessman."

Wendell cast a look of surprise, "Why, Tig, managing all those jobs you do…. What is that if that's not running a business?"

"I'm sure it ain't the same, Wendell. I'm really not the businessman type. Besides, I enjoy what I'm doin' now, and I wouldn't begin to know how to do what you're talkin' about."

"You wouldn't need to know, Tig. I'd help you set it all up. I'd manage that part of it. Essentially, you'd work for me. We could work out a deal where I'd pay you a commission for every job. I'd keep the books, manage the supplies and equipment, and all that. You'd just be responsible for maintaining and repairing the windmills and when needed, digging wells and installing new equipment."

"Ah, I'm just not sure, Wendell."

Tig was getting conspicuously uncomfortable. He shifted his weight and shuffled his feet under the table. Tiny beads of perspiration hid under his hairline. There was a pause as Wendell nervously tipped his chair back.

"Tig, I can't do it without you, son."

Tig felt no different about the idea. He really was not interested. Wendell, however, had skillfully managed to hit a nerve. He touched on Tig's ardent sense of responsibility, his never-ending compulsion to do what he thought was the right thing—to comply. In doing so, Wendell manipulated his son-in-law. Tig struggled to push his desires down in order to please Wendell. Tig sensed imminent danger. He realized the foundation he stood on, his self-awareness, was eroding beneath his feet. His resolve began to give way to self-imposed conviction. The conversation commenced to shift.

"I guess I'd enjoy the work, but I don't know."

Tig paused again while Wendell's jaw tensed, noticeably agitated at Tig's hemming and hawing. Tig made a final attempt to thwart Wendell's insistence.

"Wendell, where on earth would I come up with the money to get all this started?"

Wendell smiled and sat back in his chair. The bait was set. He looked up at his daughter. Dottie smiled and added some hot coffee to her father's half empty cup. Wendell seized the moment.

"I'd front the cash, Tig. Matter-of-fact I've already checked into buying the entire leftover surplus from Draford. You see, son, I'd make the investment to set up the company."

Tig began to hesitate, hoping if he stalled long enough Wendell would back down. Tig glanced at Dottie for reassurance. Instead, he caught a strange twinkle in her eyes. He could have sworn he saw her nod her head, agreeing with her father. He looked again. *Yes, there*, he saw it. *She wants me to agree to do this.*

Tig would have done anything for Dottie. So, with a handshake over a cup of coffee and a slice of apple cake, Tig capitulated. Against his better judgment, he agreed to work for his father-in-law.

———

Thin ripples of light spread across the water as the heron lifted, his vast wings fanning small waves while the tips of his toes skimmed the surface. The small pond rested snug between the cedars and a craggy ridge line where large sycamores stretched lazily over the water. Their shedding light gray bark was graced with a hint of budding green. Infant leaves fluttered in the afternoon breeze.

Tig emerged from the cedar hollow and let his eyes travel across the pond. The pungent scent of wet earth and fishy water greeted him. Partially sheltered, the small spring-fed pond offered a perfect refuge for gathering wildlife. Tig walked to the edge of the clay beach, a trail of footprints in the mud following him. He sat down, the weight of his body pressing into the ground. The dank mud soaked the seat of his pants. He paid no mind to the clammy denim stuck to his skin. Instead, he took his cardboard and charcoal stick, and sketched out a small map indicating the location of the cedar hollow and the pond.

I bet catfish bite here, he thought as he rested his good hand against his chin. While watching two squirrels playing tag between an elm and a sycamore, he considered the best locations for fishing.

Tig looked down at the simple map he had drawn. His glance became a chiseled brow. He scowled and shook his head in disgust over what he had produced. His diagrams were nothing more than a few random scrawling lines which made neither rhyme nor reason. He thought about the futility of creating a list, and he set the charcoal down.

Ever since his injury, Tig had been unable to write down his ideas. He could speak them, but he struggled with putting them into words on paper. This was complicated by the loss of his dominant hand. It rendered his twisted, tortured script legible only to himself. Two deficiencies of this magnitude were tantamount to failure in

Tig's mind, double jeopardy. He considered abandoning his list altogether.

He reached for the rowel and ran his fingers across the smooth part of the metal. Back and forth, back and forth—his worry stone, his rosary. It focused and calmed him. Then, as was most often the case, something sparked inside Tig, some measure of hope, and he rallied. *No, if I quit this early in the game, I don't stand a chance.*

Tig picked up his utensils and stood to his feet. A single cloud reflected on the surface of the water resembling a dollop of whipped cream on a cup of coffee. The cloud befriended Tig, moving along with him as he made his way around the pond. At the opposite edge, the rock-encrusted ridge rose several yards above the water. At the top, Tig marveled at how the terrain spread out, lying down in fields of velvet green as far as the eye could see. Blades of soft winter wheat moved gracefully as the late afternoon breeze picked up.

Intermittent drafts of cool air disrupted the warm stillness of the day. Tig knew the shifting wind in late afternoon ushered in nightfall. He was not yet familiar enough with his surroundings to be out roaming around in the dark. So, he determined he would cut across the fields and head back up toward the house, but the hike across the field was dizzying. Adrift in a sea of grass, the short blades of wheat swayed back and forth as Tig set his sight on the simple structure in the distance.

As he approached the house, he moved up and behind to the north, walking toward the fence line along another bank of cedars. The ground between the house and the trees, about two hundred yards, was rocky and uncultivated. Jagged stones and hardened clay were interspersed with an assortment of thistle, globemallow, fleabane and buffalograss. Each added a bit of color, spring confetti sprinkled about softening the otherwise harsh terrain. The pockets of sand and pea gravel made for uneven footing. The walk to the fence was slow. The breeze turned to a chilly wind rustling the tops of the trees.

Having arrived, Tig pulled the cardboard and charcoal from his pocket. He followed the rough timber and barbed wire fence around to the east and all the way back to the house, making notes of needed repairs as he went. He documented all the breaks in the wire and split posts that would need to be replaced. Tig knew he had to be diligent, since mending fences afforded him a place to live. He worked his way along the perimeter. Within a few yards from the house, the fence intersected with another run of barbed wire and wood posts. Here, the fence enclosed a small backyard.

Tig pushed down the top row of wire and carefully stepped over. There was no grass, but the ground was more forgiving than it had been on the opposite side of the fence. The rocks were smaller, and Tig could tell that at one time the soil had been turned. Within a few yards to the southeast, the distorted windmill worked the pump. Water dripped slowly but continuously into the large trough.

The sun was rapidly dropping. The rest of the land would have to wait to be surveyed until morning. He concluded he would get an early start soon after dawn. At the break of day, he would venture around the southeast part of the land, past the windmill and back down through the wooded section to the road. He would end across from where he discovered the hollow.

Tig stopped off at the outhouse before entering the back door and walking into the kitchen. There, he set the pieces of cardboard and charcoal on the table. He opened the door to the refrigerator, not that he believed he would find anything else in there but more so because the act itself brought some strange comfort. He was marking his territory, claiming his own. Looking in, his eyes lingered for a moment on the cans of beer. Turning his head away, he thought about the remaining half can of beans. Tig closed the door deciding to wait before eating them.

The armchair near the wood stove looked inviting. He wasted no time plopping down in it. The chair was lumpy, but Johnnie was right. It was the most comfortable accommodation in the house. Tig watched the light from the window change from yellow to orange. Daylight was fading, and there was nothing much to do but look at the walls.

Tig's pants were still damp and uncomfortable. Restless, he shifted his weight. In doing so, he caught a whiff. At first, he could not identify it. Then he realized the odor was rising from his own body. The last time Tig had bathed was nearly two weeks and three states ago. He desperately needed a wash-down. He recalled that

Linda had left him a towel and a bar of soap. Exhausted but unwavering, Tig stood, stretched his sore back, and gingerly set out in search of the soap and a bucket.

The sun was hiding in and out of narrow bands of cinnamon haze gathering at the edge of the earth as Tig grabbed the pail. He moved down the eroded hill to the water trough. He focused on the liquid dripping from the pipe and kept his eyes from the menacing blades screaming overhead. The water in the trough was cold but clear. He filled his bucket and hiked back up the hill. Both the pot and kettle were filled with water and placed on the stove.

He hung his cap on a rusty nail protruding from the door frame. He scratched the jagged scar on his head, the place where hair no longer grew. Pushing what hair he had left back, he reluctantly began to undress.

Tig pulled off his boots and set them by the front door. He set his knife down on the table. He fingered the rowel on his belt, momentarily paralyzed by its power to awaken his memories. Weary, he untied the rowel and placed it next to his knife on the table. Slipping his belt off, he removed his pants. A small mound of dirt remained on the floor where he stood. His socks were so filthy they stuck painfully to his skin, to the hair on his legs. Unable to loosen them while standing up, he sat and tugged on them several minutes before they finally let go of his feet. He threw his socks, spots of blood, and hair follicles concealed beneath the grime on the floor next to the door.

As steam rose from the stove, Tig stripped off the remainder of his filthy clothes. His shirt was torn and wrinkled, its many creases outlined in dirt. He wrestled his shirt over his head. Sweat stains mixed with dirt had hardened the cotton shirt, which was stiff under his arms. Tig thought he heard it crunch as he dropped it to the floor.

When done, Tig stood naked on the cold linoleum. He was a mess. His skin was caked with dirt, and the bends of his arms and legs were embedded with black stripes of grime. His toes were webbed together with hardened mud, the result of dirt mixed with sweat. Soot and sap stained his face. A layer of dust had gathered above his top lip and brow. His eyes were gritty, and his lips cracked and peeling. Tig's hair was so greasy it no longer appeared mousy brown but black and wet with bits of debris trapped between slimy strands here and there.

He slowly added the hot water to the cold remaining in the bucket. Picking up the bar of soap, he headed for the back door. In the light of day's end, Tig stood on the frigid concrete slab between the house and the outhouse. There, he bathed himself. A chill ran up his back, not so much from the shock of the water temperature, but from the physical response when forgotten, unattended flesh is awakened.

Tig stood shivering, relishing the sensation of being touched. He passed the soap through his hair several times before it would lather. He slathered himself with the foam. The suds streamed off, chestnut hued froth flowing down from the stoop and into the yard carried on small red-dirt tributaries.

Tig looked to the sky. An old friend greeted him. Familiar and comforting, akin to the painted sunsets of his youth, magenta streaks shot across to the horizon, melding with deep shades of wine and ginger. As the cool water ran down his back, Tig closed his eyes and breathed deeply.

I am finally home.

———

The biting air woke Tig. He grabbed his jacket from the floor and added it to the blanket pulled over his shoulders. Dawn had begun to hatch and unfurl its wings of milky saffron light across the prairie. In the distance, the bawling cattle moved across the buckling fields. They traveled in a line behind a spray of sweet feed tossed from the back of a rusty pickup. The truck chugged slowly along down furrowed paths and over the hills. Just outside his partially open window a half dozen blue jays protested loudly, scolding and threatening a small black snake that slithered toward the windmill. Tig rolled over and rubbed his eyes as the early light of day struggled to illuminate the room.

Swinging his legs to the side of the bed, he slipped on the only other pair of pants he owned. He pulled on his dilapidated boots and went out back to get his shirt. He had washed his pants and shirt from the day before in left over murky bath water. They hung still dripping from the back door. He collected his shirt and hung it over the door of the oven.

With the oven on low, he stood shivering while he waited for the water in his flowered teakettle to boil. He made himself a cup of hot water. Tig warmed his hands on the chipped mug as he peered through the window watching the pink-toned blush on a peach cloud spread over the eastern sky. Wanting to get an early start and fully aware of his limited provisions, he decided to forgo breakfast. Sliding his damp shirt over his arms, he picked up his knife, cardboard, and charcoal. He threw on his jacket and pulled the front door shut behind him.

Tig faced the rising sun and began walking toward the area he had not checked the day before. As he hiked down the cracked earth to the bottom of the hill, he stopped and glared at the windmill. Its tormented squawks mocked him. Tig pressed his eyes shut and forced out the sounds.

Turning his back on the menacing machine, he proceeded east. Within fifty yards of the backside of the windmill, there was another bunch of wild cedar clumped together. They rose up an incline covering a small hillside.

Tufts of new indian grass, vetch, and sorrel covered the ground. Tig hiked up to the top and found himself on the edge of the narrowest section of a deep canyon.

Strata of ancient limestone and quartz shot through the walls of red clay. Gnarled dead trees, bushes, and branches filled the bottom, which rested a good thirty feet below him. Projecting out from under the natural rubble was an assortment of manmade debris, everything from old farm equipment to bed springs. Tig moved gingerly along the rim heading south. He continued to where the canyon extended into a scrub tree forest growing on the east side of the road leading to the house.

In this area, an elevation change flattened the canyon walls as the ravine melded into the woods. Tig noticed a small creek meandering through the shallowest end. His eyes followed the thin stream to its origins somewhere from within the trees. Glancing back, he noticed that the creek bed, with its deep red veins of clay, had an area lined with large rocks. Stepping out on one, he steadied himself. Letting the clear spring water slap against his boot, he squatted down and ran his left hand through the spring-fed ripples.

He removed the glove from his right hand. The stubbed remnants of his fingers appeared bruised, so he held them in his left hand gently, massaging his mutilated digits. His ring, middle, and forefinger had been reduced by half, each a short boney stump defined by a fleshy knot at the tip. Where his little finger used to be was a long white shiny rib of scarred flesh. His thumb had also been badly maimed. The doctor had not amputated it, believing he should salvage what he could have of his patient's hand.

Eventually, Tig's severely disfigured thumb atrophied. Now turned in an unnatural position at the joint, deformed and useless, it tucked against his palm.

Tig's neuropathy had gotten worse. The damp spring air had roused his condition. The fiery pain that frequently shot through his fingers was debilitating. He set his hand into the water. He swooshed it around for a while, grimacing until the cold numbed and put the fire out in his disfigured appendages.

He lingered, allowing the stream to move over his damaged hand. He observed how his stumps caught the water. Unlike his left, his maimed hand created unique swells as the clear liquid surged up, over, around and through his mutilated fingers. The water leapt and swirled in a beautiful dance. He could not help but marvel at how something so hideous could enable something so beautiful.

As he swirled his hand in the water, Tig caught a hint of movement out of the corner of his eye. Searching, he spotted the source. Across the pond, an armadillo waddled through the thicket along the sloping edge of the canyon wall. The enigmatic little creature was looking for worms, foraging for scorpions and other delicacies. Barely noticeable, the armadillo's color and texture provided a suitable disguise amidst the weedy terrain. The creature's bony, plated armor protected its soft underbelly as it sniffed and clawed. Intrigued, Tig studied the armadillo, observing it until its camouflaged hide merged with the underbrush, causing the animal to seemingly dematerialize.

What an odd creature, he thought.

"You are better off in there, alone and hidden away," Tig shouted. He dropped his voice looking down at his hand.

"Alone where no one can harm you."

Assured his hand would be numb for a while, Tig slipped on his leather glove and resumed his hike. He climbed back up out of the ravine and walked into the woods, following the creek until it opened up through the trees to the cratered drive leading up to his house. Tig could not remember if the fence went as far as the main road, so to confirm it, he hiked down to the end of the driveway. He crossed the cattle guard and marched out into the middle of Rte. 426. Tig turned from side to side, looking in either direction. Across the road from the entrance to his house and a few yards to the west was another dirt driveway imbedded with a cattle guard. He scratched his head and wrinkled his forehead.

I wonder who lives over there. The fences sure need some work.

Tig took out his charcoal and scratched out another unrecognizable note.

The hike back up to the house by means of the driveway took Tig past a scraggy section of rough land. Thorny vines and dense ragweed were interspersed with clusters of goldenrod.

As he continued up the weather-beaten drive, Tig noted a collection of cedar and scrub trees edged the weedy patch of land. He stopped and studied the terrain. It was the entrance to the sacred place he had discovered the day before. He stuffed the cardboard in his pocket and moved on. Shortly, he crossed over the creek, which ran through a makeshift culvert under the drive. The clay was eroding around it, revealing part of the concrete duct just beneath the surface. Further up where the weather-beaten road became no more than a path in places, a couple large Sycamores draped over the road, their branches kissing overhead.

There, the elevation changed. *This must be where the canyon bottoms out just east of here*, he thought.

The wooded area opened up to rugged terrain, wheat fields, and the windmill. The house began to rise on the horizon as Tig ascended the hilly road. The straggly hedge apple, leaned toward the west side of the structure. Savaged by unforgiving winds and drought, it cast an iridescent hue of lime green against the cement stucco.

At the top, Tig breathed heavily, his sweat escaping from under his cap as he drew close to the house. He wanted nothing more than to go directly in and sit down. He would rest, cool off, let cold water run down the back of his throat, eat a late lunch of leftover beans, and feel satisfied. This would have been feasible had it not been for the date made with the windmill. Tig knew he had to inspect the damaged blades and the gear box.

He put it off as the last thing he would tackle. Now, it loomed in front of him—the grinding, shrieking blades demanding his full attention.

Tig created a makeshift scaffold next to the windmill by laying old lumber planks he had found behind the outhouse across the water trough. After testing it for load bear and when he was certain it was stable, he climbed on top.

Nearby, two restless squirrels barked at a blue jay, while a flock of crows squawked at Tig's audacity, that he dared cover their water hole. The natural sounds provided an adequate distraction from the haunting, clawing shrieks of the windmill.

Without a ladder, Tig could not get up high enough to see in detail what needed repair. From his position, he could tell the brake linkage needed work, as did the rotor hub.

Blades would have to be replaced and the tail vane straightened out. Eager to be finished with this task, Tig eased back down off the planks and uncovered the trough. He took out his charcoal and made some notes to himself, a code for what needed repair. Tig stepped back and took a long look at the metal blades, tortured and broken above him, trying to observe any other damage.

The wind shifted slightly. Slowly the windmill turned. Screeching, crashing blade on blade, metal on metal, it faced Tig, screaming at him—familiar curses conjured from the past. Tig covered his ears and turned quickly toward the house.

SIX

"This should do it, Mr. Butler." Tig stepped off the last rung of the ladder. "I oiled the gear box, and ya should be good."

"Thank ya, Tig. The cattle will appreciate this." Delbert Butler reached out with a check in his hand as Tig put up the last of his tools.

Wendot Windmill Company was a success. Folks all over Arvita came to rely on Tig. Wendell set up one job after another. There were the initial consultations, the installation, the follow-ups, the annual inspections, and the occasional repairs. Wendell was bringing in customers left and right, and Tig handled them all. Within a year, evenings at home were considerably shorter, and the weekends were consumed with work. Tig never complained. He just kept trudging along.

Always looking for ways to expand the business, Wendell brokered some new accounts two counties away. He moved one of his farm hands over to help sort supplies at Wendot and to assist Tig when needed. The business continued to expand which required additional help. Wendell promoted Tig to manager and hired two more employees as field workers. Under Tig's supervision, they dug wells and assisted in the installation of new pumps.

With all the new accounts, having additional laborers made no impact on Tig's work load which continued in force. As manager, he was responsible for handling the details. There was no single template for repairing or maintaining windmills and pumps. Each job was as unique as the make and model of each piece of equipment.

———

Damage was assessed and documented, job orders written and specific supplies ordered. Once repairs were made, follow-up visits were scheduled to check on the efficiency of the equipment. To fulfill the demands of his work, Tig's late nights at the office became more frequent. Within a few years, Tig's weekends were spent traveling to Kansas or Colorado to manage accounts and bring back supplies. He was exhausted and alone most of the time. The strain of his continual absence was seeping into other areas of his life. Tig wasn't the only one experiencing the repercussions of his job.

"Tig, you're never home anymore!" Dottie's eyes shot fire in Tig's direction. "The kids rarely get to spend time with you. They miss you! Leon asks for you all the time. Do you have any idea how often they go to bed without seeing you at all? The days have run into weeks, Tig. Weeks they go without seeing you! Do you hear what I am saying?"

Dottie was never at a loss for words when she was angry. She understood the power of her caustic vocabulary, and she wielded it skillfully. She was so competent at verbal sparring that she frequently left her opponent speechless.

"When you signed on for this, we never agreed you would work all the time! Work, work, work. That's all you do. So that must be all that matters to you, Tig Mills!"

"I'm not goin' to discuss this with ya, Dottie."

Worn-out from a long day, Tig set his elbows on the table and held his head up. His cold food waited on a plate in front of him. His children had been in bed for hours. Dottie stomped twice around the table before forcefully setting a cup of coffee down in front of her husband. It splashed up and spilled onto Tig's hand. He jerked his hand back, his arm flying up in surprise.

"Oh, so now you want to hit me!" Dottie put one hand on her hip, drew up her forehead, peering through her constricted eyelids.

"Dottie, for Christ's sake, stop. I'm not 'bout to hit ya. What is wrong with ya today?"

"Nothing that hasn't been wrong for a long time already. What is not right is what is happening to us," Dottie snapped as she started to walk away.

"And just what would that be, Dottie? Have ya forgotten how ya wanted this? How ya wanted me to work with your father so we could have more?"

Dottie's ammunition was loaded. She had been rehearsing all week and was more than prepared to fire off a slew of angry retorts. Tig's remark drew her ire.

She spun around set to pull the trigger. Her skirt swirling around conjured up a breeze that bristled against the back of Tig's neck. Dottie turned toward Tig. She was furious. Her face red and her fists clenched. She set her sight on the target, but she stopped short. Suddenly, she was incapable of releasing her anger. Her vitriol was seized by compassion for what she saw.

Tig sat slouched over a cold plate of food, his arms barely supporting the weight of his head. Weary and discouraged, Tig's eyes were closed. Was he praying? Dottie hesitated. Her fingers relaxed. Her voice softened.

"Tig, why can't you get more help? You're doing the work of three men."

Dottie moved behind Tig's chair and gently rested her hands on his shoulders. The tendons of his neck were stretched tight. She stroked his hair and rubbed his temples. He leaned back with a sigh. The warmth from her fingers penetrated the tension in his jaw, enabling him to relax. He reached up and laid his massive calloused hand on hers. Dottie leaned over and kissed him lightly on the cheek. The leftover salt from his sweat seasoned her lips.

"Bringin' on more men is not up to me, Dottie. Your father is the one in charge of that. He's been talking about divesting and creating a subdivision for the company. This would allow all the repairs to be handled separately from new installations."

"Would this mean you would not have to do both anymore, the repairs and installations?"

"I'm thinkin' that's what it'd mean." Tig pushed his chair back from the table. "Excuse me, Dottie. I'm just not that hungry tonight. I'm goin' to bed."

Tig shuffled out of the room while Dottie lingered, her hands on the back of his empty chair. She reached for the plate of uneaten food and determined to have a conversation with her father.

———

Not two months passed before Wendell created subdivisions within the company. He hired a young man from Wichita to manage the new well accounts.

Fletcher Thorton was experienced in the business having worked for the Draford Windmill Company for many years. Tig liked Fletcher. They got along well. When Fletcher saw something that needed to be done, he jumped right in and took care of it.

There were occasions when Fletcher would offer to fill in, providing Tig an extra day off here and there. Most importantly, on a day-to-day basis, Fletcher's efficiency at his job was freeing up time for Tig. What had taken five hours to complete now took only three. Before the end of that fiscal year, Tig was back to spending his evenings and weekends working around the house and enjoying his young family. The relief of not carrying all the responsibility at Wendot, could be seen in Tig's demeanor.

———

The summer of 1953 was exceptionally hot. Ranchers and farmers across Talgart and Dawson counties were converting to electric pumps. For those who continued to use the windmill, the sweltering temperatures tested the limits of the equipment. Tig, Fletcher, and Wendot's handful of employees were kept very busy. Everyone was talking about the unyielding heat.

The only thing that diverted conversations away from the weather was news the Korean conflict had ended. Photographs of returning soldiers filled practically every page of every newspaper in every small town across the country. Hidden among the thousands of anonymous images was the face of one of Arvita's own, Johnnie

Mills. Johnnie informed no one as to when he was scheduled to come home. While other veteran native sons were celebrated with gratitude, Johnnie's arrival to Arvita lacked any sense of a traditional homecoming. His reappearance in Arvita was as surreptitious as his disappearance five years prior.

———

Carolyn shared the news.

She stood in front of her best friends, Dottie and Tig, fidgeting with excitement. Dottie did her best to share in Carolyn's enthusiasm. Tig, on the other hand, was leery. He couldn't help but wonder if Johnnie ever had any intention of telling anyone, including Carolyn, that he was back in town.

"I got out of my car, and there he was just standing around talking to Russell at the filling station! I ran across the street. I'm sure I made a fool of myself, but Dottie, I just threw my arms around his neck. And now we're going out this Saturday! Can you believe it? Johnnie's back!"

Carolyn's excitement trumped her predictable poise. She shook her arms like a little girl tasting chocolate ice cream for the first time.

"Oh, Carolyn, I'm happy for you." Dottie smiled and hugged her friend. Dottie threw Tig a glance over Carolyn's shoulders that communicated she was really not pleased with the idea at all.

Several weeks later, Johnnie found his way to his brother's house. Johnnie met his nephew and his niece for the first time. Leon was six, and Effie was four. The children sat playing on the living room floor. Tig glanced across the table, watching his children chatter and giggle. *Hmm, Johnnie and I sat and played in that same spot, but that was a lifetime ago,* Tig thought.

Time had not favored their relationship. They had grown apart, and the distance between them left Tig skeptical as to why Johnnie would just randomly stop by to visit after such a long period of no communication.

"Ya got some cute kids, Tig. Everyone must know they get their looks from their momma."

Johnnie chuckled under his breath, never taking his eyes off of

Dottie. She poured the coffee and set the pot down on the table next to a plate of warm cookies.

Tig stood and pulled a chair out for her. As she took her seat, Johnnie gave her the once over. The intention of his glare was so obvious that Dottie blushed. Tig scowled.

"So, Johnnie, Carolyn tells us you're working at Russell Preston's fillin' station?" Tig spoke louder than usual in hopes of drawing Johnnie's attention off of Dottie.

With his signature smirk, Johnnie turned quickly in Tig's direction to acknowledge him. He knew his gawking at Dottie was annoying his brother, so Johnnie turned back and looked at her more intensely. Dottie rose from her chair, gathered up the kids, and left the room.

"Yeah, for now anyway. Ya know that boy looks like I did when I was his age."

"He does take after ya somewhat. So, what all are ya doin' at the station, Johnnie?"

"Workin' on engine repairs mostly."

"When did ya learn to repair car engines?"

"In the Army. I was with the motor division. Ya know they trained us, right? Tell ya what, workin' at Russell's sure beats the Hell outta fixin' truck engines in that icy God forsaken wasteland they sent us to. I never felt cold like that before. Ain't no way I'd ever go back, between the cold and… yeah…."

Something about Johnnie is different. Tig couldn't quite get his mind around it. Was it the way Johnnie's eyes glassed over? The way his lip quivered? Maybe it was his leg. Johnnie bounced his knee up and down, nervously, nonstop as they spoke. Tig felt the tension and discomfort mounting in his brother, so he changed the subject.

"I understand you're seein' Carolyn Wilson."

"Yeah, I guess ya could say that. Hey, have ya heard from Ron?"

Tig was startled by how quickly Johnnie diverted the conversation away from Carolyn. Tig and Dottie always believed Johnnie was careless with Carolyn's feelings. Johnnie's haste was a clear sign that any relationship between him and Carolyn was very one-sided.

"Yeah, I see him around town. He and Linda are doin' well. They have a little boy now. Ya knew that right?"

Johnnie's eyes turned dark. "Hell no. How would I've known that? I've heard nothin' from him. I suppose he's your best friend now."

Tig started to respond, but Johnnie jumped right over him.

"The reason I came here was I wanted to be the one to tell ya that Wendell Harns and I have been talkin'. He stopped by the station a few weeks ago, and we struck up a conversation. He told me all about Wendot and what's been goin' on. We had to deal with drillin', pumps, stuff like that in the military. We got to talkin' 'bout how the addition of a cable tool drilling division at Wendot would make a lot of sense."

Hell, this is all I need—Johnnie buttin' into my business. Tig resolved to hold his composure and said, "I'm sure when Wendell is ready, he'll make the right decisions for the company."

There was a glint in Johnnie's eyes. "He's more ready than ya think, li'l brother." Johnnie tipped his head for emphasis as he waited for Tig's response.

Tig's jaw clenched. "What exactly is that supposed to mean?"

Johnnie smirked. "You'll see." Johnnie's eyes scanned the room as he rose from his chair. "Well, I suppose this was always your vision of success. Not mine. I see bigger than this out there. I've seen the world, and there's so much out there. I intend to have some of it for myself."

Johnnie moved toward the door, leaving Tig steeped in dread.

"The future's comin' for Wendot, Tig. Ain't nothin' ya can do to stop it." The door shut with a thud.

Dottie stood in the doorway to the bedroom listening the entire time. She moved her hands up and down the door frame, her fingers passing nervously over a large dimple in the wall. Her mind raced as her hands made out the dent Tig had created years ago, the day he received his nickname, the day he tried to punch Johnnie. Tig was still staring at the front door when Dottie stepped into the room.

"Tig, Johnnie can't be a part of the business!"

"I know, Dottie, I know." Tig spoke to Dottie, but his eyes remained on the front door.

"I'm going to have a talk with my father about this!"

Tig turned toward his frantic wife. His expression registered grave concern. He knew full well Wendell was already preparing to expand into electric pumping systems. Just a few weeks prior, he had talked to Tig about working in other states. Wendell had a habit of sporadically letting his entrepreneurial spirit express itself in a flurry of far-fetched ideas. So Tig had dismissed Wendell's chatter about opening divisions in other locations.

He meant it, Tig thought. *He was serious. How long had Wendell and Johnnie been talking?* Tig bit his lip. Then it hit him.

Oh my God, he thought. *Wendell started bringing up the idea of expanding into other states just a few weeks after Johnnie was spotted in town.*

"Dottie, ya can't say anythin'. It's my responsibility. I plan to address it with your father first thing on Monday. I need ya to stay out of this. I'll take care of this. Please."

Dottie knew when Tig meant business. She registered both the seriousness and urgency in her husband's voice. He would handle this.

"OK, Tig. I promise I'll stay out of this. The children and I are counting on you." As Tig stood up from the table, his legs felt a little weak. *What if it's too late?*

———

"I have made my decision, Tig. I am sorry you disagree but Wendot is my company." Wendell stood up to talk to Tig.

Tig felt trapped. He would not be insubordinate to his boss nor disrespectful to his father-in-law. Tig's precarious position called for a particular brand of respect. Meanwhile, he also had to concern himself with Dottie's opinion, which he knew was not going to mesh with this new development.

"So, when are ya sendin' him out there?"

"He'll be leaving next month. Everything after that will depend on how many accounts he can generate."

"So, how will this affect me?"

"I seriously don't see that it will have an impact on you at all. Johnnie's division will handle only cable drilling and electric pump systems. This is outside your purview, Tig. You just keep doin' what you do and everything will be fine."

This is a bad idea. Tig knew everything was not going to be fine. Nothing was ever fine where his bitter brother was concerned. Nonetheless, Tig acquiesced. He would continue his work uninterrupted while Johnnie scouted in California, developing a new division for Wendot.

"We're growing the business, Tig. This is exciting!"

Tig looked over the desk at Wendell and forced a smile. He felt a myriad of things, none of which was excitement. Tig's apprehension that everything was going to change was met with the sting of reality and in a very short period of time.

———

Wendell set the receiver back on the phone. "Boys! We've hit the jackpot!"

Tig and Fletcher sat facing Wendell's desk. They threw each other a look of apprehension. The small office was the hub of Wendot. Wendell's suite was the largest of three paneled rooms that served as the business center for the company. The name was changed to Wendot Drilling when Wendell moved headquarters from the office in his house. Wendot Drilling was now located in a street-front lease in downtown Arvita, conveniently located catty corner to Russell's Filling Station.

"Johnnie has landed five new accounts! This makes six in the three weeks since he has been out there. He is flirting with two more and is going to need some help. Installs are scheduled to start in four weeks. Fletcher, I have decided to send you out to work with Johnnie. A rep from Acklen Cable Drilling & Pumps will meet with you when you get there. He'll see that you're trained. Your training and certification should take just a couple of weeks. I'm thinkin' this will be a temporary relocation until Johnnie's division can bring on new hires. Let's do this for four months and see where it goes."

Fletcher's eyes widened. Stunned but hiding it well, he stood up. Reaching across the desk he shook Wendell's hand.

"Yes, sir. I'll get right on it."

Tig sat silent. "Tig, you're gonna be on your own for a bit. I know you can do it, son. You've managed just fine on your own before."

Tig hated when Wendell addressed him as "son" at work. This passive-aggressive reminder that Wendell was also his father-in-law added an extra layer of condescending weight to every decision Tig made.

Tig wanted to remind Wendell of just how difficult those early years had been for Dottie, but he pushed the words back. Tig determined the most important thing was to come across strong and self-sufficient for Wendell's benefit.

Tig stood to his feet and extended his right hand to his boss, his father-in-law. "Yes, Sir. I'll manage."

———

"Dottie, what was I supposed to say?" Tig's volume was climbing.

They had been arguing for nearly an hour. Tig shared what had happened in the office earlier, and Dottie's fiery disposition took on new meaning. She had been angry when the expansion first took place. It had taken Tig several weeks to come down from that episode of flying barbs and needling digs. Tig could not have imagined that anything could make her more livid.

He was incorrect in that assumption. Dottie's anger over this recent event was extreme. She stormed. Her face was red, her hands waving through the air. Her body language indicated her contempt, but Tig could not determine if it was directed at his decisions or him in general.

"You told me not to interfere! I did what you asked and look where it landed us! Tig, we were miserable when you were managing alone. Why would you ever agree to do this again?"

"I had no choice, Dottie!"

"Yes you did! You could've let me talk to my father and none of this would've happened. He would've listened to me."

"Ahh, so that's it, huh Dottie. Ya don't think I was man enough to deal with your father. I have to use my wife to help me manage my business!"

Dottie appeared truly shocked at Tig's remark, but she wasn't about to back down.

"I never said any such thing, Tig! What does your being a man have to do with me talkin' to my father? How did you come to that foolish conclusion? I swear, Tig, you won't reason about anything!"

"Dottie, sometimes ya act like a spoiled brat, dammit. Just shut up."

Like the whip of a snake's head, Tig's words snapped and stung. Their razor-edge teeth cut through Dottie's emotional flesh. Venom raced through her veins, threatening her lifeline to Tig. They poisoned every part until they rested in her heart.

Tig felt the anger rise in him, but for some reason he could not force it back. Immediately, vines of guilt, the infectious ivy propagating in Tig's conscience, bound and dragged him back to the familiar place of self-loathing.

He had not experienced an attack like this for years, not since before he met Dottie. Now the lethal shoots constrained him again. He tried to shake off their strangling tentacles so he could undo what he had done, but it was too late. Like stubborn weeds, guilt from the past held him fast—always reminding him of his failures.

Tig began to play them out in his mind over and over. As he rehearsed his faults, the deep-rooted monster released its poison, the power of shame. Its strength increased with the recall of every lapse in judgment, every impulsive, misguided word or deed. The very fiber of each binding cord attached to Tig's spirit with a very specific toxic message. It was a lie, but one he chose to believe—*I'm worthless*.

Dottie's fire had been extinguished. She stood breathless, tears streaming down her face. She turned to leave the room, but she changed her mind. Instead, she walked over and stood directly in front of Tig.

She placed her hands on either side of his head and positioned her face within inches of his. Then she spoke.

"Tig, if you ever again attempt to break my spirit, you will lose me." With that, she turned.

SEVEN

The tires clawed at the asphalt, spraying gravel up into the muffler. Johnnie pulled recklessly off the highway. He was somewhere in New Mexico and making haste for Las Vegas. The dilapidated gas station provided a sufficient quick stop. While the attendant filled the car with gas, Johnnie made his way to the bathroom.

As Johnnie wandered around the snack racks, the attendant was losing his battle with the windshield. His attempt to clean off the blinding bug guts and carcasses adhering to the glass was futile. He surrendered to a hazy smear just about the time Johnnie was ready to leave. After paying for a six pack, cigarettes, and a bag of chips for the road, Johnnie stumbled out to the car. The attendant watched curiously as the lanky dark-haired stranger behind the blurred windshield pulled away.

Before joining the highway, the car paused momentarily. Then, with stones rattling in the hubcaps, the dirt-caked Cadillac backed up over a worn strip of leather, embedding it solidly into the ground. The wallet, with its shallow embossed designs, hand tooled by Tig's son Leon, was perfectly camouflaged—resting in a pile of roadside debris. Before tossing it out the car window, Johnnie had stripped it of its $500 leaving behind a Social Security card and all the pictures, save one.

As the grungy vehicle rattled along the black band weaving

through the desert, a tattered photo hanging from the rearview mirror twisted and turned in the wind. Johnnie reached up and held it steady with one hand while the other hand gripped the steering wheel. He stared at the photo as he careened down the road.

"So, who's got ya now, Miss Dottie?"

Johnnie laughed out loud hysterically. The sound mimicked that of someone in search of his mind. Johnnie's lingering obsession for Dottie was intensified by the alcohol compromising his rationality. As the car weaved back and forth down the road, Johnnie entertained himself, musing over how he would locate Dottie and retrieve her for himself.

———

Carolyn sorted the mail—nothing. Not one word from Johnnie. It had been over two weeks since Johnnie left to take Tig back east. On his way out the door, he promised he would be back within just a few days—another lie. His lies started the day he said "I do."

Deep in her heart Carolyn knew he had never loved her. Had she not been pregnant, he never would have sent for her. Carolyn stood with her hands braced on the counter as she looked out of the kitchen to the living room. She had put up with his deceit, philandering, gambling, and his drinking all these years.

For the umpteenth time she questioned why she allowed herself to go through this again. Carolyn picked up a picture of her and Dottie and hot tears welled up in her eyes; her throat tightened. She could see it all clearly now. *You always looked past me to Dottie, didn't you Johnnie? You led me to believe having them come to California would be good for me, especially after losing the baby. But that wasn't it, was it, Johnnie? It was to get her out here. It was always about Dottie.*

Tears fell onto the glass frame. Disgusted, she sent it hurling across the room. Hitting the wall, it shattered, spraying glass in all directions. Once more she braced against the counter, sobbing. Then, steadying herself, she stood. Carolyn picked up the receiver and dialed.

"Yes, that would be fine. Tuesday at 3pm. I will be there. Thank you."

Carolyn took the broom from the closet. Slowly and methodically, she swept up the broken shards, which she disposed of in the trash, along with the photograph.

———

Four days after Johnnie had abandoned Tig, shortly after dawn, a cloud of dusty haze drifted up from where the dirt driveway yielded to Rte. 426. Although the vehicle was not visible from the house, Tig knew the stirred-up dirt meant someone was coming. He set his eyes on the winding drive until a spot of deep red began to bob up and over the eroded surface. Tig sat on the front stoop tinkering with an old coffee can. The container was filled with rusty nails he had picked up from around the house.

Ron's big truck pulled to a halt, grinding the stones and puffing out dirt clouds. "Hey, Tig, how's it been goin? Johnnie around?"

"Doin' fine. No, he left already."

Ron seemed a little surprised if not hurt that Johnnie had left without saying goodbye. "Oh, OK. Well, have ya eaten breakfast yet?"

Tig had not eaten breakfast. Truth was he had not eaten since the day before. He had decided he was not going to mention he had been living off of a couple cans of beans and water the entire time. Nor was he going to mention it was because Johnnie stole his food.

"No, been gettin' the lay of the land and figuring which fences needed fixin'."

Ron persisted, "How'd the food do for ya, Tig?"

"Just fine. I'd like to thank ya and Linda again for providin' it for me."

"Well good, Tig. That'll make her happy. So, ya ready to head into town? We need to check on your health care. I think that's all there's left to do, except get ya to a grocery store, of course."

Tig grimaced inside. He never imagined a day when he would be dependent on the government for his provisions.

"Ron, Johnnie and I never got around to settin' up my disability. Do ya think we could take care of that today?"

Ron looked confused at first, then agreeable.

"Sure. Tig, you'll need your Social Security card. Johnnie told me ya don't have a driver's license for identification, so your Social Security card should do just fine."

"Yeah, they took away my license after my accident. I'm not allowed to drive… ya know, in my condition."

Tig hung his head. He also never thought he would see the day when driving would be illegal for him. Just the notion emasculated him.

"I don't have a Social Security card either. It was in my wallet, and that got lost on the way out here. Blew out of the car or somethin'."

Ron began to wonder what he was getting into. *Had Johnnie and Tig not planned or considered anything? Maybe Tig is irresponsible.*

"Well, we can go to the court house, and they'll tell us what you'll need to do. We'll go there first and then get some groceries and a few extra things ya might need."

Tig was not quite sure how to tell Ron he did not have any money either. *I might just wait until we get into town to tell him I'm broke. Then we can figure somethin' out.* Then Tig said, "We better get. Need to be back by night fall."

Ron opened the passenger side door, and Tig climbed up into the truck. As Ron closed the door, he threw his hand up.

"Oh shoot. Hold on, Tig. I promised Linda I'd check the gas valves on the stove. She has worried sick over them leakin'. Be right back."

Ron ran into the house and checked all the valves on the stove to ensure they were still working correctly. As he turned to leave, he noticed the food box sitting on the table. It was completely empty. Baffled, Ron opened the refrigerator. The only thing inside were three cans of beer on the top shelf. He checked the stove, Tig's bedroom, the doorless closet—nothing. There was no sign of the food anywhere.

Surely Tig didn't eat all we left him, Ron thought. Then just as quickly as that thought dissipated, another more sinister one took its place. *Johnnie took Tig's food—and his wallet too!*

All of Tig's hedging was beginning to make sense. As Ron opened the front door and caught a glimpse of Tig sitting alone in the truck, his stomach turned. *That bastard Johnnie left his brother here alone with nothin'. What breed of hatred would conjure up somethin' that cruel?*

———

"Everything's workin' as it should. It's gonna be just fine, just fine," Ron exclaimed as he slid into the truck and took hold of the steering wheel, clenching it a little tighter than usual.

It took nearly an hour to get from Tig's house to Arvita. Tig enjoyed the ride. The morning was damp and cool. Dawn left a calling card of thick dew that covered the prairie. Early daylight cast a brilliant cerise glow overtop the mist. The bright green fields of winter wheat shimmered while the deepest gorges exhaled opaque clouds—cotton puffs spilling out over sandy ledges before dissipating. In the distance, the dense fog hovered over the river—still, as though guarding secret activity beneath its veil. As the truck rolled along, Tig was startled at how different traveling the same road was from the day he had arrived.

Traversing Rte. 426 with Johnnie was unbearable, but with Ron it was a pleasure. Letting his eyes rake over the rolling unrestrained terrain, Tig began to feel as though the prairie was putting on a show for his benefit.

At one point, while Tig was gazing out the window, Ron glanced over and was reminded of the day Dottie was pulled from the canyon. *He was so powerful then, the way he lifted her off that ledge.* Ron considered bringing it up, when one look at the broken destitute man sitting next to him stopped him short. From Ron's perspective, Tig was the one in the pit now. This being the case, the last thing Tig needed was to be reminded of the day he saved Dottie, especially since it was evident that no one was making any heroic efforts to save him.

The fog lifted by the time the red truck crossed from Talgart into Dawson County. The pink orb of morning sun grew quickly bright and intense, warmer than usual for early spring. Tig rolled his window all the way down. The breeze coming through pressed against his face, humid and cool. Tig rested his arm on the door, his elbow sticking out the open window. The fields flew by in sheets of bright green, beige and pale ochre interspersed with patches of brown and deep terracotta. The truck rose and fell as it moved up and over, around and down the stretch of dirt road. As they neared the South Canadian, a large buck emerged from the wooded river bottom. Tig gasped. Ron caught but a glimpse before the deer dove back into the woods.

"Wish I'd seen him. Len Williams said he and his sons spotted him last fall, but that buck, he's an elusive devil. What ya think, ten points?"

"From what I could see he was at least a twelve. Not sure I could have shot him, though."

Tig recalled the animal's majestic beauty. *Elusive is not such a bad thing,* he thought. He smiled.

Other than a few random comments about wildlife sightings, including some interesting observations on road kill, there was very little conversation in the truck. Ron was a relatively quiet man. At this point he was focusing his thoughts on how he could best help Tig. The more he mulled over how Tig was dumped off, left to fend for himself like a stray animal, the more furious Ron became at Johnnie.

The truck bumped and rolled, pitching stones into the Johnson grass. While coursing through clay canyons and past emerald fields, down the familiar road to Arvita, Ron deliberated. *We've got to set this right. There has to be somethin' we can do to restore Tig's dignity.*

While Ron was lost deep in thought, Tig leaned out the window and let his heart latch on to the splendor and expanse that spilled out in front of him. Tig's mind relaxed; guilt temporarily released him and allowed him to enjoy the ride. In the distance, a prairie falcon soared. Tig locked his eyes on the bird, dark wings spread wide, as it glided evenly on a current of morning air. Tig inhaled the thick atmosphere as the truck rolled on. The wind distorted his face as he hung out the open window of the truck like a carefree child. It had been many years since Tig had surveyed the rolling mounds of short grass with such abandon—with such joy.

———

"I understand.... I'm so sorry.... Yes, we will.... Please tell her we love her." Tig set the phone down while Dottie hovered over him.

"So, what did he say? Well? Tig! What did Johnnie say?"

"He said Carolyn isn't doin' well." Tig paused. "She lost the baby."

Not wanting to continue, Tig looked away. Dottie stood horrified. She knew there was more. In the midst of any unpleasant conversation, if Tig turned away it was a clear sign he was hiding something.

"Tig, what else?" Dottie's eyes registered anger behind the tears. "Tig, answer me! What else?"

"When she lost the baby, she had to have surgery. She'll never be able to have children, Dottie. Not ever."

"Oh no!"

Dottie began to sob hysterically. Tig tried to comfort her, but she just pulled away. "Dottie, I'm so sorry. There was nothin' we could've done."

Dottie lifted her head from her hands and swung around, her eyes and face swollen.

"What!? You and that damn brother of yours! You could have stopped all this mess months ago if you had just stood up to my father. Carolyn was sick when she went out there. She didn't belong out there. It devastated her that she had to get married in a courthouse with strangers and not here in her hometown with all her friends and family. To have to leave everyone behind, everything she has ever known. To have to go there with nobody but that sorry excuse for a man to watch over her!"

Dottie began to yell, snuffling, coughing, struggling to breath between her crying jag and her rant.

"All of that stress! It was all too much for her in her condition. It is no wonder she lost her baby. Johnnie could have come back here instead of making her go out there! You could have demanded that. My father would have listened to you, but you did nothing!"

"Dottie, you're not makin' sense." Tig knew he had crossed the line, but he continued.

"I can't imagine how you'd think I could control your father. It has been your father running the show all along, and ya know it. What is it ya would've had me do?"

Dottie's anger exceeded her despair. Her nostrils flared, and she threw back her head with the fury and spirit of a wild mustang. Her red mane flew around her face, taking on a life of its own, summoning the fire in her eyes.

"You will make this better, Tig. Do you hear me?" Dottie squared her shoulders and parceled out her words, "You-will-fix-this."

――――

Tig spent days trying to appease his wife. Each offering met with Dottie's wrath and her insistence that he come up with better ideas to amend the situation. Tig was frustrated since there seemed to be no reasonable solution. He had no clue what Dottie expected. Tig was still struggling to make sense of it all the night Wendell called.

"I know she loves Carolyn, but I can't imagine how in the world she expects me to undo what happened."

"Tig, she misses her best friend. Her mother believes Dottie feels guilty she wasn't there for Carolyn through all of this. She is probably taking this out on you."

"That would be an understatement. I do understand, though. Maybe I could send her out there for a visit, I guess."

"I am sure the kids wouldn't mind their Aunt Clara watching them, but I think I have a better idea. Actually it came from Johnnie."

Tig bristled. *Of course it did.*

"Johnnie is expanding the business farther south. He hopes to open up a new division near San Jose. He really could use your help managing the Sacramento accounts while he is gone."

"What about Fletcher?"

"I am bringing Fletcher back here. I would like him to oversee shipping and distribution, and I need him here to bring this department up to speed. He's been eager to get back for several months now. His mother is not doing well, and he would like to come home."

"So, what are ya sayin', Wendell?

"Just that Johnnie thought it would be great for Carolyn's health to have Dottie close. He could also use your help. Besides, if you lived out there the Mills family would be close again. It would be a win-win."

Tig's eyes widened, and he swallowed hard.

"Are ya sayin' ya want us to move out to California? You know what they think about Oklahomans in California, right? So, really, Wendell, ya want us to move?"

"Yes, that is exactly what I'm saying. Honestly, I think it's a good idea."

"What about havin' Dottie and your grandchildren way out there? Are ya OK with that?"

"I would be lying if I told you it didn't sting thinking about her being far away, but I don't see this as permanent. Besides, Dottie needs to see more than dry gulch canyons. She is young, and your family is young. Now is the best time for you and Dottie to stretch a little. California is beautiful, and you're gonna love it. You can take the kids to the beach, see the ocean, all that. Dottie has always wanted to see the ocean. And, like I said, I don't see this as permanent."

"No disrespect, sir, but ya said that last time when ya sent Fletcher. What was supposed to be four months turned into six months."

"Well, Fletcher is hardly my daughter. I don't see you kids out there any longer than two or three years. Part of what I want you to do is to train your successor. The sooner you get that done, the sooner you can come back. I just don't want you out there alone. You will do your job better if Dottie and the kids are out there with you. Besides, a wife should be with her husband."

"Ya really want me to do this, move my family to California?"

"Yes, I need you to do this. For the sake of the family business, I need you out there, Tig."

Tig stood gazing out the window onto the front lawn where his seven-year-old was playing. Leon was scampering about using an old tin cup to fill a painted bucket with dirt, the very dirt Tig had shoveled off the house and barn years ago. The idea of leaving his family homestead was as foreign as anything Tig could imagine. His family was planted on the prairie. His children's connection to the swelling earth, carved canyon walls, red clay, and bleached sand was generations deep. Tig knew—bluestem and sage, goldenrod and crown vetch, all the wild grasses and flowers hold the soil down, prevent the ground from eroding, the dirt from lifting—it is never wise to uproot what is established in the prairie.

———

Effie stood in her scratchy wool coat with one hand clenching her tattered quilt and the other holding her brother's hand. They stood silently in the pitch dark, waiting as as their parents scrambled back and forth from the house. Dawn had not yet spread its wings across the horizon. Waking birds' chatter had not yet started. Wildlife lingered silent under bushes and in trees; everything slept.

With a flashlight held in his teeth, Tig tinkered with the hitch on the back of the pickup. Dottie set a few more household items on the ground next to the truck. After everything plus one thing more was stuffed into the small cavern in the back of the U-Haul trailer, Tig leaned hard against the doors and secured the lock. Dottie took a run through the house, a once over to check that everything had been cleared out.

She hesitated in the doorway. Through the darkness Tig could make out her silhouette. Dottie wiped the tears from her eyes carefully, to avoid upsetting her children. Then she turned off the light and pulled the door shut.

Tig helped Dottie into the truck. Then one by one, he lifted his children up. A lump caught in his throat. Dottie placed Effie on her lap and Leon between her and the driver's seat. Tig stepped up on the running board and leaned in over his children, warm steam clouds coming from their noses, their mouths.

"I'll be right back. Shouldn't take more than a few minutes."

"It's OK, Tig. Go. Just go."

Tig pulled a blanket up over his family, took something from the driver's seat and closed the door.

———

The weeks prior to their departure were spent sorting their belongings, selling their livestock, listing their house, and saying their goodbyes. They gathered at the homes of friends and family, told stories, shared hopes, and cried. The church hosted a going away dinner in their honor. The Annex Hall was filled with streamers and flowers. A dinner of turkey, gravy, potatoes, corn, and pie was served on linen table cloths embroidered with little green leaves. Tig was certain the whole town was in attendance. The pastor and his wife presented Tig and Dottie with a lovely set of dishes and a cut glass water pitcher.

There was a hymn sing and games for the children. At one point, all the adults sat in a big circle and shared "I knew them when" stories. During the entire event, Tig and Dottie managed to keep their feelings in check until, at the end of the evening when the Fox Creek Ladies handed Dottie a box of leftovers—dinner... in a box.

———

Tig and Dottie spent many hours deliberating, but in the end, they made the decision to go. Dottie grieved over leaving her family, demanding her parents visit the grandchildren in California within the year. Yet even in her anguish, Dottie was convinced moving would be the best thing for her marriage and family, a new start, a promising beginning.

No matter how much Tig tried to believe moving to California was for the best, he was never convinced. Even so, he chose to act against his better judgment. On the early morning of their departure, the weight of the decision to leave haunted Tig.

———

As he made his way from the U-Haul up to the pasture past the gate and along the barbed wire fence, a thin line of white dawn shot across the horizon behind him. Two simple monuments, unadorned slabs of granite, were outlined in the shadows of the cedars behind them. A straggly oak sentinel stood alongside. Tig laid a bouquet of flowers down for Carrie Ann.

"Mother, Father—I'm leavin' today." Tig could hardly get himself to say it out loud.

"I know this is not what ya had in mind. I know ya intended for us boys to stay here, live here, and raise our families on this land. I'm sorry I have to leave for a while. I won't be gone forever."

Tig clenched his jaw, closed his eyes, forced down his sorrow and frustration. He wished he could stop the entire process. He knew deep down moving was not the right thing, but he ceased answering his gut years ago. It was easier at this point to go along with the plan, to comply—keep everyone happy

As he turned to head back down the hill to the truck, Tig determined he would make the relocation to California work. As though challenging his resolve, he turned and shouted across the prairie.

"This is my home!"

EIGHT

"Ron, do ya think we might be able to stop by the ol' homestead so I can pay my respects?"

"Ya mean your family's place? Sure, Tig, we can do that. Matter-of-fact, if I remember right, it is on this side of Arvita, isn't it?"

"Yes, just this side of the Fox Creek Bridge."

"Why, we'll just stop on our way in this mornin'."

"Thank ya, Ron."

Ron glanced over at the same time Tig turned and leaned back out the window. Ron just shook his head. *There is something special about this guy*, he thought.

Ron was beginning to realize he had been wrong about Tig. His opinion about Tig had been based on what Johnnie led him to believe: that Tig was a useless, drunken imbecile, selfish and reckless. It occurred to Ron that Tig had every opportunity to indict his brother for stealing, but he never said a word. Tig was also left alone for days with nothing but a few cans of beer. He should have devoured them if he were a drunk, but he didn't. Ron understood he was not privy to the whole story. He might never be, but Ron resolved that for his part he was going to do his best to get to know Tig—the unpretentious man sitting next to him.

Two miles west of Fox Creek, the road bottomed out and curled through a small canyon. Dirt bluffs with jutting quartz and limestone strata lined both sides of the road. As Ron pulled up and out, they were confronted with a rafter of wild turkeys doing a scuffing and scratching dance across the road. The large game birds had gathered in the marshy field, a relative smorgasbord, to ferret for wild berries, seeds, and insects.

Ron slowed to a stop. The birds' heads shot up. They stood more alert, assembled together, and moved quickly through the field, clucking loudly. They appeared annoyed, aggravated that Ron dare enter their domain and interrupt their breakfast. They made a ruckus, one in particular, an ample, bronzed-feathered Tom. He strutted apart from the others. His feathers were ruffled. His shiny plumage and his blue head shook as he gobbled, cackling expletives at the red truck. Ron and Tig looked at each other and started to laugh out loud. They snickered over the tenacious turkey all the way to Fox Creek.

Ron sat in the truck looking on respectfully as Tig mounted the hill and opened the gate to the pasture. Tig paced slowly, picking handfuls of wild flowers as he moved to the location of the gravestones. Years ago, a white picket fence was placed around the burial site. Tig stood within the fenced area, removed his cap, and bowed his head.

The truck was parked alongside the road a good distance from the little cemetery, so Ron was stunned when he could make out the bald spot on the back of Tig's skull. He had heard about Tig's accident, but he had no idea his injury had left a scar of that magnitude.

The morning dew had completely evaporated by the time Ron's truck rolled over the Fox Creek Bridge into Arvita. Overall, Arvita had not changed much, but the roads into town were paved and new stop lights were everywhere. Tig noticed a neighborhood developing on the outskirts of town, and Ron pointed out a sparkling new elementary school. A few additional stores had moved in, the movie theater had been updated, and a two modern gas stations had been added, but Russell's looked the same. Of course, Wendot Drilling was gone, and "Stewart Brothers Law Offices" was painted on the window.

The first stop in town was a six-table establishment on Second Street, Classic Diner. When the waitress came by to take their orders, Tig requested just a glass of water. Ron jumped right in.

"We'll each take a cup of coffee, an order of flapjacks with a side of ham, and two glasses of orange juice, please."

Tig's face registered concern. "Ron, I don't have enough cash at the moment to pay for that."

"Tig, I happen to know Johnnie took all your food with him. Lord knows if he even stayed long enough to help ya settle in. I also believe he stole your wallet. Which, if I recall correctly, was supposed to have enough cash in it to get ya set up. Why didn't ya just come right out and tell me what he'd done?"

Tig was embarrassed. "No good would've come of it. He's long gone, and I'm worn-out from dealin' with Johnnie all these years. Tellin' ya about what he did would just keep it all goin', and I'm done with him. I need to move on."

Ron acknowledged by shaking his head. "Now the way I figure it, Tig, you're my guest today. Been a long time since an Arvita boy has come home, and I intend to make somethin' of it. So, if you'd be kind enough to let me, I'd like to take care of some things today, startin' with this breakfast."

Tig lowered his eyes and quietly said, "Thank ya."

Ron tried not to notice how Tig struggled with his flatware, his mauled hand dropping the fork, missing his mouth, food falling on the floor. Several times Tig just picked up the pancakes with the fork in his left hand. All fingers, he crammed the food into his mouth, syrup running down his chin.

Suddenly Tig looked up from his plate and quickly pulled his hands under the table. Realizing what a mess he'd made, Tig was mortified. He dropped his head.

"Sorry for this." Tig took his napkin and sopped up some syrup from the table.

Ron started to respond but chose to wait until Tig looked back up. When he did, Ron smiled.

"Can't blame a man for enjoyin' his food. Can I get ya anything else?" At first puzzled and then pleased, Tig smiled ear to ear.

"No, sir. I think I've done enough damage for the mornin'."

Ron could not contain himself. He chuckled under his breath, then laughed, then guffawed. Tig joined right in. For the second time within a few short hours, Tig laughed till his side hurt, something that before that morning he hadn't done in years.

Before heading to the courthouse, Ron made a stop by Dan's Barber Shop and paid for Tig to have a haircut and a shave. When Tig took his filthy cap off, Dan looked past Tig's scar to Ron and just shook his head. The jagged scar sat like a long island on a sea of bald flesh. Its size gave a good indication of the severity of Tig's injury.

Tig leaned back and yielded the inflamed, itchy flesh to the barber's hands. The shampoo and warm water nearly put Tig to sleep. The shave came after the haircut. Tig could not remember the last time he had enjoyed a close shave. The razor he had been using since he left California was dull and rusty. He laid his palm to his cheek and reflected on how good it felt. Tig had forgotten what his face felt like without stubble. As Ron pulled the truck around, he noticed Tig was standing a little taller.

After getting Tig situated at the appropriate desk in the correct office at the courthouse, Ron excused himself to run some errands. He assured Tig he would be back to pick him up in time for lunch. The clerk in the Social Security Office filled out paperwork while Tig answered copious questions.

As Tig was going through the typical bureaucratic rigmarole one goes through to get assistance, Ron was working his way through the men's racks at TG&Y. Ron purchased two pairs of jeans, a set of suspenders, four plaid shirts, and a package each of t-shirts, underwear, and socks. He added four bandanas to the pile as he waited to be checked out.

Tig could see the red truck turn the corner into the town square. He rose from the off-the-beaten-track park bench where he had been sitting, basking in the sun while waiting for Ron. Ron leaned over and opened the door as Tig approached.

"How'd it go?"

"I think it went real well. I remembered my Social Security number, so that wasn't an issue. They were able to ask some questions to verify it. I'll have a disability check within a week. I hope ya don't mind, but I requested they be sent to ya. I'll also receive food stamps and WIC. Ron, I mean to tell ya, I don't want to live like this. I've always taken care of myself, and I plan to do that again. I just have to adjust to all these changes. I don't want hand-outs."

"I understand, Tig, but ya need some help 'til you get to the point when ya can be self-sufficient again. I know you'd rather not do this, but it's why these programs exist."

He heard what Ron said, but Tig could no suppress his feelings of shame. He had worried all day he might see a familiar face, run into someone in Arvita whom he had known from the past. The entire time he was in town, Tig did not make eye contact with a single person. With the exception of answering questions for the clerk, Tig did not speak to a soul. He did not want anyone to recognize him, to see what had become of him.

Tig turned toward the window. *As if all that had happened wasn't enough... now welfare.* Tig closed his eyes and trembled. Ron caught the change in Tig's demeanor.

"I thought I'd run ya by Ida Mae Parkhurst's place in the next couple weeks, see if she can use your help. She lives within walkin' distance of your house, ya know?"

"Is that who lives on the other side of 426? Well, I'll be. I didn't make that connection."

"Sure is, and she'd love to see ya. She was pleased to hear ya were back in the area."

"Thanks, Ron, but I'll need to get some things before I visit her."

Tig looked disgustingly at his grungy clothing.

"Tig. I knew you'd worry about this, so I picked up a few things for ya today while you were fillin' out the paperwork."

Tig turned and sat up higher and started shaking his head no and moving his hand back and forth above his lap.

"Now before ya say anything, let me finish. Your clothes need to be washed. Linda has offered to use her machine to do this, but if ya give her your clothes, what'll ya wear in the meantime?"

Tig stopped waving his hand.

Ron reached behind his seat and pulled out a big bag. "Here, take these. Ya can pay me back later if ya want to, but for now just take 'em."

"Ron, I just...."

Ron cut him off. "There's one more place we need to go, but first I need a burger. How about ya?"

Tig couldn't remember the last time he had eaten two meals in one day. He had been on the road with Johnnie nearly two weeks. The entire time a meal meant a bag of chips and a coke, if he was lucky. Most of the time, Johnnie would go into some roadside casino and leave Tig to fend for himself. Tig spent countless hours waiting in the car in the parking lot with neither food nor drink.

"A burger sounds great. Thanks."

On the way out of town, Ron and Tig paid a visit to the Humpty Dumpty grocery store. Ron secured brown paper sacks full of meat, potatoes, vegetables, fruit, canned goods, bread, eggs, sugar, and milk in the tool box in the bed of his pickup. Tig climbed into the cab, his mind painting up images of steaming coffee, toast, and sugar sitting on his stained Formica table in the pastel light of dawn.

Before starting the car, Ron handed Tig the receipt with the words "paid in full" jotted across it. Before Tig could object, Ron interjected.

"I have a few things I need done on that back section. Ya likely saw the fences are bad over there on the east side, closest to the house. I have some barbed wire, tools, and gaged mending wire in the back. Thought I'd leave that with ya when I drop you off. If you'd fix those fences, I'd consider us settled out, even."

Tig nodded.

"Sounds more than fair."

Ron checked his side mirror and smiled, thankful that Tig agreed. Ron wanted to help but only in a way that would maintain Tig's dignity.

"How about I come and bring ya your check next Friday. We can come back down to town and get an account set up for ya at the bank, pick up some extra supplies, maybe some new boots?"

Ron raised his eyebrows as he glanced down at Tig's shabby, weather-beaten boots. Tig chuckled. "Yup. But I can't imagine why?"

Ron threw his head back and laughed. He was enjoying Tig's wry, unabashed sense of humor.

———

The remainder of the drive back to the house was mostly quiet. Both men were enjoying the beautiful spring day. The warmth of the sun poured in through the window. The breeze carried the scent of new growth, renewed life pushing through the yielding earth. The truck rolled lazily over the hills around the bends, past emerald fields of winter wheat: jewels of the prairie. The sound of gravel road shrapnel cracking against the underside of the truck carried them along. Occasionally, the breeze would shift. Their nostrils would react to the insistence of the red talc rising from beneath them and drifting inside the cab. As familiar, close-to-home landmarks began to appear, Tig looked perplexed

"Ron, I had no idea there was such a deep ravine so close to the house. I must've missed this bridge the other day. This mornin', I was busy watchin; a hawk. I don't ever recall seein' this before."

Tig looked out his window into the ravine beneath them.

"Ya wouldn't have seen it Tig. We came the back way into the house, remember? Even so, I imagine this whole area would look a little different to ya. A twister tore it apart a few years ago. It ripped out trees and left lots of debris. Weeds and shiftin' dirt have reclaimed the wreckage now. But yeah, this canyon actually extends on up onto the property. It ends up back there behind the windmill."

"Ah, that makes sense. Why, I wouldn't have recognized this. Yeah, I named that area Dump Canyon, since it looks like that's what it's been used for all these years."

"Yeah, it has, and ya can throw your trash in there too. When ya do, I ask that ya burn it so it doesn't draw visitors, nasty varmints that ya won't want to deal with. Skunks are the worst for that."

———

The last of the groceries and supplies had been carried into the house, and Ron prepared to leave. Tig walked back down to the truck with him. Ron turned to climb into the cab when Tig reached out his hand.

"I can't thank ya enough, Ron. You're a good neighbor to me." Ron smiled as he shook Tig's hand.

"Well, that's what we are, Tig, neighbors."

Ron jumped up into the truck behind the steering wheel. He leaned out the open door toward Tig.

"Linda wants to come and get your laundry, Tig. She washes once a week. If you'll put your dirty clothes in a sack, when I come back next week, I'll take them home."

"Why, ya just thank Linda for me, will ya Ron?"

"I will, Tig." Ron patted Tig on the shoulder before closing the door and driving back down the ruddy drive.

Tig walked to the house and stood on the stoop looking out to the sky in the distance, waiting for puffs of red to dissipate, a sign the truck had taken the first bend on Rte. 426.

———

Tig bent over and wiped spring earth and bits of winter dead from his new boots as Ron rapped his knuckles against the painted red door. The view beyond the front porch opened up to the swells and valleys tumbling down to the river on the south side of Rte. 426.

This was Ida Mae Parkhurst's land. Childless and a retired school teacher, she had been living alone for nearly ten years since her husband, Frank, died. The door opened wide, and a pleasant-looking woman in her early seventies stood with a big smile.

Ida Mae's white-silk waves started high on her forehead. Her hairline rested just above a row of think age-marks, and smile lines were etched in her face. Her contagious grin pushed her thin-fleshed pink cheeks up, and her blue eyes squinted in response behind silver metal frames. She wore a pink sweater with pearl buttons over top a worn but clean house dress. Her ample tummy was too large for the ties so Ida Mae pinned her apron to the sides of her dress.

Tig looked at her shoes, black and solid, her full ankles stuffed into them. In a flash of déjà vu, Aunt Verna appeared. Tig didn't want to linger on that thought, so he quickly turned his focus to Ida Mae's face.

She was thrilled to see them. "Come in, come in! Ron, how nice to see you. Well, forevermore Tig Mills! How long has it been? I'll always remember your sweet mother Carrie Ann."

Ida Mae's eyes glanced up, lost in a memory, reflecting as she closed the door behind her guests. "I still miss her dearly."

Tig recalled the days Ida Mae and his mother sat at the small kitchen table in his childhood home and chatted about many things. Carrie Ann mentored young Ida Mae on topics that ranged from favorite recipes to the boys and how to get children to do their homework. The two women were the dearest of friends, and images of them spending time together tugged at Tig's heart.

"Good to see ya again, Mrs. Parkhurst. It's been a long time."

Ida's full outstretched arms welcomed the men through the hall, past a mahogany table with a mirror. Tig purposely did not look at himself as they walked by it and into the dining room.

The linen-covered table was dressed with a cut glass vase of wild flowers, Depression glass cups, saucers, and a cream china plate stacked with lemon bars. Tig had only been in Ida Mae's home a few other times, many years before his mother had died. Ida's husband had been alive back then.With the exception of an air conditioning unit and modern appliances, Ida Mae's home looked the same. It was still every bit as welcoming.

"Tig, Ron tells me you'll be living in the Ole' Macklin place. Guess this means we will be neighbors."

"Yes, ma'am, we are that."

The small wrinkles at the corners of Ida Mae's eyes creased, and her pupils twinkled. She reached for the plate of lemon bars and handed it to Tig. Tig took one. The tart-sweet, creamy bar awakened his mouth, and his taste buds shouted.

"This is delicious." Tig's mouth puckered. His eyes watered. Ida Mae grinned.

"Catches up on you, doesn't it… the tart." Ida Mae's eyes widened.

With tears filling his eyes, Tig's smile pulled at the deep folds beside his nose and mouth, opening them into full dimpled cheeks. He began to chuckle while at the same time trying to swallow.

The room filled with laughter.

"Ida Mae, I brought Tig by today to see if ya might have a few odd jobs that need tendin' to 'round here."

Tig interjected.

"Mrs. Parkhurst, I was hopin' I could help out. I mean since I live so close an' all."

"Why Tig, I believe I would like that. I have needed some help around here—my fences, the garden, the windmill and such. Could you work once a week?"

"Yes, ma'am, I could."

"I could pay fifty a month. Is that acceptable?"

Oh, that's so generous of her, Ron thought. *She has always been so kind.* Ron was pleased. He had no idea Ida Mae would be able to pay Tig an actual wage. *This will allow Tig to live a more normal life.*

"No, ma'am," Tig said bluntly.

Ron's shoulders tensed. *What's he doin'? For Heaven's sake, why'd he insult Ida Mae like this?*

"Excuse me?" Ida Mae appeared stunned.

"I don't want your money." Tig paused. "But I do need your help." Ron sat up straight, and Ida Mae tipped her head inquisitively.

"I don't mind workin' if you'll just help me write. Ya see, it's no secret that my hand is ruined. But it's more than that. Since my accident, I have trouble readin' an' puttin' words together on paper. I can't really read or write anymore. I can speak well enough, but I can hardly make out my own scribble. It's important that someone write down my words so they can be read... so they make sense."

"Oh, I see."

Ida Mae nodded and smiled, but Tig was not finished explaining.

"I don't care much about whether I can read well or write much anymore. Fact is at this point—I could do just fine without either. It's just that I need to write to my daughter Effie. See, I haven't seen her since before the accident."

Ron caught his breath. Tig would work just so he could write letters to his daughter? The room grew still.

"I just need to know she's OK, ma'am. That's all."

Ron and Ida Mae were speechless. The humility and wisdom of the unassuming man moved Ron. Ida Mae's smiling eyes got a little glassy. She laid her hand on Tig's gloved hand.

"We will start writing next week." She gently squeezed Tig's hand. "Next week, but I insist you call me Ida Mae."

———

Simple jobs like cleaning up debris from around the barn and pulling winter's kill from the garden were among the first chores Tig handled for Ida Mae. Tig would meet with her every Tuesday afternoon at the kitchen table, but only after his chores were completed.

Within a few short weeks, Tig began considering Tuesdays as his day for social interaction. More often than not, Tig was reluctant to go with Ron to Arvita. With the exception of Ron's visits when groceries were dropped off and Linda's occasional stop over with fresh laundry, Tig anticipated his time with Ida Mae. He never mentioned he looked forward to it. To do so might cause him to appear weak, too needy.

Tig combed back his hair and poked in the few strands that would not stay up under his cap. He pulled on his boots, tucked the rowel hanging from his belt into his pocket and headed out the door. The mid-May morning sun chased cloud shadows in and out of the fissures in the driveway. Swirls of soft gray were gathering off in the distance to the west, billowing along the horizon line. Tig made a mental note that it would be wise to get back to the house before dark.

He stepped off the stoop, onto the drive, and began to make his way down the hill toward Ida Mae's. The windmill screamed at him as he passed. Tig did his best to ignore it, setting his eyes on the wooded area and continuing on. At the lowest point, the trees were waking up. A few weeks prior, they had appeared dead, their dark trunks twisted and tortured. Ruddy shoots stretched out of the blistering bark. Opening at the tips were leaves, miniature and bright.

They fluttered freely, dancing on their new stems in the gathering breeze.

The buffalo grass, straw toned and brittle, was dressed in hints of pale green undergrowth. It was softening, the splintering stalks resigning themselves to growth, to change. The gentle rustling of their stems pacified Tig as he moved slowly past, their peaceful murmurings transcending the caterwauling windmill.

Not far in the distance, the faint sound of gurgling water just beyond the trees flirted with fat bellied robins, tempting them to come and drink. Their songs echoed off the canyon walls.

Tig inhaled deeply. The acidic cedar, sap running full, filled the air with its perfume. Up ahead, high on an old elm, a woodpecker tap, tap, tapped on the rotting trunk. The bird thrust his razor beak back and forth into the tree, feasting on a trail of ants racing up and down beneath the bark.

Tig looked past the tufted scrub, beyond the fence, where just beyond the cattle guard Rte. 426 divided the land. Unlike that on which Tig lived, Ida Mae's land was open rolling prairie. A single elm shaded her porch, and a hedgerow of cedars lined the fence behind her house. The entire balance of Ida's land was planted with winter wheat or forage grass.

As Tig crossed the road and traversed the cattle guard, the sky had covered over with a dense haze. Ida's earthen driveway curved down through the waving fields, past silky strands of tanned buckskin gamma grass. Succumbing to the wind, tufts of soft prairie hair bent over, filling the fields on both sides. A deep slate-gray line of sky edged the grassland. The light generated by the approaching storms blended with the pale-yellow sky and produced a supernatural glow across the fields. Tig stopped walking, stilling himself to take in the grandeur of it all.

Ida Mae was waiting on the porch with a short list of chores. She appeared anxious. She had grown up on the prairie. She had lived there all her life. Like Tig, Ida Mae possessed an instinct all inhabitants of the prairie shared—the foreboding knowledge of perilous weather.

"Tig, run and take care of these few things, and then please come straight back to the house."

Tig took the list from Ida Mae's outstretched hand.

The chores were nominal, and within an hour, Ida Mae was ushering Tig to the kitchen. His eyes lit up as he turned the corner. A plate of Ida Mae's tart lemon bars sat waiting on the table. The cups were filled, and the warm steam rising from them invaded the kitchen with the rich aroma of black coffee. A notepad and pen rested next to the plates.

This would be the fourth time he and Ida Mae would sit over a pad of paper. Three short letters to Tig's daughter had already been sent. The first told of Tig's whereabouts and how he was setting up house. The second letter Tig sent was a brief survey describing the land encompassing the Ole' Macklin place. The most recent letter described the changes that had taken place in Arvita.

"Tig, as you know we have been meeting here together for a while now." In her sweet schoolmarm sort of way, Ida Mae gave every indication she was going to have a serious conversation.

"I don't mean to pry, but I feel like your letters have been, well…;" She hesitated. "Impersonal."

Tig would have looked surprised, but he knew exactly what she meant, and he had been anticipating this conversation for over a week.

"Tig, why don't you ask her how she is doing? Inquire about the…." "

"The baby, Ida Mae? Ya want me to ask about the baby?"

Ida Mae blushed, shocked at how direct Tig was. She pulled back in her chair, her mouth open in surprise. She put her hand to her neck, embarrassed.

"Tig, I am so sorry. I have overstepped. I never should have…."

"It's OK. I've been expecting this. I mean, it wouldn't make sense that I'd not ask. It's just that Effie and I…." Tig dropped his eyes. "Ya see, Effie and I didn't separate on good terms. Fact is, I never saw her, not once after the accident. And Ida Mae, I said some horrible things to her. I can't imagine she'll ever forgive me. I was just hopin' that by writin' her… well, that she'd eventually write back, and we'd start workin' this out."

"Don't you think that as her father…."

Ida Mae stopped short. Unbeknownst to Tig, Ron had told Ida

Mae the entire story. She knew memories would be painful for Tig. She was stepping over the boundary, and she knew it. She had no business telling Tig what he should or should not do.

"I apologize, Tig. This is really not my business. Forgive me for interfering. Now what would you like to say…."

"No, wait, Ida Mae." Tig's leathered skin wrinkling across his forehead implied concern, but his eyes softened into a gentle smile. "Ida Mae, you've been writin' these letters for me without askin' a single question. I'm feelin' it's time I told ya what happened."

Ida Mae was taken aback. "If this is what you want."

Tig reached for a lemon bar and set it on his plate. He lifted his cup and swallowed down a long sip of coffee. Pulling his chair closer, Tig rested one arm on the table. He closed his eyes and retrieved the images from the past.

NINE

Carolyn located and negotiated the terms for Tig and Dottie's rent house. It sat on a shady street, just a couple blocks from where she and Johnnie lived. The house was small but accommodating and quite modern compared to the one left behind in Oklahoma. Tig drove into Everson, California, a small town just Northeast of San Jose in the Santa Clara Valley in late November, less than a week before Thanksgiving. It took four days to get from Oklahoma to California, and Tig's family was travel weary. The cab of the truck was as cramped as the small trailer they dragged behind them across half the continental US.

Dottie called from a gas station just outside of Everson, and Carolyn waited anxiously at the window. She raced outside, arms flailing as Tig pulled into the driveway of their new home. Carolyn pulled the truck door open so fast it nearly caused Dottie to tumble out. Setting Effie on the seat, Dottie jumped out and embraced Carolyn. Dottie was distraught by the appearance of her best friend. Carolyn had grown painfully thin. Her ribs were pressing against her sweater, her eyes sunken. Carolyn smiled wide, but her eyes belied her mouth.

"Oh, it's so good to see all of you. You must be exhausted."

Tig lifted Effie out of the truck as Dottie and Carolyn chattered excitedly. He looked past Carolyn at the house, toward the door. She caught his look of confusion.

"He's not here, Tig. He had a meeting or something this afternoon. He said he'd be home by dinner." Dottie threw Tig a look, and Carolyn quickly changed the subject.

"Come see your new home! I've made some snacks. Dottie, you won't believe the kitchen and the back yard for the kids...."

The two friends walked with Effie between them into the house. Leon stood next to his father. Tig was biting his bottom lip when the thought he had entertained for weeks crossed his mind again— *Oh God, I hope we've done the right thing.*

That afternoon, Tig unloaded the trailer. Leon, Dottie, and Carolyn pitched in best they could while little Effie played in a cardboard box setting in the middle of the living room floor. Tig managed to get the beds set up and all the boxes into the house. He took the trailer to the local U-Haul drop off as Dottie and Carolyn made sandwiches for dinner. After catching up over a light supper, Leon and Effie entertained each other making forts out of cardboard cartons.

After Carolyn had left for home and the rest of the family had gone to bed, Tig was still putting furniture together. He was taking a break when Johnnie barged in unannounced through the front door.

"Hey there, li'l brother. About time ya Okies got here!" An odor of bourbon and stale cigarette smoke followed the disheveled man into the house. "Meant to get here sooner, but ya know how it goes. I've been workin' those deals south of Fresno. Keepin' me way too busy. We should be gettin' some jobs down there real soon. Tomorrow we need to get ya all set up. Hope you're ready for doin' some real work out here, Tig. Where's Dottie?"

"She's gone to bed. What time ya wanna meet tomorrow and where?"

"Damn, was hopin' to see her." Johnnie looked around the room.

"Johnnie, what time tomorrow and where?" Tig asked again, frustrated.

"There's a little office down on Collins Road, just off Main. You'll see our equipment there, our sign. Be there at nine." Johnnie turned and walked out.

Tig pulled his truck beside the fenced supply yard. Spools of heavy wire cable and electrical cords were stored behind the tall chain link. They were large steel tubes with serrated ends, sharp like teeth. A large cable drill was mounted on the back of a trailer, which in turn was hitched to a large diesel truck.

Tig felt a surge of excitement move through him. This was the equipment that would soon be very familiar. Tig had always dug by hand. Hand digging was all that was required for shallow windmill pump wells, the very kind Wendot installed across Talgart and Dawson Counties. The wells being dug in California were deeper and required a cable tool. The thought of using this massive gear excited him.

Tig looked down at his watch. He had five minutes before his scheduled meeting with Johnnie. He reluctantly turned from the fence to make his way to Johnnie's office. Tig walked around to the front of the brick building to the main entrance. A recent hire, Dave Carlton, let Tig in and led him to Johnnie's office. As he opened the door for Tig, he stood holding the door knob, mumbling something about Johnnie being on his way.

Tig stepped into his brother's office, and his mouth dropped open. The office was a mess. Papers, ledgers, books, receipts, and unopened mail were strewn all over the top of the desk. The book shelves were disorganized, and a pile of manila folders rested next to a full trash can. The room smelled like an unopened basement—stale and musty.

Good Lord, Tig thought. *Did Wendell send me out here to sort through this chaos?* Tig pulled a chair up to the desk and sat waiting for his brother. His excitement over being out in the field with new equipment learning new technology quickly waned. He began to feel tinges of anxiety at the thought of being stuck in the office sorting his way through stacks of paper while Johnnie was out roaming the countryside.

Forty minutes later, Johnnie arrived. Tig was still sitting by the desk.

Tig received his marching orders from his brother that day. In addition to a month of training with Acklen Cable & Drilling Pumps, Tig would be managing the office. Johnnie had let the day-to-day business flounder. Account management was unheard of where Johnnie was concerned. Without the aid of a comptroller, invoices were late getting out, money was slow coming in, and bills were not getting paid.

Tig wasn't certain Wendell knew the extent to which Johnnie had let things go. After talking with Dottie about the situation, Tig decided he should have a conversation with his father-in-law.

———

"I understand your concern, Tig, but this is exactly why I insisted you move out there. Johnnie's efforts have been used to forge new business and develop new accounts. I suspected he was struggling to keep up on the paperwork, but this will not be a problem now. Not with you there."

"Wendell, bookkeepin's never been my strength. Ya know I've always been suited for the field. You've gotta understand how eager I am to train on this new drillin' equipment. I'm really lookin' forward to my orientation. Cable drillin' fascinates me. I'd much rather manage the drillin' crew than work in the office. I know I'd be good at it. Couldn't we please bring on an accountant, a comptroller?"

"I know you're eager to drill. I've seen the equipment. Remember, I was out there with Johnnie when they delivered it. I don't blame you, but that will have to wait. We don't have the money right now to hire another full-time employee. You see, I just authorized Johnnie to draw $50,000 to buy out a small drilling company south of La Jolla. Company's called Sadler's Drilling. They have the equipment, a strong client list, and so forth! Everything is already in place. So, there is no additional cash flow to bring on any new hires, not now."

Wendell's audible excitement over Johnnie's deal sent the hair up on the back of Tig's neck.

"Wendell, dear God! Tell me you're not serious. Have ya met anyone from this company? How do ya know they're legitimate, and why are they sellin' out? Did Johnnie give ya any references to check?"

Tig's tone bordered on insolent.

"May I remind you, son, who you are talking to? You are out of line. I can make any decision I want regarding this company. I own it. I do not answer to you on the decisions I make, and if you desire to keep your job, you'll see to it that you never speak to me in this tone again. What you've failed to recognize is that Johnnie has grown this company. His work has helped secure your future, son. We all need to be grateful for this. Now, I'm telling you, Tig, I need you to manage the office out there until further notice. Are you capable of doing this, son, or do I need to come out there?"

Tig bit his bottom lip. He had no options, and he knew it. *What am I supposed to do now? I just moved my family clear across the country. Somehow, I've got to make this work*

"I apologize... and yes, sir. I'll take care of it."

Three weeks passed before Tig could see the top of his desk. The months that followed found him working late, always scrambling to stay on top of things. Johnnie was perpetually off somewhere, calling in every few days for good measure. Dottie spent those first months getting the kids adjusted to their new surroundings—arranging their rooms, their books and toys, taking frequent walks through the neighborhood and enrolling them in school. Carolyn came over nearly every day and sat at the table while Dottie prepared dinner. More often than not, Carolyn would stay for supper, chat with Dottie over macaroni and cheese with hotdogs, spaghetti, or hamburgers. She would help Dottie get the kids to bed just so she could stay and visit until Tig came home, always late. Carolyn would reluctantly leave, never eager to spend another night in her empty house.

———

One evening Carolyn seemed more sullen than usual. "What's wrong, Carolyn? You are not yourself. Don't you feel well?" "Oh, Dottie...." Carolyn's voice quivered.

Dottie set Leon and Effie's plates in front of them and then pulled the chair out next to Carolyn. She sat down and took Carolyn's hands in hers.

"What is it?"

Carolyn could hardly speak.

"I've not told you, Dottie, but I'm pretty certain Johnnie is having an affair."

Dottie's face fell.

"Oh, don't look so surprised, Dottie. Johnnie has always been a womanizer. Everybody knows that!" Carolyn's face was swollen, her eyes puffy, evidence that contradicted her forced composure.

"I have had phone calls from strange women looking for Johnnie. When I ask if I can take a message, they hang up. There is more, though. . ."

There was a pregnant pause and Dottie prepared herself to bolster Carolyn.

"I went the other day to add a little birthday money I got from my mother to our savings account... and... oh, Dottie...."

Carolyn dropped her head into her hands and sobbed. Dottie leaned over and embraced her quivering friend.

"Our money has been disappearing. Our savings account has been all but emptied. We were saving for a new home... a new start. It was Johnnie! He took it! I am being forced to create a separate account, one that requires my signature. What wife should have to do this?"

"I am so sorry, Carolyn. What do you think he did with it?"

"I don't know, but it wasn't spent on me."

Effie broke out in tears, wailing in empathy for Carolyn. Dottie reached for her little girl and wiped her tears while still comforting Carolyn. That night, Carolyn stayed in Tig and Dottie's guest room. Johnnie was unaware because he never came home.

———

Three months passed before the equipment was delivered from Sadler's Drilling Company. No one bothered to contact Tig about the delivery. Tig discovered the equipment one morning as he arrived at work. Behind the chain link fence, next to where he parked his truck, was cable drilling equipment, an additional diesel truck, and a trailer. Perturbed to have seen this by surprise, Tig stormed to his office. When he threw open the door, he was shocked to find Johnnie sitting at the desk going through the files. *What the hell!*

"Howdy, li'l brother."

Johnnie boasted his signature devious grin.

"Johnnie, what're ya doin' in my office, and why didn't ya tell me the delivery date had been set? Ya know I'm responsible for signin' off on acquisitions."

"Why? Because I didn't want to bother ya, Tig. Ya been with that pretty wife of yours. Besides, Wendell knew it was arrivin' this weekend. That's all that matters."

It irritated Tig that Johnnie continued to dupe Wendell. The very thought rubbed Tig's scarred relationship with Johnnie raw.

"No, it is not all that matters, and ya know it!"

"What're ya gonna do, Tig, go running off whinin' to Wendell. I understand you've been talkin' to him about me. Bet he put ya in your place, didn't he li'l brother."

Tig looked stunned.

"What are ya talkin' about?"

"Oh, I know about your conversation. Dottie told me."

Dottie, huh. When would she'd've told Johnnie about this? When was she with Johnnie? The thoughts seared deep in Tig.

"No, Johnnie, I won't be talkin' with Wendell about this. The paperwork I file will say all that needs to be said. I'm pretty certain ya wouldn't have paid me a visit about this. So, what is it ya really want?"

Johnnie offered a condescending snicker. "I'm gonna be spendin' most of my time closing out the business—ya know, Sadler's. So I'll be gettin' an office down there to make the process easier. I won't be around much."

Johnnie stood up and walked to the door.

"What about Carolyn, Johnnie? Where will she be durin' all of this?"

"I'll be up here one to two weeks a month. She's fine with it."

I bet the Hell she is, thought Tig as Johnnie walked out, pulling the door behind him.

———

Tig was home early that night. All day, he carried around what Johnnie had told him. One thought held the weight of all Tig's imagination could conjure—Dottie alone with Johnnie. Tig anticipated dinner, his unsettled spirit giving way to dangerous notions, toxic curiosity.

He started in. "So... Johnnie tells me ya told him about my conversation with Wendall." Tig's voice was angry and accusing, and it caught Dottie off guard.

"I need to get dinner on, Tig. Now is not the time."

"No, Dottie, now is the time. Why did ya talk to Johnnie!"

Tig's exclamation and elevated voice caused the children to stop what they were doing.

"I talked to him on behalf of Carolyn. She is miserable. Johnnie treats her like dirt. I wanted him to know you've got your eyes on him. That's all."

"I know Carolyn's your best friend, but her and Johnnie's relationship is none of your business. Besides, ya had no right ever disclosin' what I share with ya in confidence, especially with Johnnie... alone!"

Tig's eyes narrowed and his teeth clenched.

"What exactly are you implying, Tig?"

Tig had gotten Dottie's full attention and now her wrath.

"Are you thinking that something went on between Johnnie and me other than conversation?"

"No... well... just tell me why ya were with him alone, and why ya wouldn't've told me!"

"He came over here. I did not invite him," Dottie hesitated. "But this is not the issue, is it Tig? This is about you and me, and you don't trust me."

Tig remained still, silent, the absence of his words screaming a deafening indictment. Dottie looked Tig dead in the eyes, her words steady and low.

"You don't trust me, do you?"

Tig said nothing. Instead, he forced the words shaping his anxiety down into his chest, into the dark places nearest his heart. He thought about how much he didn't trust Johnnie, especially where Dottie was concerned. Dottie's eyes were glassing over, but Tig still would not speak.

He did not offer absolution. He did not comfort her. Instead, he yielded to his fear of inadequacy. It held him fast and rendered him impotent. In the silence between Tig and Dottie that night, seeds of doubt were planted.

———

Months passed. Years followed. Tig's endless work increased his time away from home. He would leave before Dottie roused the children from their sleep and return long after everyone was in bed. Tig's absence was having an impact on his children, who were growing up without the advantage of knowing their father. Dottie continued to insist Tig spend more time with her and the children. Tig did the best he could, but it was never enough. For the benefit of Leon and Effie, Dottie worked to cover for Tig. She would start each day with a good attitude, but by evening she was bitter.

———

Leon was twelve when Tig started taking him to work on Saturdays, showing him the equipment, and letting him travel to the drilling sites. Leon loved it all, especially the quality time he spent with his father. He was enthralled to learn what Tig was doing when he was not at home.

Effie was not as fortunate. She, like Leon, craved time with her father, but there was never quite enough to go around. She had turned from a toddler to a little girl, and Tig missed it. Effie inherited her father's shy personality and her mother's physical beauty.

Unassuming, Effie never said much when she was passed over for Leon. She was content with an impromptu run to the donut shop or a quick bike riding demo. She absorbed as much time with her father as possible before Tig ran off to answer a business call or check on a purchase order.

Dottie spent the majority of her time with the children. When the kids were in school, she tried to integrate herself within the community. She got to know some of the neighbors, played bridge on occasion, met with the Women's League, and socialized over coffee.

Given all her attempts, she never really fit in. Moreover, nothing had the power to free her from the homesickness that continued to afflict her. Dottie missed her family in Oklahoma, their neighbors, the land—Arvita. She missed her mother most of all. Wendell had been out to California to check on the business a few times, but he always came alone. Each time Wendell visited, he promised his daughter she and her family would be able to move back within a year or so, "Once the western branch is stable." As the years passed, Dottie held Tig responsible for not stabilizing the business so they could return home to Oklahoma.

———

Tig would have given anything to dig in the dirt. Over the years, the opportunities where he got to work with the drilling crew could be counted on one hand. Instead, Tig was consumed, working furiously to keep from being buried in the details of managing the business. He never felt adequate running the business, and the additional weight of Johnnie's disorganized ventures made Tig's job all the more difficult.

Early on, Tig started finding discrepancies in the books. Receivables and deposits were never balanced and cash withdrawals were not being reimbursed. Tig suspected the worst, but he could never find enough actual data to accuse. Until he had conclusive evidence, he would not burden Wendell. To do so would give his father-in-law-boss a reason to find Tig unfit. Tig would wait and gather the paper trail.

In the meantime, Tig did whatever was necessary to keep things balanced. At times, this meant securing loans using the drilling equipment as collateral, borrowing cash from restricted accounts, or paying only portions of overdue invoices. No matter what, Tig determined that he would handle it.

To deal with his angst and nagging guilt, Tig started drinking, just a few shots to unwind before coming home. It kept him focused and at his desk so he could work longer. This was unacceptable to Dottie, but he was not open to her opinion and would certainly not entertain her criticism.

———

There were times when they tried to talk and share their feelings, but it never ended well. Even Dottie's need to share her loneliness, her pain over being so far from her family, always ended in accusations. Tig was inevitably the one blamed for Dottie being stuck in California. Likewise, Tig's frustration with their situation was quickly met with Dottie's anger over being abandoned.

The cumulative effect of their unresolved arguments created a cloak of indifference. It covered them, blinding each of them to the other's pain.

Tig began to avert his eyes whenever Johnnie mentioned Dottie. The veins rose and pulsed hard in Tig's neck anytime she was mentioned. Johnnie spotted it, an indication all was not well in his brother's marriage. Betting on a breach in Tig and Dottie's relationship, Johnnie made himself readily available.

He wagered risking his own marriage would be worth it if the take was Dottie. Johnnie began to wander in and out of town unannounced. He made every effort to stop and see Dottie whenever he was around. Using every excuse he could muster, Johnnie managed to weasel himself into his brother's house to be alone with her. Masterfully, Johnnie used any number of reasons—implying he had just seen Tig and was on his way out of town, that he wanted to see the kids before he left, that Carolyn suggested he stop by.

Nothing other than casual conversation ensued, so Dottie saw no need to upset Tig by mentioning Johnnie's drop-ins. Johnnie's social calls were always short because he made Dottie uncomfortable. Not brief enough, however, to keep Carolyn from spotting her husband's car parked on the street in front of Tig and Dottie's house.

Suspicious, Carolyn began to reroute her errands so that she could keep track of the ins and outs of Johnnie's secret visits. Dottie and Carolyn spent less and less time together. Although it grieved her, Dottie assumed it was due to Carolyn's new job as a receptionist, but Carolyn knew the real reason.

TEN

The temperate weather in the Santa Clara Valley was sought after by most but not by Dottie. She longed for Oklahoma. She coveted the sweltering Julys when clay baked beneath her feet and cicadas hummed twilight lullabies. She missed the freezing Januarys when water fell from gray domed skies and created icy stalagmite fields for as far as she could see.

Dottie put her groceries on the table and thought about it all. It was January, and she longed for the sound of snow packing under her boots. The phone rang, interrupting her snow-globe daydream. Her father was on the other end, and he did not sound like himself.

Dottie sat down hard.

That evening, she stayed up waiting for Tig. Late as usual, he came wandering in close to midnight, the syrupy smell of liquor mixed with sweat wafting around him. Dottie looked stern, yet troubled.

"What are ya up for, Dottie?" Tig recovered from a slight stumble, but Dottie caught it. He reached to hug her, and she slipped out from under his arms. "Oh, I see we're gonna play hard to get tonight, huh?"

Tig chortled. He was drunk, and Dottie was appalled. She bore her teeth down on her words. Hard and cold, they turned the air between her and her husband to ice.

"Tig, not that it would matter to you, but my mother has been diagnosed with senile dementia. It is early onset and she is not well. My father needs me, so I have made arrangements for the kids. Carolyn will watch them…. Tig, I'm going home. I'll be leaving in two days, and I'm not sure when I'll be back. So for Christ's sake, get sober so you can at least act like a father while I'm gone."

———

Two weeks later, Dottie got off the plane and walked solemnly to the gate. Tig and the children stood behind the stanchion waiting eagerly. At the first sight of their mother, Leon and Effie broke loose from Tig's side. They scooted down the ramp toward her as she emerged from the cluster of disembarking passengers. Dottie had never been separated from her children, and her time away was made more difficult by their absence.

Her face lit up as she reached her arms out to greet them. She scooped them up close to her as they chattered a mile a minute. Tig stood in front of the scene, sheepishly holding a bouquet of slightly wilted roses and day-old daisies. Rising to her feet, Dottie faced Tig head on. She left her joy with the children. All she could give Tig was a deadpan expression.

Tig's insides quaked. Something was different, changed, wrong.

"How is your mother?"

"How is my mother?" Dottie made a face as though to say, Tig you are an idiot to ask such a stupid question. "She is dying, Tig. She is dying-out-there-without-me! That is how she is!"

Tig, nonplussed, drew a blank, but Dottie was at no loss for words.

"You and my father promised we would be back by now, back home… home, not here! You both lied to me, to our children. Tig, my own mother could hardly remember me. It's too late, now!"

Dottie's eyes filled, but her anger would not allow the tears to release and run down her face, not this time.

"Dottie, do you really feel like this is the place to discuss this?"

Tig reached to hand her the bouquet, but she pulled away. Taking her children by the hand, she turned and walked off, leaving her suitcase for Tig to manage. He dropped the flowers in the trash, picked up her luggage, and followed her out.

———

Over time, Dottie's spirited disposition tempered. She and Tig seldom argued, although both wished they would. At least then they would have known the other cared enough to force a conclusion.

Instead, their marriage slipped into the abyss of apathy. They lived by rote. Theirs became a marriage of convenience, only together for the children's sake. The emotional emptiness between Tig and Dottie attached itself to their children, the consequences evident. Leon and Effie were becoming teenagers. They isolated themselves, each forging an identity apart from their bitter mother and delinquent father.

Both Dottie and Carolyn could have benefited from time spent with each other, but no one saw much of Carolyn anymore. She stayed holed up in her empty house or at her office where she answered phones, typed memos, and set appointments for her boss. She and Johnnie were long since estranged, but Carolyn just couldn't let go of the hope that her marriage could be saved.

Johnnie was as much a rogue as ever. He traveled most of the time, spending money he didn't have on women who were not his. He enjoyed his reckless lifestyle. Many times, Tig was prepared, evidence in hand, to request that Wendell fire Johnnie. Yet without fail, before Tig could act, Johnnie would bring in another account and become Wendot Drilling's hero—the apple of Wendell's eye.

———

Nine years passed since the Tig Mills' family had arrived in California. Hopes of getting back to Oklahoma had been abandoned.

Dottie's mother, Anna, had to be placed in a convalescent home. The tearful decision was made during a phone call between Dottie, her father, and her sister, Clara. To provide companionship and support, Clara and her husband moved back home to run the family farm. Meanwhile, Wendell continued as CEO of Wendot Drilling, promoting Fletcher Thorton as Manager of the Oklahoma Division and Johnnie as Vice President in charge of new accounts. Wendell's decisions were a condescending blow to Tig, who as manager of the California division would now answer directly to his errant brother.

In the midst of these changes, the California division continued to struggle, and Johnnie was insistent Wendot in Oklahoma pitch in. This was a burden for Fletcher's division, as they were not managing nearly the number of accounts as Tig's division in California. Nonetheless, they were called upon to cover short falls in the budget on several occasions. Additional funds from Fletcher's division, and bank loans being out of the question, a decision was made to trim the California division. This required a reduction of Tig's workforce by half.

Tig anguished over the plan for days. The thought of laying off loyal employees and friends made him sick. How would their families manage? How would they support themselves? Where would they go? Altruistic questions most employers, on the verge of downsizing, would ask never once crossed Johnnie's mind.

In another way however, Johnnie was supportive of the decision. Money saved on payroll would be used for upgrading and streamlining with new accessories. Tig knew more equipment would be futile without workers, but he no longer offered his opinion.

When Johnnie went into the executive position, Tig took a step back. For years, Tig felt as though his hard work had gone unnoticed. Every time he approached Wendell with his concerns about the business, the finances, the books, or Johnnie, he was dismissed.

Tig was not going to cover for his brother any longer. He figured if he gave Johnnie enough rope, he would hang himself. So Tig capitulated. Inertia and Tig's stubborn refusal to intervene accelerated the erosion of both his personal and professional life.

———

A week after Tig doled out Pepto Bismol pink slips of paper to his employees, he received an unexpected call from Wendell. "Tig, we have a problem."

Wendell went on to explain how Fletcher had been finding all kinds of discrepancies in the books. The receivables and the deposits didn't match up. The company's savings were being depleted.

Tig was annoyed at first since he had been trying to tell Wendell this for a very long time. The pitch of Wendell's voice went higher and higher. The strain behind each word concerned Tig, and he was worried that Wendell might snap.

"No disrespect here, sir, but I've been tellin' ya this for years. Someone, and let's be frank since I think we both know it's Johnnie, has been embezzlin' from Wendot. At this point, I'd say tens of thousands of dollars. He always managed to bring in new accounts, but not once did he produce a paper trail to verify his transactions. Johnnie never had to, because I did. I produced them on his behalf."

"Why on God's earth would you do that, Tig!"

"For the sake of the company, of course! I've had enough trouble shakin' this damn Okie label. The last thing this business needed was a news headline on our resident crook of a VP. And don't forget, I moved my family to California, I needed to keep my job. All this and ya houndin' me to 'make it work.' For years, I've been juggling the books. Ya left me no choice, Wendell. Ya refused the see the truth."

"What are you saying, Tig, that I was duped?"

"I think we were all duped, Wendell. Johnnie's slick. I still don't know exactly what he's spent the money on, but I'd guess it was gambling."

"Good Lord, Tig. How could this have happened right under my nose?"

"Well it did, and how it did doesn't matter compared to the issue at hand. Ya see, at this point, if we don't start sellin' off our assets, we're going to default."

"What? When were you planning on talking to me about this?!"

"Wendell, like I said, I've been tryin' to tell ya this was comin' for some time now. Ya weren't listenin'. Ya were too seduced by the potential, the shiny future Johnnie kept holdin' in front of you. Well, it was all an illusion, Wendell, and now we're in a Hell of a mess! We don't have enough money to pay the taxes on the business, and if we don't, we could go to jail. I was afraid it would come to this before you'd see it for what it is."

Wendall coughed, and his voice became hoarse. "Make arrangements. Do what you can to sell one of the drilling rigs out there. I hate to do this, but I will have to close operations here in Oklahoma. We don't have any active accounts like you do out there. I'll have Fletcher prepare to sell off everything here. God help us, we have to do what we can."

"What about Johnnie, Wendell? What do we do with him?"

"Given all this, I want to fire him on the spot. But we need to be careful, Tig. It might be better to let him stay on until we have sold enough of our assets to pay the tax bill. I think we may be able to get enough on him for the company to press charges. It will take a while to gather everything on this end. Let's try to get this put together within six months. In the meantime, cancel his credit card and set up a new checking account for the business. Just tell him we're reorganizing the accounts or something. I am going to rein him in. Let's put him off until we can figure this out."

"Yes sir."

"And Tig, do you think you can handle the cable drill?"

"I believe I can."

"Tig, you'll need to make good on the job orders that haven't been filled. Get those wells dug. You have wanted to work on site for years. Well, here's your chance. Tig, I apologize for being so muleheaded. I should have listened to you a long time ago. And Tig, there is one more thing.... Our conversation today remains between you and me.... Not even Dottie is to know."

———

One week after his conversation with Wendell, Tig showed up at work in jeans, steel-toed boots, and a hard hat. He was thrilled to close the door to his office for a while and get out on the land. The first time the bit was lowered into the bore hole he marveled at its sheer power. The massive steel bit agitated and chewed the earth with each drop, the drill spudding, digging deeper as the cable tool raised and lowered the churning shaft. Every aspect of the process—every bit of oiled steel, every echo of grinding earth—enthralled Tig. Without a doubt, he knew this was where he belonged. He questioned if he would ever go back to the claustrophobic, musty office and sit behind the cramped desk.

Having a need for inexpensive labor, Tig hired his son to work part time at Wendot over the summer. Leon, just seventeen, accommodated Tig on a site east of Everson in a small town called Petesville.

Sitting next to Tig in the company truck, Leon sensed a unique connection to his father, something he had never felt before. The drive took the better part of an hour, and Leon had his father's undivided attention. He talked about school and football and someone named Faye. Tig couldn't recall Leon ever talking to him about sports or girls.

Leon was not old enough to work the drill. He did, however, have the physical strength for the job. Inherited from his father, Leon's stature made him a perfect site assistant. Leon's job included several tasks: securing the cribbing blocks under the huge diesel truck tires to keep the massive vehicle from rolling while they drilled, carrying off mounds of debris, removing drill cuttings when the bore hole was bailed, and site clean up. Having Leon alongside was not a burden. Leon fit in comfortably with other workers. He kept himself busy and never complained. Tig could not have been more proud of his son.

One afternoon, Leon was shoveling excess dirt into a wheel barrow. Tig watched from behind the truck. Leon, with a familiar rhythm, methodically lifted the heavy saturated dirt and moved it from one pile to the next. Tig smiled, recalling his childhood, the hours of sand shoveling, and his mother's approval coming through the wave of her hand from the window. Carrie Ann could have picked her grandson out of a crowd simply by the way he handled the earth.

———

Dottie was alone at the house leaning over the kitchen sink washing breakfast dishes when the call came. Her wet hands shook as the message flew from the phone receiver.

Her father was dead.

Wendall had suffered a major heart attack shortly after breakfast. The words, like bits of sand and dirt hurled by the wind capable of embedding flesh, shot straight into her heart. Droplets of water fell from Dottie's trembling fingers, from her eyes, hitting the floor. Just as suddenly as they evaporated, her father was gone.

Dottie's brother in law called the Wendot offices to tell Tig the news. As it turned out, Tig was out of the office. He was meeting a client for a pre-drilling site evaluation, so Johnnie intercepted the call. Johnnie had been informed to stay put and work from the Everson office. Johnnie believed this was because he was to oversee the sale of one of the trucks. In reality, Wendell wanted Johnnie under Tig's nose until they were ready to press charges and sue Johnnie for embezzlement. They were well into the process of corroborating Johnnie's theft, but the plan was only four months old. Wendell and Tig were not ready yet. In the meantime, Johnnie was in a holding pattern.

Wendell died before he could fire Johnnie. So now, still maintaining the position as Vice President, Johnnie would be in charge.

Johnnie had only two thoughts while listening to the news of Wendell's death. He was now officially in charge, and Dottie would need him. Johnnie set the receiver down and scratched a hasty message for Tig. Grabbing his suit jacket and hat, he raced for the door, throwing the note onto Tig's desk where it was lost among stacks of paper.

———

Dottie peeked out from behind the crack in the door. Her eyes were brilliant green, glistening otherworldly orbs. Too exhausted from crying, and weak from anguish, she had no emotional resources left to deal with her meddling brother-in-law.

Dottie let the door swing wide. Johnnie closed it behind him as he followed her into the living room. She sat on the couch next to a box of tissues.

"I can't believe he is gone. I thought it would be mom first. How am I supposed to deal with this?"

Dottie sobbed. Her eyes and nose were raw, her face flushed. Johnnie reached for her hand. This time she did not pull away.

"Dottie, I'm so glad I could be here for you. You should not be alone during something like this."

Dottie didn't hear a word Johnnie was saying. Everything that morning was a blur. She vaguely remembered calling the school to notify the kids. She couldn't recall if she had called Carolyn. The majority of her morning was covered in father-daughter memories—blurred by a flood of mourning tears, grief washing her heart. She didn't hear the truck pull into the driveway, or the doorknob turn, but Johnnie did. He pulled her close, wrapped his arms around her. Placing his palm on her red tresses, he gently coaxed her head into his shoulder. For comfort, for a loss of what else to do, she embraced him back, and Tig walked into the room.

Nearly a year had passed since Wendell's funeral. Clara and Dottie sold the farm and divided the profits three ways. The girls each got a third. The final percentage went to retire debts Wendot had incurred and pay off taxes. Dottie made it abundantly clear that this was done to save her father's good name. As she put it, she could "give a damn about saving the Mills boys."

Tig continued to work at Wendot, which was now operating out of a single office in Everson. He spent most of his time working in the field on the drill sites. Johnnie planned to make the most out of being in charge of Wendot, but Tig quickly squelched this idea, threatening to expose Johnnie's theft and press charges.

Johnnie was never sure just how much Tig had on him. He may not have considered his brother a threat had Tig not shown him a copy of the ledger and the report Wendell had been working on. To save what was left of the company, but mostly to keep his wife from additional grief, Tig successfully blackmailed his brother.

Tig was not successful, however, at getting the image of his wife embracing Johnnie out of his head. Nor could he put aside the insinuations Carolyn made certain to share with him, regarding the ongoing liaisons between Johnnie and Dottie. Tig and Dottie slept in the same bed, but he could not recall the last time they had held each other. As much as he tried, he could not evoke the actual memory, but he never forgot how it felt—her warmth, her energy, how it strengthened him.

———

He looked into the glass of bourbon in front of him. The ice was nearly melted, almost gone. He ran his hands along the mahogany counter. Its edges were worn from years of lonely drinkers, hanging on, imploring commiserating bartenders.

Tig's half-eaten burger and fries sat cold on a greasy plate. Tig was only one of three left in the dimly lit tavern.

I should be home, but why bother? I"l just wait till they're all in bed. This is the routine anyway. So, why not give them what they're expecting?

Tig's stubbornness was working calluses into his heart. Like shoveling sand, like dealing with death, like losing Dottie, he just kept pushing--drinking the pain down. He ordered two more before he stumbled out to his truck.

Johnnie was miserable working in the office and exactly what Tig wished would happen did. The monotony of working behind a desk five days a week was more than Johnnie's restless spirit could tolerate. Two years after Wendell's death, Johnnie tendered his resignation.

Tig was thrilled. His brother would no longer be an annoying fixture at Wendot. Johnnie found a job selling swimming pool covers to hotels and country clubs. Assigned to the Northwest Territory, which included central and northern California, Johnnie traveled extensively but remained based out of Everson. Tig preferred that Johnnie leave the state, but Johnnie had no intention of distancing himself from Dottie.

Nonetheless, Johnnie was out of the office, and for Tig, this was a first step.

———

Leon spoke to his father about working full time after graduating from high school. Tig was pleasantly surprised. At nineteen, Leon could drive the truck and work the drill. Leon enjoyed it so much that Tig could easily imagine his son taking over the business someday.

Dottie pushed for Leon to go to college, but after a great deal of cajoling, Dottie partially conceded. Leon could work at Wendot for the first year out of high school but no longer. This would give Leon a chance to build up savings before starting at California State University.

Tig was getting to know his son, but Effie remained a mystery. As a little girl, she had been inseparable from her mother. Dottie had taught Effie everything she knew about sewing, crafting, cooking, and fashion, about all the things Dottie believed girls would love to know. With all the attention Dottie lavished on her, Effie wanted more, needed more.

She craved a relationship with her father. She longed to know him, hear him say she was valued and loved. Effie would often throw Tig a look indicating a question was coming. Then, she would stand and wait.

This confused Tig and made him nervous, causing him to appear preoccupied. Her father's apparent disinterest stifled Effie. At the point of expressing her thoughts, she would drop her head and turn away. This miscommunication ritual happened with devastating frequency. After the age of ten, there were no conversations between Tig and his daughter, just obscure expressions and swallowed words. While Tig and his son were growing closer every day, the chasm between Tig and his daughter expanded.

———

Tig was finishing another late dinner, balancing tepid meat on a fork in one hand with a profit and loss report in the other. The window in the kitchen looked out to a well-past-midnight sky. The house was quiet. Leon was staying with a friend, and Tig assumed Dottie and Effie had both retired for the night.

He set his paper down to pick up his beer. Dottie and Effie were standing on the opposite side of the table. Their white cotton night-gowns glowing in the dim light. They appeared to hover, apparitions of the same soul at different ages. Dottie's hair, nose and mouth were replicated in her daughter, but Effie's eyes mirrored her father's. Tig startled and nearly choked.

"Ya scared me to death. What're ya two doin' up at this hour?"

Dottie put her arm around Effie. "Tig we need to... um... we have...."

Effie put up her hand and stopped her mother. With a facial expression that conveyed more determination than Effie had ever let her father see, she stepped forward.

"What mom is trying to say is...."

Effie swallowed hard then straightened her back. "I'm pregnant."

Tig had the air knocked out of him. He shook his head in disbelief. "No, no, nah ya can't be pregnant. You're too young."

"She is seventeen, Tig, and she is indeed pregnant. The doctor confirmed it today."

Tig inhaled deeply but unevenly. Dottie reached and pulled Effie back close to her, bracing for Tig's exhale. After a pause that felt like an hour, Tig let loose. He stood up and planted his palms on the table. Leaning over, he spoke, every word a crescendo.

"Why in the Hell would ya go an' get yourself pregnant? Don't ya think we've got enough problems around here?! We can't afford this mess!"

Dottie pulled Effie tighter. Before she could rebuke Tig for his tone, he launched again, this time with more aggression than Dottie had seen in years. She feared for her and Effie's safety.

"Who is the father? Let me guess. That no good, li'l bastard that's been hangin' around here! Is that who you've been whorin' with?!"

"Tig, I will not allow you to speak to our daughter like this! If you were around more...."

Tig slammed his fists on the table. The plates and flatware jumped and came back down with a crash.

"You're-her-mother! I've been working myself to the bone. Where in the hell've ya been?"

Tig and Dottie were screaming over top of each other. Effie began to sob. She wiped her eyes on her sleeve and bawled.

"Get this taken care of, ya hear me! I mean it. We're not gonna be the family in the neighborhood with the unwed pregnant teenager! And so help me if I get my hands on that little…."

"Tig, stop! I mean it, stop! You're drunk, and you don't know what you're saying. Besides, she is too far along. She is going to have to carry this baby full term."

Tig walked around to the opposite side of the table. Dottie raised her hand up as a threat should he come any closer. Tig bent down till he was eye to eye with Effie. All of his anger, the volume compacted, reduced to a low growl.

"Effie. I… said… Effie! Look at me!"

Effie raised her head, her tear-filled eyes locked on her father's.

"You're such a disappointment. Do ya have any idea what ya've done, how ya've threatened the welfare of our family with your self-ishness? Ya listen here, Effie. I won't provide for one more soul under this roof. Understand? So ya better make arrangements to put that… that bastard child up for adoption. And I don't wanna to see your face durin' any part of this."

Tig swept his hand back and forth in front of his daughter's belly.

"Do ya hear me, Effie? Just stay away from me. No daughter of mine is a whore." Dottie's eyes flared.

"Tig, for Christ's sake what are you sayin'!?"

Effie broke into a wail, pulled away from Dottie, and ran into the bedroom.

"Tig Mills what is the matter with you? How could you say such a thing? I swear I don't even know you anymore. Why do I put up with you… with this!"

Dottie hurled the empty beer can across the room.

"I want you out of here, Tig! You need to go! Go stay somewhere else till you realize what's important in your life. Take your damn beer and go!"

Dottie picked Tig's coat up off the couch and threw it at him as she turned toward the muffled whimpering coming from behind the bedroom door. Without hesitation, Tig stuffed his paperwork under his arm, picked his coat up off of the floor and slammed out of the house.

———

Tig's story hung suspended in the air, saturating the atmosphere in Ida Mae's kitchen. "That was the last day I was in that house. I got a hotel room that night and never went back."

Ida Mae sat frozen to her seat. A long silence ensued. Outside, the wind rattled the storm cellar door and whistled through the clapboards, but the only sound in the kitchen was the soft simmering of the tea kettle. Speechless and absorbed in thought, Ida Mae's face was somber and her eyes distant.

Tig looked remorsefully out the window. He fixed his sight on the black clouds that had risen and were churning in the sky. The wind increased. An eerie green-gray lit up the fields, the gusts whipping the grass. *There will be no time to write today.* Tig thought. *All the better.*

"I need to head up there and secure the house. Will ya be OK here by yourself, Ida Mae?"

Tig's words snapped Ida Mae back but not completely. Her voice softened and monotone, her eyes conveying a deep sadness.

"Why yes, um, I have the storm cellar should I need it." Ida Mae took a foil package from the counter.

"Here, Tig. I've wrapped up some lemon bars for you."

ELEVEN

Tig carefully tucked the wrapped lemon bars into his shirt and stepped off the front porch. He raised his eyes toward the foreboding soupy clouds congregated overhead. The vast fields of shivering blades of grass radiated a supernatural golden luster against the black horizon.

Since Tig was acquainted with this bizarre light, he picked up his pace, kicking red dust heedlessly over the toes of his new boots. Flashes of lightning lit the stormy skies. The thunder grew louder, deeper. Swollen drops of water started to fall from the sky. They smacked the thirsty earth, leaving dimples in the dirt. The intensity of the increasing rain struck Tig's shoulders, smarting where it hit. The downpour came in sheets. Tig could see it sweep across the fields in the distance. He ran in an attempt to beat it to the cattle guard but failed.

The heavens opened full, and five weeks of withheld precipitation came at once—a deluge of water. Tig's new buckskin boots darkened, washed and stained by the slurry coursing down the drive. He was drenched through and chilled to the bone. He ran across the slick muddy Rte. 426, straining to keep his balance on the slimy clay.

The grasses and weeds on either side of the road were now fully bent over, hugging the ground, bowing to the raging heavens. Navigating the uphill drive to the house became a battle of wills, Tig's against nature. The uneven driveway was no longer passable. Within minutes, the eroded clay and deep gashes in the surface filled with water. The road was no longer recognizable. It had become a torrential stream. There was no way to gain any traction.

Tig reached for the scrub trees sprouting along the border of the disintegrating road. He grabbed hold and pulled himself off of the slippery surface. Once to the side, he stood up, tottering as the water poured down his face, blurring his vision.

He decided to work his way up through the woods and around to the house. The lapse of time between the lightning and thunder was decreasing—the flashes blinding, the sound deafening. Tig picked up his pace. His heart was racing. Rain had filled the floor of the wooded area. The ground was soggy and marshy, but the twigs, rocks, and weeds along the surface provided provisional reinforcement for his footing. The wind screamed, and then... all went still.

It was a horrifying silence Tig knew only too well. He waited, considering which way to go, and then the hail came. Ice pellets small at first were thrust from the sky; within seconds, intermittent large balls of ice were being hurled every which way as the angry storm raged. A hideous otherworldly roar shook the trees. Overhead, the clouds churned, and Tig knew—*A tornado! Run!*

He dug the toes of his boots into the mud and turned toward Dump Canyon. He ran, slogging through the draw until he reached the canyon wall. The mud sucked at his feet and legs as he grasped anything he could along the earthen bank, seeking an anchor, all to aid him in progressing deeper into the gorge.

Time ran out. The roar was over the top of him. Tig dropped to his knees, pushing himself against the clay wall and tucking his head under his arms. The cedars bent over. The topmost branches of the elms shook violently, then they let go. Thrown by the wind, they whipped overhead, joined by trash, leaves, and shingles being hurled across the canyon.

The windmill screamed, unsuccessfully resisting. A powerful gust grabbed a blade, twisted it, and ripped it off. Torn metal was lashing, screeching, and swearing at the wind. It was flung, whirring across the ravine where Tig lay.

He shook, tightening his eyes as a metal blade came crashing to the ground. Pinned against the wet earth, slurry washed down over him. Hail pelted his arms and back. The raging winds above and around him pressed him down, covered him with debris.

An odd sense of déjà vu overtook him. Tig grew increasingly agitated, his insides screaming, begging God to be spared the vision that was determined to arise. He tried to shift his weight and his thoughts, but to no avail.

The tempest, the memories—neither would let him go. Sinister and unforgiving, what had been buried deep resurrected from Tig's memory. He turned his torso and his face to the sky. As he rolled, the lemon bars smashed against his chest, warm and sticky like broken flesh. The phantoms ascended, covering his mind with darkness. And, against his will, Tig recalled… everything.

———

It was a typical October afternoon in Everson, cool but not cold. Tig had been staying at the Green Valley Motel for nearly three months. Dottie was in no way ready to allow him back into the house since he had made no effort to reconcile with either her or Effie. At this point, the only connection Tig had with his family was through Leon, who was working with him full time at Wendot. Leon drove Tig's old truck while Tig drove the company pickup. Since Tig and Dottie had separated, he and Leon would take turns picking each other up for work.

Tig had stayed out a little longer than usual the night before. He stumbled in just before dawn. Dottie was clearly annoyed when he called at four in the morning and asked for Leon.

"Do you have any idea what hour it is, Tig?"

"Just have Leon pick me up at the motel, will ya, Dottie?"

"I thought you were picking him up here today?"

"I was, but something has come up. So just have him come by here. I'll be ready by six."

"I'm sure I can imagine what." Click.

Tig would never get used to Dottie cutting him off. He dropped the phone on the receiver and flopped down on the bed. Reaching over, he guzzled from the half bottle of Jim Beam on the nightstand. The tepid liquid slipped down, stinging the back of his throat. Tig grabbed the rowel dangling off his belt and twirled it around in his fingers.

"I'll show ya, Dottie. I'll work my way out of this, and we'll all move back home."

Groggy, Tig let his head drop back on the pillow, and he passed out. He would have been happy to stay there all day had it not been for the thud on the door.

"I'm comin'."

Tig pulled his boots up, threw on his ball cap, and grabbed his coat. He took hold of the half-full bottle and stuck it into his back pocket. It was a self-prescribed elixir, just in case. Struggling to steady his gait, Tig opened the door.

'Hey, Leon! How's my boy today!"

Tig's breath and exaggerated, somewhat distorted words told Leon all he needed to know. "I'm glad I'm drivin', Dad. Maybe we should cancel this trip out today."

"Nonsense, Leon. We've gotta stay on top of these jobs to keep Wendot in business. Ya know that. We're goin'. I'll be fine. I just need some coffee."

Tig and Leon were scheduled to drill a well in the small town of Campton located in the valley just east of Everson. The landowner had met with them the week prior. Everything was ready for drilling a shallow well, one hundred feet or less, into the soft rock strata, typical for the region.

Leon and Tig drove over to Wendot and picked up the diesel truck and rig. At one point, Wendot possessed two trucks and three cable drilling tools. Tig had sold the newer equipment when the company was in trouble. Now there was just a single rig left with a cable tool, bit, bailer, extra drill string wire, and a mounted deck engine on a 1955 seven-ton diesel truck. They had been using it for every job since Wendot consolidated its assets and downsized. The equipment was old but was inspected regularly for frays in the drill string wire, malfunctioning parts, or bit and casing cracks.

Leon kept a detailed check list for inspections and maintenance.

It was his job to look over the cable tool and drilling components before every job, while Tig managed the maintenance on the truck.

As Leon unlocked and opened the company garage, Tig was feeling a little unsteady. Handing over the truck keys, Tig conceded that Leon should drive. Within a half an hour, everything was loaded, and Leon was sitting high behind the steering wheel of the truck. On the way out of town, Leon pulled into the local truck stop. He slipped out of the cab, while Tig's snores intermittently fogged the window. A few minutes later, Leon hustled back across the parking lot juggling a couple styrofoam cups of coffee and a bag of glazed donuts. He had hoped the sugar would energize his father, help him burn off the remains of the night before.

"Thanks, son. I'm just not hungry today, but the coffee will do just fine."

The drive out of town was quiet. Leon was lost in thought while the Beatles serenaded them from the radio. Tig dozed leaning against his door, his face smashed against the window. Occasionally Leon would glance hopelessly at his father, sigh, and turn back to his thoughts. As they approached the site, Leon roused his father.

"Dad, we're almost there. How do you want to work this today?"

As a rule, once they arrived on the site, they would pinpoint the bore hole location. Leon would navigate, while Tig backed the rig into position.

"Dad?"

Tig startled. He jerked his head back, drool running down his chin. Embarrassed, he wiped his mouth with the back of his hand and sat up straight. Leon reached over and tapped his shoulder.

"Dad, how do you want to work this today?"

Tig turned with a jolt, facing Leon.

"What do ya mean, Leon? Ya know how we do this. We'll handle this the way we always do. I'll get the truck in place. You'll handle the cribbin', and we'll both raise the mast and tighten the cables, and then…."

"I know what comes next, Dad."

Realizing the futility of furthering the discussion, Leon slipped out from under the steering wheel. He hopped down out of the cab and walked around behind the trailer.

Tig slid over behind the steering wheel and rolled down the window. He leaned out and called to Leon. "OK, son, ease me back now."

The big truck heaved and hopped slightly as Tig put it in reverse. Leon began to motion for him to back up but quickly threw his hand up, indicating that he should stop. Tig hit the brake and leaned further out the window.

"What's goin' on back there, Leon? Hey what's goin on?"

"I don't know, Dad. They didn't level this out. We're not sittin' right. I think we have too much of an incline here."

Tig put the truck in park and jumped down out of the cab. He sauntered back to where Leon was studying the ground.

"See, Dad?"

Leon pointed out the back tires on the driver's side that were dug into the ground and then the tires on the opposite side barely making contact.

Tig groaned, frustrated.

"This will be fine, son. I've seen some of the best wells drilled on more of an incline than this. We're only goin' a hundred feet or so."

Tig walked back to the cab of the truck, while Leon bit his lower lip and shook his head with trepidation. Respectful of his father's authority, Leon proceeded to direct the truck and trailer into position over the location of the bore hole. Once in place, Tig hastily put the truck in park and climbed out. Leon had already started to get the large weighty wood blocks down to crib the truck and trailer tires. Tig and Leon had just moved to the driver's side when the truck lunged unexpectedly. Slipping out of gear, it began to roll. Tig jumped back and ran up toward the cab.

"LEON! Get away from the truck!"

Before Tig could get the cab door open, the incline along with the load-bear on the trailer caused the truck to rock. Tig watched it all happen. He was helpless.

Leon had leapt backwards and out of the way of the truck, but in doing so, he placed himself in direct line of the trailer. The steel mast of the cable drill was directly over the top of him. The truck rolled over with a sickening thud. A dirt cloud formed up and around the truck, covering Tig, blinding him. Leon looked up. The weight and force of the overturned truck fishtailed and flipped the trailer, sending the massive drilling equipment crashing down directly on top of Leon. After a single gasp, Leon was crushed.

Tig heard it before he saw it. "Oh God! Noooo!"

Tig ran to pull Leon out from under the pile of steel. Panicked, he fell on his belly. Still blinded by dirt filled eyes, he called out to his son in desperation.

"Leon! Leon, I'm comin'! Hold on, son! Hold on!"

Tig inched beneath the upturned trailer, pushing under the mangled metal until his body was wedged between bars of steel. Dirt filled his mouth and burned his eyes. His hands clawed over the stony ground, searching for flesh. He twisted and pushed with his legs, freeing himself from the steel. He thrust through closer to where he knew his son lay. He forced his body to contort and conform to the small spaces within the wreckage.

Tig stretched his arm out, his hand digging around metal and through debris, groping for his son. He shook his head, trying to clear the dirt from his eyes. He could barely see Leon's arm extended through the dusty haze. Inching his way farther under the debris, Tig jammed his torso between several thick wire cables and the gravel beneath him. Extending his hand as far as his arm would allow, he managed to touch Leon's cold fingers. The dirt settled, the dust cloud began to disperse, and Tig caught a glimpse of his son's crushed skull. Tig cried out in agony.

"Le-on! My son! Oh God, please, no!"

Wrenching his back, Tig torqued his abdomen and stretched his shoulders. He rolled his body to one side, forcing his weight up against the wire cables. He could hear the dull crack of his rib as he turned and flopped over onto Leon's chest. Taking hold of both his son's arms, he was determined to pull Leon out.

Tig resolved to drag Leon from behind as he inched out backwards from under the tangled web of steel bars and wire cable. As Tig's fingers wrapped around his son's wrists, the truck jerked and slid further down the incline. The pile of debris from the upended rig shifted and fell hard on top of Tig's right hand. As he screamed out in pain, a section of thick steel casing hovering precariously over his head released, swung down and cracked against his skull.

All went black. All was silent.

———

The clouds had moved past. The wind laid down. Scant flashes of faraway light and faint claps of remote thunder echoed from the edge of the earth. Directly overhead the night sky revealed a drape of black ink with glitter stars sprinkled about. The grasses stood up, raised their heads, and shook themselves off in the gentle breeze. The cedars stretched. The leaves of the hardwoods rustled, dropping tiny globes of water onto the spongy forest floor. A raccoon blown from its nest scampered through the downed limbs and up a nearby tree. The prairie, irrepressible and resilient, recovered quickly and settled in for the night.

Deep in the eroded ravine of Dump Canyon, Tig lay perfectly still, his eyes sealed shut, covered over with mud. While the thunderstorm raged, Tig relived the horrific details of the day his son was killed.

Everyone referred to it as a terrible accident, but Dottie blamed Tig for Leon's death. In this case, Tig agreed with Dottie. He carried inside the culpability of an irresponsible drunk, a wanton father who could have-should have saved his son.

He had managed to suppress the details of the tragic event for months. Now the emergent memories caught him off guard, spinning him off balance, sucking him in like a tornado. Tig's head swam. Reeling, he trembled uncontrollably. He pressed his knees deeper into the earthen wall and submitted to the ripped branches and gnarled debris that hemmed him in from behind. For the night, Tig became one with the storm-ravaged canyon.

Hours after the thunderstorm abated, the internal tumult for Tig continued. In the early light of daybreak while magenta and purple bands painted the dawn, Tig lay bound by the darkness of his memories.

The images of the accident and Leon's broken body were so real. The pain was so palpable, Tig retched. Lying in his purge, he began to weep. Isolation overtook him. For the first time since the accident, since Leon's death, Tig cried for his son.

He sobbed. He wailed, his anguished groans all but eviscerating him. Mournful howls rose from the canyon. Carried on the breeze, they combined with distant reverberations of thunder, the laments of earthen vessels and heaven.

"Oh God, forgive me. Oh God...."

———

The pickup bobbed and rocked back and forth, backlit by midmorning sun. Its wheels spinning through sludge, it chugged up the driveway to the house, the bottom half of the truck dipped in chocolate earth. Ron pulled up as far as the windmill, stopped abruptly and clamored out of the cab.

"Good Lord, Tig, is that you? Are ya OK?"

A grave look of concern overtook Ron's face.

Tig had just climbed out of Dump Canyon, and he was standing aimlessly in the middle of the road, exhausted from fighting—the storm within and outside of him. His appearance was alarming. His clothes were coated in muck and debris. Mud was caked in his hair and on his skin. His eyes appeared as two slits in his face, his mouth a gaping hole. Red clay was so thick on his clothing, his legs resembled the eroded driveway. Tig let out a groan as he moved toward the truck. His joints were stiff and his head ached.

"Ya must've had quite a night! Ya could've gotten killed down there with all that stuff blowin' 'round. Tig, here, get in the truck. We'll head over to the house. We can get ya cleaned up there. Have a warm shower, a good meal. We'll have plenty of time later to pick up debris around here."

"I don't think it hit up here, the house...."

Tig's face cracked as he spoke. He pointed towards the house and clumps of mud fell off his arm. There was junk blown against the small building on all sides. New chunks of cement stucco were missing, evidence the house had taken a beating. A section of roof had blown off, but the walls stood.

"A small tornado set down just west of here, but the winds were bad everywhere. Thought for sure it would rip your house right out of the ground. The gusts were fierce enough, that's for sure. I guess that old thing is stronger than we figured. Sure enough, Tig, your house weathered the storm and prevailed."

———

Tig searched until the sweat ran freely down his neck, his back. His face was flushed from the heat. The sun beat unforgivingly on his shoulders. It had been two days since the storm, and Dump Canyon was still sopping wet. The humidity was so thick at the bottom that it was difficult to breathe. Tig spent the entire morning there, searching, scouring, determined to locate the broken blade from the windmill. He was preparing to climb back up out of the gorge for lunch when the slight motion of a small snake caught his eye. The reptile's gray-black body matched the dull metallic surface he slinked across.

Ahh, there it is, Tig thought as he moved toward his prize. Nestled in a tangled mess of briars and an old truck chassis was the single galvanized steel windmill blade that had snapped during the storm. Tig maneuvered himself through the clutter to where metal rested on metal. He picked through the rubbish and retrieved the twisted, deformed blade. Satisfied, he worked his way back up to the house.

Tig kept a bucket of tools on the concrete slab behind the back door. From there, he selected a well-used hammer. Setting the contorted blade on the ground, he began to pound, steadily, methodically. Starting from the top and working his way to the bottom, Tig hammered, flattening the windmill blade.

He held it up in front of his face, inspecting his work. Not completely pleased, he set the blade back down and spent another thirty minutes tapping out the creases and folds in the tortured metal. Each tap was made with the determination of a metalsmith creating something of great value. Once again, he held it up. *Yes,* he thought. *This is good.*

Carrying the metal like a baby, Tig headed down the hill toward the windmill. He stopped and glanced up at the disfigured machine as though seeking its permission. The windmill towered over Tig, broken and silent. Tig carefully knelt down and set the blade flat on the ground. He ran his hand over its smooth metal.

Taking a nail from his pocket, he dragged the point over the surface, scratching and etching the object. He took the hammer and tapped the nail, deepening the scratches in the surface until the lines were chiseled into the steel. He took his hat off and wiped his forehead with the back of his gloved hand. Looking up at the sun, he nodded his head.

Carrying the windmill blade, he hiked down the drive to the wooded area, the entrance through the cedars, the door to the sacred room, and to the sanctuary among the trees. He held the etched side of the blade close to his chest with his injured hand and forced back the brush with the other. He put his head down and pushed through to the opening.

Rays of light dropped from above and lit up the center of the space. The ground was soggy and the scent of wet cedar was overwhelming. New growth had added a mossy green luster to the leaves and twigs carpeting the floor. Tig sighed at the beauty and solemnity of the place. He moved reverently to the middle and knelt down, the moisture from the ground penetrating his pants, saturating his knees.

He took the blade and let it rest on the ground. He removed his shirt and rolled it up. Laying the fabric over the top of the galvanized steel blade, he brought the hammer down several times, driving the piece of metal into the ground. Standing to his feet, Tig stepped back. The blade stood erect, jutting out of the ground—a marker. Tig arched his neck and looked up through the middle of the trees to the sky. The near noon sun overhead cast vivid rays of light through the oculus. Tig smiled, believing he had garnered God's approval as a near perfect circle of light embraced his memorial.

"This will be our place, Leon."

Tig let his eyes move around the wall of cedars. He breathed in deep, letting the pungent scent of wet earth and bark fill his lungs.

"You would've liked it here. Maybe we can meet here? Maybe here I can find the words for the conversations we never had."

Tig nodded his head, confirming for himself and in agreement with God. He took off his glove and sat down on the damp ground. He would linger a while. Tig placed his mangled hand on the blade. The cool steel against his flesh caused his throat to swell, his eyes to burn. In silence, he slid his ravaged fingers slowly over the scratched surface of Leon's epitaph, "Dear Son."

TWELVE

Tig's presence began to have a noticeable effect on the Old Macklin' place. Immediately after the storm, he cleared the debris from around the house. Trash, shingles, torn branches, leaves —all were pitched into Dump Canyon. Tig hiked into the gorge to where the trash was heaped in a pile. He took the three cans of beer out of the pockets of his overalls and poured them over the debris. He struck a match, stepped back, and tossed it in. The trash burst into flames, tongues of fire shooting upwards, lapping at the sky.

Tig walked back up to the house, stood on the stoop, and watched. Smoke and flames mingled below him just beyond the stilled windmill. He put his hands on his hips and stretched his back. The cool morning breeze flirted with the curtains in the open bedroom window. Acrid dead leaves, wet earth, sweet sage, wild flowers, and pungent smoke combined and anointed the air. It was a natural perfume, the scent of the surrendered past—wed to the fragrance of new growth.

Tig took a deep cleansing breath and closed his eyes. The crackling of the fire, the twittering birds, the scampering squirrels, the soft swishing grass, and the rustling leaves all flowed together in a chorus that embraced Tig. Peace engulfed him, and his heart recognized the melody…. It was the song of the redeemed.

———

Downed limbs had taken out several sections of fence. Ron was set to move the cattle to the east pasture, and fence maintenance was part of Tig's agreement with Ron. So, Tig made the repairs a priority, but managing barbed wire fences was a challenge Tig had not foreseen. He had been working for weeks to gain strength and coordination with his left hand. If anything could train him to become ambidextrous, he figured it would be working with gnarly posts and thorn-laced barbed wire. The stretch of fence separating his small yard from a wooded section of pasture was the perfect place to practice.

Over and over again, Tig would contort himself in any number of positions, leaning against and wrapping around the weathered oak posts to create tension in the wire before stapling it down—securing it in place. The first few days, his hips and torso took a beating. When he removed his shirt, blood stains marked the bruises and scrapes down his side. Although gloved, his left hand was scratched as though he'd dug through wild roses all day. By the end of the week, Tig was getting the hang of fence mending, although he did discover one very unique hazard—scorpions.

"I see ya, ya nasty little critter!"

The minute Tig took hold of the post, the scorpion scuttled to the opposite side. Tig tried to shake the arachnid out of the wood, but the scorpion promptly disappeared. Figuring he had hidden deep in one of the cracks, Tig wrapped his arm around the post to pull it straight. The minute Tig tightened his grip, the scorpion surfaced and stung his inner arm, a reminder of who owned the post. Wincing, Tig continued working the fence. This scenario occurred frequently, frustrating Tig that he could not seem to outwit the menacing pests.

As the summer heat mounted, Tig invented a way to thwart the burning stings. He stuffed thick strips of torn fabric down the inside of his shirt sleeves. He figured he would rather be covered with sweat than welts.

———

One morning after Ron and Tig inspected the fence repairs, they returned to the house for a cup of coffee. They were sharing tales when Ron noticed Tig's shotgun leaning in the corner.

"Tig, I've been meanin' to talk with ya about goin' huntin' with me. Nice lookin' shotgun ya got there."

"I think a huntin' trip would do me some good, but I can't use that shotgun anymore, Ron. I tried. I just don't have the strength in my hand to handle the kickback…" Tig glanced at the shotgun with disappointment in his eyes. "Too dangerous."

Ron looked to the corner, squinting and screwing up his mouth. "Hmm. What about a rifle? Could ya learn how to shoot a rifle?"

"Ya know, I reckon I could. A rifle would be smaller and much easier to handle."

"I've got several rifles. How about tradin'? Would ya be interested in tradin' me your shotgun for a bolt action 22?"

Ron knew by the look on Tig's face that he loved the idea.

The men agreed, and Ron brought the rifle over the next day, along with an old sawhorse. With Ron's help, Tig learned how to hold the rifle with his left hand. After a couple weeks of practicing, holding, and carrying the rifle safely, Tig and Ron decided to try target shooting.

They set up the sawhorse about fifty yards from the west side of the house. Tig scavenged a bunch of cans from Dump Canyon, which they set in a row along the top of the two-by-four. Standing under the hedge apple tree, they fired off a few rounds at the rusty cans. They had quite the brouhaha, creating puffs of gun smoke, shooting at bottles and other junk. They laughed hysterically as the whizzing tins were sent flying in all directions. Tig and Ron were doing more than spending an afternoon together, they were bonding as friends.

In less than six months, Tig had gotten quite adept at shooting the rifle. Ron came by one morning to drop off more fence wire and discovered Tig standing over a sizzling frying pan. Tig was grinning from ear to ear.

"How 'bout some fried squirrel, Ron? I hit it at twenty five yards." Ron just smiled and sat down at the table set for two people.

———

Tig continued to do chores for Ida Mae, although there were no letters written to Effie for several weeks after the storm. Ida Mae did not press. She believed Tig would come around when he was ready. It was Tuesday, and the ice in the lemonade was melting quickly. Only a couple quarter size pieces remained in the glasses by the time Tig stepped onto the front porch The late spring sun was conjuring heat waves over the sweating fields, the mud in the road cracking from the blistering heat.

"I have somethin' here for ya, Ida Mae."

Tig reached out his hand. A large cube of cheese wrapped in wax paper, sticky from the heat, was offered as a gift.

"Ya know I get food stamp allotments. Let's me get dairy goods and the like. There's always more cheese than I can use. Thought ya might make somethin' good outa this."

Ida Mae grinned and graciously accepted the block of cheese from Tig, who was smiling big.

"I bet I could make a fine casserole with this cheddar. Maybe you and the Carsons could join me some evening for supper?"

Tig smiled, nodding in agreement.

"Ida Mae, I figure if it's OK, I'd like to commence writin' to Effie."

"I would love to help you with that, Tig." Ida Mae was so pleased. She had been concerned for weeks that she had frightened him off with her admonition regarding the context of his letters.

"Most of what needs to be done this week is in the barn and out of the sun. So why don't we spend time on your letter first, and you can get to the chores before you leave."

Tig dictated a letter to Effie that afternoon. Ida Mae was pleased with how Tig's words to his daughter had softened. He spent little time on the logistical ins and outs of the day. Rather he talked about his deep sorrow over the loss of his son, her brother. He mentioned how he longed to have her and Dottie back in his life; he lamented over not having met his grandchild. Most poignant was the final line of the letter, simple and eloquent: "Effie, please forgive me."

Ida Mae sealed the envelope, addressed it, and handed it to Tig. He stuck it in his pocket.

Ida Mae peered out the window as he headed up the drive. Her heart swelled for the sorrow Tig carried, and she whispered a prayer on his behalf.

Tig took the letter back up to his house and set it in plain view on the formica table. That Thursday, Tig requested that Ron drop it by the post office.

———

Throughout the summer, repairs were made to the house; hinges were fixed, broken glass replaced, and linoleum tacked back down. Tig spent some of his money to buy a bag of cement, which he used to patch all the cracks in walls in both the interior and exterior stucco. Ron gave him pieces of corrugated tin for repairing the roof. Two weeks later, Tig bought a half gallon of cheap white paint and repainted all the walls inside his house—two coats over the bleeding fissures in the front room. He cleaned all the appliances and the creosote out of the wood stove. He borrowed tools from Ida Mae and planted a small vegetable garden.

When Ron mentioned how Linda had convinced him they needed to lay some gravel in front of their house to keep the dust down, Tig asked if he could scrounge a little. He took the leftover gravel and spread it along the incline, the most eroded section of the driveway.

Not a great deal was done to beautify the place, but Tig did transplant a young sapling cedar from the woods to the west side of the house for shade. He also dragged a volunteer rose bush from Ida Mae's garden and stuck it in the ground next to his front door. It was obvious to the Carsons and Ida Mae that Tig was doing more than just tending to perfunctory repairs; he was turning the Old Macklin' place into "Tig's Place."

The windmill was dormant all summer. Since Tig's water supply was limited, Linda continued to wash his overalls, jeans and shirts. He felt it inappropriate for her to launder his underwear, so he washed those in a bucket behind the house. Linda was bringing back Tig's laundered clothes one morning when she surprised him with a small hand-braided rug for his bedroom.

"The Fox Creek Ladies made this for you, Tig. They love doing things like this. They asked me if I could drop it off for you. Isn't this nice?"

She held it up for him to inspect.

"I'll say. Thank 'em for me, won't ya, Linda?"

Linda placed the rug in Tig's hands, and he laid it next to his cot while Linda looked on. As her car hopped and weaved in a cloud of dust down the driveway, Tig moved the rug and laid it under the kitchen table. That night he took his boots off before eating supper. While downing a bowl of canned soup, Tig rubbed his bare feet across the rug and smiled.

———

Hiking aided in staving off bouts of loneliness, so Tig frequently took long walks. His quiet strolls centered him. They untroubled his mind, doused him in tranquility. On an early July afternoon, Tig walked his gnarly driveway to just beyond the cattle guard. With his new buckskin cowboy hat shielding his eyes and a faded bandana around his neck soaking up the sweat, Tig rolled up his sleeves and stood taking in the halcyon prairie. The sun was bleaching the fields, the soft green grain relinquishing to golden beige. The wheat swayed gently back and forth. Heat-burned vegetation mixed with dusty earth, dormant hay and goldenrod created the familiar essence of late summer, fall-is-coming-potpourri. Tig breathed in deep and set his eyes on the horizon. Outside the cultivated fields, untamed territory tumbled out in knolls and draws. Tussocks of soft purple-silver bluestem, wispy field hair, sprouted atop peeled back terrain of blood-red earth, a hairy epidermis on intermittent cliffs of clay. Stretches of chewed down pasture seasoned with clumps of sage welcomed the bottom land, where ribbons of dark chocolate ground embraced the river.

His eyes searched across the swelling hills. Conjuring up a flash of wild auburn mane, Tig lamented. How could he have let go of all of this, of her? His love for Dottie was as feral as the land. Why had he ever sought to tame it with something as superficial as financial gain?

THIRTEEN

Tig lay in a coma for two weeks suffering from severe head injuries and internal bleeding. His mangled hand, recovering from emergency surgery, rested in thick bandages across his chest. His head was wrapped in gauze. Tig slept unaware.

Day after day, Effie waited silently by his side, straightening his bedding, tucking her father under the drab hospital-issued blanket. On the day Leon was buried, the machine next to Tig measured his breaths, the beats of his heart in thin blue lines. In a small cemetery on the edge of town, the lifeless body of his first born, a casket covered with violets and roses, was lowered beneath the sod.

Dottie's grief consumed her, and she held Tig responsible for the accident that took their only son. Dottie convinced herself Tig was a murderer; whether directly or indirectly, it was all the same to her. She could not imagine Tig without blood on his hands. Her wrath and pain were so intense that she could not bear to be in the same room with him. Carolyn was incapable of consoling her friend, while Johnnie's solution was to commiserate with Dottie via embrace.

"Johnnie, I've made a decision. I am leaving Tig. I'll never be able to look at him again without seeing him as Leon's murderer." Dottie's eyes were emotionless.

Dottie had always been impulsive, so this knee jerk reaction didn't surprise Johnnie. Although he fully enjoyed the idea that she might become available, he was certain she would not go through with a divorce.

What he didn't know was what had taken place prior to the accident. Dottie had kept Effie hidden, so Johnnie had no idea his niece was pregnant nor did he know anything about the argument that forced Tig to rent a room. The reality was that Dottie's indifference toward Tig had been growing steadily. The apathy, the expanding emptiness in Dottie's heart over the years, left a chasm well suited for accommodating repulsion.

"Why don't ya give this some time, Dottie?"

Dottie would have been surprised at this statement, being that it was the most benevolent thing she had ever heard Johnnie say with respect to his brother. However, she was too covered over in contempt to hear it. In her mind, Leon's death justified what she had intended to do for a long time—leave Tig.

"Johnnie, I have filed for divorce. It was bound to happen sooner or later. I've placed the house up for sale. I'm moving away from here, Johnnie, away from all of this. I'm taking Effie with me. I'll be gone before he leaves the hospital. I've contacted the insurance company and the hospital already." She paused.

"I've signed Tig over to your care, Johnnie. You'll need to go and complete the paperwork."

"You what!? No! Hell no. I'm not gonna be responsible for him and his mess."

"I'm afraid you would have to take care of him at some point anyway, since you are his next of kin. You can sign him over to the state's care if you wish. But then…."

Dottie got a glint in her eye. She knew full well who was manipulating whom.

"…The state would garner his disability pay and the insurance from the accident."

Johnnie hesitated. His face cracked a smile when he realized there might be something in it for him. "You know, Dottie, maybe you're right."

"Good. Then it is settled. I'll be gone within a couple weeks."
"But Dottie, how will I contact and update ya?"

"Once I have a forwarding address, I'll leave it with the hospital.

Good luck, Johnnie." Johnnie reached out to hug Dottie. Not interested, she turned suddenly and walked off.

———

On a quiet street in Everson, Tig and Dottie's little house sat empty on the first day of Tig's rehab. Dottie only visited the hospital to expedite the paperwork ensuring she would be completely free of Tig. The day before she moved, she signed the last of the forms.

Dottie never turned back as she pulled out of the driveway with the little U-Haul hitched to her car, all her material belongings bobbing behind. As she and Effie drove past the Wendot office on their way out of town, Effie began to sob, huge tears running down her face. Dottie stared straight ahead, her eyes the deepest tone of jade. She reached over and laid her hand on her pregnant daughter's leg but said nothing.

———

Tig had been in rehabilitation for nearly two weeks. Confined to a sterile blue room, he sat looking out the curtain-less window, the white shade pulled up tight. An empty light flooded across the highly polished linoleum floor.

Why hadn't they come? He knew Leon was gone, but no one had confirmed it. The words had never been spoken. He had not seen nor heard from Dottie or Effie. His calls went unanswered. Carolyn and Johnnie had stopped by shortly after he gained consciousness but only for a very brief visit. The friction between Johnnie and Carolyn as they stood detached from each other at the end of his bed only depressed Tig. He was thankful when they turned to leave.

———

Sleepless nights filled with terror yielded days of medicated stupor, and time passed. One morning after breakfast, Johnnie came bounding unexpectedly into Tig's blue room.

"Well, looks like they're feedin' ya well enough."

Tig rallied quickly. He wasn't in the mood for Johnnie's obnoxious remarks. He had more important things on his mind. Finally, someone was there to answer his questions.

"Johnnie, why haven't I heard from Dottie? Where is she? No one's told me anythin'. I know Leon is gone, but what about the funeral? What's happenin'?"

Johnnie pulled a chair up next to Tig's bed and plopped down in it. Johnnie's breath smelled like his 2am binge.

"Brother, she's gone, long gone. She just packed up and left."

Tig's face went ashen. "What do ya mean, gone? Johnnie what do ya mean!"

"Ya see, Tig, she just couldn't tolerate bein' around ya any longer. I mean can ya blame her? Ya murdered your own son. I tried to stop her, but she took Effie and cleared out."

Tig sat motionless. He couldn't breathe; he couldn't cry. His emotions froze. Stunned, eyes not blinking, mouth partially open, Tig stopped hearing. The blood raced from his limbs, and he went cold. The only feeling left was a slow steady throbbing in his right hand.

Johnnie continued to ramble.

"I'm sure the doctor told ya that you'll be discharged in a week. Dottie signed ya over to my care. Of course, neither Carolyn nor I have room for ya at our house. So, I put a call in to Ron Carson. Ya remember the Old Macklin' place we used ride out to? Well, I asked Ron if ya could live there, told him ya would have disability coming in sooner or later. He was hesitant at first. I think he was worried about havin' a gimp livin' out there. I could hear Linda in the background. I'm certain she talked him into it. I laid this all out for Carolyn, told her I'd be drivin' ya back out there in a couple weeks. So, there ya have it in a nutshell. You're in my custody, and we'll be goin' back east to Oklahoma. Should be quite an adventure, don't ya think?"

"Get out, Johnnie! Get out now! Just leave!"

"Sure thing, li'l brother, but I'll be back in a week. Be ready to go, ya hear? Oh, and I'll run ya by the insurance office so ya can sign a check. You'll also need to close out your account. We're gonna need some travelin' cash."

Johnnie reached over and condescendingly patted Tig on the shoulder.

———

The nights were torture, and the days were endless, and Tig had all but given up. He mostly sat in a drugged haze staring out the window. *What have I done? Why did ya have to leave?* Two weeks from the day Johnnie had stormed into Tig's room, a battered Cadillac sat in the patient pick up drive at the hospital. Johnnie threw Tig's paltry belongings into the trunk of the Cadillac. The nurse assisted Tig, who crawled reluctantly into the front seat. Johnnie started up the engine. Despondent, Tig sat holding tight to the rowel tied to his belt loop. In a gas station lot just past the hospital, Johnnie doled out three pain pills to Tig—two more than prescribed.

"Johnnie, do ya think we can at least stop by the cemetery, so I can say goodbye to Leon?"

"I don't see why not. It may be a long time before ya get back out here."

At the outskirts of Everson, the blue Cadillac drove past a serene cemetery covered in trees. A drugged Tig slept, his head resting against the window. Johnnie had no intention of stopping.

———

When Johnnie abandoned him in Oklahoma, Tig had lost everything save his life. But the night of the storm while huddled in the canyon, Tig realized he had been given a second chance. Stripped down as it were, it was an opportunity, a way to accept his circumstances and make the best of things. He believed there was a chance that someday he could embrace life again.

He determined to set out to do just that—slowly, methodically, Tig made every effort to live with intention and gratitude. Difficult at first, Tig made deliberate choices to be thankful. Through practice and over time Tig's responses became rote.

He felt his senses begin to sharpen. He saw more, felt more, perceived more. He became aware of his capacity for joy. His moments of fear dissipated. The urgency that for so long had dictated his life was trumped by a need for quiet contemplation. Every morning he would visit the sanctuary, sit and talk to Leon, talk to God. Tig concerned himself less with what could have been and celebrated what was, no matter how simple or unadorned. Tig slowed down but was finally catching up with life.

———

At the beckoning of spring, the Red-tailed Hawk swooped and screeched, diving for prairie voles as they darted through patches of canary-yellow ragwort. A spotted fawn at the edge of the woods paused, ready and alert. She stood camouflaged against the gray lichened tree trunks and the remains of winter's composting terrain. A surfeit of baby skunks scampered about the chilly floor of Dump Canyon.

All too soon, the cool prairie winds shifted and spring graced seamlessly into dog days. The harbingers of summer had departed, changed, giving way to fields of Indian blanket topped with fluttering Monarchs and scissortail fly catchers flittering in cloudless skies above shiny red sand plums, their skins pulled taut.

Tig sat on the front stoop, scuffing gravel under his feet. The sun had set, but the dense July heat had not abated. He considered sleeping outside. He crossed his arms and leaned back against the door, looking up into the star-filled night, the big sweeping sky of the prairie swathing the slumbering land from horizon to horizon. The baying of a lone coyote pierced the thick atmosphere.

Tig closed his eyes and listened until all he could hear was the haunting nocturnal sonnet. He smiled with wonder. *Had anyone else heard the song?* He reflected on all he had witnessed since he'd arrived, all that lived and thrived around him. Tig had captured them all in his heart, offerings from the prairie, from God, and they were filling the empty places, the longings.

FOURTEEN

Tig was stacking a pile of small logs and branches against the outhouse when Ron walked up with a box in his arms.

"Ya surprised me! Didn't hear ya drive up."

"Sorry 'bout that. Didn't mean to startle ya. Looks like you're gettin' ready for winter already."

"Yup. Felt a chill in the air this mornin'. It'll be September soon, and sometimes it can get cold early."

"You're wise, really."

"Whatcha got there?"

"Oh this, yeah. I finally got around to findin' those tools ya needed."

Ron set the metal box down. Tig thanked him and started rummaging through the contents. There were miscellaneous nuts and bolts, rolls of wire, rope, a variety of wrenches, screwdrivers, and some cutting tools.

"The blades and parts should be in next week."

"Thanks, Ron. This'll do just fine."

———

The next week, Ron dropped off a ladder and a box of mechanical parts shipped from Aerometer's Windmill Company. Before leaving,

Ron set some extra pails near the back door. He had Tig help him move an old porcelain footed tub to the cement pad near the outhouse. The rusted claw feet plowed through the yard leaving two equally spaced furrows behind them. Both Tig and Ron stood bent over with their hands on their knees, huffing and puffing once the tub was in place. The chips in the finish and the layer of rust stains made no difference to Tig. He was pleased with the newest addition to his house.

"Man needs a decent bath once in a while."

Ron was a little embarrassed, since both men knew the tub was Linda's idea. Regardless, the thought of a hot bath in his own tub appealed to Tig.

"Thank ya, Ron. And um, give my thanks to Linda. Not that she had anythin' to do with this." Both men tried to stifle their laughter so as not to add to their back pain.

"You've really fixed this place up, Tig. Good to see you've settled in. Ya know word is gettin' around town that you're back. Some folks would love to see ya."

Tig looked startled, then concerned.

"I'm not ready to see anyone else, Ron. Things have changed for me since the storm. I believe it's best that I be by myself right now."

Ron's eyes flashed a brief look of disappointment.

"I understand, Tig. We'll keep it this way as long as ya want."

Tig turned away as he mumbled a faint thank you. Ron knew better than to further the conversation. He couldn't imagine what went through Tig's mind most of the time. He had come to believe, however, that Tig assigned himself to seclusion as a type of penitence. Tig was a recluse by choice. Ron's misunderstanding of what this meant caused his heart to ache for the simple man he cared about.

————

The ladder leaned precariously on top of makeshift plank scaffolding spread over the water trough. Tig ascended. He disassembled the gear box and removed the last of the damaged blades from the fan, dropping them to the ground. At that point, he climbed back down, juggling the gear box in his bad hand while holding on to the ladder with his good one.

Tig sat on his stoop surrounded by gears, screws, bearings, washers, and the disassembled gear box. He brought a glass of lukewarm iced tea to his mouth and drank generously as he mentally cataloged the objects spread about. Tig looked over at the fan-less tower. *I haven't drawn water from this well in nearly four months. Ron's been bringin' me water in that portable water trough since I got here. It's an inconvenience for the Carsons. I won't continue imposin' on them.*

Driven by this thought, Tig determined to repair the wind mill. He had become fairly agile with his left hand. However, the small gears and bearings would prove a challenge to the motor skills of his once dominant hand. Minutes grew into hours. The job started early in the day, dragging late into the afternoon. Tig gathered up his work and the remaining parts and carried them into the house, his back aching from sitting hunched over on a cool cement stoop all day. Transferring his project to the table, he turned on the overhead light, grabbed a piece of bologna from the refrigerator, and continued piecing the small machine back together. Six hours later, at two in the morning, he held the repaired and reassembled gear box in front of his weary eyes, inspecting it one last time. *Now we're ready!* Setting it down, he shuffled off into the bedroom, flopped on the bed, and fell fast asleep.

———

The clanging outside the bedroom window alarmed Tig. He jumped up from the cot and grabbed the rife resting in the corner. Not bothering to look out the window, he bolted through the front door, gun up, ready to shoot.

"Whoa, whoa Tig. It's me!"

"What in God's name are ya doin' here at this hour, Ron? Who's managin' the cattle?" Ron was stooped over with his palms on his lower back, catching his breath.

"Tig, ya near gave me a heart attack. I had Jay and a couple other hands take care of things this mornin' so I could come over here and help ya hang this new windmill fan. I figured you'd be stubborn enough to repair that gear box, but you'll need some help gettin' it all put back together. And judgin' from that dangerous jerry-rigged scaffoldin' ya got set up over there, it's a darn good thing I came around. Now please set down that gun!"

Tig was reticent to agree to Ron's help as he turned and slipped the gun inside the front door.

"Yeah, I suppose you're right 'bout that. I got the box repaired, though. Took near all night, but it's done."

"I knew it would all come back to ya, Tig. This fan came in yesterday, late, and I was gonna surprise ya with it. Guess ya surprised me first. Lord have mercy!"

Ron broke out in one of his contagious bouts of laughter, drawing Tig into the guffawing. Both men made a commotion.

"Here, how about helpin' me get this out of the back of my truck."

Tig slipped his boots on and met Ron at the truck. They unloaded and mounted the fan within an hour. Together they disassembled Tig's makeshift scaffolding and cleared the stagnant water out of the trough. The morning breeze picked up and caught the rudder, systematically turning the fan in the opposite direction.

Tig and Ron looked up and watched the restored machine begin to dance. The axis began to rotate; the blades caught the wind and spun effortlessly. No longer tortured, they whirred and hummed. Within minutes a slow trickle of clear water ran from the discharge pipe and flowed into the trough. The sound of the purring blades and the dripping water was beautiful, a lullaby for the wind—for Tig.

"Now, that's more like it!"

Tig beamed. This was the first job he had worked on since the accident. He allowed a hint of pride to show. Ron caught it. Knowing full well how important this event was, he stuck out his hand to Tig. Confused at first, Tig hesitated then reached out in return. Ron firmly shook it.

"Fine job there, Tig. Fine job. Now how 'bout a cuppa coffee."

The two men sat on the front stoop of the house, laughing and carrying on all morning, watching the windmill spin. Ron no longer identified Tig as someone in his care, someone needing assistance—benevolence. Rather he saw Tig as his friend, a man he enjoyed spending time with, someone he could respect, the very things he no longer felt for Johnnie.

———

The letters started arriving in June, not long after Carolyn had left. They spilled out onto the floor just below the mail slot in the door; they lay scattered among the bills and junk mail. After deciding to leave Johnnie, Carolyn hired a private detective to gather information for her case against her wayward husband. She was not surprised in the least when she received information that Johnnie had stopped in Las Vegas for an extended stay. With all the proof she needed, Carolyn filed for divorce. Johnnie's departure from Vegas and his remaining journey back to Everson were monitored. A brown sedan sat parked across the street from Johnnie and Carolyn's house, an envelope sitting on the front seat next to a balding man.

The rattling of a loose muffler caught the attention of the occupant in the sedan. He set down his newspaper and watched as the long blue convertible drove past and pulled into the driveway. Johnnie had been gone for nearly seven months to Oklahoma, a trip that should have taken no longer than four weeks. Over the time he was gone, he had successfully squandered all of his and Tig's money. He only left Vegas because a stop was put on his credit card, a bank draft that would have drained what little was left of his and Carolyn's savings.

Johnnie's Cadillac had seen better days. The finish, pelted by sand and rock, was chipped and scratched. Smear from bird droppings and smashed insects covered the windshield and the grill. The car was filthy inside and out. The torn upholstery, covered in dust, flapped back and forth. Loose junk, bottles, half empty bags of chips, and dirty clothes filled the back seat. The debris was kept from blowing out of the car by the weight of a battered suitcase thrown on top. Johnnie looked as dilapidated and disheveled as his car. He hadn't shaved in days. His hair was stringy and overgrown. His once brilliant black eyes were clouded. He had lost considerable weight. His cheeks were sunken, his jawbone pressed tight against his skin stretching his chapped and cracked lips taut.

He flung the car door open, grabbed his suitcase from the junk-bed backseat where it rested, and walked to the front door. Juggling the key, he turned the knob. As he stepped in, he slipped and nearly lost his balance on the letters strewn across the floor.

"What the... huh? Carolyn! What the Hell is this mess?" The musty house was disturbingly still.

Johnnie dropped his suitcase and started gathering the letters into stacks when the doorbell rang. "I figured you saw me drive up. Just wanted to surprise me, didn't you? Come in here, baby."

Expecting to find Carolyn on the other side, Johnnie threw open the door where stood a stocky balding man.

"Jonathan William Mills?"

"Yes."

"You have been served."

––––––

Ron shared with Linda over dinner about how Tig had frightened him to death with the rifle. Linda couldn't wait to tell her girlfriend Betty about it. Betty told the story to Eleanor, who was a member of the Fox Creek Ladies Auxiliary, and in no time at all, hearsay was flying around Arvita. Tales of the crusty recluse living in the Old Macklin' place were not new. They had actually started circulating within weeks of Tig's arrival. However, this latest addition painted Tig Mills as an outlaw. Rumor was he brandished a gun and would shoot anyone who dared trespass on what he now considered his land. Ida Mae tried to squelch the stories, but the mystery was far too seductive.

Yet, the Fox Creek Ladies took a particular interest in Tig. He was always at the top of the list to be the beneficiary of their charitable projects. In the short time since Tig was back, he had received, via Linda, two food baskets and a "care" package full of soap, deodorant, toothpaste, and disinfectant cream, along with personal items and a pair of rubber boots. He was grateful, always reminding Linda to thank the ladies for him.

Unfortunately, the growing myths, particularly the most recent installment replete with a loaded rifle, contained an element of truth and a dark side. The gritty reality of the deformed man who had a part in the death of his own son was, for many, repulsive and evil. Swiftly, the gossip cultivated a corporate fear of Tig.

―――――

By mid-autumn, additional boxes of food and other gifts from the Fox Creek Ladies would show up randomly on Tig's driveway. Too frightened to approach his door, gifts were delivered during times when he was either with Ida Mae or sleeping. He was very grateful for the gifts, but the way in which they were left fostered his isolation. Tig became further withdrawn, cloistered in his little house on the hill.

Ida Mae and Ron tried to encourage Tig to get out, but the community's fear of him held him back, gave him cause for concern. Tig no longer bore guilt, but the scars from his past still stung. They had an impact on his choices and affected his responses. Tig was not confident he could handle the stares and whispers of those who engaged in half-truths and titillating hearsay.

―――――

By first frost, Tig had stopped going into town altogether. He was satisfied to stay hidden. He looked forward to the red truck grinding the gravel on his driveway every two weeks, his weekly letter writing time at Ida Mae's, and his once-a-month visit from Dan the barber. Between these opportunities for human companionship, Tig spent his time with the land, resting in it, hiking, mending fences, working his garden, and making repairs around the house.

There were days when Tig's longing for his family was so acute he could barely function. He missed Dottie, frequently seeing her face, her smiling eyes in his memory. Tig knew Dottie well enough to know he would likely never see her again, but he could not help thinking about her every day. He struggled to jettison his thoughts of her as they surfaced, for he knew they had the power to cover him in regret. He wondered if he would ever not ache for her, for his children… his grandchildren.

Alleviating anguish was Tig's most difficult challenge, making his daily visit to the sanctuary essential. Since creating a memorial for his son, the protected hollow, the tranquil oratory in the woods, had become an altar. Tig never felt alone there. Rather, he felt strangely comforted. The sheltered sanctuary evoked a sense of solace that provided Tig a place to commune, share his pain and his deepest regrets.

At times, the dappled peat floor sprouting Leon's marker summoned Tig's deep sadness. He would let himself consider things that would never be and he would mourn. Those days, he would season the earthen mat beneath his feet with salty tears. Sometimes the soft light penetrating from above would invite him to rest. In those moments, he would sit quietly, humming Carrie Ann's favorite hymns. On occasion, he would lie flat on his back like a ten-year-old staring at the sky, letting his imagination make ephemeral art out of patches of ethereal fluff. Sometimes, he would shout out loud, his hopes declared to the universe were witnessed by cedar sentinels. Other times he could do no more than whisper to clay dust filtering through useless fingers.

———

Brittle chestnut-brown leaves, the swan song of autumn, crumbled under Tig's boots as he moved past the windmill. The blackjacks and elms were nearly barren, their jagged intertwined trunks, umber squiggly lines painted against the cold winter sky. Blackbirds were gathering, peppering the stubby khaki straw and sienna terrain with their bodies, black-winged specks. Off in the distance, fields of dried-up grass rippled like lamb's wool, dressing for winter.

Weaving through long strings of barbed wire, wild sumac flourished, its foliage as bright as the red enamel truck weaving along Rte. 426. A flash of crimson turned and moved up the drive, the body of the truck striking color against the dormant neutral background. The black rubber tires churned up dirt road clouds, setting the birds to flight: swooping, gliding masses of black stipple on a canvas of gray wash. The pickup came to a stop in front of Tig's door. As Ron and Linda pulled brown paper sacks from the front seat, Tig trudged up the hill, a mantle draped over his arm.

Linda handed a bag to Ron and stood staring at the blanket Tig was carrying. "That's quite the quilt you have there, Tig."

"Hey Ron, Linda, yeah this is another gift from the Fox Creek Ladies. This time they left it down by the windmill. I believe this is handmade. The colors match the land, and look at this."

Tig held up the quilt for them to see. The quilt was comprised of triangles within triangles of calico muslin. All the triangles came together to form a single large earth-toned star in the middle.

"Why Tig, that's a Lone Star quilt! My how lovely." Linda ran her fingers over the quilt, all the while ogling it.

Tig grinned and tipped his head, watching Linda covet the blanket.

"It's a beauty, isn't it? I do believe the Fox Creek Ladies have outdone themselves. I'll tell ya what, Linda, I really don't need somethin' this elaborate. Why don't ya take it?"

Linda looked surprised.

"Absolutely not, Tig! That quilt was made for you, and you must keep it."

Ron shook his head back and forth in disbelief behind Linda's back. "Yeah, she says that now, but ya better keep your eye on it 'cause she may just make off with it while you're not lookin'!"

Linda reached over and playfully punched Ron's arm. The men laughed as Tig folded the quilt and set it on the stoop.

"Here, let me help ya with those." Tig grabbed a bag of groceries from Ron. "How much do I owe ya?"

Ron set the bags on the table, and Tig followed him back out to the truck, while Linda continued to run her hands over the quilt.

"Let's make it an even twenty today."

Ron never told Tig exactly what he spent. He always shaved some of the cost off. Tig held out a twenty-dollar bill, which Ron stuffed into his pocket.

"By the way, Tig. I bought ya that bag of dog food, but I don't have a clue why."

"There have been a few stray dogs roamin' around. I feel bad for 'em. They get a rabbit or squirrel once in a while. Saw one carryin' a mole or mouse the other day. Thought I might just leave some food out for 'em."

Ron's face turned serious.

"Tig, ya can't do that. Those dogs could be rabid. Just a few weeks ago, several ranchers at the co-op were complainin' about wild dogs. They said those dogs are capable of takin' a baby calf, and given the opportunity, they won't hesitate to tear a sheep apart. Ya best not leave any food out. Matter-of-fact, please make sure ya burn your trash often. Those dogs are dangerous and need to be put down."

Tig's brow furrowed with disappointment, but he nodded in agreement nonetheless. "I understand, Ron. I don't want to make this worse."

"I'm concerned that ya have already seen them around here. Ya need to be careful out there. I'm gonna bring a hand gun next week. I'd feel better if you'd keep it with ya."

"Thanks. Hey, before ya leave, do ya think we might be able to drive over to my folk's old place sometime, so I can pay my respects before snow comes?"

"Sure, Tig. I'll pick ya up next week."

———

The fire had gone out of the small stove sometime during the night. Tig's hand and knees throbbed with arthritis, a familiar burn. He pulled back the patchwork quilt and got up from bed. The light from outside the window seemed abnormally bright for early morning. Ron had helped Tig cover all the windows with plastic sheeting to shield out the cold. The thick opaque sheets puffed in and out against the glass, making soft sucking sounds.

Tig, eager to understand the source of the light, slipped on his pants and boots and headed to take a look outside. He put a pot of water on and stoked the fire in his wood stove before venturing out.

Moments later, he stood in the door way looking out over a breathtaking winterscape. The heavens had delivered a late autumn snowstorm, covering the desolate landscape in a cloak of white. The gnarly trees, the eroded clay, the draws, the canyons, heaving-earth with its bluestem hair all wild and feral, all yielded to the quieting snow. The prairie was hushed as abundant snowflakes, heavy and wet, drifted down, soothing the spirited terrain.

The cold was exhilarating. The air was thin and sharp and stimulated Tig's lungs. Bits of melting ice tingled against his skin. The steam from his nostrils rose and swirled, dancing around fat snowflakes falling lazily from the seamless white sky.

The raw beauty was overwhelming, and Tig could not contain it. He lifted his hands above his head as though attempting to gather it all to himself. Irrepressible joy overcame him. Turning his face upwards to the source, the white-veiled unknowable, Tig laughed out loud.

———

Ron was right on time, mid-morning. His red truck washed with slush made soft crunching sounds as the tires flattened the snow on the driveway. Tig pulled the door shut to the house, sending small icicles to the stoop. Inside the cab, steam rose off two cups of hot coffee siting in a cup rest, fogging up the windshield. Ron wiped the inside of the window with a bandana.

"Early this year. Snow's bad enough the kids are gettin' out of school today."

"First time I've seen snow in a long time. Sure is beautiful, but I can't recall the last time I've seen this much white before Thanksgiving."

"Tig, I brought ya that handgun I mentioned. It's just a little 9 millimeter, but it'll protect ya from those dogs and snakes an such. Oh, an here is a box of extra shells" Ron handed Tig the gun with a glance of concern. Tig carefully slid the small weapon into the side of his boot.

"I appreciate this Ron. I'll be keepin' it with me."

The windshield was catching plump snowflakes. Disintegrating into small puddles of water upon contact, they ran in slushy trails down the glass. Captured by thwacking wipers, they collected into small drifts of icy pulp where the glass connected to steel. The truck skidded along, making new tracks down the drive.

At the intersection to the road, the land sprawled out in front of them. Virginal snow covered the hills leading to Ida Mae's and beyond. Intermittent stubble shot out from the sugar-coated terrain, and dark dormant trees leaned naked to the east, bent over as though misshaped from the snow collecting on their limbs. Tig closed his eyes and let the image imprint, adding it to his collective memory—visions of the harsh and exquisite land he loved so much.

"Speaking of Thanksgiving, the kids aren't gonna make it home, so Linda and I will be joinin' Ida Mae for dinner. She tells us ya plan to be there as well."

"Yes, I will be. I told her I wouldn't be any good cookin' anything, but I plan to bring some flour and cheese. She's makin' those noodles, ya know."

"Oh yes, I know. She's got quite the reputation in these parts for those noodles!"

My mom used to make noodles. Hers were the best in the county. I'll bet that is where Ida Mae learned to fix 'em.

Tig turned to the side window. He could almost smell them stewing in chicken broth on the stovetop. Steam curls of home cooked goodness seeped through the cracks around the windows and out into the snow-packed yard where Tig and Johnnie played until their noses and fingertips were numb. Their mother's noodles were the only thing powerful enough to retrieve them from outside. Carrie Ann would sit across from her sons watching as their cold, red hands held tight to the warm bowls. She delighted in seeing her sons devour her simple, soothe-the-soul concoction. Tig smiled at the thought.

Ron pulled into the driveway of the old homestead. A dim light glowed from the front window.

"I contacted them earlier this week. They said it wouldn't be a problem at all. Ya go ahead, Tig. I'll wait here."

Ron sat in the truck watching through ice crystals gathering on the window as Tig slogged through the snow to the small pasture and on through the gate. He leaned against the fence that surrounded the small cemetery. The oak tree that had for so long guarded the graves was barely hanging on. Its weathered limbs were heavy, burdened with snow. Tig took a bandana from his pocket and wiped off the stones.

"Mom, Dad, well it looks like I'm gonna make it out here on my own. I didn't think I could survive without Dottie and the kids.... I guess I'm stronger than I thought. I've got good friends here. The Carsons and Ida Mae, they've helped me this whole time through so much. I couldn't ask for better friends. It does get lonely sometimes though. But you'd know all about this, wouldn't ya?"

Tig reached down and ran his fingers over his mother's name.

"I won't be back until spring. I'll bring some wild flowers with me when I come. Maybe they'll let me plant some here."

Tig lifted his head momentarily and glanced down at the house. A small window looked out over the pasture; a flicker of light radiated from somewhere behind the glass. His heart raced back to his and Dottie's first snowfall as newlyweds. They had stood looking out from behind that very window, the one that opened their bedroom to the vastness of the prairie. They were two young lovers marveling over the exquisite winter wonderland stretched out in front of them before climbing back under the covers.

Tig turned back to the gray-as-the-sky tombstones in front of him. *I just have to get through this winter first.*

———

The snow had cleared by Thanksgiving. Ida Mae was waiting by the front window. She spied Tig trudging down the frozen dirt road toward her house. He was carrying a bag of flour and a large hunk of cheese wrapped in paper.

Not long after he arrived, Ron and Linda made their entrance. Linda worked with Ida Mae in the kitchen, while Tig and Ron sat in the front room talking. A roaring fire added to the warmth that radiated throughout the house. The strong comforting scent of turkey and stuffing made Tig's stomach growl. Several times, the sound emanating from Tig's gut was so loud the men laughed.

"Tig, I brought ya some old magazines. I think you'll enjoy lookin' at 'em."

"Thanks, Ron. That'll give me somethin' to do this winter."

"Tig, I've been meanin' to ask. Have ya heard anything back from Effie? I mean those letters you've written. Any word?"

Tig looked down and sighed. "No, not a word."

"I'm so sorry, Tig. I shouldn't have asked. I just thought...."

"It's OK. I didn't expect to hear from her, especially since she's livin' with Dottie. I'm gonna keep on writin', though. Maybe sooner or later...."

Ron clearly did not understand the full conversation, but his respect for Tig continued to grow.

––––––

That evening after a satisfying dinner with friends, Ron drove Tig back up to the house. "Thank ya, Ron...." Tig paused. "I don't think I've ever had a better friend."

Ron reached over and caught Tig by surprise when he shook his hand. "It's been my pleasure, Tig."

Tig climbed out of the cab with a paper sack containing a pie plate of leftovers and a mason jar full of noodles. Ron smiled as he drove all the way back down the drive.

Tig stirred the embers and threw a new log in the wood stove. He snatched a piece of pie from the leftovers plate and carried it with a cup of coffee over to his shabby arm chair. Next to him on the floor sat the stack of magazines. He picked up one to look it over, when he suddenly set it back down and got up. Tig walked to his bedroom and pulled the quilt from his cot. Settling back down in his chair, he pulled the handmade covering up over his lap.

Other than to note the pattern, Tig had never really studied the quilt before. Under the soft light, the stitches revealed the craftsmanship. It captured his attention. The colors represented those of the prairie, all the shades resonating with the land: sienna, ochre, beige, sage, cream, terracotta, and soft blue. *Obviously, these small pieces of fabric were carefully selected.* Each piece of cloth had been meticulously cut and sewn together by hand. The calico triangles repeated over the entire surface of the blanket's topside, coming together to form a single large star. Around each small patch were lines made up of tiny dots of white thread. Each stitch was perfectly measured and spaced, the tension between each piece of thread the same.

This is likely the most valuable thing I own. Tig pulled it up over his torso and indulged himself with a piece of Ida Mae's fresh apple pie. He set the plate down and settled back in the arm chair. The exquisitely crafted quilt, an heirloom, lay draped over his lap. He propped his feet up on a bucket, drank his coffee and perused a used magazine. Gazing at the glowing embers, Tig mulled over the events of the day, and he felt like a very rich man.

———

December brought more snow. The first few inches barely covered the stubble, but the temperatures were so cold the snow never melted. When the second blast of cold air shot down from the north, it ran into a warm front rising from the Gulf. The two air masses met over the top of Tig's house. The clouds heaved sheets of rain that froze upon contact. All night long the trees heaved and cracked, the tortured sounds of nature so haunting Tig could not sleep. He sat in his dark house watching from the window. The next morning, layers of shiny glaze encased everything the rain had touched, as gorgeous as it was treacherous. Even walking was hazardous. The ice made a precarious infrastructure for the next snowstorm which arrived two days later, when layers of gray clouds claimed the sky and dropped eight inches of heavy wet snow.

With enough wood and food supplies, Tig decided to wait it out. With the exception of tending to emergencies, such as using broken branches and a shovel to continually knock the snow and icicles from the roof, Tig stayed holed up in his house. The conditions prevented his weekly visits with Ida Mae, who was also staying put until weather conditions improved. Trips to Arvita were discouraged since business across Talgart and Dawson counties had been brought to a halt. Ron was preoccupied with keeping the cattle cared for in such unforgiving conditions, so he only stopped by to see Tig a few times.

His visits were limited to brief checks on Tig's welfare. He would drop off a few food items, some eggs, milk or bread and head straight back to the ranch.

As the month progressed, Linda became concerned Tig would be spending Christmas alone. She implored Ron to speak with Tig about the matter.

The week before Christmas, Ron skidded up Tig's drive, snow and ice packed solid under his tires. The mid-morning sun was bright but deceptive, for the rays of blinding light bouncing off the snow possessed no warmth. Tig had just put water on for coffee when he heard the truck door shut. Tig ushered Ron through the door and pulled a chair out from the table. Ron was pleasantly surprised at how snug and warm the little house had stayed despite the unyielding frigid temperatures outside.

"How about a fried egg sandwich? I was just fixin' to make one for myself. Wouldn't be any more work to make two."

Ron started to decline but saw the eagerness in Tig's expression. Ron realized he needed to accept Tig's hospitality as much as Tig needed to offer it.

"Sure. Sounds great."

Tig turned the crackling eggs while Ron shared his and Linda's concerns about the holidays.

"She just doesn't want ya sittin' up here all by yourself over the holidays. Tig, I don't understand why ya won't just join us for Christmas. I can come and pick ya up."

"Ron, I realize what Linda is tryin' to do, and I appreciate it. I know you'll have your family there, your kids. I just don't think I'm ready for that. I doubt I'll ever be."

Tig's expression changed, enough to disturb Ron. "There are just so many holidays in the past that…."

"No need to go further, Tig. I understand. I know Linda will be disappointed, but she'll also understand. We never want to force ya to do anything that would make ya uncomfortable. Ya mean too much to us."

At first Tig looked confused. Then his face broke into a smile. "Thanks, Ron."

"Now, do ya have enough food to get you through the New Year?"

"I could use a few things."

Tig took a small piece of paper from the shelf. Ron had learned to decipher most of Tig's scrawl. "I'll be runnin' to town before the weekend. I'll gladly pick these things up and drop them off." "

"Thanks, Ron. Here's a twenty. Now let's eat these eggs while they're hot."

————

Christmas Eve was bitter cold and bright. The moon reflected off the snow, backlit and shimmering against a cloudless indigo sky. Tig stood on his front stoop shivering, exhaling clouds, looking to the heavens. Star gazing, he searched for the biggest, the brightest. Tig contemplated the Christmas story. He wondered if he were to find it, the brightest star, could it lead him, a less than wise man, to the child? Tig thought about the infant in the manger, about the baby he had never seen. He recalled images of Virgin Mary holding the swaddled babe. He pictured Effie in his mind, all glowing, enraptured by her infant. *How old would my grandchild be now? Nearly two years old, toddling, speaking? What words would she, would he say? Does the child bear a resemblance to Effie, to me, or maybe to Dottie?*

"Where are you now, Dottie? Are you holding our grandchild in front of a sparkling Christmas tree?"

The frigid air stung his eyes; now blurred, the stars all ran together. Tig turned and walked into his empty house. On the table was a small crèche, a plate of cookies, and a candle that Linda had Ron deliver. Tig lit the candle and sat quietly by the table. The flickering flame comforted his heart but did not alleviate the loneliness.

Maybe I should have accepted Ron's offer, he thought.

————

Gilded light spilled out from the small windows of the church as each parishioner held a single lit candle up into the darkness. Christmas had arrived. Eager families and excited children filed out of the church as Ron gathered his family. Once back at the house, everyone made a beeline for the kitchen. There, Linda had chowder warming up and plates of cookies set on the counters, all ready for the celebration. Everyone huddled in the kitchen except Ron, who ran back and forth from the house with packages in his arms. As he readied to leave, Linda walked out to the truck and stood next to the open window.

"Thanks for understandin', Linda. I shouldn't be long."

"You stay as long as you need, Ron. I'm so proud of you. Give him our love." Linda kissed Ron through the window and stood waving as he drove off.

———

The crush of snow under truck tires was a familiar sound. Tig rose from the table and walked to the door. Ron was just getting out of the truck.

"Merry Christmas, brother!"

Brother? Tig's heart leapt and a smile spread from ear to ear. "Ron, why are ya here and not with your family?"

"Because I needed to be here for a time, to help ya celebrate!"

Ron stood at the door holding an arm full of packages covered with bright paper and sparkling bows. Tig ushered him into the house. They set the packages next to the arm chair. Tig grabbed a chair from the table and was pulling it over when Ron turned to head out the door.

"Wait, aren't ya gonna stay for a bit, at least for a cup of coffee?"

Ron smiled.

"Oh, I'm not leavin'. I just need to grab one more thing from the truck. Ya go ahead and start that coffee. I plan to stay and visit for a while."

Ron pulled the door shut behind him. Tig was so blessed his throat tightened. *What a great friend.*

A scuffling sound came from just outside on the stoop, then a whack on the door.

"Ron, ya don't have to knock again…."

Tig's words were captured mid-air as he stood speechless in front of the open door. Ron was grinning, while the bright-eyed puppy in his arms squirmed to get down.

"Merry Christmas, Tig!"

FIFTEEN

Tig named his pup Spur. When Ron asked why he gave his dog that name, Tig replied, "He just gives me a reason to get up and go."

The eight-week-old—a spotted mutt, part retriever, part boxer—immediately took to Tig. He was a smart whelp, and he trained easily, except with regard to the bed. Every night, Tig would give Spur a dog biscuit and settle him down on the floor at the foot of the cot. Every morning, Tig would awaken with the weight of his dog on top of his feet. The fact that the cot was not large enough for the two of them made no difference to Spur. He lay flopped on the quilt with his paws hanging off the edge.

During the cold months of winter, Tig spent many hours sitting on the floor with Spur playing tug-o-war with an old sock. Sometimes, the two would wrestle in reckless abandon, toppling chairs and spreading magazines across the linoleum. Tig would ultimately laugh until he cried at his dog's stubborn determination.

Boundless energy coupled with a puppy's need to chew made Spur something of a menace. It certainly put Tig's meager furnishings at risk. Spur wanted to chew on everything. Tig was always after him when he caught him gnawing on the legs of the table, the chairs, and the cot. One night, Tig came back in from the outhouse to discover his dog had found the holes in the arm chair. Tufts of cotton wadding were spread all over the house. Tig intermittently laughed and then scolded Spur, who jumped around excitedly. It became a game for Spur to grab hold of each piece of soft fluff Tig attempted to poke back into the chair.

Spur would generally sit under the table while Tig ate. Every so often, Tig would reach down with a piece of bread or meat, which Spur would swallow whole. His tail wagged so hard the plates skipped across the table top and the coffee would slosh out of the cup. Tig would talk to Spur about everything, and Spur was content to listen. Every evening after supper, he happily curled up next to his master in the arm chair. The two sat like old friends, warming themselves by the wood stove. With Spur by his side, Tig's loneliness abated. He still desperately longed for his family, but believed he finally had someone with whom to share his disappointments.

———

Spring found Tig and Spur outside roaming the fields, the woods, and Dump Canyon together. Spur went everywhere Tig went, including the sanctuary. A piece of rawhide or an empty peanut butter jar was all that was needed to keep Spur occupied until Tig was ready to leave. As Tig would turn to pass through the cedars, Spur would pick up what remained of his treat and follow him out.

Ron and Tig were planning an autumn hunting trip, so Tig felt the need to initiate Spur's field training. The dog had no problem in the retrieving department. No matter what Tig would throw, Spur would come bounding back with it held loosely in his mouth. Knotted socks and an old baseball once belonging to Ron's son became the favorite fetching items. However, Spur needed to become accustomed to the sound of the gun. Tig started by randomly hitting pieces of old metal with a hammer when Spur was distracted. The first time Tig did this, Spur jumped back and began to bark incessantly. After several daily episodes of this noisemaking event, Spur became used to the sound. So, on a cool April morning, Tig decided it was time to test Spur against the sound of the rifle.

Tig stood rifle in hand, dog by his side. "Stay, Spur."

Spur sat looking up his master, having learned this meant he was to remain still until Tig released him. Tig raised the gun and took one shot. KA-POW. Zing-whiz. The bullet struck the can, propelling it spinning into the air. Tig lowered the gun. Spur had not moved.

"Fetch, Spur!"

Spur took off in the direction of the sawhorse and came bolting back with a stick in his mouth. *This is going to take some work.*

He reached down and scratched Spur behind the ears.

"You stayed put while I shot the gun. Good boy, Spur. You've still got more to learn before I take ya huntin', but this'll do for now. Let's go get ya a treat."

Spur was so excited that the entire back half of his body wagged.

Spur was never on a leash. It was not needed, since he was so well trained. When out walking, he never wandered beyond Tig's line of sight. Whenever Tig let Spur out of the house to do his business, he would come back and sit on the front stoop waiting for Tig to let him in. Ida Mae gained Spur's approval with the first ham-hock she offered him.

Just the mention of her name would send Spur into a happy dog dance around Tig's feet. Spur always accompanied Tig to Ida Mae's, where he would sit on the front porch sleeping or watching birds flit across the fields. Whenever Spur heard Tig and Ida Mae coming toward the door, he acted as though he had not seen them for weeks. Spur's entire body would shake, and at times, he could not restrain himself from howling with excitement. This was the same response he would have when he saw the familiar red truck bobbing up the driveway. Spur made a beeline for Ron, circling him, tail wagging, sniffing Ron's crotch and generally just making a happy nuisance of himself.

"How are ya, Spur?"

Ron bent over and rubbed the dog's head with both his hands.

"He's growin' so fast. He has to be pushin' sixty pounds by now. What a good lookin' dog ya are, Spur!"

Spur's tongue flopped back and forth as he panted with delight.

"He's figured out how to fetch when I shoot. He brought back a squirrel for me the other day."

"Is that so? Well then, I guess we'll be ready to take him huntin' with us this fall."

"We did have an incident though. Spur's convinced skunks are cats he can actually catch."

"Oh no…. He didn't?"

"I wish I could tell ya that, but he did, and it has taken me nearly two weeks to get the smell off of 'im. He got down in Dump Canyon after a rain and chased down a young one. Ya could smell that stench for miles and for days!"

Ron was laughing out loud at his mental picture of the whole event.

"I made him follow me up here and get into the tub. I scrubbed him down for well on an hour. That night, I made him stay outside. First time I ever tethered that dog. Tied him to the hedge apple tree. He howled all night. Kept everything breathin' awake. But I made him stay out there. I just couldn't let him in. He reeked so bad, likely woulda made me sick!"

Tig screwed up his face. It was so ridiculous looking that it triggered Ron's funny bone. He laughed so hard his eyes began to water.

"I did everythin' I could think of to rid that smell. I even rubbed cedar branches on him, hopin' the oil would cover that foul odor. Nothin' worked, save lettin' it just wear off."

Tig and Spur were devoted to each other, and everyone knew it. All the myths circling around town about Tig now included his constant companion, a lovable yet protective hound. The Fox Creek ladies were always on top of the developments. Tig mused how they must have approved of Spur because care packages occasionally included dog biscuits or a squeaky toy.

————

Since the delivery of the quilt, baskets were left for Tig every three weeks like clockwork. They were always placed in the same location by the windmill. Tig appreciated the thoughtful donations left for him. As far as he was concerned, cans of fruit cocktail, packages of fancy soup, hand lotion, and chocolate were specialty items. There were also boxes containing much needed supplies like aspirin and Ben Gay. They were greatly relished, particularly because Tig would never have been able to purchase them. He began to notice the gifts were also becoming increasingly personal. Once, he found a bottle of shaving lotion rolled up in a washcloth. Another time, he was given a pair of new socks, then a new belt and suspenders. Tig was insistent about relating his gratitude, so Ida Mae and Linda faithfully passed along his appreciation to the Fox Creek Ladies.

———

Tig continued to write Effie. After a year of weekly letters, he decided to cut back and write only two times a month. He had not received one letter back in response, but this had no bearing on his decision to limit his letters. He and Ida Mae both felt that if he were to write less frequently, he would have more to say. Tig wanted desperately to hear back from Effie, but he never expected he would.

When he had last saw her, he had made it all too clear he wanted nothing to do with her. His letter writing had become more an act of restitution than anything else. So he and Ida Mae continued to write. He wrote to Effie about Ron and Linda, Ida Mae and Spur, and all his adventures, the wild beauty of the prairie, and the peace found amidst cedar sentinels in the sanctuary.

Tig's letters were the sum of his days, a journal written two or three pages at a time for his daughter. He would carry each letter back up to his house, where he would place it on the table in clear view until Ron came. Trips to the Post Office were tagged onto the supply runs into Arvita.

Every two to three weeks, Tig would hand Ron a twenty-dollar bill, a small supply list and his letters to Effie. Both Ron and Ida Mae were overwhelmed by Tig's tenacity, his unyielding commitment to writing his daughter. Likewise, all of Tig's friends were saddened that he had not heard back.

———

News traveled quickly, especially if it had a bit of titillating gossip potential attached to it. Sometimes the community, particularly the Fox Creek Ladies, knew more about current events surrounding Tig's life than he knew himself.

This was brought to his attention on a June afternoon while sitting across from Ida Mae's open kitchen window. Tig was enjoying the scenery as Ida Mae arranged glasses of lemonade on a tray. She turned and set the tray down gently on the table. Her movements were more an act of reluctance than that of concern for her sparkling Depression glassware.

Tig looked through the soft green glass holding the pale yellow liquid and out to the fields. The colors mixed together and strangely mimicked the color of the pasture with its copious yellow wildflowers. The warm breeze wafted their sweet ginger scent through the kitchen window.

Tig had been coming once a week for three years to assist Ida Mae with chores around her place, her land. He had never accepted a single dollar for his work. The companionship, food gifts, and Ida Mae's continued support in drafting letters to his daughter were compensation enough.

Besides, visiting Ida Mae was a pleasant reprieve from the struggles of his rather primitive lifestyle. She kept a clean, comfortable home and had a flair for hospitality. He enjoyed her soft upholstered cushions and the oily sheen on her mahogany furniture. Coupled with her kindness, this nurtured his self-esteem. He knew his time with Ida Mae had engendered a change for the better in him.

For her part, having known Tig's mother, Carrie Ann, Ida Mae felt a particular bond to Tig. With no children of her own to dote over, Ida Mae enjoyed doing things for Tig. She believed Tig living nearby was not a coincidence. He was a gift to her, and she easily accepted him as her own.

Ida Mae looked long and hard at the man sitting at her table. His skin was leathered and cracked. His teeth were stained and chipped. She observed how he ran his chafed, calloused hands over his knee, his joints painfully swollen. Although nearly twenty years his senior, most days Ida Mae appeared younger than Tig. His clothes were mostly clean, but they were threadbare with holes at the seams, knees, and elbows. His felt cowboy hat, sitting next to him on the table, was misshaped and stained with red clay and sweat. His boots and leather gloves were scuffed and discolored. Tig had few earthly possessions and basically no monetary worth. He was a recluse, an indigent, an aging hermit who preferred the music of nature to the sounds of human discourse. *He might well have been a poet*, Ida Mae thought, *a gentle observer of hidden things*. She studied him as he sat mesmerized by the view and her heart ached. He never deserved to end up like this, she thought.

Tig was unaware of Ida Mae's penetrating stare, her pursed lips, the ripples of concern emerging on her brow.

"Tig, before we write today, there is something I need to tell you." Tig looked up startled but smiling.

"Sure, Ida Mae."

"Tig, you know I hear a lot of talk around town and church."

Ida Mae stopped. She looked pained, which caused Tig to lean over the table. "Is everything OK? Are ya OK, Ida Mae?"

She inhaled deeply.

"Tig, you likely would not know this but Clara's best friend, Debra Bailey, still attends Arvita Congregational."

"Dottie's sister, Clara?" Tig shrugged his shoulders as though it made no difference to him.

"Yes. Her best friend. Debra is a member of the Fox Creek Ladies Auxiliary. I guess she and Clara have been staying in touch. It seems she has been talking to Clara about you, sharing with her all the things the women have been doing on your behalf.... "

She paused.

"...Which is clearly against the 'Right hand not knowing what the left hand is doing' rule!" Ida Mae dropped her head and mumbled the last part under her breath in disgust.

Tig's eyes narrowed. "And?"

"Apparently Clara felt Debra needed to know that this past spring... Dottie remarried."

The last two words out of Ida Mae's mouth struck Tig straight through the chest. He turned his eyes to the window and swallowed hard. Ida Mae wished she could take back the words, but it was too late.

Tig had already frozen and sat mute, captive to his thoughts. Ida Mae unobtrusively reached over and placed her hand on his. The two sat in silence for nearly fifteen minutes. Then, Tig turned abruptly as though roused from a deep sleep. He spoke with absolute clarity.

"It's for the best. We need not discuss this again. Now, how about that letter to Effie?"

As Tig was leaving, Ida Mae handed him the sealed envelope along with a small bag of apples. He turned to Spur, who was lying with his legs draped over the edge of the porch.

"Come on, boy."

Spur stood up and ambled off the porch steps following Tig back up the road. Ida Mae stood in the opening, watching until Tig topped the hill. Taking a flowered hankie from her apron, she wiped her eyes before shutting the door.

Tig took a detour on his way back to the house. He turned abruptly and headed into the cedar hollow. Pushing his way through the scrub and past the evergreens, he stood looking down at the sunlit patch in the middle of the clearing.

"I need ya to stay, Spur."

The dog acted on command and lowered his body to the ground. Tig set the bag of apples down and reached for his belt. Never taking his eyes off of Leon's marker, he felt around until his fingers met the sharp edge of the rowel. Ripping it from his belt, he looked down at the object resting in the palm of his hand. He knelt down. Using his fingers, he clawed feverishly into the dirt. In a small depression directly in front of Leon's marker, Tig buried the rowel.

———

Time moved slowly and seamlessly on. At four years, Spur weighed in at close to one hundred pounds. His dangling paws dragged the floor as he spread across the bottom of Tig's cot at night. Spur had worn the delicate quilt triangles paper thin. A dark, dingy stain covered one third of the well-loved blanket, its threads embedded with dirt and dog hair. The quilt had been washed only twice, but its detailed stitches were pulled and frayed in places from constant use. Several patches had started to separate from the rest. None of this bothered Tig. For him, the wear and tear, the stains were proof of Spur's devotion.

With the exception of Spur being added to the mix, nothing much at Tig's house had changed over time. He had not acquired any additional furnishings. Nothing about his trappings would indicate any adjustment in his income. Bits of stained cotton batting extruding from the Naugahyde arm chair continued to vex Spur. The table legs remained etched by Spur's "puppy chewing days." The appliances had gathered a few more scratches, and the kitchen chairs still teetered, their legs never planting evenly on the floor. Although better maintained, Tig's house was as stripped down as it had been the day he arrived, and yet, for Tig, it was as comfortable as an old shoe. He had made it his home.

———

Every spring, Tig would patch the cracks in the walls and wipe the red clay from the floors. He would take the plastic off the windows and tack any loose tin on the roof. The windmill was always inspected after the winter to ensure water drizzled freely from the discharge pipe. He mended the fences and attended to the chores both at his house and at Ida Mae's. Dirt was shoveled from Dump Canyon and used to fill the deepest erosions in the driveway. Tig cleaned seasonal debris out from around the shallow edges of the pond while watching the geese migrate. Using an old screen, he sieved off soggy leaves and algae, which he hauled in buckets to the compost pile. Tig spent hours mixing compost into the soil of his small garden, dropping seeds in the carved dirt rows—beans and tomatoes—and adjusting his rain catchers, old buckets set along the east fence line.

When work was done, Tig would take Spur fishing. They would sit on the highest side of the pond, a lookout over the prairie. Waiting for catfish to bite, they'd watch the murmuration of the starlings over the fields, sweeping movements of visual sky music, individual black notes amassing in crescendos over fields of bright green winter wheat. Down below, a red clay rift weaved through the field filled with spring rain reflecting a perfect cerulean sky. Occasionally, a swift fox dashed between the draws, a streak of golden fur chased by the black tip of his tail.

At times, Spur would take off after a mousy-toned jack-rabbit, scooting unaware through mesquite vine sprouting along the sandy creek bottom. A predictable breeze would sweep across the rolling terrain. It stirred up a dance of gray-green in the tops of the Black Jacks, the breath of air sending their hairy pollen caterpillars to flight, forming soft hills of stringy fiber at the base of the trunk. Bits and pieces cast off by the tall oaks were eagerly picked through and carried off by a congregation of nest builders. Tig and Spur sat enraptured by it all, waiting until dusk before heading home, always wanting to catch the red ball falling, the summoning of nightfall.

————

Summer heat brought endless hours of water bucket lugging. Carrying a five-gallon pail with his good hand, Tig would hike down to the windmill. Not far behind, Spur would sniff things out along the way.

Determined to catch some of the water splashing from the bucket, Spur would position himself directly beneath Tig. Attempting to dodge the dog, Tig would move quickly. Water sloshed up and over the rim. The shifting weight of the bucket sometimes caused Tig to lose his balance and stumble. Waves of water would pour out of the bucket all over Spur. Tig would howl with laughter at Spur, who stood soaked, looking like a wet rat. In turn, Spur would shake with delight sending a shower of water all over Tig, who laughed bent over, holding his gut. The regularity of this sport would have become annoying to Tig had it not been so amusing and refreshing. Ultimately after each episode, the two would traipse back to the house for lunch, sopping wet and remarkably cooled off.

After a bite to eat, Tig normally headed out to work the garden. Spur understood that when Tig went to his knees it was time to play. While Tig weeded the squash and picked tomatoes, Spur would drop his ball in the dirt right under Tig's nose. After throwing the ball several times, Tig would ignore Spur and act disinterested.

At that point, Spur would attempt to bury his ball under the okra stalks. When Tig waved his hat and fussed, Spur understood it as a signal; it was time to play ball again. Spur would gather his muddy ball in his teeth, carry it over and drop it on Tig's feet. This routine took place every time the two visited the garden. Spur never grew tired of it, but in truth, neither did Tig. Rather than shaking his head, Tig would just fill his basket with vegetables, shoo Spur out past the garden gate, and head back to the house. Later, with a glass of iced tea and a bowl of water, Tig and Spur would sit under the shade of the hedge apple tree. Looking out over the pasture, they'd watch the lazy cattle grazing, silver haired grass tickling the under-bellies of Angus as they ambled slowly toward the pond.

Late afternoons were often spent collecting sand plums and wild berries for Ida Mae. Tig and Spur would walk the fence line along Rte. 426 and pick the fruit, shaking a stick around the base of the vines hoping not to be bit or stung by territorial critters living there.

———

In late summer, Tig lugged buckets full of sand plums down the road to Ida Mae's house, his gloves stained crimson. She turned the tart fruit into sweet jam. In return for his gift, Tig was always given six jars of her delicious concoction, a sweet elixir that kept summer alive in the dead of winter. Tig displayed two jars of the ruby preserves on the shelf near his stove. The others he saved and stored under his cot as gifts. Much to their delight, he had surprised Ron and Linda with a jar one Christmas. Ron went on about it so much, Tig continued to hold back a jar for him every year. Tig also passed one along to Ron to give to Dan the barber and requested that one be left at the Post Office.

———

As everything swelled in the mid-day heat, summer afternoons yawned into early evening. After a day of foraging for wild fruit and berries, Tig and Spur hiked back to the house backlit by July's luminous lavender-ruby sky. Halos of gnats swarming around them, they moved unaffected up the hill. On the stoop, Tig would stop and check Spur for ticks, the gentle giant of a dog rolling his eyes in delightful submission.

Once inside, Tig prepared a simple dinner, often fresh tomatoes, cucumbers and okra. As the final light of day dropped below the earth, Spur chewed happily on his ball while Tig sorted through the daily yield from his garden. Spreading the harvest out on the table, Tig separated out what he felt he would use. The excess was divided into two bags. One was offered to Ida Mae to use or share with the Fox Creek Ladies and the other given to Ron to distribute at the church.

Once all had been organized and put away, Tig and Spur would move back out to the front stoop. Tig would stretch out his legs with Spur spread out next to him. There they would sit, in the dark lingering heat of a late summer day, listening to a mourning dove cooing lullabies to restless crickets and cicadas.

"Listen. Ya hear that Spur? The prairie, she's serenadin' us. Yes sir, she is, she surely is."

Tig yielded to the sounds, letting them embrace him with tranquility as he stroked his dog's supple fur. Spur, content, lay snoring at Tig's feet.

———

Hunting trips with Ron were the highlight of every autumn for Tig. Ron would pick Tig and Spur up early, before dawn. Tig always had a cup of coffee and a piece of toast ready for his friend. Ron sat at the humble table and drank Sanka from a steaming chipped mug. Meanwhile, Tig changed into the camouflaged pants and jacket Ron brought for him to use. Ron would rack Tig's rifle above the shot gun behind the seat before the three would eagerly climb into the truck. Spur was as excited as the men, sitting high next to Tig with his nose smearing the glass, determined to wedge it just above the window. The hunting lease was about forty minutes away. This gave Tig and Ron time to talk as they drove. Off they'd go down the road, telling yarns while bands of crystal blue morning sky rose and caressed the horizon.

Tig never shot a deer. His gun was not strong enough to take one down. He wasn't certain he could have shot one anyway. Over the years, he had watched too many gather at the pond to drink. Their eyes, so large and bright, were always watching with an innocent beauty.

He came up on a doe early one morning in the woods near the pond. Tig stood very still and watched the earthen toned mother curl around her spotted newborn fawn. Nested in a pile of leaves, the fragile creature with spindly legs was smaller than Spur. A nearby male was set to flight by the rustling of dried leaves under Tig's boots and the scent of dog. The agility of the animal as it leapt past trees and over splits in the forest floor took Tig's breath away. Tig's aversion to hunting deer kept his excursions with Ron limited to those of the bird or small game variety.

———

The men and dog would walk for hours over the hills, through the draws, along the floors of small canyons, into wooded areas. Spur would run ahead and scare up the quail for Ron, while Tig kept an eye out for squirrels and rabbits.

The cold air against their skin was invigorating. The leaves had changed to deep russets and golden yellow, so that the light distilling through them took on a tint of amber. The broad-leaved trees contrasted against evergreen cedars with golden tips and fire engine red sumacs. By this time of year, the fields were exploding with broomweed, acre upon acre of bright yellow. Along the edges of red dust roads were rows of wild sunflowers and volunteer gourds twisting their way around barbed wire, their plump leathered fruit hanging off shriveled vines.

By mid-day, they would stop to eat. Ron and Tig set out on every hunting trip with the intention of ending up on the river beach for lunch. River water flowed in chiseled out areas in the center of the riverbed, leaving wide caramel-colored beaches on both sides. Spring thunderstorms had toppled diseased trees along the shore, and torrential rains pushed them into the watershed. The excess water dissipated rapidly in the summer heat, leaving the crooked trunks and scraggly branches planted in the sand along the river's edge.

Linda saw to it that each man had a sandwich and two thermoses, one with coffee and one with soup. There was always a special treat for Spur, who planted himself between the two men while they ate. The copious deposits of natural debris positioned around the three accommodated a variety of creatures with more than adequate shelter. Often, wild game would join them. Over the years they saw everything from coyotes, armadillos, lizards, geese, and even an elusive beaver.

Fortunately, Tig would always fire a command to Spur, keeping him from chasing creatures he shouldn't. One time, neither Tig nor Ron saw the armadillo before Spur took off after it. He cornered the armored rascal and ended up getting a nasty scratch across his nose. The armadillo would have taken Spur's eye had Ron not shot the sharp-clawed, leathered grub-eater. The most unexpected lunch-sighting for both men and dog, however, was a wild boar that encouraged them to hastily pack up their lunch and move on.

———

More often than not, their kill didn't amount to much, maybe a squirrel or two, a few rabbits, a half dozen quail, and once a rather scrawny turkey, of which they were rightfully proud. This limited bounty did not seem to bother the men. What they lacked in meat for the freezer, they gained in memories—watching Spur chase a lizard along the beach; tracking the movement of wildlife via fresh prints in the sod; spotting a Road Runner scurry across a back road; listening to a hawk screech overhead; smelling the mix of leaves blended with freshly plowed fields; laughing over the other stepping in fresh manure.

These were the most valued returns from their trips together, memories made by best friends. The drive back was always spent recapping the events of the day. The road home always took them due west directly into the setting sun. Cloud-arrows unfurled and shot bright rays of magenta and deep amethyst through the windshield. They spotlighted Ron and Tig as they recreated their hunting scenarios and laughed. Spur's wet nose was glued to the window of the truck as it rumbled over gravel-covered roads, past fields basking in purple light.

———

Over the course of time, there were the occasional storms, periods of seemingly endless heat and bone-cracking cold. There were hours consumed with visiting good friends, storytelling around a picnic table or in front of a fire. Many days Tig spent alone with his dog at his feet in the quiet, still behind the four walls of his little house. There were dates that awakened painful memories and moments recalled for their lighthearted celebrations. For Tig, it all balanced out over time. The day-to-day rituals of living grew as comfortable as his arm chair, as satisfying as a breath of cool morning air.

———

Tig's trips to the sanctuary continued uninterrupted. Every morning possible, at dawn, before attending to anything else, Tig would push his way through to the hollow. Rain or shine, the haven in the woods would greet him with its sheltered light and oily pungent scent. The light cast on Leon's medal revealed seasons of change, how it had weathered over the years. The etched marks were shaded with patina and had grown darker over time, but the metal blade beaten by hail and strong winds still stood erect.

Tig saw to it. He treated the makeshift memorial like a gravesite. He stabilized the marker when needed and carefully tended to the ground around it. He often carried an extra bandana with him to wipe off any debris or bird droppings. On Leon's birthday, special occasions, or for no other reason than just a desire to feel close to his son, Tig always left something special. He would position an empty peanut butter jar, or a toy taken from a cereal box, some little thing he whittled from wood. He left objects commemorating some of Leon's favorite things. At times, Tig would leave a message scribbled on a scrap piece of paper. Everything was placed on the ground directly under the words "Dear Son."

SIXTEEN

Blinding sun reflected off of the December snow enveloping the prairie. A pair of vibrant cardinals flittered between bush and tree just outside of Tig's frosty windows. The sight of the male's brilliant red body set against the backdrop of white and gray was nothing short of magical, particularly on Christmas Eve. The snow had come hard and fast all morning covering everything in sight.

For the first time in five years, Tig had agreed to attend a Christmas dinner at Ida Mae's house. He had been mulling over his decision for weeks, weighing back and forth if he had made the right choice.

Wiping the frosted glass with his mangled hand, Tig peered through the window as Spur dragged his body lazily off the quilt.

"Well buddy, it's Christmas, and we have a date with Ida Mae."

The minute Spur heard her name, he sprang to life, whining and bouncing around Tig's legs. "Hold on there. We have to get ready first."

Tig glanced out the window again, peering through a small tear in the plastic sheathing. Reluctance was fighting to control his resolve, but Tig was a man of his word, so he dismissed the thought and moved from the window. He heated some water, then poured it from the kettle into a bucket and bathed himself.

He shaved and combed back his hair. He opened a small bottle of shaving lotion which he used only for the most special occasions. He rubbed some under his chin and tucked the bottle back into the closet. He pulled out his weathered jacket along with a new scarf and leather gloves, given to him earlier that year, found in a box near the windmill. He took two jars of jam from under his cot and put one in each pocket. He retrieved a small paper bag from just inside the back door. It was filled with native pecans found and gathered from along the east fence line.

Tig pushed his arms through the sleeves of his coat. This was a sign to Spur that an adventure was forthcoming. Spur's entire body wagged as he anticipated the turning of the doorknob. Tig picked up the sack and opened the door to a blast of cold air, immediately clearing his head.

A bucket overflowing with evergreen cuttings, cedar, mistletoe, sprigs of curly dock, and clusters of sumac berries sat on the stoop. Tig had collected the cuttings for Ida Mae since he knew how much she loved decorating her table. Carrying the sack of pecans under his arm, he took the handle of the bucket and stepped out into the fresh snow, which compressed and crunched under his feet.

"Come, Spur. We're goin' to Ida Mae's."

Spur leapt off the stoop and ran out ahead of Tig, dragging his nose through the white powder. He knew the way, but every few steps he would turn just to make sure Tig was following. The two moved past the stilled windmill and through the whispering trees. Halfway down the drive, they crossed over the culvert, a small string of ice threading through it. A fat raccoon waddled back into the woods as a two tag-playing squirrels sprang limb to limb. They launched clumps of snow, which plopped to the ground, leaving soft divots in the smooth blanket of white. Tig and Spur passed by the brambles and the bushes, each sprawling growth topped with bright snowy caps. Where the driveway merged onto Rte. 426, fresh tire tracks turned and two narrow ditches led the way to Ida Mae's house.

"Looks like Ron and Linda have beaten us over here, Spur."

Tig and Spur sloshed their way to the house, the snowy tread marks oozing red mud.

"Merry Christmas, Tig!"

Ida Mae's face lit up. She stood in the open door with her red apron, blushed cheeks, blue eyes, and her soft silver white hair. She could have passed as Mrs. Claus.

"Why don't you take Spur around to the back door? He can stay in the kitchen today."

Ron was waiting at the back to let Tig and Spur in. Ron and and Linda's married children were all at their in-laws, so knowing her friends would all be alone, Ida Mae planned a Christmas Eve dinner at her house.

Ron reached for Tig's coat as he came through the pantry. "So good to see ya, friend. Merry Christmas!"

Tig smiled and returned the greeting with a hearty handshake.

Ida Mae had gone back to tending to the stove, and Linda was preparing potatoes. Tig took a deep whiff. "Is that ham I'm smellin'? Mercy, that smells good!" Tig made a face that made Ron laugh.

As Tig turned the corner from the kitchen, he saw the Christmas tree. The evergreen was lit with colored lights and sparsely decorated. He walked over and set his jars of jam and the bag of pecans down. A fire crackled in the hearth; above it on the mantle was a bough of holly. He stepped back to take it all in.

This was the first Christmas tree Tig had seen since before the accident. There had been so many others before that. He suddenly flashed back to an image of Effie, just a toddler reaching for the shiny glass ornaments on the little tree he and Dottie had placed in the living room of their first home. He had picked his little girl up and held her close, letting her chubby little fingers sweep over the prickly needles. She had squealed with delight. Dottie and Tig had joined in... and then Leon.... Leon. The nostalgia caught Tig off guard and stung the deep recesses in his heart. He suddenly felt lightheaded and terribly homesick, but could not determine for where or for whom. Ron caught the faraway look in Tig's eyes.

"Can I get ya a glass of punch?"

Tig's legs went weak and he sat down. "Sure."

He was beginning to regret his decision to come when he heard Linda and Ida Mae laughing. They were arranging boughs of green in the center of the dining room table. Tig's old bucket sat on the floor next to the polished mahogany legs of the table. Tig stepped into the dining room just as Ida Mae pulled out a sprig of deep red sumac Tig had dried for her.

"Oh Tig, these are absolutely beautiful!"

She held it up in front of her eyes and sighed. "Frank used to do this for me."

Ida Mae's tone softened and her countenance dropped as she recalled the memory.

Tig felt his feelings being echoed by hers. He realized she, like him, like everyone, has places inside, areas in the heart that memories fill. Only the most sacred of recollections permeate the deepest regions of loneliness and heartbreak. He knew these types of memories. These are the most vivid of remembrances. They are illuminated by the fire of loss, by what could never be—they burn, they cauterize. This is what healing and mending a broken heart requires, that one not be afraid to face the memories. Tig understood.

"Tig, thank you for these cuttings. This means so much to me!"

"You're welcome, Ida Mae. I'm glad ya like 'em."

———

The meal was a feast, one that Tig would long remember. The conversation and laughter around the table was so much more than could have been hoped for. Later in the afternoon, presents were opened. Tig gave the pecans to Ida Mae, who went on about all the ways she would use them. Ron and Linda gave Ida Mae a cut glass candy dish filled with chocolates. She oohed with delight. As the dish was passed around, Tig handed Ron and Linda each a jar of jam. Ron grinned and snatched Linda's jam from her hands. The two commenced in a playful tug-a-war. Ida Mae gave everyone homemade fruit cakes wrapped in wax paper and tied with red ribbon. Tig held it to his nose and inhaled deeply, reflecting on how long he could make the treat last. Then, Ron took an odd shaped package out from under the tree and handed it to Tig.

"This is from Linda and me. Just be careful openin' it."

It was a shiny new saw, something Tig had needed for a long time. "This will be well-used, Ron, Linda. Thanks!" Tig beamed.

Finally Ron pulled out a big box covered in wrapping paper. He set it on the kitchen floor in front of Spur. They all laughed as the dog tore into the paper, obviously smelling the homemade dog biscuits hidden inside.

While Ron and Tig were still chuckling over Spur, Linda and Ida Mae set a chocolate red velvet cake with cream cheese frosting out on the table. Fluffy peaks covered the cake like waves of Christmas snow. Everyone hovered around the table as Linda let the knife glide through the cake, the blade clinking against the plate after each slice. Thick pieces were set on porcelain Christmas plates. Ida Mae and Linda carried the cake and coffee into the living room as they all gathered around the Christmas tree. Tongues of fire shot up between two logs, hissing and crackling while embers glowed from beneath. Tig brought his fork up to his mouth and closed his eyes. The creamy frosting combined with the dense rich chocolate was a taste so divine he wished for it, for all the memories of the day, to linger.

———

The knock at the door startled the guests but apparently did not surprise Ida Mae. She was expecting the unannounced visitor. Everyone stood up as Ida Mae answered the door. Standing in the opening was a tall, dark haired young man.

"Oh, Jeffrey, hello. Thank you for coming out on Christmas Eve. Do come in and let me introduce you to everyone."

The stranger stepped into the entryway and took his hat and gloves off.

"Ron, Linda, Tig—this is Jeffrey Hudson. He and his wife just bought your folks' old place, Tig. I wanted you to meet him since I know you go there to pay your respects."

"Hello."

Tig reached out his hand.

"I'd heard someone bought the ole' Mills place," Ron chirped.

Tig rolled the words over in his head—*The ole' Mills place*. It sounded so odd.

"Where'd ya move from?" Ron asked.

"My wife, Lynn, and I, we moved from down near the Texas border. Been workin' on the house for several months. Just finished in time to move the family in before Christmas."

Workin' on the house? "What ya doin' to it? I haven't been down there in a while, but I don't recall seein' any changes."

Tig was eager to know what had been done to his childhood home.

"Oh we've just been updatin' it some. Most of the work has been on the inside, so it wouldn't've been noticeable. Last couple months, we've added on some more space."

"Why that sounds wonderful, Jeffrey," Ida Mae smiled. The young man, slightly embarrassed, lowered his eyes.

"I knew everyone would be here and I wanted Jeffrey to meet you. I met his wife last week at an Auxiliary meeting. Oh yes, that reminds me what you came for. If you will please excuse me?"

Ida Mae scurried out of the room. It would have been terribly awkward had Ron not spoken up. "So what kind of work do ya do, Jeffrey?"

"I am an electrician by trade. I've applied for a job at Milford Electric, in Arvita."

"Yes, I know the company. They've done some work for a friend of mine, Butch Ross. Yeah, worked on his ranch. He speaks well of the company."

Ida Mae came back into the room with a box in her arms, which she handed to Jeffrey.

"OK. Well, here you go. I know she needed them soon. I hope these will work for her. She may need to cut them before she starts her class. Please tell her how much I appreciate her invitation. I'll not be able to attend this time, but I hope to be there next month. I can catch up then."

Ida smiled as Jeffrey took the box.

"Oh, and would you also please take this fruit cake back to your lovely family?" Ida Mae reached over and picked up an extra fruit cake setting on the hall table. "Please tell Lynn I look forward to getting to know her better."

"Thank you, I will. Merry Christmas!"

Everyone in the room returned the gesture, wishing the young man a wonderful holiday as he turned to leave. As he was going through the door, he turned back to Tig.

"Sir, you are welcome to visit the cemetery anytime you wish."

SEVENTEEN

R on pulled the truck up in the drive, and Tig slid out of the cab. "Stay, Spur. I'll be right back."

Ron sat quietly reading a newspaper. Spur sat at his side while Tig sloshed through the early spring snow to the small cemetery. It was the beginning of March and his first visit to his parent's graves in nearly six months. The winter had been exceptionally cold and wet, making the trek to the cemetery a burden, particularly on Ron whose cattle needed his full support.

While Tig walked back to the truck, he noticed the changes Jeffrey mentioned had been made to the house. The back had been extended out a few feet. Where the small dining room window used to be there was now a bay window that curved out from the front of the house. An attached garage stood where the carport used to be. Tig was pleased to see the rose bushes were still where his mother had planted them.

There was one small addition that brought a smile—a single rope swing with a tire attached hung from the Sycamore behind the house. Tig was thankful there were children living in the house again. He had been told the house had not seen children since he and Dottie moved to California.

He was still smiling when he pulled himself up into the truck. "Looks like they're doin' a good job on the place."

"Yeah, it sure does. By the way, I heard from Butch that Jeffrey here got hired at Milford. He must be pretty good 'cause they only hire the best."

As they backed out onto the road, Ron pointed out a small painted sign at the corner of the driveway. "Hey Tig, look at that!"

The sign read, "The Original Mills' Homestead." Tig was elated. As they headed back up Rte. 426, Tig thought, *I might just have to add Jeffrey Hudson to my list of friends.*

———

Once all the snow melted, the clouds withheld crucial spring rain, and the prairie began to dry up. Most of April and May were relatively arid. The seasonal drought played havoc with crops throughout Talgart and Dawson. Weather in northwest Oklahoma was known to change in an instant, and long seasons of no moisture could be abruptly met by angry thunderstorms and torrential downpours.

This is exactly what happened. For nearly the entire month of June, it rained every third day, the purging clouds soaking, saturating, and attempting to drown the prairie.

———

By late-June, water lay stagnant in Ida Mae's fields and filled the deep erosions in Tig's driveway with red slurry. The sanctuary was covered with a half inch of water. The small stream that trickled through the culvert into Dump Canyon had grown into a racing brook. It jumped its banks and sent water coursing downstream. The excess flooded the pond. Elms, oaks, and sycamores stood with their root-feet covered with muddy water.

Mallards and Canadian geese were swimming in the fields just west of the house. The trough and rain buckets were full, but the water was not needed for the garden. It had enough of its own, so much that the tomatoes and cucumbers had drowned.

Rain water seeped through the roof into every room of Tig's house. In a constant battle to keep the floor dry, Tig set pans and pails in strategic locations to catch the leaking water. Although frequently rotated, they were unsuccessful. The drips continued to plague him, playing "catch me if you can" with the buckets. In the end, the dribbling water won and gathered in puddles collecting mold. This set off an allergic reaction reaction in Tig. His lungs filled with congestion causing frequent bouts of painful hacking.

Water sitting in the ditches and draws became hotbeds for the rapidly multiplying mosquito and fly population. Tig bailed water from every place he spotted it collecting, striving to keep the mosquito larvae to a minimum. Spur was always muddy. After three attempts to clean him off in the tub, only so he could roll in the muck again, Tig gave up. Spur ran around with mud caked to his fur. Everything, including his dog, was a soggy, sloppy mess.

———

Summer did not wait for things to dry up. The soaring temperatures in late July sucked the moisture from the earth, resulting in dense unbearable humidity. The air was so thick, Tig could wring the sweat out of his shirt after spending thirty minutes outdoors. For Tig, there was no sleep to be had at night. Between his nasty cough, the plague of mosquitoes and the wet heat, getting chores done was nearly impossible. The heat drained every ounce of his energy. He felt weak all the time.

Tig and Spur were sluggish and sedentary, reserving energy just to manage the sultry days. After a morning of diminishing returns in the garden, Tig sat with Spur on the front stoop dipping bandanas in cool water. He was rolling one up to place on the back of his neck when the sound of spinning tires buffing packed clay caught his attention.

Spur got to his feet and fired out a warning bark. Tig rose to study the mud-covered beige pickup bobbing and sloshing up the drive. The truck was unfamiliar. The afternoon sun was throwing a glare on the windshield, hiding the driver. Tig carefully cracked open the door behind him, his rifle leaning in the corner at the ready. Tig wondered who would possibly be visiting at this time of day in the middle of the week. The only vehicle in five years that had ever driven up the driveway was Ron's... and Johnnie's.

As the truck pulled around in front of the house, Spur started wagging his tail, giddy with excitement, certain someone had come to see him. The truck pulled to a stop, and the door opened. Tig placed his hand on Spur's head and gave a stern command.

"Stay, Spur. Sit."

"That's quite an obedient mutt you've got there, li'l brother."

"His name is Spur. What do ya want, Johnnie?"

"Now is this any way to treat your brother? I drove all the way out here just to see ya, Tig. Are ya gonna ask me in or not?"

"What do ya want?"

"I've got news for ya. How 'bout we talk over a glass of water? I'm parched. This damn place never changes. Summers still hot as Hell."

Tig opened the door and ushered his brother in. Johnnie sat down at the table while Tig poured the water.

"I'd like to say I like what you've done with the place, but it doesn't look any different than when I left. 'Cept maybe for the water on the floor."

Johnnie laughed sarcastically. Tig saw no humor in anything Johnnie said. He was certain Johnnie had an agenda, and he would get to it sooner or later. Tig was hoping it would be sooner. *Get to it, Johnnie and leave* was all Tig could think as he set the water in front of his ruthless brother.

Tig's veins were filling with the blood of anger; it pulsed up his neck and pounded in his head. Dark feelings began to rise up in him, ones Tig had long since laid to rest. But just the presence of his brother resurrected them afresh.

He swallowed hard. *God let me be merciful,* he thought. Tig knew nothing good could come from entertaining thoughts of revenge. He would never be able to change Johnnie.

Only Johnnie had the power to change himself, and he clearly wasn't interested.

Johnnie jabbered on about all his adventures in Las Vegas, as if Tig did not know it was his money and Carolyn's savings he had squandered. Tig sat mute while his half-drunk brother blathered on.

As Tig half listened, he was seized by how Johnnie was nearly unrecognizable. His brother was wearing the effects of his reckless selfishness, the evidence of his depraved life. Johnnie had lost weight; his knuckles and wrist bones protruded and stretched into long bony fingers. Deep worry lines were chiseled into his forehead. There were furrows at the sides of his nose and hatch marks all around his puckered mouth. His eyes were sunken with dark circles beneath them, but it was Johnnie's pupils that were most alarming. Once dark and deep, full of lust for discovery and adventure, they were now hollow looking and void.

Sadness drained the hot blood from Tig's pounding temples and concern washed over him. Tig was jarred by his sudden sense of compassion. The vacuous look on his brother's face, Johnnie's present condition, clenched Tig's heart and softened his resolve. His brother was broken.

"Are ya hungry, Johnnie?"

"Huh?"

"I was askin' if you're hungry."

"I can make us a baked bean sandwich. Ya know, the kind we used to have when we were kids?"

Johnnie didn't know where to put Tig's kindness.

"Ah, sure sounds great. Not much more on the menu, I imagine." Johnnie smirked.

Tig shrugged and laughed it off.

"Nope. That'd be at the diner ya passed an hour ago."

Johnnie chortled, surprised by Tig's wit.

While Tig made sandwiches, Johnnie ran outside. Tig thought his brother had gone to the outhouse, but as he turned to set the food down, he noticed Johnnie drinking from a bottle he had pulled out from under the seat. Tig sighed and set the plates on the table.

For a brief time, there was a sense of connection between the two as they sat at the little table eating bean sandwiches. Johnnie talked on, and Tig listened and nodded. Johnnie never once asked about Tig how he was or how he had survived the last five years. Tig was aware of Johnnie's lack of interest, but it really didn't matter to Tig anymore.

During the lunch, Spur had taken his place under the table and was pressing against Johnnie's legs.

"Tig, get that mutt off'a me!"

Johnnie reached down to swat Spur, but Tig was ahead of him and had already gotten Spur to move out from between the table legs.

"I suppose ya heard Dottie remarried."

Tig dropped his head. *Of course Johnnie would have to bring this up.* "Yes, I know all about it."

"She lives in a fancy house in northern Oregon. A place like that, yeah she must have gotten some big money from the insurance company, Leon's death an' all."

"I wouldn't know, Johnnie."

"How could ya not know? If she got anythin', ya would've gotten some too. So what did ya do with it, Tig?"

"I have no idea what you're talkin' about, Johnnie. Can ya please just drop it?"

Johnnie went dark.

"The Hell ya don't, Tig. I'll find out. Be sure of it. Some of that money is rightfully mine. Dottie signed ya over to my care, so I'm due."

"Johnnie, does it look like I have come into some money? There isn't any."

Tig invited Johnnie to join him on his afternoon walk down to the pond and along the fence line. Tig figured the air would do his brother good or at least get him off the subject. Tig remembered he needed to go and inspect the fences. He would have put it off, but he couldn't stand to be stuck in the house one more minute with his drunken brother. Johnnie declined, stating it was way too hot, and he would rather rest. He mentioned he planned to stay one night and head back out the next morning.

Tig hoped an afternoon nap would facilitate an earlier departure. Johnnie's history of thievery did cross Tig's mind, but he quickly dismissed the thought since there was nothing left for Johnnie to steal. Tig didn't own anything of any value, save the quilt which was dirty and nearly worn-out.

Tig never kept any money at the house. His meager disability checks paid for a few groceries, dog food, propane, and a few extra items on a rare occasion. There was never any extra to stash away. Besides, Tig did not want his brother staying the night, and if that meant leaving Johnnie alone for an hour in the house to rest... so be it.

———

Tig and Spur headed out together, while Johnnie made himself comfortable in the arm chair. Shortly after Tig pulled the door behind him, Johnnie was up stalking his brother from the window. As soon as Tig was out of sight, Johnnie scoured the house. In the bottom of Tig's closet was a bank book. Johnnie opened it greedily, certain he had found what he sought after. He caressingly carried it out to the table. Sitting down, hoping to savor the moment, he opened the cover to expose an empty ledger—nothing.

In anger he hurled a glass against the wall. Shards flew everywhere. *He must have hidden it or buried it*, Johnnie thought. He tore the stuffing out of the arm chair and ripped through Tig's clothes. He went through everything Tig had, upturned the furniture, and pulled the shelves off the wall.

Exasperated, he picked up Tig's gun. *This will be worth something*. Rifle in hand, Johnnie stormed outside in frustration. He threw the gun onto the front seat of his truck and in exchange grabbed two bottles of whiskey. Back in the house, Johnnie grabbed a bottle and settled into what was left of the arm chair.

———

Tig and Spur were back from their rounds within the hour. Tig opened his front door and stepped in. Bits of glass crunched under his feet. He stopped short and immediately threw out his arm restraining Spur.

"Stay here, boy."

Spur waited on the stoop as Tig stepped back in. Standing just inside the door, Tig took a look around, his mouth gaping open. His house had been ransacked. Johnnie was asleep, a near empty bottle of liquor in his lap. Tig walked over and shook him hard.

"Johnnie! John-ee!"

"What the hell! Ya tryin' to give me a heart attack, li'l brother?"

Tig, still strong as an ox, especially when he was angry, grabbed Johnnie by his shirt and pulled him to his feet.

"I want ya out of here, now. Do ya hear me? Now!"

"Sure, Tig, if that's the way ya want it. But you're not gonna keep me from what I'm due. I'll find that money you're hiding from me. It's rightfully mine, ya know?"

Johnnie was clearly inebriated, but Tig did not give it a second thought. He put his knuckles to Johnnie's back and pushed him out of the door, across the drive, and up against the truck. Holding his clenched fist to Johnnie's throat, he narrowed his eyes.

"Don't ya ever come back around here again! Do ya hear me?"

The anger in Tig's eyes, coupled with his raw strength, was frightening.

"Sure, li'l brother, if that's the way ya want it, Te-ga."

Johnnie fell into the truck and fumbled for his keys. He started the ignition, pulled the truck around, and turned to head back down the drive. He drove as far as the windmill and stopped suddenly. He leaned out of his window and yelled, "Spur, here boy!"

Spur took off running. Tig was too stunned to respond quickly enough. Within seconds Spur was coming up alongside Johnnie's truck.

Everything moved in slow motion.

Johnnie's head disappeared, and in an instant, he leaned back out again, this time with Tig's rifle in his hands. He took one shot at close range. Spur went limp and dropped to the ground.

"That'll suit ya, ya stupid mutt. Told ya I'd get mine, Tig."

In that instant, for Tig, there was not enough oxygen to sustain him. He gasped for air. He could not make a sound. Johnnie put the truck in gear and sped down the drive. Tig clamped his teeth and tightened his jaw. He reached down and methodically pulled the handgun from his boot. Steadying it with his right hand, he took aim and fired two shots, low, at the back tires of Johnnie's truck.

The truck swerved and careened down the last few yards of the driveway. Turning recklessly onto Rte. 426, it skidded and swayed as Johnnie floored the gas pedal. The tires spun on the gravel-packed clay and the truck jerked forward, accelerating faster than Johnnie expected.

As he approached the bridge over the ravine, Johnnie strained to focus his blurred vision. He mistook the tall end of the guardrail for a deer. He jerked the steering wheel swiftly to the left, overcorrecting. The pickup slid into the oncoming lane.

Johnnie hit the brake hard, the wheels skidding off the side of the shoulder. The front end was forced against a large boulder. It crunched against the rock, ripping into the rim and bumper of the truck, exploding the tire. The hub cap hurled into the air, landed and rolled down the gravel. The force of the tire giving way threw Johnnie to the opposite side of the road and into the guardrail.

In a panic, Johnnie grabbed the wheel and yanked it to the left, propelling the truck back again across the slick clay. This time as the pickup flew across Rte. 426, there was no barrier to stop it.

Johnnie laid on the brake, but the clay and gravel offered no traction. The truck's locked tires slid over the shoulder and plunged into the canyon, rolling several times, throwing Johnnie from the passenger side. His head hit the door as he flew out, but it was the neglected debris, the accumulation of years of refuse that killed Johnnie. He died when his body was impaled by gnarled black jack limbs.

———

Tig heard it all: the screeching tires, the crunching metal, the loud deadening thud. And he knew exactly what had happened. Tig dropped the gun and closed his eyes. He turned quietly. Barely lifting his feet, he walked into the house. He picked his knife up off the floor and carried it into the bedroom.

The quilt had been thrown in a heap in the corner. Picking it up, Tig thoughtfully spread it evenly across the dusty linoleum. He sat down beside it. For a few minutes, he rubbed his hand back and forth over the end of the quilt. Taking his knife, he made a cut in the quilt just above the stained area on one end. He made another cut on the adjacent side.

Standing up, he stepped on one end of the patchwork bedding and pulled the other with his left hand, tearing a large rectangle out of the quilt, an area all stained and worn—Spur's part of the quilt.

Tig folded the torn section over his arm and carried it out of the house. He walked slowly down the hill toward the windmill.

Spur's body, still warm, was stretched out on a rough section of gravel. Tig set the quilt down and lovingly picked up his dog and laid him over on it. Then Tig got down on the cool clay and laid the side of his face against Spur's body.

As Tig closed his eyes, he was certain he could hear them, the sounds of the rabbit hunt, the dull thuds of clubs against flesh and fur—Hell's music. Black billowing clouds of dread rose up in him. They covered and asphyxiated him. Dark and impenetrable, they sealed his eyes, his mind, shut out the light. There was no bed to hide under this time, nowhere to run away to. He could not save himself. The violent sounds of death, of loss, grew louder. They pounded behind his ears, in his throat. They came from inside his throbbing head.

Tig wrenched his neck back and opened his mouth to let them out… "Nooo!" And the rabbit screamed.

———

Tig lovingly rolled Spur up in the scrap of quilt. Struggling for his balance, he bent over and carefully picked the bundle up. Tig moved slowly down the drive. Late afternoon clouds had darkened, and it began to rain. The earth already damp, the road was quickly soaked. The gushing clay slurry made it difficult to walk, so Tig moved to the weedy side of the driveway.

By the time Tig got to the bushes that led to the sanctuary, red stains were seeping through the quilt. Sweat and rain mingled with Spur's blood and ran down Tig's arms. With determination, he forced his way through the brambles. Thorns and jagged branches dug at his skin and snagged the quilt as he pressed on. He twisted and turned to maneuver his way through. The weight of the bundle pulled on his lower back. His neck ached, but he kept going. The last of the cedar branches spread open at the will of his shoulder. Tig staggered to the center, rain pouring in from overhead, and set Spur down gently next to Leon's marker.

"I won't be long, Spur."

Tig pushed his way back out of the hollow and trudged up the driveway to the house in the pouring rain. In a daze, Tig paid no mind to the clashes of thunder that rumbled through him or the dangerous, blinding flashes of light. He just walked on, beyond the house and around to the backside of the outhouse. There he took hold of the shovel.

———

Soaking wet and flush, Tig dug his shovel deep into the earth next to the bulging shroud. Tig knew how to dig. Shovel after shovel, he dug the heavy wet clay up out of the hollow. His head was pounding and nausea was vexing him, but he did not stop. He dug far deeper and wider than he needed but Tig was dazed and sick, and as far as he was concerned it did not matter. He just needed to dig.

He finally let the shovel fall. His good hand was bleeding. His shoulder and back were cramped. He knelt down and protectively rolled the bundle until it tumbled into the hole he had dug. He stood up, his heart pounding hard in his chest, in his throat. Slowly, he stepped back and worked an old baseball out of his pocket.

"Ya were a good one, Spur, a good friend. Don't know what tomorrow will be like without ya, buddy. Just not certain."

Tig swallowed down the lump and forced the words out. "But I'm thankful for our time together, sure am...."

Tig dropped the tattered baseball into the hole. Salty rain ran down his face. "I'm gonna miss ya."

Tig picked the shovel back up and sank it into the wet clay. Lifting and dumping, he shoveled the dirt. Tig gave the clay back to the gaping hole until a small mound rose from the floor of the sanctuary. Tig sat down and sighed. Too sick, too weary, too broken to make the trek back up to the house alone, Tig lay down.

———

Ida Mae never heard the accident happen. She might have, if all her windows had not been closed and her air conditioner had not been running. It was actually a passer-by who spotted the overturned truck in his rearview mirror three days after the accident. He immediately turned up the next available driveway, Ida Mae's house, and pounded on the front door.

Ida Mae called the police and then called Ron. Linda took the call. She ran and checked the barn, but Ron was visiting with Butch Ross, out with the cattle somewhere. She had to wait for him to return before she could give him the message.

When Linda relayed the message to Ron, Butch offered to go along, in case they needed more man power. The police and emergency vehicles were already there and working the accident by the time the red pickup arrived at the scene. Ron pulled along the side of the road and parked behind the Sheriff's car. The Sheriff was writing something on a notepad.

"Jim, what happened?"

"Hey, Ron. Horrible accident, apparently the truck overcorrected and skidded off the road. Went straight down into the canyon."

"Who was in the truck? Did anyone survive?"

"Only one person in the truck. No survivors. They found him hanging in the trees down there. The body was pretty torn up. Been out here for a few days. They've taken the remains away already. Gonna have to be an autopsy to confirm the identity. But here's the darndest thing, Ron. Papers in the glove compartment show the owner of the truck is Jonathan Mills. Not sure yet, but we're guessin' it was Johnnie drivin' that truck. Had no idea he was back in town. Haven't seen him for years!"

Ron's eyes widened. He was noticeably shocked. "Neither have I, Jim."

Ron looked concerned. Random thoughts were struggling to coalesce. *Why is Tig not down here? We are within walking distance. Wouldn't he have heard this?*

Jim's voice ripped through Ron's thoughts. "I am so sorry, Ron. I know how close the two of you were."

"Yeah, we used to be real close." Ron was becoming unsettled.

"Ron, there is something else."

The Sheriff reached into his car and pulled out a metal box. He carefully set it on the hood.

"Not sure how this managed not getting thrown from that truck. We just got it out of the cab. Amazing that it stayed intact while that truck rolled. Here, take a look."

He opened the latch and lifted the cover. Inside were dozens of letters still sealed in their envelopes. "They're a little soggy, but you can see they are still intact."

Ron looked stunned.

"Jim, do ya mind if I spend a minute lookin' through these?"

"Not at all. Take your time. I'm gonna be here awhile."

"Thanks."

Ron rifled through the letters. Envelope after envelope held a letter Tig had written to Effie. The postmarks indicated they had been sent, but they had never been opened. Ron started to feel sick as he fingered through dozens of letters representing years of a father's determination to reconcile with his daughter. In the bottom of the box, the envelopes were a different shape and color. Ron pushed Tig's letters aside to find a separate stack, not sent by Tig, but rather addressed to him. The name, "Effie Mills" was written on the corners of the pink envelopes. They were also sealed.

Ron stood looking over the letters with absolute disbelief when the sheriff walked up with a gun in his hands.

Startled, Ron inquired, "Jim, where'd ya get that?"

"Why, it was also in the truck. We're needin' to run a check on it, make sure it wasn't stolen, used in a crime, so forth."

Tig's rifle? Ron's mind was racing in a hundred different directions.

"No need, Jim. That's my rifle. Actually, it belongs to Tig. I traded him that rifle for a shotgun a few years ago."

"Well, what the Hell was Johnnie doin' with it?"

Ron was getting increasingly agitated. Tig's whereabouts were foremost in his mind.

"I'm sure I don't know. Hey, Jim, sorry but I've gotta run. May I take these letters for Tig?"

":Not just yet. We've gotta hold on to them for a bit, formalities you know?"

"Oh, yeah, right. Thanks Jim. Hey, let me know if I can be of any help on this."

Ron shook the Sheriff's hand and quickly ran across the road. There, Butch and some other ranchers were standing around pointing and staring into the ravine. As Ron approached, he thought about how the deep gulch snaking through the woods connected to Dump Canyon just below Tig's house. Ron tapped Butch on the shoulder.

"Hey, Butch. We need to go."

He looked confused until Ron made a face that indicated it was urgent. Ron threw his neighbors a tip of his hat as he and Butch hustled back to his truck.

———

Ron could tell something was not right before he got out of the truck. Things were too quiet, too still.

"Butch, I need ya to wait here 'til I see what's goin' on."

Ron opened the door of Tig's house. The small front room was in shambles, broken dishes, cotton batting strewn across the floor, and there was blood. Ron quickly ran into the bedroom, then to the outhouse—no Tig, no Spur. *Oh God, where is he?* He tore back through the house waving his arms, motioning to Butch to hurry and get out of the truck.

"Something's happened, but I'm not sure what. I don't like the looks of any of this. We've got to find Tig. Ya head down toward the canyon, and I'll start by the windmill. He'll have Spur with him, so call for both."

———

The two men frantically began searching. Their calls to Tig and Spur could be heard reverberating thru the trees, off the house, and over the fields.

"Tig! Spur!"

"Tig! Spur! Here boy!"

They combed the area for nearly two hours with no luck. Ron was very agitated and showing visible signs of apprehension. He caught up with Butch back at the house.

"Did ya see anything? Any sign at all?"

"Not a thing, Ron. This ain't good."

"I know, and I'm not leavin' here till we find him. He wasn't with Johnnie, so where in the Hell did he go?"

"I can't imagine, Ron, but I'm right beside ya till we find him."

"Let's circle back around but this time, let's do it in an organized way. We'll go down to the cattle guard and work our way back up the drive. You take the east side. I'll take the west. Let's push back through the dense areas all the way to a clearing, then come back to the road. We'll move a little closer to the house. If we don't find him, we're gonna have to send for help."

Starting at the intersection of Rte. 426, they began to move slowly up the road. Every few feet, they pushed back into the vegetation, the woods, the brambles, the soggy grasses. Butch was coming out of the backside of the woods into the shallow part of Dump Canyon when Ron saw it. Caught in the bushes on his side of the road was a small strip of quilt. Ron pulled it off of a thorny vine and studied it.

That's from the quilt he got from the Fox Creek Ladies. I'm sure of it, Ron thought.

Without hesitation, Ron bent his arms up in front of him and pushed through the bushes. When he got past them to the cedar row, he could see where a couple limbs were bent. He put his head down and went under. What he saw on the other side astounded him.

"What the…? Good Lord. Tig!"

Ron ran over to Tig, who lay unconscious between a pile of dirt and a piece of metal sticking out of the ground. Tig was soaking wet and cold. His lips were blue. Ron feared he was dead. *No. No. Tig, come on.* He checked for Tig's pulse. It was weak but still there. Ron turned his cheek toward Tig's mouth and nose. Tig's breaths were so shallow they were barely discernible. Ron pulled his slicker off and laid it over Tig. Then standing up, Ron put his fingers to his mouth and whistled as loud and long as he could.

Butch heard the whistle, turned, and ran toward the sound, calling out to Ron as he went. Ron was pushing out of the cedars to meet him.

"No, don't bother comin' through this tangled mess. He's here but unconscious. Go take the truck and get to Ida Mae's. Call for an ambulance. After ya call, bring me back a scythe or somethin'. We need to get these vines cut down, so they can get him outta here. A scythe, a rake, a saw—Ida Mae should have somethin' that would work. Hurry, please hurry."

He tossed Butch the keys and turned back into the hollow. Ron sat down in the mud next to Tig and placed his hand on his friend's shoulder.

"Hold on buddy. Hold on."

EIGHTEEN

"How is he?"

Ron looked up. Ida Mae and Linda had just arrived.

As the paramedics were carrying Tig out of the hollow, Ron sent Butch back with his truck to gather the women and meet him at the hospital. He climbed up into the back of the ambulance and rode next to Tig.

They rushed Tig in as a nurse directed Ron to the nondescript emergency and outpatient waiting room. Generic chairs with soiled upholstery lined the stale blue walls. Four scratched end tables held small stacks of previously owned magazines. Ron was weary and soaking wet. He had pieces of leaves, sticks, and cedar twigs stuck to him, as though he had been sprayed by a shredder. He picked a chair near a window and walked over, leaving a trail of mulch in his wake. Ron had been resting his head in his hands when Ida Mae and Linda walked up. Idae Mae tapped him on the shoulder. She was frantic.

"So, how is he?"

Worry was spread across her face.

"Yes, how is he? And Ron...," Linda furrowed her brow. "What is all over you? Where have you been?"

"I've not heard anything yet on Tig's condition. This—" Ron picked leaves off his sleeves. "—it's a long story."

Ron proceeded to tell them how the man they found dead was Johnnie—how his truck had crashed in the ravine. He told them how the police found Johnnie's identification in the glove compartment. He explained how he knew something bad had happened when the sheriff found Tig's rifle in Johnnie's truck, but Tig was nowhere to be seen.

"I knew this meant Johnnie had been with Tig. Those two have never gotten along since I can't remember when. I never told ya this, but Johnnie stole Tig's wallet and all his food when he left Tig here. He never stayed to help Tig settle in. He took off in the night, takin' everythin' his brother had save his clothes and a couple cans of beer and…."

"That son of a bitch stole the food we sent up there for Tig?" Linda's eyes narrowed—her words were full of contempt.

"Yes, he did. But there's more, something I feel is far worse." Ron sighed.

Ida Mae's worried brow narrowed. "What would that be, Ron?"

"The sheriff found a box of letters in Johnnie's truck. Ida Mae—all those letters you helped Tig write—all those letters I mailed—they were bein' forwarded to Johnnie's house! Apparently, Dottie left Johnnie and Carolyn's address as hers and Effie's forwarding address. Carolyn wasn't there, so the letters collected, and Johnnie never saw that Effie got 'em."

"Oh no."

Ida Mae took on a look of concern. Her hands began to fidget. "How could he have been so cruel?"

"There's more."

Linda's face expressed disbelief that it could be worse, while Ida Mae stood dumbfounded.

"Effie had been writin' to Tig all this time too."

"What!"

The nurse at the desk hushed Linda, reminding her she was in a hospital.

"What? Ron, how do you know this?"

"All her letters to Tig were also in the box, each one still sealed," Ron said as he shook his head.

Ida Mae threw her hand to her throat, dropped her head, and sighed. "How? I mean, well, how could this happen?!"

"All of Effie's letters were sent in care of Mr. and Mrs. Johnnie

Mills. I'd lay odds that since Dottie made Johnnie legal custodian for Tig, and since Tig had no permanent address, she would have instructed Effie to send her father's letters to Johnnie's care. She did, and he hoarded them, probably just for spite. I've got to believe the only reason he would've brought them out here now, after all these years, would be so he could use 'em somehow to extort somethin' from Tig. Though I can't imagine what. Apparently, Johnnie either chose not to use the letters or he never got the chance."

"Excuse me, are you Ron Carson?"

The doctor walked in and stood directly behind Linda. He had approached unnoticed, his wrinkled blue cotton scrubs melding with the faded walls. Ron stood up quickly.

"Yes, I am Ron Carson. How is he? Is he gonna be OK?"

"Mr. Mills is going to be fine, but it will take a couple weeks. He has a bad case of pneumonia. Apparently, he has had it for a while, but was unaware he was sick. He must have been showing signs, but regardless, it's a good thing you found him when you did. One more night in the soggy environment where you found him, and he would have died."

"Oh, thank God."

There was a consolidated sigh of relief from the group.

"How soon can we see him?"

"He needs to rest. He's on heavy antibiotics and breathing treatments. He needs his sleep. I've ordered no visitors until tomorrow afternoon. Be assured he is stable now and in good hands."

Ron picked a cedar sprig off his shoulder and handed it to Linda. "Well, I guess we can all go home and get some rest. I'd love to get cleaned up."

Linda glanced down at the twig in her fingers. "I still don't understand how you managed to get covered in this stuff."

"I found Tig in the woods, in a natural clearing in the middle of a ring of cedars. There was somethin' special about that place, obviously even more so for Tig. He's the only one who can tell us about it."

"Hmm, I see," Linda said as she pulled another twig from Ron's collar. "By the way, who's taking care of Spur? He must be going nuts in the truck."

There was a long painful silence.

"I'm pretty sure Spur is dead. That's where I found Tig. He was lying unconscious next to a small mound of freshly dug dirt, and Spur was nowhere to be seen."

The words were so implausible they took a minute to penetrate Ida Mae's thoughts, but they did.

"Nooo, not that." She began to cry. Linda's eyes were filling too.

"Hasn't that poor man lost enough? How? How could Spur possibly have died? He was healthy as an ox just last week? What is going on?" Linda was exasperated.

Ron shook his head. "I don't know, sweetheart, but I intend to find out!"

––––––

Ida Mae paced the floor of her kitchen. She prayed she had made the right call. Ida Mae was known for her capacity to avoid butting into other peoples' business. On more than one occasion at the Fox Creek Ladies Auxiliary meetings, she had shut down the gossip train. Now she was in deep, but her love for Tig meant more than her stellar reputation. The knock came before Ida Mae was convinced she had done the right thing. Nervously, she opened the door.

"Ida Mae, I hope you know what you're doing."

"Oh, I am so glad you came. Will you please come in? We need to talk. I have tea in the kitchen."

––––––

Warm sunshine was spilling across the shiny floor but the room was cool. Tig was resting peacefully and comfortably for the first time in over five years in a real bed. Ron stood patiently outside the hospital room. The nurse lifted Tig's oxygen mask from his face, adjusted his bed, stepped out, and invited Ron in.

Ron had asked Linda if he could have some time with Tig before anyone else arrived. She agreed, offering to pick up Ida Mae and bring her to the hospital to visit later.

Ron stepped through the door and Tig smiled. His voice was weak. "Ron."

Ron pulled up a chair next to his friend's bed.

"Tig, I'm so glad you're gonna to be OK. How're ya feelin' today?"

Tig turned his head, tears running down his face. He whispered, "I killed him."

Ron leaned over the bed.

"What? Tig, what are ya sayin'? Who?"

"I killed Johnnie, Ron. I shot my brother...."

Tig was overwhelmed with grief. Ron was confused. He stood up and placed his hand on Tig's shoulder.

"Tig we don't need to talk about this now. You're working yourself up. Ya need to rest."

Tig shook his head vehemently. His voice was raspy, his words delivered on shallow breaths. "I need to tell ya."

"Tig, Johnnie just ran off the road and wrecked. You didn't kill him."

"Yes—I did. I shot his back tires so he'd lose control of the car. I knew he was drunk, and with no tires, he'd lose control and crash."

Tig paused and then sobbed.

"I wanted him to die. Oh God, I wanted my own brother to die."

"Tig, I'm certain that's not the way Johnnie died. What was he doin' up there anyway? What'd he want?"

"He came lookin' for money. Thought I'd been sent insurance money from the accident. He tore my house apart and...." Tig closed his eyes. "...he shot Spur."

Ron could barely stand the agony Tig was enduring. "Oh, Tig, I'm so sorry, so sorry."

Ron put his hand on Tig's shoulder and stood by the bed next to him. When the sun began to cast long shadows on the floor, Ron was still standing silently next to Tig.

———

The door cracked open, and Linda stuck her head in. She and Ida Mae had arrived just a little before dinner. Linda had Butch run up to Tig's house and get the quilt from his cot. She laundered it and had it draped over her arm as she and Ida Mae entered the room. Linda spread the damaged quilt over Tig.

He smiled. He felt comforted beneath it. Even with a big hole in it, the quilt was no less stunning. "Thank ya, Linda."

Ida Mae drew close to the bed and threw her arms around Tig's neck.

"You have to get better, you hear me? We have sand plums to process in a couple months!"

Tig smiled and whispered. "Lord, I hope I'm up and around by then."

A chuckle spread through the room, loud enough to rise above the hum and whir of the medical equipment. Tig laid his head back in relief at their laughter. He knew their friendship had the power to heal.

The door burst open, and a jovial nurse entered with Tig's dinner tray.

"Can they stay while I eat?"

"Absolutely. If you folks would like you can get some hamburgers from the hospital cafeteria and bring them up here. Here, I'll point you in the right direction."

Linda smiled and said, "Sounds like a great idea. We'll go grab some food and be right back."

The nurse held the door. Linda and Ida Mae pulled it behind them as they walked out arm in arm.

As the women left, Ron reached over and laid his hand on Tig's shoulder. "Tig, if ya don't mind me askin', what was that place? I mean where I found ya. Ya never spoke of it before."

"The hollow?" Tig smiled and tipped his head.

"Yes, the natural clearing in the cedars."

"That place, Ron—that place is my sanctuary, my altar. I've gone there every mornin' for years. In the beginnin', I mostly mourned there. I grieved for those I'd lost and lamented over how I'd lost myself. Over time, I needed to be there at the break of dawn. It—God—drew me there. It became the place where I'd say thank ya

Lord for all I'd been given. Where I would think about the folks I love and honor—those I've lost. While the mornin' sun was risin', I'd let go of my fears... and pray for strength to hold on to my hopes. And Ron, that's where I'd ask for my family—Ida Mae, Linda, and you—to be blessed...."

Tig turned his eyes toward the window. "It's where I'd go to pray."

Ron was overcome by the thought of Tig kneeling in the forest on his behalf. He might have said as much to Tig had the door not opened again.

"Food's here!" Linda's cheerful disposition burst into the room.

Having just been introduced to a part of Tig he never knew existed, Ron stood deep in thought near the window. Meanwhile, the women pulled up trays and spread out the burgers. As though part of a typical routine, Ida Mae reached down into her handbag and pulled out a jar of her homemade pickles.

"Can't do without these!" she cackled.

Her serendipitous yet signature hospitality had everyone in stitches.

The last amber rays of sunset filled the room as the friends began to disperse. Before Ron left, he tapped Tig on the foot.

"Thank ya for those prayers, brother."

———

Five days had passed, and the doctor made an announcement that Tig would be able to go home in a week. Ron and Linda scurried to get their guest room ready for Tig, but Ida Mae had a different idea. Cool air had finally broken weeks of rain and humid heat. The windows throughout the hospital had been cracked open, and the breeze carried the fresh air into the rooms and through the hallways. It was a Sunday afternoon, and visitors scurried about the shiny floors, moving in and out of patients' rooms, juggling flowers and balloons. Ron and Linda brought Ida Mae with them to visit Tig after church. When they arrived, Tig was sleeping.

"I suppose we could go and come back later?"

Linda looked to Ron for his opinion, and Ida Mae jumped in.

"Do you think I might visit with him alone? Would you mind if I just stayed behind? I could leave with you later today when you come back."

"Are you sure you want to stay here that long by yourself, Ida Mae?" Linda reflected concern.

"I'll be fine. I have some reading I want to do, and I have some other things that will fill my time. I have appreciated you carting me around but please don't wait for me. You go ahead. I will see you this evening."

Ron nodded his OK. "There's quite a bit I need to catch up on. Since all this commotion started, I've gotten behind on some chores. This'll actually work out well."

"Yes it will," Ida Mae mumbled.

"Excuse me. Did you say somethin' Ida Mae?"

"No, nothing really. You go ahead. Ron. You and Linda have a lovely afternoon."

———

Ida Mae stood outside the door waiting. She checked her watch. Maybe she wouldn't come. She turned to see the figure moving down the hall. Ida Mae smiled. The woman in a dark jacket with the hood pulled up over her head nodded.

"I am so glad you decided to come."

Ida Mae reached and opened the door to Tig's room and ushered the woman in. Tig was still asleep. Ida Mae stood reverently by the door as the woman made her way over to the foot of Tig's bed. She stood quietly, observing the man who lay before her. She scanned the bed, her eyes resting on the missing corner of Tig's quilt. She took her hands from her pockets and ran them respectfully and lovingly across the torn edges.

"What happened?" She whispered, looking to Ida Mae with a look of concern.

"Yes, I know. I was disappointed to see this too. He cut a section out of it when his dog died. He wrapped him up in it before he buried him."

"Oh."

The woman put her hand to her heart, dropped her head, and sighed. "I see."

Ida Mae nodded, encouraging the woman to move to the side of Tig's bed. The hooded woman quietly positioned herself next to Tig. For a period of time, she just stared down at the man as he slept. She reached for his hand but quickly drew back, giving the indication she wanted to give the visit a second thought. Looking over to Ida Mae she sighed and bit her lip. Then she shook her head from side to side indicating she couldn't do it. Ida Mae tipped her head, and a compassionate ache filled her eyes. She smiled gently.

She mouthed, "Go ahead. It will be OK. Really."

The woman turned and slowly reached over and rested her fingers gently on top of Tig's mangled hand. As soon as she felt the weathered calloused skin beneath her fingers, tears rolled down her face and spilled onto the tattered quilt.

Her touch startled Tig who roused. He opened his eyes, blinking. He struggled to stay awake. Then he realized *she* was there. He forced his eyes to focus as he studied the woman by his side. She quietly lifted the hood from her head. Tig caught his breath.

"Effie—Effie is that you?" Tig reached his hands up towards the woman's face. Effie silently took her father's hands in hers. "Oh Effie. I've hoped for so long…."

Tig's frail voice reached across the room and touched Ida Mae's heart. She knew it was time. She opened the door and backed slowly out into the hall before closing the door gently behind her.

Ron and Linda came bounding down the hall. Linda carried a box of chocolates in her hands. Ida Mae sat quietly on a chair just outside the door to Tig's room.

"Did ya have a good visit?"

Ron smiled and reached for the doorknob. Ida Mae lightly placed her hand on his. "Not now, Ron."

Ron and Linda looked confused. "Is he OK?"

"He has never been better." "

"Huh?"

"Let's go get a cup of coffee. My treat."

———

"So you're tellin' me Effie is up there with Tig right now?" Ron and Linda's eyes widened.

"How, how could she've gotten here so quickly? I mean it has only been a few days, right?" Linda asked.

"I know it seems confusing, but you see, Effie has been here for a few months."

"How could that be?"

"You had no way of knowing, but you met her husband over Christmas." Linda looked totally surprised.

"Yes, Jeffrey is her husband."

"But he said his wife's name is Lynn!" Ron was getting frustrated.

"Effie's real name is Evelyn. When she moved back here with her daughter, she decided she wanted a fresh start, so she asked to be called Lynn."

"She had a girl? Tig has a granddaughter!" Linda gasped.

"Yes, he most certainly does, a beautiful granddaughter, Ellie. You see, when Dottie remarried, Effie did not get along with her new stepfather. She threatened to leave, but she knew she had little Ellie to care for. She couldn't do it on her own. Dottie suggested that she and Ellie go to live with her sister, Effie's aunt. Clara had just lost her husband unexpectedly, so she welcomed the idea of having her niece and grand- niece come live with her. Arrangements were made, and Effie and Ellie moved to Durant to live with Clara. Effie graduated from high school in Oregon. So, while Clara watched Ellie, Effie took a class or two at Southeastern University. That's where she met Jeffrey Hudson. They married within a year. All the while, Clara kept up with her friends here in Arvita. Her best friend, Debra Bailey, is a Fox Creek Lady. Clara and Debra chatted all the time about what was going on in Arvita. Of course this included all the goings-on with Tig.

Effie wrote Tig, but she never heard back from her father, so she believed he meant it when he said he didn't want her in his life. Even with these thoughts, she never stopped hoping they would reunite. When she heard the stories of how he was living here, she begged her Aunt Clara to let her send special little gifts to the Fox Creek Ladies so they could deliver them to her father. Clara agreed and sent them to Debra on Effie's behalf, but no one else knew where they came from. As far as the Fox Creek Ladies were concerned, they were separate donations Debra had gathered. Furthermore, no one had a clue Effie lived with Clara, not even me, except Debra of course who was sworn to secrecy.

In the last two years, Dottie got a settlement from the insurance company, a life insurance policy her father had taken out on his grandchildren unbeknownst to either Tig or Dottie. Dottie was the beneficiary for Leon."

Ron's mouth dropped open and then his lips curved up in a slight smirk.

"Oh, so that was it! Somehow Johnnie must've found out about this and figured Tig would've gotten some too. That's why he ransacked Tig's house! This all makes sense now!"

"Yes, I guess it does. Tig never got any of the money, but Dottie did. She sent Effie a portion of the insurance money as a belated wedding gift. Effie always wanted to come back to Dawson County to the family farm, so when she got the money she had Jeffrey scout out jobs here. Meanwhile, they offered the owners of the Old Mills' place a very generous amount for the farm. Jeffrey and Effie ended up buying the farm last fall. They started remodeling it before moving in the first of December. They live there now."

Ron and Linda were dumbfounded. Ron could not stop shaking his head. "Dear Lord, all this time. They've lived there for eight months? Why didn't she just go up there and get him? And why didn't ya say anythin' sooner—tell Tig about her bein' here?"

Ron was riled up. *What's the matter with these people!? All Tig has been put through, all the relentless unnecessary sufferin'. Why?*

"Ron, it was not my place to tell Tig. My first real conversation with Effie wasn't until March after the snow started to clear. I had only met her briefly at a meeting prior to that. The first thing she asked of me was that I respect the fact that it was her responsibility to make contact with her father. She made me vow to tell no one, most importantly not Tig."

"OK, I understand, but why didn't she go up there and get him?"

"You have to remember she had not gotten any of his letters.

When I met her, she was convinced her father hated her and had disowned her. She knew Tig blamed her for his break-up with her mother. He moved out right after the argument with Dottie over Effie's pregnancy."

"But you knew he was givin' letters to me to send to her. You even knew what they said. Why didn't you tell her?"

"I did, Ron. And she told me it made a huge difference. Part of the reason Effie moved here was to try to reconcile with her father, but these things take time. Effie and I talked a great deal about the letters Tig and I wrote to her. I told her everything, even how the only compensation he wanted for his work was for me to help him. When I met with Effie in April, she was preparing to go and get him. The rumors the Fox Creek Ladies spread about Tig, and his gun caused Jeffrey to forbid Effie to go alone to see her father, so they were arranging a time to go together."

Ron was incredulous.

"This still doesn't answer why she didn't go. What happened?"

"Yeah, what's kept her so long?" Linda piped in.

Ida Mae nodded her head and bit her lip, hesitating to speak.

"The weather for one—Jeffrey and Effie were fixing up their house when they ran into some problems due to all the rain. They had to repair some damage, and this caused some delays. Also, in April, Effie discovered she was expecting. She was just miserable with morning sickness for weeks. Both she and Jeffrey believed the stress of meeting and trying to reconcile with her father might be too much. They decided to wait until she was further along. They intended for Effie to reunite with Tig this fall.

As for me, as I said, I had no idea she had been living with Clara all that time. I didn't even know she was back in Arvita until Debra let it slip. She just happened to mention the woman named Lynn, who was on the schedule to teach a class for the Auxiliary, was actually Clara's niece. Debra had no idea I knew Clara. I just put two and two together. Once I learned this, which was just a few days before Christmas, I have been doing everything I could to unravel Effie's misconceptions and undo the lies she'd heard about her father. That is why I invited Jeffery over to pick up supplies. I knew Tig would be at the house all cleaned up for

Christmas dinner. I wanted Jeffrey to see the real Tig, a gentle civilized man."

Ron was noticeably embarrassed.

"I apologize, Ida Mae. I didn't mean to sound like I was accusin' ya. It all seems so sad to me."

"I know, so sad and unnecessary, but for the most part we don't have a say in what life offers us. We all know how things can spin so quickly out of control sometimes, and we certainly cannot choose the consequences of our decisions. We do, however, decide how we will accept what life doles out. We can choose to live in grace, and I think Tig is the best example of this I know."

"You're right, Ida Mae," Linda smiled. "That's how he is, isn't he?"

Ron wasn't quite finished asking questions. "Effie must've known Johnnie had the letters. Wasn't she forwardin' them to him?"

"She was. She just assumed all these years that Johnnie was delivering them to her father. This was part of the problem. She thought her father just didn't care to answer. When you mentioned the box with the letters they found at the accident, I met with Effie to clear all this up."

Ron sat with his chin resting between his thumb and his forefinger, shaking his head in disbelief. "Has she been with Tig a long time today?"

"All afternoon. I think there's a lot of reconciliation and catching up going on."

Linda looked over at Ron and then back to Ida Mae.

"I would like to meet her, Ida Mae. Tig's kids were so young when they left Arvita, and we didn't know his family that well anyway."

Ida Mae looked thoroughly pleased.

"I am certain that can be arranged."

———

On Monday morning, Ron got a phone call from the sheriff's office requesting that he stop by. Ron was asked if he would deliver the metal box full of letters and the rifle back to Tig. There was little left of anything else from the accident, but what could be salvaged would be given to Tig at a later date. After signing the paperwork, Ron had a few questions.

"Jim, what was decided about the accident?"

"Ron, Johnnie was intoxicated and should never have been out on those roads. He hit a boulder and blew out his front tire. He lost control of his truck. He would have been charged with manslaughter had there been any other victims, but since his recklessness took his and only his life, there is nothing left to do."

"Did ya say a front tire?"

"Yes, sir, I did. The front tire on the driver's side."

Ron could not get Tig's confession out of his mind. *I don't get it. Tig was convinced he'd shot the back tires of Johnnie's car. Maybe because he was so sick, he was delirious and didn't realize what was happenin' at the time. That doesn't make any sense, though. How would someone imagine shootin' a gun, two times, for that matter?*

Ron would not rest until he figured this out.

———

On the way home from the sheriff's office, Ron pulled into Tig's driveway and parked the truck. He got out and walked up to where Tig said he was standing when he fired the gun. Not trained in forensics but smart enough to envision the path of a bullet and the distance it might travel given the specific conditions—Ron began to search. He tracked through the trees on both sides of the drive for nearly three hours. He was determined to find some indication that a bullet might be embedded in something in the vicinity. Frustrated and needing to get home, he climbed back up into the truck. Not wanting to drive all the way back up to the house, he decided to back out onto Rte. 426 and turn around. As he was watching his side mirrors, he noticed the fencepost next to the cattle guard was tipped in an odd way. He stopped the truck and got out to straighten it.

"Well, I'll be damned."

There in the middle of the fencepost was a bullet hole. The bullet was lodged deep in the splintered wood. The force had split one whole section off from the side of the post. Ron took out his pocket knife and dug the bullet out of the weathered hardwood. Holding the .9 mm caliber bullet between his fingers, he shook his head.

"Ya sure did try, didn't ya? Thank God ya failed."

Ron took a deep breath and put the bullet in his pocket.

————

The day before Tig was to be discharged from the hospital, Ron called Effie's husband and asked him to meet him at Tig's place. The land had dried out some, but Ron told Jeffrey it would be a good idea to wear his boots, nonetheless. When Jeffrey arrived, the two walked together down the eroded wet clay and into the area where the Cedars formed the clearing. The thorny bushes had been cut back the day they removed Tig from the sanctuary, so the path was relatively clear. Ron led the way, pushing back the evergreen branches so that Jeffrey could move into the hollow.

"Oh my goodness, this is…"

"Amazin' isn't it?"

In the middle of the natural clearing, directly under a single source of light, was a repository. The ground around Leon's marker was covered with things, lots of things. A collection of commemorative objects and keepsakes was laid out in rings around the etched blade—little cars and toys, empty boxes of Cracker Jacks, a new baseball, an old calendar photo of a dump truck, a used T-shirt with Wendot printed across it—dozens of items. All were offerings of Tig's affection. Leon's marker shot up through the middle. The only area under the small patch of sun not covered was a small fresh grave.

"I am so glad ya brought this to my attention. This is it, isn't it?"

Jeffery reached down and placed his hand on the weathered windmill blade. "Yes, that's it. Here, let me help ya get that."

Ron and Jeffrey together tugged and pulled until the sanctuary floor relinquished the marker. Ron took a bandana from his pocket and wiped the mud from the steel. Then he respectfully handed the blade to Jeffery.

"This should work just fine for the time bein'. I'll put it in the ground today. It can stay there 'til the stone comes in."

"Thank ya, Jeffrey. I ordered it yesterday, so it shouldn't take too long to arrive. It's gray granite, as close to the color of this blade as I could find, and it'll read, simply 'Dear Son.' Just the way Tig would've wanted it."

"Good. The new marker should fit up there just fine, right next to Carrie Ann's stone. Lynn, I mean Effie—gonna take some getting used to sayin' this—is pleased. She said her father will be able see it from the new room, his bedroom, just off the back of the house."

———

The nurse's aide was gathering Tig's belongings when Ron walked in.

"Mr. Mills, I think this just about does it. We will put everything in a bag for you. We should have the wheelchair up here in just a minute."

As she was leaving, Ron pulled his chair over next to Tig's bed. "So, are ya ready to get outta here?" He laughed.

"Ya bet I am."

"Tig, before they come to get ya, I've gotta coupl'a things I need to give ya."

Tig's smile changed to a look of confusion.

"First, let me give ya this."

Ron took the bullet out of his shirt pocket and placed it in Tig's hand.

"This is one of the two bullets ya shot at Johnnie. The other one must be in a tree, Lord only knows where."

Tig started shaking his head and was about to say something when Ron stopped him by putting up his hand.

"I know ya told me ya meant to kill him, but we'll never discuss that again. Fact is—ya didn't. The sheriff said Johnnie ran into somethin' and blew out his front driver's side tire. The back tires were fine. Ya never shot 'em, Tig. Maybe it was because ya were sick and didn't know it, but ya missed them by a mile. I pulled this bullet outta the fence post."

Tig shut his eyes and caught his breath.

"Thank God, oh thank God…. And thank ya, Ron."

"No need to thank me, brother. Now, there's somethin' else."

Ron carefully set the metal box up on the bed and opened it.

Tig stared in disbelief. "My letters, all my letters to Effie, but where? How?"

"Johnnie had 'em, Tig. He had all of 'em. He never forwarded them on to Effie. And he didn't send hers to you either."

"What? What letters from Effie?"

"She'd been writin' to ya too, Tig."

"She never mentioned this to me in our conversations over these past few days. Matter-of-fact, whenever I asked if she got my letters, she just changed the subject."

Tig looked confused.

"Tig, Effie knew about what Johnnie had done and how the letters were found. Ida Mae told her. When I offered to give Effie this box, she declined. She said she wanted to wait to talk with ya about 'em. She thought the two of ya might want to read 'em together sometime. In the meantime, she felt ya should have 'em."

Tig immediately started riffling through the box. He pulled out a light pink envelope and held it up in front of his eyes, studying the script, moving his mangled fingers across his name. He drew the letter to his face and pressed it against his cheek. Tears ran freely over the envelope. Ron patted Tig on the shoulder and stepped quietly out of the room.

———

Tig's family and friends were waiting in the lobby as they wheeled him around the corner. He held tight to the metal box resting on his lap. Ron, Linda, and Ida Mae stood to one side, grinning ear to ear and holding a big green plant, a gift from the Fox Creek Ladies.

The nurse rolled Tig to the middle of the lobby, directly in front of Jeffrey who stood with his arm around Effie, a slight bulging promise barely visible at her waist. Next to her, a bright eyed little red-head, the spitting image of Dottie Harns, wiggled about, a toy rag doll hanging from her small hand.

"Dad,"

Just the words caused Tig's heart to quicken.

"I want you to meet your granddaughter, Ellie Genelle."

Effie squatted down so she could look her little girl straight in the eyes. "Ellie, this is your Grandpa Tig."

Effie took the doll from Ellie's arms and gently nudged her toward Tig. Ellie stepped forward and timidly stretched out her hand. Tig took her small hand in his calloused palm. She grinned and captured Tig's heart with her smiling green eyes.

"Nice meetin' ya, Ellie."

She quickly stepped back under her mother's arm and reached her hands up. As Ellie turned around, she held her rag doll tight to her chest. Effie had swaddled it in a small blanket, an earth-toned quilt delicately stitched with fabric stars. The covering looked strangely familiar.

Tig glanced down at the threadbare quilt on his lap.

———

A cool northwest wind moved across the prairie. It blew against the rugged limestone extruding from red clay bluffs and over the rolling hills dressed with spotty mounds of sagebrush, indigo and yarrow. It sent the Russian thistle tumbling into the draw and lifted the wings of the red-tailed hawk soaring over golden prairie sunflowers—to where the land lay down to greet the sandy banks of the river. It wafted through the windows of the small clapboard house, filling the sheer curtains.

They billowed and rose like spirits dancing in the current. Visiting the small room, the breeze kissed the freshly painted walls and fanned the polished bureau. It skipped across the braided rug and rose. And there, it fell gently, coming to rest on an earth-toned quilt—delicate calico triangles forming a single, lone, star—folded at the end of the bed.

Outside, just beyond the window, atop a small hill, the bluestem and indian grass waved, brushing softly against granite and galvanized steel; rejoicing. For with the wind came the promise--change was coming--relief for a scarred and weary land.

ABOUT THE AUTHOR

Sunni Mercer holds an MFA in painting and sculpture. She has taught Art History and has written for museum exhibits. Sunni is an NEA Regional Fellow whose art has been exhibited in galleries and museums in the U.S. and abroad. Her work has been the subject of dozens of articles in a variety of national publications. As an assemblage sculptor, Sunni uses language as a source of inspiration to create what has been referred to as sight poetry. Now, Sunni has chosen to use her art as the impetus for her stories. As a skilled storyteller who draws attention to the details, Sunni now offers us works of fiction—assemblages of provocative characters facing unique challenges.

Sunni lives and works in Oklahoma. You can learn more about her art and her books at sunnimercer.com

THELMA

FROM SUNNI MERCER'S NEXT NOVEL

The tightly secured box sat waiting on the table. Denise rotated the package carefully, examining the top and sides before sliding the paring knife down the seam. The cellophane tape split, and the flaps were freed. The box released a puff of mildew, accumulated from years in the attic. Denise gave a dusty exhale as she pulled back the tabs.

Stuffed in the top were four stained cotton floral napkins wound around a set of Depression glass salt and pepper shakers. Denise held the milky green vessels close to her eyes. She could barely make out the worn embossed letters. Setting them aside, she pulled out an old handmade sock monkey, faded and frayed, one of the button eyes missing. Denise gave the well-worn toy a squeeze. Thunk. A small smooth stone enmeshed in the sock's torn wool had fallen back into the box. Denise bent to retrieve the shiny piece of quartz, and that is when she saw it—the book.

A small black leather journal was resting snuggly, well-hidden in the bottom of the box. She carefully removed it. The leather edges were brittle and disintegrating, its frail pages filled with hand-rendered script. Denise sat down and stared out the window for a moment. As she wrapped her fingers around the cover, feeling the book's delicate binding, her mind traveled back to an overstuffed cabbage-rose sofa and gooey, caramel-apple pie. She closed her eyes, uncertain she had the authority to examine the treasure she held gingerly in her hands. Fixed, she let the gravity of the moment sink in. She carefully turned over the fragile cover, and encountered the River Maiden.

———

Twenty-four-year-old Jackson Fillman Sr. introduced himself to Thelma Reynolds at the Benson County Swing Dance. Thelma wore a swishy Charleston dress and Sally Shoes. The combination of her short frock and two-inch heels accentuated her lanky extremities. Jackson caught a glimpse of her from across the room—the long-legged girl with a graceful neck and uncommon features. Thelma stood behind her sisters like a crane protecting her young. As Jackson moved toward her, Duke Ellington's "Diga Diga Doo" sent couples running onto the dance floor.

Jackson never took his eyes off Thelma. He made his way across the crowded room, weaving and ducking past jive-dancing couples with arms flailing. As Jackson drew closer to Thelma, he became more intrigued. She appeared shy; her head slightly bowed. There was a freshness about her—her wholesomeness an indicator of innocence. Jackson stared at her like a wildcat considering the chase.

Thelma watched Jackson approach. She stood breathless. She had spotted him earlier, and she had studied him. Now she watched him out of the corner of her eyes. Among all the eligible, courting-age-men, it was Jackson's blond hair and obvious charisma that caught Thelma's attention. As he reached for her hand, Thelma couldn't help but notice the sparkle in his blue eyes and his beautiful smile—all teeth. Jackson hastily pulled her onto the dance floor. The air was thick, laden with cheap perfume and cigarette smoke. Ambient laughter and heels clicking on wood accompanied the clarinets as Jackson pulled Thelma against his chest.

Thelma could not figure out what Jackson saw in her. Jackson could turn an eye with his boyish charm and handsome features, but Thelma considered herself to be plain. She was taller than most of the girls her age, big-boned and broad-shouldered. She kept her wavy black hair pulled back behind her head. Invariably, a couple rogue curls would escape the hair ribbon and fall loosely against her forehead. Her thick, black eyebrows and high cheekbones were her prominent facial features—but her eyes were the most mysterious of her attributes.

Thelma's pupils were gray, the color of river slate accented by specks of sandy gold. Her eyes had a distinctive clarity to them. No one looked at Thelma's eyes. They looked through them. This would often cause people to stare longer than normal when addressing her. So, Thelma habitually looked down when she spoke to people. She did this—not in a dismissing way but rather out of deference—to avoid awkward moments.

That night at the dance, when Jackson took Thelma's hand for the first time, she did not look down. Thelma looked Jackson straight in the eyes, and she seized his heart.

———

At barely sixteen, Thelma married Jackson Fillman Sr., a handsome, vicious man. Their first baby came that next year. While Thelma learned how to mother an infant, Jackson scrambled to find employment to provide for his growing family.

He took his first job as a construction worker for the railroad. The more perilous the work, such as building and repairing elevated tracks, the better the pay. Jackson always volunteered to take the most dangerous jobs, work that placed him at risk on a daily basis. The responsibilities were intense, and the constant stress plagued his nerves. This combination of navigating treacherous environments along with his unstable, thrill-seeking mentality shaped within Jackson an arrogant invincible spirit. His mood swings were more difficult for Thelma to navigate than the demands of her colicky baby. She had never known anyone who could sleep a full day only to follow it with sleepless days of nonstop reckless behavior.

Thelma was in her third month of her second pregnancy the first time Jackson Fillman Sr. stayed out all night. Following that episode, the aroma Jackson frequently wore home served as evidence. Thelma was convinced, her blue-eyed sweetheart had a penchant for the bottle.

Jobs were becoming scarce and the crash of '29 created a widespread panic. Resources were drying up and all too often Jackson found himself without work. Frequent unemployment caused Jackson to feel vulnerable. Unwilling to accept failure Jackson manifested his self-perceived weakness into anger and depression. His antidote was a shot or two of whiskey. Jackson's self-medicating with alcohol did not keep him from working. He managed to function well enough. It was the introduction of opium that led to Jackson's disintegration.

———

In a last-ditch effort to provide, Jackson moved his family from the city to a small house he had inherited in the country. Relocating meant Jackson would no longer have to pay rent. Taking this into account, he packed up his pregnant wife and little boy and moved them to Clayton County. As the black Chevrolet Coach turned off of Post Road, spraying gravel over the dirt driveway, Thelma could see nothing but promise. There waiting for her was a pretty little two-bedroom tenant house with white clapboards and black shutters. A wild, honeysuckle bush grew out front. *We will be happy here, raising our family—setting down roots.* Little time passed before those roots began to rot, drowned by Jackson's addictions.

———

By the time their second son, Jackson Jr. was born, Thelma had endured months of drunken brawls in her living room. The young family's resources were nearly depleted. Jackson could no longer be counted on to provide for his family. So, Thelma set out to find work. With only a seventh-grade education and two small boys to care for, housekeeping seemed to be the best alternative for Thelma.

———

The small house Thelma lived in was on a five-acre tract of land between two large farms. The dairy farmer to the west had recently stopped by Thelma's house. His wife had taken ill, and he could not manage the farm and the household. He offered to hire Thelma for cooking and cleaning and to help care for his wife. Thelma agreed, providing she could bring her son Lil' Jackson.

"He won't be a problem, Mr. Burns. You can be assured of that. I really do need this job. Thank you for askin' me."

Mr. Burns had a reputation around Clayton County. He was

known to be a kind, soft-spoken, godly man. He was of medium height but had solid shoulders and strong arms. Mr. Alford Burns managed a prosperous dairy farm. Every morning from her kitchen window, Thelma watched the black and white Holsteins line up in the distance, marching toward the barn. Mr. Burns had the fattest cows she had ever seen. On more than one occasion, she noticed him pat the cows on the back and talk to them as they gathered at the feed bin.

Mr. Burns wore overalls with boots and a faded ball cap on his head. The cap was more pink than red. Whatever insignia had been on it had worn off ages ago. His overalls resembled what car repairmen wore, dark brown, one-piece, zipped up the front. He always carried a bandana stuffed in his back pocket. Mr. Burns wore this ensemble every day but Sunday.

On Sundays, he donned a dark suit, pressed white shirt and silk tie. His shiny black shoes completed his church ensemble. Mr. Burns was distinguished looking, waiting by his red Ford truck with his Bible tucked under his arm. When his wife, Lilly, was ready to leave for church, he would open the truck door. He would gently reach for her arm and help her into the front seat. Mr. Burns never missed a Sunday.

Alford and his wife had inherited the land they lived on from her parents, but he and Lilly built the farm from the ground up. Over the years, they raised two sons, teaching them how to manage the farm business. Lilly had dreamt her sons would stay close by, but the boys chose otherwise.

The boys married and moved with their families to New York City and Philadelphia. Alford and Lilly's gracious farmhouse was mostly quiet now except on holidays when the driveway and dining room table were filled. On those days, happy, ruckus sounds would spill from the house. Regardless of Lilly's disappointment in her grandchildren living so far away, the Burn's home was always a joyful place.

Thelma craved the harmony the Burns cultivated—a consistent, nurturing environment. Thelma knew time spent there would be good for her and Lil' Jackson.

———

As Thelma began her new job, she established a morning routine to ensure she arrived on time each day. After getting her oldest off to school, she tucked a piece of white bread, a small chunk of cheese, an apple, some crayons, and a piece of newspaper into a small dish towel. She tied the corners of the towel together, gathered up her youngest, and headed off to work. As she and Lil' Jackson walked along the dirt road, Thelma would call out make-believe names to the Holsteins. She would talk to the cows as they stretched their necks through the fence. Six days a week, with a toddler in tow, she trekked past a mile of barbed wire and wooden posts to get to work. Thelma walked to work in the morning with a light heart, but she returned home at the end of the day with dread. While she was changing for the good, Jackson continued to corrupt.

———

As mid-spring approached, the meadows filled with burdock thistles and clusters of Queen Anne's lace. The wafting scent of apple blossoms quickened Thelma's heart. Her strolls past the fields were like visits to a garden. The morning sun was a warm cape thrown over her shoulders—the rustling grasses along the sides of the dirt road bowed to her as she passed. Thelma treasured her walks to work. She came to believe the distance between hers and the Burns' house was a conduit leading to safe places.

———

One night after a cruel beating, Thelma lay on her back staring into the dark. Jackson lay next to her snoring and sputtering liquor-laced spit onto his pillow. The heat and humidity wafting through the window caused the sheets to stick to her bruised skin. Summer was approaching.

Thelma knew better than to disturb Jackson's fitful sleep. She lay still mulling over in her mind a different route to work. She would take her son and walk behind her house through an empty pasture.

At the corner, she would cross the fence and move down along the banks of the Susquehanna. She would travel back up to the road just beyond the bridge, where she would enter the Burns' property from the other side.

Visualizing her new route could not keep her mind from replaying Jackson's fit of rage from earlier that evening. He was angry that his coffee was not hot enough. Raging, he had grabbed the cast iron skillet from the stove. Jackson swung and hurled hot grease all over the table, just missing the children but scalding Thelma's arm. Before going to bed, she had moved around the table to get a small apple out of the bowl. She stood in a daze, wondering how she would ever get the grease marks out of the tablecloth.

The next morning, she picked up her pace, eager to get out the door. She wanted to have some extra time along the river. Thelma tied a thin scarf around her toddler's neck and tucked his pants securely into his rubber boots. She stopped for a moment and stared at the little cherub eagerly gazing up at her. Enraptured, she couldn't help but smile.

"You sure do look like your father. With those blond curls and deep blue eyes, you could be your father's twin. Jackson Jr. was sure the perfect name for you, little one."

She took Lil' Jackson's chubby hand in hers. They headed out, letting the screen door bounce against the house a couple times as they exited. The morning sun was bright, and the doves were cooing. With the exception of a few steaming cow piles and prickly weeds here and there, the stroll across the pasture was refreshing. The pungent scent of hay and earth mixed with cow manure was strangely comforting.

Thelma and Lil' Jackson moved down to the tree line and soon were among tall pines and thick hardwoods. The leaves were beginning to fill in, creating a forest canopy. The warm sun stroked the damp forest floor in dappled light. She could see the shimmer of water through the tree trunks. From where Thelma stood, the river was not very wide, no more than the size of a large creek. Parts were filled with large gray slate and granite rocks. Water tumbled through and around them, spilling out into shallow pools with small smooth stones reflected from below. The flow widened upstream especially at the bridge. A short distance upstream from the bridge, a confluence created sections of the river that were still, dark green, and deep.

As they approached, the gurgling tributary became more pronounced. The muddy banks slurped as the Susquehanna quenched her shoreline.

Ahh, the river beckons.

Thelma smiled.